Romantic Suspense

Danger. Passion. Drama.

Murder At The Alaskan Lodge
Karen Whiddon

Safe In Her Bodyguard's Arms
Katherine Garbera

MILLS & BOON

MURDER AT THE ALASKAN LODGE
© 2024 by Karen Whiddon
Philippine Copyright 2024
Australian Copyright 2024
New Zealand Copyright 2024

First Published 2024
First Australian Paperback Edition 2024
ISBN 978 1 038 90769 1

SAFE IN HER BODYGUARD'S ARMS
© 2024 by Katherine Garbera
Philippine Copyright 2024
Australian Copyright 2024
New Zealand Copyright 2024

First Published 2024
First Australian Paperback Edition 2024
ISBN 978 1 038 90769 1

MIX
Paper | Supporting
responsible forestry
FSC® C001695

Published by
Harlequin Mills & Boon
An imprint of Harlequin Enterprises (Australia) Pty Limited
(ABN 47 001 180 918), a subsidiary of HarperCollins
Publishers Australia Pty Limited
(ABN 36 009 913 517)
Level 19, 201 Elizabeth Street
SYDNEY NSW 2000 AUSTRALIA

Cover art used by arrangement with Harlequin Books S.A.. All rights reserved.

Printed and bound in Australia by McPherson's Printing Group

Murder At The Alaskan Lodge

Karen Whiddon

MILLS & BOON

Karen Whiddon started weaving fanciful tales for her younger brothers at the age of eleven. Amid the gorgeous Catskill Mountains, then the majestic Rocky Mountains, she fueled her imagination with the natural beauty surrounding her. Karen now lives in north Texas, writes full-time and volunteers for a boxer dog rescue. She shares her life with her hero of a husband and four to five dogs, depending on if she is fostering. You can email Karen at kwhiddon1@aol.com. Fans can also check out her website, karenwhiddon.com.

Visit the Author Profile page
at millsandboon.com.au for more titles.

Dear Reader,

I've always loved fishing. Where I live, it's mostly lake fishing, but I've never forgotten a fishing trip/vacation my husband and I took to Painter's Lodge on Vancouver Island, Canada. We fished in Alaska as well, but it was an excursion off a cruise ship, not a stay-and-fish-type thing. Not only did we catch large salmon (mine was twenty-two pounds!), but the scenery and the experience made this the most unique vacation I'd ever taken.

That's why I decided to kind of re-create that experience for this book. *Murder at the Alaskan Lodge* takes place at a fictional Alaskan fishing lodge. I drew upon my memories, and while I did have to take a few liberties with the location and the fish, I enjoyed meeting Maddie Pierce and Dade Anson. Writing about them not only learning to navigate their new reality but also falling in love and keeping each other and their guests safe was like a dream come true. I hope you enjoy reading this book as much as I enjoyed writing it!

Karen Whiddon

DEDICATION

To my ultimate fishing buddy for life, Lonnie.
Catching those huge salmon was one of
my favorite things ever!

Chapter 1

Today would be the day her spectacularly craptastic life took a turn for the better, Maddie Pierce thought as she waited impatiently for her luggage to show up on the rickety airline carousel. It had to because it certainly couldn't get any worse. Unless they lost her bags. Hopefully not, because even a hostile universe couldn't be that cruel.

Scowling, she reminded herself to keep a positive attitude. Which was extremely difficult since in the space of a few weeks she'd not only lost her awesome job working for the top commercial land developer in Dallas, but also, as she'd flailed about trying to figure out what to do next, her boyfriend of two years had dumped her for someone else.

She'd loved her job. The boyfriend, not so much. She suspected they'd each been placeholders for the other, filling in until something better came along. Sure, the timing had sucked, but Maddie couldn't really blame him.

As for the land developer, the company had sold to an even larger developer that was moving north from Houston. Massive restructuring had taken place, and entire departments were cut. Maddie's had been one of them.

Desperate to stay in the game, she immediately began the search to find something similar. Aware she might have to relocate, she'd even branched from commercial real estate development and included residential. At her lowest point, she'd sent out over two hundred and fifty résumés. All to an alarmingly lackluster response.

Busy living in the fast-paced world of up-and-coming young executives, Maddie hadn't managed to save much money. She'd barely be able to make next month's rent, and that would be if she didn't pay utilities or buy groceries.

She began looking at other jobs (bartending, office work, waitressing) to tide her over. And then a certified letter had arrived, informing her that she'd inherited half of an old, remote fishing lodge up in Alaska. Which was about as far as she could get from Dallas, Texas, and remain in the United States. At this point, leaving and starting over actually suited her just fine. And even though the will inexplicably stipulated she'd need to live there one entire year before owning her half outright, she figured she could use that time to regroup and evaluate.

A new opportunity, she'd told herself, every time she'd wondered about the cold or the ferocious wild animals she'd heard were everywhere in the Last Frontier. Good luck, like the stars had magically aligned or something to save her butt. No job, no boyfriend, and her luxury apartment lease had just ended. Since she'd never known the grandfather who'd left her the lodge, both his passing and the certified copy of his will had been an utter surprise. Especially since he'd never made even the slightest attempt to contact her, not once in her entire twenty-five years.

Serendipity or a random lightning bolt of fate, whatever. All signs were screaming that the time had come for a major change. So, with no other choices, Maddie had closed her eyes and taken the leap. Instead of placing her belongings in storage for her eventual return, she'd sold or given almost everything away. With the last of her funds, she'd booked a one-way ticket to Anchorage. As soon as she snagged her suitcase, she'd be meeting the man who'd inherited the other half of Grady's Lodge. She found his name intriguing. Dade Anson. She pictured a kindly older man, heavyset and wearing glasses, taking her under his wing and showing her the ropes. After all, not only had she never been to Alaska before, but she'd also never even set foot in a fishing lodge. Or really even gone fishing.

She had, however, done her research. Surprisingly, she'd learned fishing lodges, especially those catering to wealthy clientele, made a ton of money. This was where she knew her skills working for a land developer were likely to come in handy. She figured she'd modernize the place, do some advertising, and by the time her year had passed and she could sell, Grady's Lodge would be a completely different type of place. Trendy, popular and profitable.

Her life seemed to have done a rapid 360.

Until the text messages had started coming. If not for the weird, vaguely threatening texts, all from different, unlisted numbers, she'd be on cloud nine. The texts had started soon after she'd firmed up her decision to go. She'd since learned there was an app people could use to text and remain anonymous. Part of her wondered if Dade, was sending them. If he thought texts would scare her away, he was sorely mistaken. She'd decided to ignore them. So far, nothing had actually happened. And here in Alaska, she knew she'd be out of reach.

Finally, her suitcase dropped into the carousel and

moved toward her. Once she'd grabbed it, she turned and took a deep breath.

Now to start the next phase of her new life. Part owner of Grady's Lodge.

This Dade guy had said he'd be waiting for her in a dark green Jeep Wrangler, parked right outside the baggage claim area. Pulling her luggage after her, she hurried toward the exit door, anticipation making her pulse race.

Outside, she inhaled, liking the crispness of the air, the way the light seemed different, making everything appear sharper, cleaner, somehow. Spotting the Jeep, she hurried over.

She shouldn't have been surprised when a man the size of a grizzly bear got out of the green Jeep. After all, this was Alaska. But still… This had to be Dade Anson. Not quite the kindly, older man she'd pictured.

The sight of him made every nerve in her body tingle. Astonished, she stopped dead in her tracks. Hot and dangerous, so much so that she thought this couldn't be real. For one thing, he was the largest man she'd ever met in person. As in, Jason Momoa's size, tall and massive with broad shoulders, a muscular body and the same kind of long, wavy, dark hair. He even had the same rugged face, compelling eyes and commanding presence.

Staring, she tried to collect herself. Men who looked like him didn't really exist in real life outside of Hollywood, did they? Clearly, they did. In the person of one Dade Anson, the man with whom she'd be spending the next year.

Taking a deep breath, she forced herself to move forward. "You must be Dade," she said in her best professional voice, holding out her hand. "I'm Maddie Pierce."

His huge hand completely engulfed hers. His fingers

were calloused and rough. Though he could have crushed her hand, he simply shook it firmly before releasing her. With a quick flash of a smile, he reached for her bag, hefting it easily into the back seat.

"Welcome to Alaska," he said, apparently completely unaware of his effect on her. "We've got a little over a two-hour drive before we get to Blake. Which means if you need anything before then, it's best to get it here in Anchorage."

Still a bit stunned, she tried to think. "I think I'm good, thank you."

He nodded. As his impersonal gaze swept over her, he opened the passenger-side door and stepped aside. "Great. Then let's get started."

Wondering how on earth this man had known her grandfather, she climbed up into the Jeep and fastened her seat belt. When he got in the driver's seat, his presence filled the interior of the vehicle. For one brief moment, she wondered if he'd fit. But despite his sheer size, he settled in easily behind the wheel.

He met her gaze, sending a jolt of attraction straight through her core. "Are you okay?" he asked, making her realize she might still be staring.

Flustered, she nodded. "I'm just a bit tired. It's been a long travel day."

"I can imagine." Starting the engine, he pulled away from the curb. Navigating traffic, he didn't speak again.

The urban environment of Anchorage surprised her. She'd read that Ted Stevens Anchorage International Airport sat five miles to the southeast of the city, but nothing could have prepared her for the sheer size and breathtaking beauty of the huge mountains that rose in the background. Where she'd come from, there was a saying that everything was bigger in Texas, but she guessed whoever had coined that phrase had never been to Alaska.

While she'd done her research on fishing lodges, she'd barely bothered with the state's most populated city.

Meanwhile, Dade Anson wasn't much of a conversationalist. In fact, he didn't talk at all once the initial introductions had occurred.

Twenty minutes passed. Then thirty. While Maddie had never been the kind of woman uncomfortable with silence, for whatever reason she felt the urge to fill the quiet with words. After all, she had a lot of questions.

"Did you know my grandfather very long?" she asked, turning to look at him.

"Almost my entire life," he replied, his voice clipped and his attention still on the road. The hustle and bustle of the city had given way to what she guessed might be the suburbs. Soon, she figured they'd leave even that little bit of civilization behind.

"You must have been very close." Of course, they had to have been. After all, Dade had been bequeathed the other half of the fishing lodge. Truth be told, Maddie had no idea why she'd been left anything. She'd never known her maternal grandfather. Growing up, this had brought her a lot of pain. She didn't understand why he never even attempted to contact her. Her mother had refused to talk about him, even though he was her own father.

"We were." Now Dade glanced at her, his gaze dark. "He was like a father to me."

Not sure what to make of that statement, Maddie nodded.

As she twisted her hands in her lap, she wondered why

she felt nervous. Maybe because she was about to go off into the wilderness with a man she didn't know.

"Better get used to it," she muttered under her breath. Her life had been nothing but one change after another lately. She'd always considered her self-confidence one of her best strengths, but these days some of her nerve seemed to be slipping just a little.

Maybe more than a little. A lot. That was what she got for letting so much of her identity get tied up in a job.

"I'm sorry, did you say something?" he asked, his brows lowered. He glanced sideways at her.

"No," she lied, unwilling to admit that she'd been talking to herself. "Not really."

Though a muscle worked in his rugged jaw, he finally nodded. "Okay."

She waited for him to say something else, anything, but he didn't. Nope, definitely not a talker. Which actually was much better than someone who chattered on non-stop about nothing. She'd worked with a few clients like that. They'd been exhausting.

The long day of travel must have taken its toll on her. One moment, she'd closed her eyes to rest them, and the next, she was jolted awake when the Jeep hit a pothole or something hard. She let out a muffled scream, not entirely sure where she was for a second.

Glancing around, noting the giant man with muscular arms in the seat next to her, now staring, she remembered. Alaska. Alone in what now appeared to be the middle of nowhere, with a man she didn't truly know. Both of his hands gripped the steering wheel as he navigated an increasingly rutted road that wound through nothing but trees. If anyone lived out here, the houses weren't near the road.

"How long was I out?" she asked, covering a yawn with her hand. Her shoulders felt stiff, and she rolled her neck to try and help with that.

"No idea," he replied, his impersonal tone matching his expression. "Possibly an hour. Maybe longer."

She sat up, still trying to get the kinks out of her neck as she took in the landscape. A narrow slice of blue sky was visible through the forest. While it appeared they were still on pavement, she wondered if that would soon give way to gravel or dirt. "Are we getting anywhere close to Blake?"

"Not really." He waited a moment, and then he laughed. The richness of the sound washed over her, making her shiver. "Just kidding. We're almost there."

"I can't wait." Her first real Alaskan village. She'd done as much research as possible on the area and the fishing lodge she'd inherited. Research on real estate had been her specialty in her previous job. Blake was the only place even remotely close to the fishing lodge and where they'd get supplies. From the photos she'd seen online, it appeared to be a charming place. Like something out of a holiday card, except in need of some sprucing up.

Thinking of that brought something else to mind. "Does it snow a lot here?" she asked, even though she already knew it did.

"Define *a lot*," Dade replied. "I mean, it snows in the winter, of course. And in the fall. Sometimes in the spring. That's why the lodge is only open from May until September."

She knew all this. Again, she'd done her research. But

she liked hearing him speak. The husky timbre of his voice did things to her. Pleasant things. Damn.

"Dallas doesn't get much snow," she commented. "I have to say, even though I checked out the stats online, I'm not sure how well equipped I am. I'm not a big fan of the cold."

The incredulous sideways look he gave her revealed his thoughts about that. "You've got some time to get ready," he said. "We're just about to open for the season. But yeah, there's going to be snow eventually. Definitely more than you're used to in Texas."

She nodded. "Tell me about the lodge. I tried to look it up online but couldn't find much. There are several larger fishing lodges in the general area, and they all have a major web presence. But not Grady's."

He snorted. "Grady wasn't big on the internet. We don't get it where we are, and he never wanted it brought in."

"What?" Now he'd managed to surprise her. "No internet?"

"Nope. No Wi-Fi. I think there might be dial-up or something, but who has the patience to deal with that?"

Not good. Considering her plans to set up a website and do some advertising, this wasn't good at all.

"What about in Blake?" she asked. "Do they have Wi-Fi there?"

"They do. But since it's a good thirty-minute drive or more, there doesn't seem to be a point. If people need to reach me, they can call on the land line. It's the most reliable."

Since she couldn't fathom this, she tried again. "You can get email on your phone, right? And use your cell to access websites?"

"We don't exactly get much cell phone service out there

either," he told her, the glint in his eyes telling her he was clearly enjoying himself. "We use a satellite phone when outside for emergencies, but that's it. One of the reasons businessmen like to escape to our lodge. It truly is getting away from it all."

"Wow." She didn't know how else to respond to that. All of her research and she hadn't seen anything relating to modern conveniences.

"Trust me, it's better this way," he said. "You'll see."

While she had her doubts, she knew better than to voice them. "I guess I won't have much choice."

The dense forest began to give way to a house here and there. Some were actual log cabins, others more elaborate wood-frame homes. None of them were brick, like most of the homes back in Dallas. She guessed brick might be hard to get out here.

"We're getting close to town," he said. "If you don't mind, I'd like to stop. I need to fill up with gas and pick up a few supplies. Since we open in a week, I had to place the usual big order. We're pretty much booked up for the entire season."

Impressed, she nodded. "You don't do any advertising, do you?"

"No need. Most of our clients have been coming here for years. Before them, their families. The other clients are strictly word of mouth. We like it that way."

She knew better than, as the newbie partner, to immediately vocalize any plans she might have to change things. She'd need to take time to settle in, learn the ropes, see how things were run. Then and only then would she have enough knowledge to decide to make improvements.

As they crested a steep hill, he pointed. "Watch for it."

And then she saw Blake, Alaska, below them. A cluster of buildings along a single street, with a few side streets that appeared to be residential. One stop light, she saw.

Blake was much smaller than she'd imagined, and less picturesque without the snow, but still charming. They drove down Main, past several small businesses, and pulled up in front of a red wood building with a large sign proclaiming Murphy's General Store.

"Come on inside," Dade said, his voice slightly warmer than it had been. "You can meet some of the locals."

Since she'd been traveling for what felt like forever, she knew she didn't look her best. But aware she couldn't refuse and appear unfriendly, she unbuckled her seat belt and reached for the handle.

To her surprise, he opened the door for her, waited for her to get out and then closed it. "This way," he said.

Maddie had always considered herself a confident woman, but right now she felt like a small child about to walk into her first day of kindergarten.

He held the door open and gestured at her to precede him.

Stepping inside, her first impression was of a rustic kind of cozy warmth. There was, she saw, a little of everything. From handmade quilts to hunting supplies, food and medicine and everything in between. Including both men's and women's clothing.

"Hey, Dade!" A stocky man came out from around the counter and clapped Dade on the back. "And this must be your new partner."

Partner. Dade struggled not to wince. Watching as Maddie chatted with Kip, thoroughly charming the store owner, Dade clenched his hands into fists and told himself he couldn't just walk away and leave her there. He'd known before he'd even met her that he wouldn't like her much. How could he, when she hadn't even once bothered to try and have any kind of relationship, even a long-distance one, with her grandfather?

He'd been less than thrilled when Grady had told him he planned to leave the granddaughter he'd never gotten to know half of the fishing lodge. But Dade had loved Grady more than anyone else on this earth, and if doing that made the old man happy, who was Dade to argue?

When Grady died, Dade's entire world had shattered. Grady had been everything to him, and Dade felt his absence keenly. Nevertheless, he'd done what he'd been tasked to do and made sure Grady's last will and testament had been filed with the courts. Puttering around the lodge that Grady had built, Dade had still been struggling with the loss when he'd received the news that Maddie Pierce, estranged granddaughter and co-heir, had agreed to the terms of the will and was on her way to stay. For at least one full year.

Which Dade thought would feel like an eternity.

Though Grady had always talked wistfully about her, Dade had never gotten over the simple fact that she hadn't cared enough, not once, to even pick up the phone and call. Or send a single letter. Never mind visit. It had seemed as if she were trying to pretend that her grandfather didn't exist. That didn't sit right with Dade.

Anyone who could blow off a man as great as Grady Pierce wasn't worth Dade's time. Where the old man appeared able to forgive and forget, Dade couldn't. Not about something as important as this. Sure, Maddie might be far prettier than he'd expected, and sexy as hell, but he'd already made up his mind not to like her. Meeting her bright blue eyes, so reminiscent of Grady's, felt like a slap in the face every time.

Once the year stipulated in the will had passed, Dade planned to make her an offer, buy out her half of the lodge and send her packing. She could go right back to Texas, where she belonged.

For now though, they were stuck with each other. Which promised to be interesting.

Once Kip had rounded up all the items from the list Dade had given him and shown Maddie where to find the local baked goods and jams and jellies, Dade loaded everything into the back of his Jeep. He told Kip he'd see him soon and opened the passenger door for Maddie. Once again, his polite gesture appeared to surprise her. Maybe if she'd spent even a little bit of time with her grandfather, she'd have seen how Grady had been polite to a fault. He'd instilled the same manners in Dade.

Once they'd pulled away from the general store and were headed north on Main, Dade noticed that Maddie had again fallen silent. Good. Maybe she'd go back to sleep. He found making small talk with a total stranger exhausting.

"Eventually, we'll get used to each other," she said. Brushing her thick, dark hair away from her face, she sighed.

Startled, he glanced at her, wondering if she'd read his mind.

"Your expression gave you away," she told him, flashing a sly smile, her eyes sparkling.

What could he do but laugh? To his surprise, she

laughed with him. The light, feminine sound brought both a sense of comfort and of uneasiness.

They both went quiet again as they left Blake behind.

"The road gets even rougher from here on out," he warned her. Since his description, at best, was an understatement, he wondered how she'd react once they started being bounced around. He had to give her props, though. Despite what had to have been a long day of traveling and now riding in the Jeep, she hadn't complained. Not once.

For the next few miles, the pavement got worse and worse, becoming almost nonexistent in places. Deep potholes and jagged ridges tested the Jeep's suspension. Eventually, they would reach a combination of dirt and gravel, which became treacherous in the rainy season and downright dangerous when it snowed.

Out of necessity, he slowed the Jeep down. Though she didn't comment, she glanced at him. For the first time, he noticed her death grip on the door handle.

"Are you all right?" he asked.

"I'm fine." Her clipped response told him otherwise.

"Soon, we'll be crossing the Neacola River," he offered. "It's pretty scenic."

And then they hit a deep rut. Because he'd allowed himself to be distracted, the Jeep front tire hit hard. This sent them both bouncing. Only the seat belts kept them from hitting their heads.

Maddie let out a muffled curse. Then, apparently embarrassed, she shook her head and looked away. "You weren't kidding about the bad roads," she said.

Worried about his undercarriage, Dade pulled over. "Wait here a second," he said. "I need to make sure that didn't damage anything. This Jeep is fairly new, and I want to take care of it. I'm usually paying better attention than that."

He got out, walked around the exterior of his vehicle, then crawled under. A brief inspection revealed everything appeared to be fine.

Relieved, he got back inside and buckled up.

"Do they ever fix the roads?" she asked. "I mean, I'm guessing our clients have to travel this way, too, don't they?"

Our clients? Though, at first, the words hit him wrong and he took exception, he realized she was right. As of now, they were both the hosts. The clients would be their clients.

"They do," he answered. "But most of them have been coming here for years, so they know to be careful. And as far as your question about repairs, if we want anything like that done around here, we have to do it ourselves. Every once in a while, Blake gets together a group of citizens and fills in the potholes. Snow and cold always come after and mess everything up again."

She frowned. "It's weird to me that there's no state or county maintenance for the roads."

"Oh, I'm sure there is in some places. For sure in Anchorage and Fairbanks and all the other heavily populated areas. Alaska is a huge state. There's a lot of wilderness and remote areas. Since they can't possibly get to them all, most of us Alaskans pitch in and do our part." He didn't even try to hide the pride in his voice.

"It's so beautiful here," she said, gazing out the passenger window. "I don't know if you've ever been to Dallas, but it's super flat. I love the hills and mountains and all the trees."

When he thought of Texas, he thought of heat. Lots of hundred degree summer days and winters with rain and no snow. Since he much preferred cold weather to hot, he didn't think he'd make it in Texas. He had to wonder how Maddie would fare here in Alaska.

The steadily inclining road began leveling out, which meant they were approaching the Neacola.

"Here's the bridge," he pointed out, unnecessarily. "And down below, there's the river."

As they reached the other side, he pulled over so she could take a look. "Lots of tourists stop here and take pictures to post to their social media. Just in case you wanted one."

"I'm not a tourist," she pointed out, making no moves to get out of the Jeep. He noted she didn't claim not to have any social media. "Though that is a stunning view."

"It is." He nodded. "There was an accident here not too long ago. A car went off the bridge and ended up in the river. One person was killed and another survived."

Turning to look at him, she tilted her head. "Was alcohol involved?"

"No. It's a long story, but the guy who made it stayed. He's now married to the new doctor in Blake."

"You'll have to tell it to me someday," she said, her blue eyes bright, her expression quizzical.

"Or better yet, you can hear it directly from them." Looking away, he cleared his throat. "I'm sure you'll meet them eventually. Especially since you're going to be here an entire year."

This made her wince. "You make it sound like I'm serving some sort of sentence."

"Aren't you?" he asked. "You might as well level with

me. I suspect you wouldn't be staying that long if your grandfather's will didn't have that stipulation. Am I right?"

She met his gaze. "I don't know," she answered quietly, her expression thoughtful. "They always say when one door closes, another opens. That's kind of what happened to me. I'm ready for a new start."

Appreciating her honesty, he nodded. "All right then. Are you sure you don't want to take a look at the river?"

"I'm sure. Maybe another time."

He waited a moment longer before shifting into drive and pulling back onto the road. "We're lucky we have good weather today. With no rain or snow, we only have about twenty more minutes before we reach the lodge."

"I didn't realize you were that far away from Blake." She glanced back at the river. "And how is a fishing lodge located such a distance from the water?"

Her question made him grin. "The river curves," he said. "Grady built his place on the river bank several miles upstream. You'll see."

She stared at him, as if she wasn't sure whether he might be joking. "I see."

"Have you ever been fishing?" he asked.

Slowly, she shook her head. "Not really. When I was a teenager, one of my boyfriends took me out in his boat while he fished, but I never actually tried."

"Was it a lake?"

"Yes. He caught some largemouth bass and a catfish on a line he strung between two empty milk jugs." She grimaced. "He wanted me to cook them, too, but I'd rather eat my fish in a restaurant."

Not sure how to respond to that, he settled on a non-committal nod. "Well, we have to cook our own fish up here. And our clients'. It's one of the services we provide to our guests."

For a second, she appeared taken aback. "I guess I can learn. Salmon, right?"

"Mostly, yes. Some people like to have it smoked, and there's a place in Blake that does that for them. They even ship it home if they want."

"That's a nice service," she said. "But I'm wondering why the lodge doesn't cut the middleman and offer this service instead. That way, we could get a cut as well."

Not sure how to respond, he considered not even bothering to dignify her statement by replying. But then again, she needed to understand where he stood on things.

"We're not out to gouge our guests," he told her firmly. "We offer a great experience for a fair price. People who book with us know what to expect. Most of them are repeat visitors, who know who does what and for what price. We're not going to suddenly tell them things have changed and will now cost more."

To his relief, she didn't have an answer for that. Yet. Somehow, he suspected she would eventually.

They drove along for several more minutes in silence. He'd just begun to feel comfortable when she spoke again.

"I'd like to examine the books."

"What books?" he asked.

"Your ledgers. I assume you do keep them. Where you log income and expenditures."

Somehow, he kept a straight face. "We don't keep records of any of that," he said, only half joking. "I mean, sure. We log income from guests. And we keep receipts from grocery bills. But it's a pretty straightforward operation. No frills. So not too much to examine."

She stared at him for a second too long. "Is it safe to assume you—we—do make a profit? Or is this your way of telling me that my grandfather operated this fishing lodge for fun?"

What could he do but laugh out loud? Even if having to explain all of this made him want to put his head down and curse the cruel twist of fate that meant he had to deal with her and her questions.

When he'd had his little forced chuckle, he kept driving. Jaw clenched, eyes on the road. Though she hadn't known about Grady's will. And since she hadn't met him, no way could she have understood a man like her grandfather and the joy he'd found in his small business.

At first, he could tell she was trying hard not to push him. But then, when he didn't elaborate or explain, she shook her head. "Why did you laugh?" she finally asked. "I wasn't trying to be funny. I simply asked an honest question."

"I know," he replied, shaking his head. Then, as he saw what looked like hurt flash across her beautiful face, he sighed and relented. "We make a profit, believe me. Even though Grady loved what he did, like everyone else, he had to make a living."

"Then why wouldn't you want to make more money?" She sounded genuinely puzzled.

"Money isn't everything," he said. Then, as her frown deepened, he decided to try to redirect the conversation. "Look, you just got here. You haven't seen how the place runs or gotten a feel for our clientele. Why don't you give it some time, learn everything you can about our operation, and then you can make suggestions about changes? Does that seem fair to you?"

Her gaze shadowed; she finally nodded. "You're right, of course. I'm sorry. I tend to be a little…over-enthusiastic."

"Better than apathy," he said, finally smiling a genuine smile. "You actually have a lot to learn."

Though she nodded, he knew she didn't have the faintest idea. Which was okay because he'd teach her. And he suspected she'd be ready to leave long before the designated period of one year had passed. Which wouldn't work out for him, as that would mean the lodge would never become his. The will stipulated both had to remain, and if one left, they willingly had to sign the lodge over to the other with nothing in return.

Since there was no way in hell Dade planned to go anywhere and he suspected she would never give him the lodge without some sort of payment, he'd do whatever he had to do in order to convince her to stay. Because after one year had passed, either party could sell. Then and only then, the lodge would be his.

Chapter 2

In the few weeks that she'd spent getting her affairs in order before she'd boarded a plane to Anchorage, Maddie had done extensive research on various Alaskan fishing lodges. She'd settled on two that she wanted to eventually emulate. Both of them were upscale and luxurious, providing accommodation and entertainment for both the anglers and their families.

At first, she'd found the idea of vacationing at a fishing lodge repellent, something that she'd never, ever be interested in doing. But as she'd delved into reading about them, she'd warmed up to the idea. Who wouldn't—with the opportunity to visit a spa or go on a wildlife tour, attend yoga classes and eat healthy, chef-prepared meals? Fishing, which might not be for everyone, appeared to be optional. With which she definitely could get on board.

While she understood her grandfather's lodge was rustic at best, she understood the potential. All she'd need to do was convince her new partner, Dade, of the opportunities ahead of them and then bring in investors for funding. Soon, they'd be operating one of the best Alaskan fishing destinations ever!

The future looked bright. And maybe it was due to the spotty cell phone service, but the threatening text messages seemed to have stopped. She hadn't gotten one in two days.

Everything would finally work out. And yes, she did have a lot to learn. Though, no matter what her new partner thought, she wouldn't be catching or cooking fish. She had no interest in fishing, and cooking wasn't one of her life skills. The guests certainly wouldn't appreciate anything she fried up and tried to serve them. Once Dade sampled something she'd made, she knew he'd agree.

She'd more than make up for her lack of those skills with her others. She might not be a homebody, but she did excel in seeing overlooked potential. And she was a damn good decorator, skilled at hosting and making people feel welcome. All in all, she'd be a valuable asset to this entire operation. Dade would eventually learn that for himself. Right now though, she supposed she had absolutely everything to prove.

"Here we are," Dade said, gesturing to a faded wooden sign that read Grady's Lodge, 5 Miles, with a large arrow pointing down a rutted dirt track that disappeared into the trees. "Hang on," he told her, making the turn slowly. "It's a bit rough going from here on out."

For whatever reason, she suddenly felt nervous. While she'd done an exhaustive internet search for her grandfather's place, she hadn't been able to learn much. Of course, she hadn't even known of its existence until a few weeks ago. At least she'd been able to ascertain Grady's Lodge was real.

Her heart pounded. She sat up straight. Now she'd finally lay eyes on her inheritance.

Despite their slow speed, mostly a crawl, they bounced along the road, if one could even call it that. More like a path or trail. She made a mental note to make sure the way in was one of the first things repaired or improved. A nice couple of layers of asphalt or cement would go a long way to helping guests reach the lodge.

"People don't mind driving on this?" she asked, earning her an incredulous glance from Dade.

"You're in remote Alaska," he replied, as if that explained everything.

"I see." But she didn't. Gripping the door with one hand and the dash with the other, she tried to keep from hitting her head.

Since she'd studied numerous websites and photos of other fishing lodges, she had a pretty good idea of what to expect. Even if the only photos she'd located on the internet of Grady's were old and faded. As they pulled up to a medium-size frame home, she tried to see past the main dwelling to the rest of the property. She couldn't see anything, not even the water. There were just too many trees.

As soon as Dade shifted into Park, she opened her door and hopped out.

Dade exited a little more slowly, grabbing her luggage from the back. "Follow me," he said. "I'll show you to your room."

As he opened the door (unlocked, she noted) and flicked on the light, she eagerly stepped inside and took in the room. Small but neat, with older furnishings, it definitely had a masculine vibe. Every item in the room was functional. Nothing unnecessary or decorative. Even the artwork on the walls appeared to be photographs of various fishing expeditions.

Moving closer to one, she studied the picture of a grinning older man with his arm around the slender shoulders of a teenaged boy holding one of the biggest fish she'd ever seen. Glancing at Dade, she realized the kid had to be him. Which meant the man must have been her grandfather. His craggy face appeared kind, and she saw traces of her mother in his lopsided smile.

"I regret not ever meeting him," she said sadly. Someday, she'd ask Dade if he knew why Grady hadn't ever reached out, but not today.

"He was one of a kind," Dade said from behind her, his voice husky with emotions. "I'm sorry that you never got the chance to meet him."

She shrugged, pretending his words didn't sting. Damned if she'd point out to her new partner that her own grandfather had never expressed the slightest interest in getting to know her. Which was why she'd found his bequest a complete and utter shock. None of this made sense.

Where Dade fit in, she wasn't yet sure. Judging from the photograph, he'd been around here for a long time. A sudden thought shocked her, making her turn. "Are we… related somehow?"

"What do you mean?" he asked, frowning.

"Are you Grady's son or grandson?" She pointed toward the photo.

For a moment, he simply stared at her and didn't answer. Finally, he lifted his chin and shook his head. "No. Not by blood, at least," he said. "He raised me like a father, and I consider myself his son. But there's no actual relation."

She felt a prickle of rancor hearing that, even without knowing the story. Her grandfather Grady had raised this man and loved him like a son. While Maddie had been forgotten and unwanted. Silly to feel like that now, since she couldn't miss what she'd never had. She guessed he'd left her half of this place as a way to make amends.

"I can give you a short tour," he added. "But it's really not a big house."

Nodding, she looked around. A small kitchen sat to the left of the living room, and a short hallway led to the bathroom and bedrooms.

"Is that where I'll be sleeping?" she asked.

"Yes. There are two bedrooms. Yours is on the right," Dade said, turning on the light and then depositing her bags on the double bed. "There's only one bathroom, which we'll have to share, but it's a solidly built house."

"Thank you," she told him, smiling slightly at his description.

Then, as she noted the cowboy hat hanging on the bed post, she took a second look.

"Was this…" She looked around, swallowing hard. "My grandfather's bedroom?"

"Yes. Mine is next door. This is the largest one."

She went slowly around the room, unable to resist touching some of the personal things on the oak dresser. A large stone, worn to smoothness by water. An old paperweight, gold shavings in a heavy glass globe. And a small clock, made of some kind of petrified wood. All occupied places of honor.

The bed appeared to be a queen rather than a full. A colorful, quilted comforter had been neatly folded at the end of the bed. It looked well-worn and homemade.

"There are clean sheets," he said, still standing in the doorway. "But I didn't empty the closet or the dresser. I wasn't sure if there might be something of his you wanted to keep."

Unsure how to respond to this, she swallowed. "What about you?" she asked. "You were close to him. Please, take anything you want."

He met her gaze. "Thank you. I appreciate that. But Grady already gave me everything I wanted."

Which meant she'd have to do what? Go through her grandfather's things? Toss them? "Is there a place where we can drop them off as donations? That way, someone else would be able to use them."

Expression thoughtful, he nodded. "Yes. We can take them to Kip at the general store. He'll be able to distribute them."

"Oh good." She didn't try to hide her relief. "I'll bag them up so the next time we're in town we can take them. That way, I'll have room for my own clothes."

He turned to go, his hand on the knob as if he meant to close the door behind him.

"Wait," she said, suddenly and absurdly afraid of being in this room alone. "When can you show me around the rest of the lodge?"

His gaze was steady as he studied her. Though she still found him a bit unnerving due to his sheer size, he'd been nothing but kind.

"I thought you might want to rest up first," he replied, his husky voice making her insides quiver. "Get unpacked, settle in. There's no rush, is there? It's not like you're going anywhere anytime soon, right?"

She knew he was right. In fact, earlier she had been looking forward to a short nap and then unpacking. But she hadn't expected the sudden swell of emotion at knowing she'd be going through the personal things of the grandfather she'd never known. She wished he'd left her a letter, something, anything to explain why he'd never once reached out to her.

Pushing the sudden longing aside, she grimaced. "You're right, of course. Thank you."

Without another word, he nodded and left, pulling the door closed behind him.

Alone in the small room, she went back to the dresser and pulled open the top right drawer. Inside, she found white, black and grey men's socks, all rolled up in pairs. She sighed, wondering why she felt so much like she was trespassing.

When Maddie had been a child, her mother had moved them around a lot. Maddie had gone to so many different schools she'd almost lost count. It seemed like just as she'd started fitting in and making friends they'd move again. And then once again, she'd become the new kid. The outsider.

She'd often longed for the kind of stability that came from deep roots, from family. The only thing she'd known about her grandfather was that her mother, Vanessa, refused to discuss him. This had led Maddie to believe Grady must have been some sort of monster. Her mother never attempted to dissuade her from that assumption. Right up until she died, she'd refused to say anything good about where she'd come from or the man who'd raised her.

Now, it appeared there were two sides to every story.

Water under the bridge, Maddie told herself. She opened another dresser drawer, saw the boxer shorts neatly folded inside and closed it. She'd do all her unpacking later. For now, her own things could remain inside the suitcase.

To reach the small bathroom that sat in the hall between

the two sleeping areas, she had to leave her room. Hoping Dade wasn't in there, she gingerly opened the door and made her way out. To her relief, Dade had stacked clean towels and a washcloth on the counter for her.

After washing her face, scrubbing off the makeup, she went back to her room with the intention of at least trying to nap. But on the way there, she made a sudden detour to the kitchen. Underneath the sink, she found a box of white kitchen-size trash bags and took three. No time like the present. She had way too much nervous energy to even consider she'd have any luck at sleeping.

Putting a staunch lid on her emotions, she got to work.

It took much less time than she'd thought to empty the dresser. It helped that she worked fast, giving zero thought as to the man who'd owned these things. They filled up one trash bag.

Once she'd finished that, she moved on to the nightstand. Opening the small drawer, she found, instead of clothing, a silver medallion on a chain and several old, faded photographs. She almost slammed the thing shut, but curiosity got the better of her.

She took out the necklace first, studying the medallion. It appeared to be a Saint Christopher pendant. A large man with a child on his shoulders and a staff in one hand had been etched into the metal. Interesting. She remembered reading somewhere that many people wore them as a symbol of safe travels and protection.

For whatever reason, she found the medallion beautiful. Instead of dropping it into the bag with the clothes, she placed it back into the drawer for safekeeping.

Now the photographs.

She took them out carefully, afraid she might damage

them. The first one was of her grandfather, though much younger, standing next to someone who had to be Maddie's mother. She appeared to be a teenager, maybe about fifteen or sixteen. Since Maddie had never seen pictures of her mother when she was young, she was taken aback at her innocent beauty.

And then she looked at her grandfather. The love in his expression as he gazed at his daughter came through as loudly as if someone had printed the words in red on the picture. Maddie studied it, noting the familiar stubborn look on her mother's face. Her crossed arms further attested to her mood.

The next photo was of her mother alone. Still young, but maybe a few years older than in the first one. In this one, she wore a denim jacket, and a rebellious glint shone in her eyes. If Maddie were to choose a word for this one, it would be *trouble.*

There were two more photographs. The next one seemed to be the oldest of all. Taken in black-and-white, it showed Grady Pierce as a young man, with his arm around the woman who must have been his wife. She'd died in childbirth, and Maddie's mom had never known her. Again, this picture embodied the word *love.*

Finally, the last shot was of an infant, lying alone in a pale pink onesie. Studying this, at first, Maddie thought it must have been her mother as a baby, but gradually she realized she'd seen the same picture in the baby book her mother had made. It was Maddie, a few months old. How her grandfather had gotten this, Maddie had no idea. As far as she knew, her mom and grandfather hadn't spoken after a pregnant and angry Vanessa had left Alaska for the lower forty-eight.

Though Maddie hadn't thought much about any of that since her mother had died, learning of the inheritance and her estranged grandfather's death had brought back a powerful curiosity about what had happened all those years ago to cause such a rift. Now, she'd likely never know.

After placing the pictures back in the nightstand next to the necklace, Maddie grabbed another trash bag and moved on toward the closet. The sight of all the men's clothes hanging neatly in there nearly stopped her short. But then she shook her head and began taking them off the hangers and shoving them into her bag.

She used the third bag for the shoes, coats and hats, feeling both guilty and accomplished once she'd cleared the space out. Now she had room for her own things, but a sudden wave of exhaustion had her rethinking the idea of a nap.

It had been a long day. Heck, it had been a long couple of months, if she were honest.

Kicking off her shoes, she gingerly climbed up onto the bed, closed her eyes and hoped she could sleep. Her scattered thoughts kept crowding her mind, but she forced herself to clear her head. She'd allow herself thirty minutes in an effort to try to sleep. If she wasn't out by then, she'd give up and finish organizing her new bedroom.

Alone again in the kitchen of the small house in which he'd lived for most of his life, Dade once again wondered what Grady had been thinking. He missed the man with a fierce ache, but damned if he understood him. Giving half of the lodge to that woman, an outsider from the lower forty-eight, could cause irreparable damage to everything Dade—and Grady himself—held dear.

She didn't belong. She'd never belong. One look at her perfectly done makeup and fashionable, impractical clothing revealed that. Maddie might be easy on the eyes, but everything about her screamed *big city*.

Hell, Grady himself had never even met her. Dade found it hard to respect someone who'd never made one single attempt to contact her grandfather. Not one letter or phone call or visit, even as the man grew older and frailer. Since his daughter Vanessa had passed away, Maddie was Grady's only remaining blood relative. He'd never stopped hoping to eventually connect with her. But his letters had gone unanswered, and he'd finally given up and stopped writing. His daughter Vanessa, Maddie's mother, had turned her against him, Grady had lamented. Since Dade knew all too well the story of Grady and Vanessa's estrangement, he'd simply nodded. Hell, Maddie hadn't even cared enough to notify Grady of Vanessa's passing a few years back.

And now, after Grady was dead and buried, she'd finally come. Several months too late. Even worse, in order for her to meet all the conditions of the will, Dade would be stuck with her for one entire year. And while he suspected she'd be more than happy to sell him her half of the place, he wouldn't be surprised if she attempted to gouge extra money from him. She'd never understand that deep connection he had to the lodge, to the wilderness and the water, the eagles and the fish. To the land.

Dade's roots ran deep, into the earth and sky. His ancestors had hunted and fished in these parts for hundreds of years. Somehow, Grady shared the same connection. The older man had taught a young Dade how to hunt and to fish, how to respect the sacrifice given by the deer and the elk and the salmon. How to honor the land.

Grady had been the only family Dade had ever known. He didn't remember much about his birth parents, only that they'd abandoned him when he'd been too young to take care of himself. Somehow, he'd ended up here at the lodge, a scared and half-frozen five- or six-year-old boy. Not knowing what else to do, the older man had taken him in.

At first, he'd thought he was only going to stay through the winter, while Grady quietly searched for his parents. Secretly, Dade loved being fed and warm and treated like he mattered. He'd hoped he never had to leave.

Despite Grady's attempts to locate his people, no one had ever come forward. Dade became part of Grady's family and part of Blake. He'd emulated everything the older man did, his honestly and honor, the way he became everyone's friend.

Dade owed Grady a debt he could never repay, not in this life or the next. He had raised him as his own and Dade had always felt that, for as long as he lived, Grady's Lodge would be his home. Dade wouldn't let anyone take that away from him. Especially not Maddie Pierce.

Right now, he found the woman a bit of an enigma. He'd been prepared to completely dislike her, and her willowy sort of beauty had come as a shock. He'd been alone too long, he thought, judging by his body's instant reaction to her. Since that would be the kind of complication they could both do without, he'd forced himself to try to study her impassively, without judgment. Truth be told, Maddie Pierce reminded Dade a little of himself, all those years ago. He'd spotted a certain kind of vulnerability in her gaze, when she didn't think anyone was looking.

Shaking off the foolish thoughts, Dade knew he had to be practical. After all, for the next year, they were going to be a team. They had less than a week to get to know each other before the first round of paying guests arrived. He'd need to get her up to speed on how the lodge was run, what the guests expected and her part in making all of this happen.

Honestly, he could use the help. He'd somehow managed to run it by himself last season, since Grady's illness had robbed him of his strength. Watching the man he thought of as a father grow weaker had just about killed Dade. Alone, he'd managed to keep his chin up and appear happy for their guests. He'd successfully finished off last season, but it hadn't been easy.

However, none of that compared to having to watch Grady die. All of Blake had attended the funeral, but Grady's granddaughter had not. Dade had asked Grady's attorney to reach out to her, which he had. She hadn't replied back. In fact, none of them had heard a peep from her, until she'd learned she'd inherited part of the lodge.

To ward off his increasingly dark thoughts, Dade left the house and walked out to one of his favorite places, the boat docks. Here, several outboard, flat-bottom boats awaited the next group of fishermen. Dade had spent the past several weeks working on them, making sure the motors ran smoothly and had plenty of gas. He'd cleaned them up, too, polishing the sides and the seats until they shone.

He climbed into one and sat. Instead of starting it up and puttering out into the river, he simply glanced back at the lodge and tried to picture how this fishing season would go. There were six cabins, all facing the river and the boat slips. He'd already gotten a head start on readying them for guests, airing them out after the long winter, dusting and sweeping. The beds were not yet made up, but all the clean linens had been placed in each one. The small bathrooms still needed cleaning, as did the kitchens, but it wouldn't take long to do that. Especially now that he had some help.

Fishing season would be starting soon. The first group of guests had been staying here for years. Several of them had even come in for Grady's memorial service. This would be the first season open without him. Dade was determined to make certain it ran smoothly. Even with Maddie Pierce here. *Especially* with her here, he corrected himself. If she was going to be a partner for the first year, she'd be putting in the time and the work.

At least she appeared game. He had to hand it to her for that. He'd halfway been expecting her to sweep in here with a major attitude, full of entitlement and lofty expectations.

Luckily for them both, so far she didn't seem anything like that.

He'd let her get some rest and settle in, and then he'd show her around tomorrow before putting her to work. They had a lot to do to ensure everything would be perfect on opening day when the guests arrived. More than anything, he hoped she could help him out with the cooking. While they kept the menu simple, Grady had been a talented cook. His pan-seared salmon had been the most anticipated dish for every guest.

Speaking of work, as a matter of fact, he might as well get started. Heading toward the first cabin, he figured he had enough time to finish cleaning, plus make the bed up, before it would be time to head back to the main house and see about preparing the evening meal.

Since he'd done quite a bit of work on this unit already, he only had the bathroom left. Everything had been thoroughly cleaned after the close of last season, but dust accumulated over the winter months, and he wanted the shower, sinks and commode sparkling.

Once he'd finished with the small bathroom, he spritzed the mirror, wiped it and stepped back to look at everything with his best critical eye. He even checked the mini-fridge, now plugged in even while empty, which guests used to store their own beverages or snacks.

Pleased with the results, he grabbed the clean sheets and blanket and made up both beds. After he'd pulled the plaid comforters up and arranged the pillows, he exhaled. One down and five left to go. With two people per cabin, they could host up to twelve people at a time. Usually, their groups weren't quite that large, but as luck would have it, the bunch coming at the end of the week would have them operating at capacity.

Once he closed the cabin door behind him, he made his way home.

Back at the main house, he moved quietly, just in case Maddie might be asleep. Since she'd closed her bedroom door, he figured she likely decided to take a nap. He couldn't blame her. Dallas to Anchorage was a long flight.

With the ease of familiarity, he got out Grady's old cast-iron skillet, the rice maker and a bag of microwavable frozen green beans. Two large salmon fillets, some long-grain rice and steamed green beans would be their dinner tonight. He got started cooking, focusing on the familiar motions.

"That smells amazing," a soft voice behind him said. For whatever reason, his body sprang to instant attention.

"Thanks," he managed, keeping his back to her so she wouldn't notice his arousal. Cursing himself, he knew he had to get this under control before it became the kind of problem no one needed. Especially not him.

"It's salmon," he said. "We eat a lot of it around here."

"I love salmon." She came closer, until her slender hip bumped his. "Sorry," she said when he quickly stepped sideways.

A quick glance revealed she'd focused her attention on the stove.

"Are you frying that?" she asked. "I've never had fried salmon."

"It's blackened. Grady taught me to make it," he said, glancing at her to see her reaction. "Your grandfather was a really good cook. I hope you inherited that skill from him."

This made her laugh. The light, feminine sound was like the first chirp of a bird announcing spring. He couldn't help but stare, both enthralled and frightened.

"What?" she finally asked. "Why are you looking at me like that?"

Shrugging, he told her the truth. "It's been a long time since we had a woman around here."

"Women don't come here to fish?"

"Not often. Every once in a while, one or two accompany their husbands," he said. "But mostly, it's just men."

She studied him, her expression intent. "Do these women ever come back? After their one time, do they return the next season?"

He didn't even have to think about it. "Not often. I'd have to say there are only a few women who truly want to spend their vacation time fishing."

"You don't say." She cocked her head, the gleam in her eyes giving him a warning. "That must be why the other upscale fishing resorts have activities for women to enjoy while the men fish."

"We're not an upscale fishing resort," he said. "We never have been. Our guests come here for one reason only. To fish."

Instead of arguing, which he kind of expected, she simply stared at him. He could almost see the wheels turning inside her head. Yes, he knew about these other types of fishing resorts. They were luxurious, with amenities neither he nor Grady had ever wanted to have and prices more than double the cost of Grady's Lodge. Which was fine by him. Each type of lodge occupied their own niche. He and his guests preferred things the way they were.

He took the fish off the stove, made two plates and carried them to the table. "Come on," he said. "Let's eat. I'm guessing you have to be hungry."

Again, she flashed that smile. "Starving," she agreed, pulling out a chair and dropping into it. "This looks amazing."

Since he ate salmon so often he'd grown tired of it, he shrugged. "It'll do."

"Do you have any wine?" she asked. "A glass of pinot grigio would go great with this."

"I haven't picked up the beer and wine yet," he said. "I usually just keep that stocked for the guests. I can get you water or iced tea."

She frowned. "Water is fine. You don't drink?"

"Not anymore," he said, hoping she'd leave it at that. He grabbed a couple of glasses, filled them with cold water from the refrigerator and carried them over to the table. "I hope you like the fish."

Taking the hint, she picked up her fork and dug in. He did the same, trying not to watch her while she ate, but unable to help himself.

Concentrating on her meal, she didn't speak again until she'd cleaned her plate. "That was delicious," she said. "You're a really good cook."

Sitting back in his chair, he grinned. "Thanks. I can't wait to eat something that wasn't cooked by me."

Though she smiled back and nodded, he swore he caught a trace of worry in her expression. He really didn't know what he'd do if she claimed she didn't know how to cook. He wouldn't be surprised, but he needed a helpmate here, not another guest.

"I know you said you haven't really gone fishing, but you might like it," he told her, changing the subject. "After all, you're going to have to do a fair bit of it."

She laughed, as if she thought he was kidding. When he didn't laugh along with her, she stopped. "You're serious. But I don't understand. Why on earth would anyone want me to go fishing with them? I'm a complete novice, or worse. I'd have no idea what to do."

"We've got a few days to teach you a few things," he said. "Sometimes, the guests want someone to drive the boat. That way they can concentrate on fishing."

"I'm thinking you're going to have to be the boat driver." Twisting her hands in front of her, she grimaced. "Honestly, I don't know how."

"I can teach you," he said, making his tone firm.

Her eyes widened. "I supposed you can," she replied. "But I doubt I'll be nearly as good as someone like you, who must have years of experience. Why would any fisherman want to deal with me when they could have a pro like you?"

"We have six boats. When we're full, they're all out at the same time. I can only pilot one."

"What about the other five?" she asked. "If they all need drivers, what do you do? Even if I were to drive one, that leaves four others. Are there other employees who could handle them?"

Slowly, he shook his head. "We have no employees. For years, it's been just me and Grady. Now it will be you and me. Most times, the fisherman handle their own boats. It's just every once in a while that they request one of us take them out. We just have to be prepared for when that happens."

"Maybe it won't."

While he hated to dash her hopes, he wanted to make sure she understood the reality. "Most likely, it will. We'll go out tomorrow so you can learn. It's actually pretty easy. They're all outboards."

She gave him a blank stare. "I don't know what that means."

"You'll learn. I promise. Now about the rest of it, we've got five cabins left to clean and get ready. We've also got to do a lot of meal prep right before the guests arrive. After that, we'll take turns on cooking duty."

"That's a lot," she commented. "Do you have a menu already made up?"

"We do." He smiled, hoping she could see his approval. He'd halfway expected her to claim she didn't know how to cook either. "We tend to stay pretty basic, nothing fancy. A lot of salmon, since it's so plentiful here. I'll show you a copy of it later."

Expression dazed, she nodded. "Thanks. I'm still a bit groggy from all the traveling. But I'd like to take a walk around the place, if that's okay. Maybe check out the cabins and the fishing pier."

Fishing pier? She meant boat docks. He decided to let that one pass. She'd figure out soon enough that around here, they fished by boat.

"Sure," he replied. "Are you ready to go now?"

"I am."

"Perfect." He grabbed a couple of cans of bear repellent and handed one to her. "Never go off without one of these."

Looking up from reading the label, she made a face. "You're joking, right?"

"Joking? I'm afraid not. You're in Alaska now. Bears are everywhere. Believe me when I say you don't want to get mauled by one."

Eyes wide, she nodded. "Just to be on the safe side, I'm sticking with you." She lifted up her can. "And I can assure you that this will always be in my hand."

"Good."

"I'm glad we ate," she said, her tone teasing. "At least I've had a good meal before my life flashes before me."

Despite himself, he smiled back. "I'm glad you think it was good. Let me get this cleaned up, and we'll go."

Chapter 3

"I'll do it." Maddie pushed to her feet, grabbed their plates and carried them over to the sink. She took a quick look around, hoping for a dishwasher, and when she spotted one, she let out an audible sigh of relief.

"I'm glad there's something I can do to contribute," she said, rinsing off their plates before stacking them inside. "I think I read that it doesn't get dark at this time of the year until late. Is that right?"

"It is," he replied. "The sun doesn't set until after ten in May."

"I think I like that." She finished stacking everything in the dishwasher. Eyeing the cast-iron skillet, she tried to figure out the best way to clean it. "Can this go in the dishwasher?" she asked, holding it up and turning toward him.

"No." He pushed up from the table and came over, taking the frying pan from her. "I'll take care of cleaning that later. And show you, so you can clean it when you use it."

Though she nodded, she couldn't help but wonder what he'd say if she told him she hadn't realized she'd be cooking for people other than herself. Honestly, she'd figured the lodge would have some kind of staff, even if it were minimal. Cooks and housekeepers at the very least.

Obviously not.

After washing her hands and drying them on a dish towel, she took a deep breath and pasted a smile on her face. While she hadn't been entirely sure what to expect, even her most basic expectations hadn't been met.

Which was okay, she told herself. Because change would be coming.

On the way out, she saw a huge stack of mail on the counter. There were magazines and envelopes, more mail than she personally got in a week.

"That's a lot." She gestured. "How often do you get mail out here?" she asked.

"It depends on the weather," he answered. "I try to pick it up once a week in town, though this time it was more like ten days. I grabbed it yesterday while we were there."

"In town? You don't have a mailbox?"

He glanced at her sideways. "This is remote Alaska," he said, as if that explained everything.

"And? What, do they bring the mail in by float plane?"

"Sometimes," he replied. "It all goes to Anchorage and is distributed from there. I take my outgoing stuff into Blake, and about once a week, they truck it to Anchorage."

Which gave an entirely legitimate meaning to the term *snail mail*, she thought.

"We might be accessible by road right now, but it's not that way always," he continued. "In winter, we're often cut off for weeks at a time. Or longer. Which means our mail service can be hit or miss."

"No mail and no Wi-Fi. How do you pay your bills?"

Unsmiling, he eyed her. "I have them set up on automatic payment. The ones that aren't, I know when they're due, and I can pay them by phone if necessary."

"But you said that Blake has Wi-Fi, right?" she asked.

"Yes."

"Okay." Before she even spoke, she knew he wasn't going to like her suggestion. But she didn't see any reason why they couldn't begin to move out of the dark ages and into modern times. "If Blake has it, and they're not that far away, it shouldn't be too difficult to get service out to the lodge. Have you ever looked into it?"

"No." He crossed his arms. "Sometimes it's a good thing to unplug from all that."

"I agree," she said. "For a while. But decent internet is an absolutely basic requirement for a normal life."

Shaking his head, he stared at her. "Slow down. You haven't even been here twenty-four hours, and you're already trying to change things."

"But for the better," she pointed out, her cheerful tone in direct contrast to his surly one.

"Come on." Clearly unpersuaded, he opened the door and gestured for her to precede him. "At least take a look at the place before you start thinking about what you want to change."

"Sorry," she said, though she wasn't. As she swept past him, she couldn't help but wonder why he had so much resistance to such a minor thing. Most people regarded internet as a convenience.

Outside the main house, all she could see were trees, which made her wonder why the home hadn't been built close to the water. He took her down a long, windy path through the forest. Bits of bright blue sky were visible through the leafy canopies. Despite herself, as they walked, she felt a sense of peace come over her.

Finally, they turned a corner and reached a clearing.

Now, she could see parts of the river, a glittering blue thing shimmering not too far in the distance.

He stopped, and she noticed the small cabin, tucked within a strand of evergreens. Made of rough-hewn logs, it had a rustic feel. The covered front porch even had a couple of rocking chairs.

"Here's cabin one," he said. "They're all identical. This is the only one I've had time to get ready. We'll tackle as many of the others as we can tomorrow."

Climbing up onto the front porch, wood creaking under her feet, she barely heard him. She opened the front door, found the light switch and stepped inside.

The blue-and-green plaid comforter was the only spot of color in the room. Everything, from the log walls to the area rug on the floor, appeared to be in some shade of brown or tan. A small, white mini-fridge sat near the door.

She walked around the room before taking in the small but sparkling bathroom. Even the shower curtain continued the same monochrome color scheme, right down to the pictures of deer and moose on the beige fabric.

"Well?" he asked from behind her. "What do you think?"

That he'd even ask her opinion surprised her. "I love the comforter," she said truthfully. "It adds just the right pop of color to the room."

He nodded. "They're new. Grady ordered them right after last season ended. He died before I could show him how great they look in every cabin."

Though he kept his face expressionless, she could hear the sadness in his voice. "You miss him, don't you?" she asked softly.

"Yes." Turning away, he walked back outside, leaving her alone in the cabin.

Though she really wanted to get out her tablet and begin making notes of small tweaks she wanted to make, she knew now would not be the right time. Dade had already accused her of coming in and immediately wanting to make changes. While he wasn't wrong, she knew she needed to pick her battles. She'd check out the rest of the lodge, make her notes in private and maybe even speak with the first round of guests about their preferences. She suspected doing that would carry a lot more weight than if she simply came up with stuff on her own.

Outside, Dade waited for her on the balcony. He stood with his back to the door, leaning on the railing and staring off in the direction of the river. She noticed a large, stone fire pit with a circle of at least twelve oversized rustic wooden chairs.

"I like this," she mused. "I can see roasting marshmallows over the fire."

"More like beer and sausages," he said without turning around. "Let's move on. We've got a lot of ground to cover."

"Lead the way." If all the cabins were exactly the same, she hoped he wasn't going to show her the other five. Especially since he'd said they'd be cleaning them tomorrow.

To her relief, they walked past all the others, which were just like he'd said, carbon copies of each other.

They were headed toward the water, she realized. Due to the curvy path and all the trees, she only caught occasional glimpses of it shimmering bright and blue.

Another turn and a large, corrugated metal building came into view, with the path leading right up to its door.

"There's where we store the boats in the winter," Dade pointed out. "I started working on them a couple of weeks ago, one at a time. I made sure each was up and running before I put it in the river. We also have a couple of golf carts in there that we use to ferry guests from the main house to the cabins."

Though she smiled and nodded, she realized all her research had failed to prepare her for the actual reality of this place. Instead of managing various employees and fine-tuning the lodge's customer service, she'd be working in the trenches, doing the jobs she'd wrongly assumed would be performed by others.

She'd have no choice but to roll with the punches. She'd learned when she'd first entered the competitive field of commercial land development that she'd have to work hard and smart if she wanted to get ahead.

But then, look where that had gotten her.

More trees, another curve and then ahead, the river and the boat slips. There were ten, six of them filled by boats. The watercraft all appeared sturdy and serviceable to her inexperienced eye. They were all made of metal, with an outboard motor on the back end. While they didn't look very comfortable, she supposed they were perfect for fishing.

"They're jon boats," Dade said. "The most common boat in Alaska. They're cost-effective and tough, easy to navigate, and bouncing off the occasional rock doesn't hurt them."

"Bouncing off the..." She shook her head. "And you expect me to learn how to drive them? With so many boats, why don't you hire locals to come help out? It doesn't make sense to have only two people, one of whom has never done this before."

"It'll all work out." He sounded confident. Or delusional. She couldn't decide which. "Grady and I worked this way for years."

"Grady knew what he was doing," she pointed out, barely keeping the panic from her voice. "What is the reasoning behind not hiring a couple of guys from town?"

"If we actually have a need, we have some people we can call. But like I told you earlier, most of our clients are regulars. They know their way around the river and prefer to take the boat out on their own. It's only occasionally that we get a group that wants someone to accompany them. Those tend to be first-timers."

Maybe there was hope. "Do you have any first-timers coming this year?"

"I'm not sure." He shrugged. "I'd have to check the reservation book. I know the first group is all return customers."

This startled her enough that she stopped walking. "Book? As in paper? You don't manage your reservations on a computer system?"

"Nope." Eyeing her, he grimaced. "That'd be kind of hard to do with no internet."

Which boggled the mind. "How do people make reservations anyway?"

He gave her a sideways glance, tinged with amusement. "They call or leave voicemails. We don't give out our cell numbers, just the landline, since that tends to be more reliable. I check the dates they're wanting in the book to make sure we have room. If we do, I write them down and confirm with them. Pretty simple."

"Like they used to do back in the days before people had internet." Dazed, she tried to understand. "Look, I get that Grady must have been old-fashioned. Sometimes, people can get stuck in the past and refuse to modernize."

"Maybe so," he agreed. "But everything has worked perfectly, so why fix something if it's not broken?"

Since she had a feeling she couldn't persuade him, at least not yet, she simply nodded. She had to wonder how much business the lodge lost each year due to the lack of convenience in making reservations.

"Would you like to go out in one of the boats?" he asked. "I really think you'll enjoy seeing the river."

Looking from him to the fast-moving water, she finally succeeded in staving off her fear and agreed. "Just promise me you'll take it easy. I'm not really comfortable off dry land."

"You can swim, right?"

Though sorely tempted to lie and say no, she reluctantly nodded. "I can."

"We'll be wearing life jackets anyway," he said. "No need to worry."

"I'm not." Which wasn't entirely true, but she didn't want to reveal all of her weaknesses up front. Water was supposed to be soothing, right?

They got onto one of the boats, and he retrieved a couple of life vests from under the seat. They put them on. She sat down and watched while he untied the boat, started the motor and pushed away from the dock.

At first, she clutched the sides of the bench seat, her heart pounding. But as they puttered along at a steady pace, she exhaled and began focusing on the beauty of their surroundings. The way the boat parted the water, the rich greenery on both sides of the river, the sheer majesty of the rock cliffs studded with occasional trees.

All of this somehow soothed her. For the first time, she thought she might partially understand the lure of this remote and wild place.

Seated in the back of the boat near the motor, steering them, Dade seemed to blend with the wildness of the landscape. He belonged here, she realized, a sudden pang of longing making her catch her breath. He belonged here in a way she herself had never been able to anywhere she'd lived.

To chase away her sudden sadness, she did what she always did. Chitchat.

"This really is relaxing," she said brightly, pasting on a cheerful smile. "I'm so in the habit of constantly checking my social media feed that it feels weird not to."

"But kind of nice, too, right?"

She nodded. "Yes. You're right. There is something to be said about being unplugged."

The words had barely left her mouth when her phone pinged, announcing a text. Despite herself, she instantly tensed, resisting the urge to grab it and check it. It had to be her stalker. No one else would be texting her. All of her friends knew she'd gone to Alaska. "How am I getting text messages where there's no cell service?"

He shrugged. "It comes and goes. I told you, texts get through more than anything else. I really don't know how all that works. When we want to be sure to have a working phone, we carry a satellite phone with us."

"I see."

This would be the one time she wished her cell service wasn't working. On the plus side, at least she knew Dade wasn't the one sending them.

Though she tried her best to ignore her phone, when

it sent the reminder ping, she pulled it out and glanced at it. The mystery person had messaged her again. Short and to the point.

You don't belong here. Go home. Or else.

Dade couldn't help but notice Maddie's strange reaction to getting a simple text message. She'd immediately tensed up, a flash of fear in her eyes. She'd immediately looked down, clearly trying to hide it. When her phone pinged again, she'd snatched it up, almost angrily. And then, the instant she read the message, her entire expression changed. Gone was the relaxed, awestruck woman enjoying the beauty of nature. She looked, he thought, miserable.

Dade didn't like it. He didn't like it one bit.

"Old boyfriend?" he drawled, before he could help himself.

"No," she replied, clearly distracted. "Ever since I got notified about Grady's death and my inheritance, I've been getting random texts." She met his gaze. "They're all from different numbers, none of them valid. I know because I've tried to call them back. Apparently, there's an app you can use to send texts anonymously."

He frowned. "These messages, are they threatening?"

"Only vaguely. In the beginning, whoever is sending them warned me not to come to Alaska. I haven't gotten one in three days, so I thought they'd given up." She showed him her phone and the words on the screen. "Now they want me to go home."

"Why?" he asked. "There has to be a reason."

"I have no idea." She shoved her cell into her back

pocket. "To be honest, I kind of thought you might have been the one sending them."

At first startled, he realized he couldn't blame her. If their situations had been reversed, he would have suspected the same thing. "I'm not," he replied. "Truthfully, while I'm not entirely happy about the terms of the will, I admired and loved Grady. If this is what he wanted, then this is what he's going to get."

Their gazes locked and held. While clearly she hadn't cared for her grandfather, he mentally dared her to say anything derogatory about him.

To his relief, she didn't. Instead, she ducked her head, appearing to withdraw into herself. Continuing to pilot the boat, he left her alone.

Finally, she lifted her chin and sighed.

"Where did you go to school?" she asked, out of the blue.

"What?" He stared at her, keeping his expression blank as he skillfully navigated around a fallen log. "Are you seriously changing the subject so you don't have to discuss those texts anymore?"

"Maybe. But I'm also curious."

"I went to school here, in Blake." He sighed. "And that's it. No education beyond high school, if that's what you're asking."

"It is." She smiled.

Not once in his life had he ever regretted staying at Grady's Lodge after finishing up high school. Grady had generously offered to pay his way through college, if he'd wanted to go, but Dade hadn't ever bothered to apply. He'd known for years what he wanted to do with his life, and he didn't see the point in spending time and money getting educated to do something else.

When he looked back at Maddie, she'd resumed studying the passing landscape. Slowing the boat, he pointed. "See those rocks over there? Just past them, the river gets really deep. We catch a lot of salmon there."

"Clearly, I didn't do enough research," she mused. "I focused on what I'd need to know to run a fishing resort from a management standpoint. I'm afraid I didn't take the time to learn the million small details that I need to know, like what kind of fish we catch the most, how they're caught and what the guests like to do in their off time."

Since she sounded more bemused than forlorn, he took pity on her. He even found himself smiling at her. "You'll learn. I'll help you. We're a team now, remember?"

Slowly, she nodded, her blue eyes locked on his. "Thank you."

"Keeping our guests happy is what matters," he continued, turning the boat around to head back to the dock. "Sometimes, after a day of fishing, after dinner, they like to sit around that fire pit you saw earlier. They drink beer, grill sausage and trade fishing stories until they turn in for the night. Once they go to bed, I make sure and check that the fire is out."

"Do you join them?" she asked.

"Sometimes Grady and I did." A pang of grief, sharp and deep, sliced through him. "In better days. Last season, he was too sick to do much."

She went quiet again. Part of him had hoped she might ask a few questions about her grandfather, at least pretend she cared. Instead, she averted her face and gazed out at the water.

He wished he knew why she despised Grady so badly. Maybe someday she'd tell him. He didn't know her well enough to press her.

Back at the slips, once he'd tied up the boat, he helped Maddie disembark. As they walked back toward the house, Maddie yawned several times, covering her mouth with her hand.

"I'm sorry," she said, noticing him watching. "It's been a really long day. Even though I napped earlier, I'm still pretty beat."

They reached the main house. Once inside, he turned on the TV.

"Satellite?" she asked, yawning again. "I mean since you don't get decent cell service, and I don't see any giant antennas, what else could it be?"

"Yes, satellite. It's spotty sometimes, but the only way to get any channels at all." He noticed the way she kept glancing at her bedroom door. "If you're tired, we can talk again in the morning," he finally said.

"I'll keep that in mind," she replied, smiling through yet another yawn. "But I'm thinking, if you're able to have satellite TV, wouldn't it be possible to add an internet package?"

He nearly laughed out loud. She didn't give up, did she?

"Maybe." He shrugged, acting disinterested. "Actually, I have no idea. I've never checked. Grady was dead set against it."

"Well, since Grady is no longer here, maybe we can see?" she suggested gently. "Not only can internet access really help this business, but it'd be great for your guests and for personal use as well."

He had his doubts about that. Since he'd already voiced them at least once, he wouldn't again.

"If you want to check into it, then knock yourself out," he finally told her. "Bear in mind, we're going to be really busy the next few days before the first set of guests arrive."

"Hopefully, it won't take long to find out. I'll need information on your satellite TV provider, if you don't mind. Like the account number and their customer service phone number, that sort of thing."

Weary of the entire subject, he looked at her. So exhausted she swayed on her feet, she took advantage of his tiny concession and jumped in with both feet.

"Not tonight," he finally said. "Get some rest and we'll revisit the idea tomorrow."

"You promise?"

"I promise," he replied. "To be honest, unless the cost is ridiculous, I think having decent internet out here would be helpful."

Her smile lit up her entire face. Once again, his body went full-on DEFCON 1.

"Thank you," she said.

Temporarily unable to speak, he simply nodded.

"How much longer until the sun sets?" she asked, turning away to look out the window. "I want to go to bed, but it feels kind of weird to do it with the sun still so bright outside."

Composing himself, he checked his watch. "It's barely nine, so you've got another hour. The curtains in the bedroom are blackout, so with them closed, you'll barely be able to tell if it's light or dark."

Still, she hesitated.

"We'll be making an early start in the morning," he

said, to nudge her along. "I figure we might as well get in practice. Fishermen like to get started as soon as possible."

"Early? How early?" she asked. "Will the sun be up?"

"I was thinking six," he replied. "And yes, sunrise is around five forty-five. We have long days this time of the year."

Despite her visible drooping, she still made no move to head to her room. Eyeing her, he thought about simply scooping her up and carrying her there, dropping her unceremoniously on the bed.

Except he wasn't that much of a Neanderthal.

Neither spoke. Silent battle of wills? Or maybe she was simply too exhausted to speak.

Finally, she dipped her chin in a nod. "Sounds good. I'll set my phone alarm."

After she excused herself, closing her bedroom door, he went back to the kitchen. He couldn't stop thinking about the text messages she'd mentioned getting. It really bothered him. He could see why she'd thought they might have come from him. Who else wouldn't want her here?

No one but Grady's attorney had known about the will. And Stuart Schmidt, the lawyer, had been one of Grady's oldest friends. Even if Stuart had downed a few too many beers in a bar one night, Dade still couldn't think of a single person in Blake who'd give a damn who Grady left the lodge to.

Whoever was sending Maddie the texts had to be someone from her previous life in Texas. If so, at least while she was here in Alaska, she'd be safe.

He knew he shouldn't care, but he did. Because he knew Grady would have wanted Dade to keep his granddaughter safe.

The next morning, after Maddie took her turn cooking and made them a simple breakfast of fried eggs and toast, they headed out and got busy readying the rest of the cabins. With both of them working, they were able to knock that particular chore out in a little under three hours.

"That was a bit of a workout," she said, smiling up at him as they walked back toward the main house. "But I like the sense of accomplishment."

Though he wanted to point out how great that was, since they'd be doing this after each set of guests left, he didn't. "What are we having for lunch?" he asked instead. "And I'm wondering if you'd had a chance to think about dinner, too."

Just like that, her smile vanished. "It's still my turn to cook? Even though I made breakfast?"

"Yep," he nodded. "We each take a day, remember? Today is yours. Tomorrow mine."

Her expressive sigh had him hiding his own smile. To his shock, he kind of liked her. If he could manage to ignore how she'd hurt Grady with her stubborn refusal to have anything to do with him.

"I forgot about the cooking rules," she finally said. "I don't know if you noticed or not, but I'm not really comfortable in the kitchen. I'll have to look through the cupboard and see what I can make with what we have."

He took pity on her. "For lunch, sandwiches are fine. Or soup. And I defrosted some ground beef, if you want to use that for dinner. We have a pressure cooker, too. Believe it or not, Grady kept a notebook with his favorite recipes. You're welcome to take a look at that if you like."

"Thank you." She glanced sideways at him. He noticed she kept her bear repellent clutched in one hand, always ready. "Is there anything you'd particularly recommend that's easy?"

"We have all the ingredients for you to make chili mac in the pressure cooker. It's quick and easy and generally lasts for a few days, when it's just two of us. It's also a guest favorite, though you have to double the recipe."

They'd reached the house. Inside, he went straight to the refrigerator, grabbed a can of diet cola and handed her another. "The first guests arrive on Friday," he said. "The rest of this week, we're going to plan out a menu, grab supplies and make sure we're as ready as possible."

After lunch, which consisted of a can of tomato soup warmed on the stove and grilled cheese sandwiches, he double- and triple-checked the list he'd compiled from all the times he and Grady had gotten ready for the start of fishing season.

Once he felt sure he hadn't missed anything, he showed her the list, explaining how many guests would be arriving and what they'd be served for meals. When she pointed out he'd left off paper towels and toilet tissue, he almost hugged her.

"Thanks," he said instead. "Every year, I forget something and have to go back. I'm thinking you just saved me having to do that this time."

"You're welcome." She beamed, his thanks seeming to energize her. "Are we going into town to pick up supplies now?"

"No, not until tomorrow. I thought we'd leave right after breakfast. This afternoon, I thought we could sit down and go over the menu for the first bunch. They'll be here Friday afternoon through Tuesday morning."

"Four nights?" She asked, appearing surprised.

"Yes, and three and a half fishing days."

"How many guests?"

He didn't even have to go check the log. "Eight. They'll be using four of the cabins. The Hilbarger family. Four generations of them. They've been coming here for years. They always want to be the first group of the season."

"What do they know about me?" she asked, leaning forward with both elbows on the table.

Surprised, he tried to figure out how to best answer. In the end, all he could give her was the truth. "Grady talked about you a lot. One of his biggest regrets was that he never got to meet you. But beyond that, no one knows anything else."

She recoiled at his words.

"Grady didn't want to meet me." Her flat voice and stony expression told him she believed every word. "He never made a single attempt to reach out. Not one. He didn't attend my high school graduation, or my college one either. He never sent one single Christmas card or birthday card or even a letter."

Dade stared at her, letting his disbelief show. "You're mistaken. I'm sure he did. I sat with him at that kitchen table many times while he wrote you. He tried to write you at least once a month when you were younger. I know for the last few months of his life, he wasn't able to write much, but he tried."

"What?" She shook her head. "If he did, he must not have mailed them. Because none of them ever made their way to me."

"I've no idea why you never got his letters or cards, but he sent them. I took them to the post office in Blake myself. Maybe he had the wrong address. I remember him saying it changed over the years."

Expression still shuttered, she shrugged. "We moved a lot, but I'm pretty sure we always had a change of address form in with the post office."

Unless someone had kept them from her, he thought, deciding not to say that out loud. Maddie would figure it out for herself. Or she wouldn't. Either way, he supposed it didn't really matter now. Any chance she and Grady might have had at forging a relationship had vanished with Grady's death.

Except this bit of knowledge changed things a little for Dade. Knowing she hadn't intentionally shut Grady out helped ease some of the bitterness that had festered inside Dade since he'd met her.

Though, realistically, he knew it shouldn't matter, it did. Maddie and he were partners, for at least a year, no matter what had happened in the past.

Chapter 4

The next morning, the soft ping of an incoming text message woke Maddie. Instinctively, she reached for her phone, rubbing the sleep from her eyes so she could see.

I see you haven't left Alaska yet. You'd better get going, and quickly, before something awful happens.

Her heart skipped a beat. Another veiled threat.

Until recently, she hadn't even suspected Dade might been the one sending them. But why wouldn't he? After all, if she left before her one year was up, he'd get the entire lodge as long as she signed it over to him.

Working in the cutthroat business world of commercial property management, she knew forcing her out would have been the modus operandi of many of the executives she'd worked with.

She couldn't say she would have blamed Dade either. It couldn't be easy to have devoted your life to something only to lose half of it to a complete outsider.

Except now she wasn't so sure it was him. Even if the app had some sort of scheduling capability, Dade had been nothing but pleasant to her. If he truly wanted to chase her away, she would have expected him to be rude and condescending. Instead, he'd made it clear that they would be a partnership. He wanted to honor her grandfather, a man he'd clearly loved.

But her growing certainty that Dade wasn't texting her begged the question—who was?

Some of her former work colleagues had been cut-throat. And when she'd been laid off, they'd acted like she'd ceased to exist. They wouldn't return her texts, never mind phone calls. Not a single one of them even knew she'd inherited property in Alaska. If they had, she suspected they wouldn't have cared.

Theo, her ex, was now engaged to his side chick. From what she'd been able to see on social media, the two of them were expecting a baby and over-the-moon happy.

As for friends... With her demanding career, Maddie hadn't made time for much of a social life. Between work and Theo, she hadn't had the energy for anything else.

Which meant if no one from back home cared about her move to Alaska, it had to be someone here.

She made a list of possible suspects in her mind while in the shower. Maybe Dade had a girlfriend, someone who was upset at the idea of another woman sharing his home for twelve months. Or a really loyal guy pal who felt Dade should have been given the entire fishing lodge.

A short list, she thought ruefully. And neither one seemed all that plausible. After all, whoever it was had to have gone to extraordinary lengths to get her personal cell phone number.

In reality, she didn't have a clue. But she figured she'd eventually find out. Because she definitely would stay here the entire year in order to meet the stipulations in the will. It would take more than a few vague texts to run her off.

Glad it wasn't her day to cook, she dried her hair and walked into the kitchen to find Dade already there, making pancakes.

"You're just in time," he said, smiling. She felt the warmth of that smile all the way to her toes.

"I like your cooking day best," she admitted, heading for the coffee maker. While her coffee brewed, she watched him as he poured the batter onto an electric griddle. He handled himself with ease, as if long used to knowing his way around a kitchen. There was definitely something sexy about a man like that. Especially one as ruggedly handsome as this one.

Nope. She shut that thought down. They were going to be working side by side for twelve months. Desire was the last thing they needed to bring into the picture.

As they ate breakfast—delicious, by the way—and talked, she found it interesting how she and Dade tiptoed around the subject of her grandfather. With every comment about Grady, Dade made it clear how much he admired the man. As for her, she couldn't seem to rid herself of the hard, cold nugget of resentment that sat like a festering lump inside. While Dade claimed Grady had been writing her letters, she had no proof of that.

He'd been kind enough to think of her in his will, but it was too little, too late. While she certainly appreciated the bequest, if she were honest, she would have liked to have known him. Growing up, she hadn't had much of a family. Just her mother, a woman who'd been more preoccupied with having a good time than spending time with her daughter.

All of that was in the past now, and Maddie believed in moving forward. She'd been given the opportunity to start a completely new life, and she'd seized on this with both hands. Dwelling on what might have been would only drag her down.

First thing she wanted to do was get them set up with the internet. And the whole cell phone thing perplexed her, so she'd also like to find out what, if anything, she could do to make it be more reliable.

"We'll deal with that later," Dade said, gathering up the dishes and carrying them over to the sink. For now, we've got to get ready for our guests. Lots of cleaning to be done."

Though back in Dallas she'd paid to have someone come clean her apartment, she managed to nod, hoping she appeared enthusiastic. Apparently, she didn't fool Dade.

"It shouldn't be too bad," he said, grinning. "With the both of us working, we should get those cabins done in no time. By the way, it's your turn to do dishes."

"I'd rather clean up than cook, any day," she retorted. "After we get all the cabins ready, can we sit down and go over the info I need to get internet?"

"We'll see." The non-committal answer had her shaking his head.

"Passive aggressive much?" she muttered.

His answering bark of laughter told her he'd heard.

Surprisingly, cleaning the cabins and setting up the beds wasn't as bad as she'd imagined. By the time they'd finished, she even felt a sense of accomplishment. Dade inspected the ones she'd done and gave her a thumbs up. "Good job!"

They went back to the house for lunch. While Dade made them a couple of BLTs, she pressed him for the satellite TV information. "I'd really like to get started making a few phone calls," she said.

"I know. But we still have a lot of work to do. I'll try and look for that tonight, once we're done for the day."

She knew better than to groan out loud. This was her job now. Until she learned the ropes and felt competent, she'd do what needed to be done.

True to his word, they spent the rest of the afternoon planning out the menu and making sure all the necessary supplies were on the shopping list. For once, she appreciated that all the meals were rustic and simple, since her culinary skills were, too.

By the time Dade announced they were finished, she knew the satellite TV customer-service line would be closed. Which meant she'd have to try again in the morning.

Once again overwhelmingly glad it was Dade's day to cook, she sat and watched TV while he grilled them some hamburgers. They ate dinner in what she thought felt like a companionable silence. Every time she looked at him, the sharp tug of attraction that zinged through her came as a surprise. Prior to coming here, she'd had a type. She'd tended to date well-dressed, blond men who worked in finance or real estate. Drop one of them on a deserted island, and she doubted they'd survive. With his shaggy dark hair and muscular build, Dade was about as opposite of that as a man could get.

If she were in his shoes, she might have been resentful that an intruder from Texas had swooped in and taken half of what he likely considered his. But instead, he'd been polite and considerate, accepting the situation with grace. Instead of trying to run her off, he'd taken the time to let her know what would be expected of her.

They worked well together and made a good team.

Even though the will had made it plain they both had to stay one long year, if either of them left, the lodge would go to the other. Dade could have decided to make her life miserable so she'd go back to where she'd come from. Then he would inherit it all and could go on running the fishing lodge the way he'd always done.

Except she didn't think one person could do this alone. Heck, she doubted two people would have an easy time of it. Once the first set of guests arrived, she'd have a better perspective on things.

For the first time in a long time, when she went to bed, she couldn't shake the feeling that things were all going to work out fine. There weren't any more text messages either. She could only hope that there wouldn't be.

That night, when she fell into bed, she knew she'd sleep well. It had been, she thought, a surprisingly good day.

In the morning, she woke up in a great mood. Though outside the sky had only begun to lighten, she got up first and grabbed a quick shower. A trip to town sounded like a lot more fun than she would have ever imagined. She'd always loved shopping, and even though they'd only be getting supplies for the lodge, she hoped to have time to purchase a few things to personalize her new bedroom. After all, it wasn't like she'd brought any decorative items with her.

By the time Dade woke, she'd already started breakfast. This time, she'd decided to keep it simple. She made scrambled eggs and toast, along with some sausage patties. Sipping her coffee, which for some reason tasted better than it ever had, she hummed under her breath as she prepared the meal.

Dade wandered into the kitchen just as she'd put the sausage patties in the frying pan. He made a beeline for the coffee maker, but halfway there he stopped and turned, eyeing her.

"You're up early," he commented.

"Breakfast is cooking," she chirped, hiding her smile at his surprised expression. "Grab your coffee and sit. It'll be ready in a few minutes."

"That sausage smells great." Carrying his mug to the table, he never took his eyes off her. He sat, using his hand to brush a lock of his dark hair away from his craggy face. He looked unbelievably masculine and too freaking handsome for her peace of mind. She had to swallow hard and turn away. Time to force herself to focus on her cooking so she wouldn't burn anything and ruin their meal.

She could have stood and watched him eat, but instead made her own plate and sat down across from him. He ate fast, appreciation on his rugged face. Again, she caught herself sneaking looks at him, unable to shake the twinge of attraction.

"That was good," he finally said, after pushing his empty plate away. "Thank you."

"You sound surprised," she teased. "I don't think anyone could screw up scrambled eggs and toast."

This made him laugh. And, like everything else he did, he didn't do that halfheartedly either. He threw back his head and laughed, the deep, richness of the sound washing over her like waves on a tropical beach.

Flustered more than she should have been, since she suddenly found herself wondering how enthusiastically he made love, she busied herself collecting their plates and carrying them over to the sink.

If he noticed how she avoided looking at him, he didn't comment. Instead, he pushed to his feet and grabbed her arm.

"I've got those," he said. "It's my turn. Remember, whoever doesn't cook does the dishes."

"Not this time." Needing to keep busy, she waved him away. "You go ahead and get your shower. I've already had mine."

Dropping her arm, he eyed her. "Okay, but you still have to make dinner."

"That's fine."

He didn't move. "Are you all right? You seem really motivated today."

All she wanted was for this buzz of desire to go away. It didn't bode well that she'd never felt anything like this, not in any of her other relationships, including the one with the man she'd believed she'd eventually marry. Until he'd dumped her.

Dade was still watching her, and she realized he'd asked her a question. Depositing the dishes in the sink, she took a deep breath and turned to face him. Annoyed that she had to actually brace herself for the butterflies in her stomach, she forced a smile. "I am. Both all right and motivated. For whatever reason, I'm really looking forward to going into town."

"Why?" he frowned. "You were just in town the other day, when you first arrived here."

"I enjoy shopping." The truth never hurt. She glanced over at their lengthy list. "Are you sure the general store will have all of that stuff in stock?"

His frown smoothed out. "Yep. We place a large order every year right before the start of the season. Kip knows it's coming, so he makes sure to have everything we'll need."

Damn. Part of her wished he were old and unattractive. The rest of her figured she might as well relax and enjoy the view.

Then, while she was still internally reeling from her visceral reaction to him, he pushed to his feet, flashed her a smile and disappeared into the bathroom.

A moment later, when she heard the shower start up, she allowed herself to sag against the kitchen counter. What was wrong with her? Sure, a month and a half had passed since she and Theo had broken up, but she definitely needed to get over this. The two of them were going to be stuck with each other for an entire year. She needed to keep reminding herself of that. And she might not know much about being a business owner, but she knew combining pleasure with work wasn't ever a good mix.

By the time Dade emerged from his shower, she'd finished cleaning up the kitchen. Out of habit, she'd tried scrolling social media on her phone. To her surprise, a few new posts had popped up in her feed before she lost the connection. She sighed as she dropped the phone into the new, cross-body designer purse she'd purchased at the Galleria right before leaving for this trip. Hopefully, she could take advantage of the internet access in town and see about getting something set up. She knew a guy back in Dallas who specialized in websites for businesses, so she'd get him to give her an estimate for one for the lodge.

The lodge. Better known as Grady's. Now hers and Dade's. She picked up some of the cookbooks and began leafing through them. Several were quite old and had some interesting recipes inside.

"What are you doing?" Dade asked, bringing her out of her thoughts. He strode into the kitchen, wearing a tight-fitting black T-shirt, jeans and boots. His hair had clearly been towel dried, giving it a tousled—and sexy—look. Staring at him, her mouth went dry. Dang, dang, dang.

"What?" she managed to ask, smiling. She babbled about finding what she wanted to make for dinner later and complimented him on the well-stocked kitchen.

If he noticed her scattered disposition he didn't comment. Instead, he seemed irritated as he turned around and went back to his room.

When he returned a few minutes later, he asked her if she was ready to go. When she said she was, he scooped the car keys off the counter, flashed another one of those smiles and headed toward the door.

Shaking off her daze, she followed after him, trying not to notice how good his backside looked in those faded jeans.

Once inside his Jeep, she buckled in, mentally giving herself a stern talking to. "Let's do this," she said, resisting the urge to give him a high five. Turning her face away, she concentrated on watching the landscape go past. Mile by mile, she began to relax. If she could manage to keep her mind out of the gutter, she could do this thing.

Dade still wasn't sure what to make of Grady's grand-daughter. Maddie wore impractical clothing, looked as if she'd be more at home in a metal-and-glass high-rise, but she didn't shy away from hard work. Sometimes, she seemed a bit bewildered, maybe even lost. Like earlier at breakfast. She'd kept sneaking looks at him as if he'd suddenly sprouted horns. When he'd gone in to take his shower, he'd actually checked himself out in the mirror to make sure he didn't have something on his face.

He didn't. Which meant he had no idea why she'd been staring.

By the time he emerged, she'd thoroughly cleaned the kitchen and was flipping through one of Grady's old cookbooks.

"I think I've found what I'm going to make for dinner later," she said, smiling slightly. "I've already checked and made sure we have all the ingredients."

"If we don't, you can get whatever else you need while we're in town."

Her smile widened, which made his body stir. "We do. You keep a well-stocked kitchen here."

"We do." His response came out slightly curt, since he had to regain control of his suddenly raging libido. To give himself a minute, he strode back into his room and pretended to be looking for something. Deep breaths and staring at the picture of him and Grady that he kept on his nightstand helped.

When he reemerged, she'd finished leafing through the cookbook and had taken a seat at the table.

"Are you ready to go?" he asked. To his relief, his voice sounded normal.

"I am." Again that devastating smile, sending a bolt of heat to his gut.

Asking himself what the hell was wrong with him, he pulled his keys out of his pocket. "After you," he said, gesturing toward the door.

Following her out to the Jeep, he couldn't help but admire her shape in those jeans. Which was perfectly normal, he thought.

Once he'd started the engine and they pulled away from the lodge, he enjoyed watching the way she studied the landscape with the enthusiasm of a tourist. He wondered how she, a Southerner, would adjust to the often brutal winters of his beloved state. He guessed he'd find out soon enough. First, they had to get through the fishing season.

"Any more of those texts?" he asked. Though he kept his gaze fixed on the road, he caught her quick intake of breath.

"Not since yesterday. It said they could see I haven't left Alaska yet. And then a vague threat if I didn't get going."

He didn't like that. Not one bit. No one had the right to threaten his partner. No one at all.

"Who all knows you're here?" he asked, drumming his fingers on the steering wheel."

She didn't miss a beat. "You. Only you."

This surprised him. "You didn't tell any of your friends? Or people you worked with? What about your family?" He also considered asking about a boyfriend, but for some reason that seemed too personal. If an ex was the person sending the texts, he guessed she'd have figured that out already.

"My mother passed away a year ago," she said, her voice level. "And the people I thought were my friends all vanished when I, uh, lost my job."

"Because you were coming here?" he asked, navigating his favorite hairpin curve easily.

Now, she hesitated a moment before answering. "No. Before that. My company reorganized, and my position was one of the ones that were let go."

Since she didn't sound angry or bitter or even sad, he nodded. "That all sounds like it worked out for the best. Otherwise, you might not have been able to come to Alaska."

"I guess so." She sighed. "Though, it didn't seem like it was at the time. I had to process several life changes all at once."

He waited for her to elaborate, but she didn't. Though curious, he didn't want to press her. She'd tell him whenever she felt ready.

Once in town, he went directly to the general store and parked. "I called ahead," he said. "Kip is expecting us. That way we won't have to wait while he gathers everything up."

"Good thinking. But I'll still have time to look around a little, right? I'm hoping to buy a few personal things."

Surprised, he opened his door and went around to her side, doing the same for her.

"Thanks," she said, lightly placing her hand on his arm. "You have great manners."

Then, while he puzzled over the bolt of electricity that shot through him at her touch, she sailed on into the store, leaving him to follow along after her.

"Good morning," Kip said, beaming at them from behind the counter. "I'm glad you called, Dade. Though to be honest, I'd started putting the usual stuff together a few days ago. We're all looking forward to our small influx of tourists."

"Me, too," Dade replied. "We both are. Right, Maddie?"

Maddie had wandered over to the area where local artists' paintings, sculptures and other crafts were displayed. She looked up, clearly preoccupied, and nodded. "Of course."

Her response made Kip grin. "How's that working out?" he asked. "The whole partnership thing?"

"It's a work in progress. But we've already got the cabins ready for the first round of guests, the boats are running great, and all we need to do is stock up our supplies, and we should be good to go."

Kip's grin widened as he took the hint. "Well then, I guess I'd better start loading up your Jeep."

"I'll help you." Dade felt a pang. In better days, he and Grady had done most of the carrying and loading. It had only been the last few years that Grady's failing health had made him unable to lift much.

The entire time Kip and Dade made multiple trips from the storeroom to the Jeep, Maddie continued shopping, apparently oblivious. Dade considered asking her if she'd mind helping, but decided not to. After all, she'd be unloading it along with him once they got back to the lodge.

Once everything was loaded, Kip tallied up the total, and Dade paid. He'd just finished tucking the receipt in his pocket when Maddie came up to the counter, carrying several paintings, a small sculpture and a couple of quilted pillows Mrs. Ashworth had made.

She deposited her haul on the counter and waited patiently while Kip rang her up. She used a credit card and signed her receipt. Accepting the plastic bags containing her purchases, she smiled brightly at Dade. "Ready?"

The irony of her question didn't escape him. "Yes. Let's go."

"Wait, I almost forgot," Kip interjected, after handing Maddie her receipt. "More mail came in for you. Let me go back and get it."

He hurried off to the back room.

"Did he mean me?" Maddie asked Dade, frowning. "I mean, I put in a change of address form at home, but I wouldn't think I'd be getting any mail yet."

"I think he meant the lodge," Dade replied. "Though I have to say, it's unusual to get mail more than once a week."

"You got quite a few things," Kip announced, carrying a cardboard box full of envelopes and things. "It looks like it's the usual fishing magazines that Grady always liked to subscribe to, catalogs and junk mail, plus several pieces of regular mail."

"Thanks," Dade said, accepting it. "I haven't even had time to go through the stack you gave me the other day."

Kip laughed. "Probably just bills anyway. I know how that goes."

Carrying the box outside, Dade placed it on the back seat of his Jeep. By the time he climbed in, Maddie had already buckled her seat belt. With the sun lighting up her dark hair, she looked more relaxed than he'd ever seen her.

She smiled when she saw him looking at her. "Everything I bought today will help personalize my bedroom. I'm happy to be putting my own touch on it."

That last sentence brought back memories. "Grady was on an HGTV kick for a while," he said. "It seemed like just about every couple on every single show wanted to put their own touch on something."

"Oh, I know." She laughed, the lighthearted sound like a breath of fresh air. "I used to watch those shows all the time, too." Then, sobering, she made a face. "It's funny, but I get it. Staying in Grady's former bedroom felt... odd. I'm hoping when I get it decorated, it might feel more like home."

The echo of loneliness behind her statement resonated with him. He considered himself lucky that he was driving. Otherwise, he might have done something foolish like pulled her close for a hug.

Back at the lodge, the two of them made several trips back and forth, carrying supplies from the Jeep to the house. Most of it went to the kitchen pantry, though Dade set aside all the various fishing and boating supplies to take out to the storage shed.

Once they'd gotten everything put away, she'd taken her new purchases into her bedroom. "I'll make lunch in just a little bit." And she closed her door behind her.

Her comment about lunch had him glancing at the clock. Surprised to see it was a few minutes after noon, he realized he'd worked up an appetite. He was curious to learn what she'd make for the midday meal, but he decided to go ahead and take the fishing and boating supplies down to the shed. He wanted to bring back up one of the golf carts, too, since they were getting close to the arrival of the first set of guests.

When he got back, he found her in the kitchen, stirring something in a mixing bowl. "I hope you like tuna salad," she said, smiling brightly. "I found a recipe in one of the old cookbooks, and since it looked easy, that's what I made."

"We had tuna?" he asked, since he didn't remember ever buying any.

"Well, no. But there's a lot of canned salmon, and I figured it would be close enough."

Salmon salad. He had mixed feelings about how that would taste. But seeing her bright expression, he'd choke it down and compliment it no matter what.

While she made their sandwiches, he couldn't make himself stop watching her. The largest city he'd ever visited was Anchorage, and he'd never seen a woman quite like her. Beautiful, sexy, yet also fearless, she carried herself with the kind of confidence most people her age could only aspire to. The interesting thing was he suspected some of that confidence was all for show. He'd seen how nervous she'd been about going out in the boat.

And despite her expensive clothing and perfect fingernails, she hadn't shied away from cleaning the cabins. She'd also tackled the chore of doing her share of the cooking without a single complaint.

To his surprise, the salmon salad tasted great. "You've just found another way to use the most plentiful fish in these parts," he told her. "I really enjoyed that."

Her cheeks colored. "Thanks. Finding new things to make is more interesting than I thought it would be."

While she took care of cleaning up, he carried the box of mail to the table and began sorting it. Bills went in one stack, junk mail in another and everything else in the middle.

One envelope in particular caught his eye. Handwritten, it was addressed to both Dade Anson and Maddie Pierce. "Weird," he said out loud, turning it over in his hands before grabbing the letter opener. Inside, a single piece of good quality paper had been folded in thirds.

Shaking it open, he saw it had been typed in a font designed to resemble handwriting. Which in itself was weird, considering the text of the letter was an offer to buy Grady's Lodge for a substantial amount of money, signed by a vice president of a large property investment company in Anchorage.

His first thought was that it had to be some sort of scam. He didn't think that offers of this sort were presented in such an unprofessional manner. Grady had used an attorney in Anchorage to make up his will and Dade figured anything related to the lodge would have been sent to him.

Did Maddie have something to do with this? Did she really think she could circumvent the terms of the will so easily? Eyeing her as she cheerfully puttered around the kitchen, he found that possibility hard to believe.

But then again, he really didn't know her that well.

Once again, he read the strange letter. Where had it come from? And how had they known about the fact that he and Maddie would be partners, at least for the next year? While most everyone in Blake had attended Grady's funeral, only a few people were even aware that Maddie would be coming to help out, which was how Dade had put it.

He'd told no one about Grady's will or that he and Maddie would be partners in running the lodge for the period of one entire year.

Which meant this offer had to have come from someone Maddie knew. When he got to town again, he'd bring the paper with him. Once he had access to Wi-Fi, he planned to do some research on the internet. He needed to find out if this investment company even actually existed.

Maybe, he thought, Maddie's idea of getting internet at the lodge might be a good thing after all.

Right now, though, he needed to talk to her.

"Do you have a moment?" he asked, keeping his voice pleasant despite the anger swirling inside of him.

"Sure, what's up?" Carrying a dish towel as she dried her hands, she crossed the room.

He handed her the letter without saying a word. Reading it, she went absolutely still. "How did this person know about the ownership change?" she asked, turning the paper over in her hand.

"I was hoping you could tell me," he replied, arms crossed.

Immediately, she realized what he'd inferred. "You think I reached out to these people and asked them to present their best offer, don't you?"

"Did you?" he asked, letting some of his anger show in his voice.

"Of course not." Lifting her chin, she met his gaze. "Just like you, I'm well aware of the conditions of the will. If I don't keep my part of the agreement, the lodge goes to you. And vice versa."

Gaze steady, he nodded. "Since Grady knows I'd never sell, he didn't put any stipulations on if we jointly decided to sell it. So maybe you somehow think you can convince me to sell. Having someone send an offer arriving around the same time you do is a bold move."

"I just told you, I had nothing to do with it." Her eyes flashed as she dropped the letter onto the table. "You may not know me very well, but I don't lie. If I do something, I can promise that you'll know it."

Slowly, he nodded. He believed her. "I apologize," he finally said. "I just don't know what to think."

And then her phone pinged, announcing a text.

Chapter 5

The sound made Maddie's entire body tense. "Bad enough to be accused of something I didn't do," she said. "But now this. I don't even want to look at my phone."

"Would you like me to look at it for you?" he asked, his gentle tone completely different from the hard accusation of a moment before.

If she'd been at her old job, and he'd been a coworker, she'd have told him off with a scathing remark. But that life had ended. Without saying anything else, she nodded and handed over her phone.

"I need your passcode," Dade said. "Unless you'd rather key it in yourself."

"3535," she said.

After typing it in, he tapped on the text. Leave now or die, it said. He read it out loud. "Sounds like he or she is upping the ante."

"Yes. I've been trying to tell myself it's going to be okay as long as they didn't escalate to real threats. Saying *leave or else* is very different from saying *leave or die*."

"I agree." He glanced at the letter. "I wonder if the two things might be related."

"Interesting." The more she thought about it, the more it made sense. "I worked in real estate development back in Dallas. People can get very cutthroat. If someone got it into their head that I'm standing in the way of them buying this lodge…"

"Except everyone around here knows I'd never sell," Dade said. "So why hasn't anyone been threatening me? Trying to push me out?" He hesitated before continuing. "Quite honestly, I think everyone in Blake believes Grady left the lodge entirely to me."

Blinking, she stared at him. In retrospect, she figured she should have been surprised, but she wasn't. Instead, she felt hurt. "Don't you think we should tell them? I mean, why else would I be here?"

"I don't know," he replied, holding her gaze. But she suspected he did.

"What happens here at the lodge is none of their business," he continued. "Because Blake is such a small town, people like to gossip. Our inheritance is private. They don't need to know anything about what Grady did."

Was that pain she heard threading through his gruff voice? For the first time, she realized having his beloved Grady leave half of his home to a granddaughter he'd never known might have hurt him.

"I'm sorry," she began, trying to find the right words to let him know she understood. But then the rest of what he'd said about Blake and small-town gossip penetrated. "Please tell me you haven't let them all think I'm your girlfriend or something."

"My partner," he clarified, a muscle working in his rugged jaw. "That's all I've said."

She groaned out loud. "Partner, girlfriend, they're all the same thing."

"Does it really matter?" he asked. "I don't like letting other people know anything about my personal business."

"*Our* personal business," she clarified. "And while I do understand your reasoning, at some point, I'd like everyone to understand who I actually am and why I'm here."

Expression bleak, he shook his head. "Why? You know as well as I do that after your year is up, you're going to sell your half of the lodge and go back to the lower forty-eight."

As she'd learned to do in her former career, she took a deep breath and mentally counted to ten before speaking. Burning bridges was rarely advantageous.

She could stand up for herself without doing that. Yet she didn't want to give away all of her plans for this place, not this soon. Dade would only be resistant, which would obstruct any forward progress.

"You don't know that," she finally said, her voice level. "This might turn out to be my calling."

At least he didn't scoff or roll his eyes, as some of the men she'd worked with over the years might have done. He simply studied her and finally inclined his chin in a quick nod of agreement. "Grady must have thought so."

"About that," she began, deciding it was time to try and get some answers. "Do you have any idea why? I never knew him at all. My mother raised me, and quite frankly, she hated him. She told me he killed her boyfriend, my father, and that she could never forgive him for that."

Quiet now, his expression thoughtful, he studied her. "Did you ever look into that story? There were various news reports published, I know."

"No," she admitted. "I heard that story for years from my mom. Ever since I was small. She passed away eighteen months ago." Swallowing, she pushed away that ache. "After my mom died, I never had a reason to look into anything about her past. To be honest, since I'd never heard from Grady, I didn't even tell him about his daughter's death."

"He knew," Dade said. "Believe me, he knew."

"What are you not telling me?" she asked. "Please. It was a long time ago, but I deserve to know the truth."

"I can only tell you what Grady told me. I believe him, since there was a full police investigation, and Grady was cleared of any wrongdoing. I'm sure you can look all of that up online next time we're in town."

"Or once we have internet." She crossed her arms. "But for now, let me hear what you know."

Nodding, he took a deep breath. "Your father—your mother's boyfriend—liked to drink. One night, when he was inebriated and your mother was pregnant with you, he attacked her. Grady intervened."

The version Maddie's mom had told her had been completely different. Fascinated, Maddie waited for him to continue. She hadn't known either her father or her grandfather, but she still felt emotionally connected.

"They fought," Dade continued. "He went after Grady with a broken beer bottle. Grady shoved him away, hard, and he hit his head on the cast-iron stove. He died instantly. Your mother wanted Grady charged with murder, though it was self-defense."

"You say Grady was cleared of all wrongdoing?" she asked.

"Yes. But your mother never forgave him. She stole all the money Grady had and ran away, moving to the lower forty-eight. Grady only ever heard from her when she needed money, which he sent. When he learned he had a granddaughter—you—he even traveled to Texas to try and meet you but was turned away. Over the years, he sent letters and cards with checks inside. The checks were cashed, so he knew they were received."

Maddie wasn't sure how to react. "I never knew," she said. "She didn't give me any of the letters or cards. I grew up thinking my own grandfather wanted nothing to do with me." Despite her best effort to remain emotionless, her voice broke and her eyes welled up with tears. "I never knew him." She let the tears stream down her face. "All those years wasted and for no reason."

With a muttered oath, he pulled her into his arms. "Don't cry. Please, don't cry."

She allowed herself a moment of weakness, taking comfort in his embrace. His strength, the sheer size of him, made her feel tiny and protected, even though she'd always considered herself a tall woman. She let herself sob, releasing all the emotions she'd kept locked up inside of her. Losing her mother, then her job and the man she'd thought she would marry. And now this, learning she'd lost something she hadn't ever had. A grandfather who'd actually cared about her.

Standing with her body pressed up close to his, she gradually became aware that something changed. The air around them, electrified. Conscious of every corded muscle, she heard the hitch in his breathing at the same time he shifted his body.

She tried to step back at the same moment he did. She looked up. She might have pulled his face down to hers, or he might have met her halfway. Either way, their mouths met and electricity sparked.

More than sparked. Blazed. She forgot her own name, where she was, everything but the delicious sensations of his lips moving over hers.

And then Dade abruptly lifted his head and stepped back.

Dazed, she stared at him. That had been a kiss unlike any she'd experienced in her twenty-six years. She suspected it would be all she could think about and dream about for quite some time. Already, she knew she wanted more.

Except Dade, with his shuttered expression and heaving chest, appeared the epitome of regret.

"That shouldn't have happened," he said.

Slowly, she nodded. "You're right." Because of course he was. They had to work together for the next twelve months. They couldn't chance complicating things with kisses. Or sex.

Which might turn out to be one of her deepest regrets. Because judging by the way her entire body wanted him, *craved* him, if they were ever to come together that way, it would be magical.

Her desire for him would be one more thing she'd have to throttle. Luckily, she'd always had a willpower as strong as steel. Heaven knew, she was going to need every ounce of it.

Because Dade was still staring at her as if she'd grown two heads or something, she managed to summon up a small smile. "Let's make a deal. How about we pretend that never happened and never, ever mention it again?"

The relief in his expression should have been amusing. Instead, she felt stung. Another bit of foolishness on her part.

"Deal," he agreed. "Now if you'll excuse me, I've got a lot to do. Tomorrow is a big day. I'll see you in the morning." And then, he turned and walked away.

True to his word, he made himself scarce the rest of the day. She wondered if he'd even show up for dinner, but then because she knew he had to eat, she went ahead and cooked. To her surprise, she found she enjoyed using Grady's old cookbooks. The recipes were not only simple, but tasty.

Pan-seared pork chops, baked potatoes and green beans soon had the small house smelling amazing. With no idea where Dade might be, she went ahead and set the table for two. If she had to eat alone, so be it. She'd make him a covered plate and put it in the fridge for him to enjoy later.

But just as she put the finishing touches on everything, Dade strolled into the kitchen. "That smells great," he said.

She swallowed hard and pasted on her own friendly smile. "Thanks. It's ready, so you're just in time."

"Great." After helping her carry the food to the table, he took a seat.

As they ate, some of her tension dissipated.

"Another one of Grady's recipes?" he asked, after cleaning his plate. "I seem to remember that one. Very good. I enjoyed it."

"It was, and thanks." Pleased, she made no move to help when he began clearing off the table. Tonight, she planned to hole up in her room and read for a bit before going to bed early.

"Good thinking," he commented when she told him her plans. "Tomorrow's going to be a big day."

Though it felt like retreating, Maddie left him there

doing dishes. She changed into her pajamas and climbed into bed with a thriller she'd started on the plane.

About an hour later, she heard the television come on in the living room. Judging this to be a good time to wash her face and brush her teeth, she headed to the bathroom.

Once she'd taken care of her evening ablutions, she went straight back to her room, even though she wanted a glass of water. She figured if she got thirsty later, she'd head to the kitchen after he'd turned in for the night.

Instead, she drifted off to sleep almost immediately. When she next opened her eyes, it was just before dawn. She sat up in bed and stretched. Nothing like starting the day with a sense of purpose and anticipation. Today the first set of clients would arrive. Surprisingly, she had butterflies in her stomach. The kind she used to get before a really big presentation at work.

She showered, put her hair in a neat French braid and then joined Dade in the kitchen.

As usual, her first sight of him caused an instant jolt to her equilibrium. How such a large man could move so gracefully, she'd never understand. It was his day to cook, which she counted as a good thing, since he'd be making the first dinner for their guests.

Guests. She'd trained herself to use this word, instead of *clients*.

Before she'd left Dallas, she'd purchased and downloaded several books on the hospitality industry on her Kindle. Most nights, before she went to sleep, she read them. She'd learned early on that most of the topics they dealt with didn't apply here. Except for the sections on making guests feel welcome. Those she devoured, figuring she could definitely put those principles to use.

"Are you okay?" Dade asked, eyeing her from the stove. "You look lost in thought."

She made herself a cup of coffee. "I'm a little bit nervous. But I'm really looking forward to meeting everyone."

Her comment made him smile. "They're good people," he said. "And I'm sure they'll be thrilled to finally meet Grady's granddaughter."

While she wasn't too certain about that, she held her tongue. She had no idea what her absentee grandfather might have told these people about her, but she'd prefer to let them judge her on her own merits.

After breakfast, Dade went down to the storage building. He came back driving a large golf cart that she hadn't even known they had. "It's for ferrying the guests to their cabins.

Shortly after ten, two large white passenger vans pulled into the drive. Maddie joined Dade on the front porch to greet them.

At the same time, doors opened and people began spilling from the vans. All men, varying in age from elderly to teen. They were in a jubilant mood, joking around with each other and hollering hellos to Dade.

Beaming, Dade greeted them, shaking hands and doing that back-clapping thing that men always did. She watched from a distance, unsure despite her voracious reading on how to be a good hostess.

A man with a shock of wavy white hair approached her. Smiling, he looked from Dade to her and back again. "I'm Elwood," he said, holding out his hand. "Who might you be?"

"I'm Maddie Pierce," she replied, trying for the right

combination of friendly and professional. "Grady's grand-daughter."

"Grady's granddaughter?" Elwood exclaimed, his voice booming. "Well, I'll be. Pleased to meet you."

Just like that, all conversation ceased. One by one, each man turned to stare.

Dade hurried over to join her. "My bad," he said. "I meant to do introductions. Hilbarger family, this is Maddie Pierce. And you heard right. She is Grady's kin. And she and I are partners here at Grady's Lodge."

Stunned to hear him finally say the words out loud, she smiled. "Yes, we are."

Now they all began talking at once as they rushed her, hands outstretched. A couple of the younger men had an appreciative glint in their eyes. But by and large, they all seemed friendly.

She shook hands, made small talk and finally began to relax. All the while, Dade stayed by her side. Which she appreciated more than she could express. She hadn't realized she'd be quite so nervous, but she thought she hid it well.

All in all, a perfect start to a new beginning. She'd even left her phone on her nightstand, just in case another one of the texts came through. She refused to allow anything to ruin this day.

Dade watched with a sense of relief as his longtime customers absorbed Maddie into the fishing family. He'd wondered how they'd adapt to this change, especially this group since they'd been coming here the longest. He'd worried most about the older men, some of whom seemed set in their ways. The younger guys had taken one look at

Maddie's beauty and had just about fallen all over themselves to get close to her.

This shouldn't have bothered him, but it did.

He kept his mouth shut and stayed back, letting them all greet her.

After a few moments, Dade announced that he was ready to take the first group of guests to their cabins. Since the single golf cart couldn't hold all of them at once, he'd have to make two trips. "You know the drill," he said. "I should have brought the other one up, but I forgot."

"We can walk down," one of the younger men volunteered, elbowing the teenager next to him. "We'll let Gramps and the uncles ride."

"If the other one is running, go get it, and I'll drive one," Maddie offered quietly.

Dade shook his head. "I appreciate that. We'll definitely do that next time. It's all good for now."

Then, before she could ask him what else she could do to help, he walked around to the back of the main house. A moment later, driving his white, four-seater golf cart, pulling a small trailer, he rolled up beside the group and beeped his horn. "Hop on in, gentlemen," he said, grinning.

While the oldest men in the group climbed in, Dade jumped out and began loading the trailer with the guests' bags.

"We'll carry our own," Jason, Elwood's oldest grandson, volunteered. "Come on, guys. A little workout won't hurt any of you."

Once Elwood, his two brothers and a couple of their sons had taken a seat, Dade started toward the cabins. None of them felt the need to fill the silence with small talk, which was one of the things Dade appreciated about the older men in this group.

As they pulled up to the first cabin, which Elwood and his brother Floyd always shared, Dade hopped out. Once they'd identified their bags, Dade carried them inside.

"We want to get in at least a couple hours of fishing before lunch," Elwood announced. "Are the boats all ready?"

Immediate fishing was another Hilbarger family tradition. Elwood asked this same question every year. "Yes, sir," Dade answered. "And I've set up bait boxes and tackle boxes in the same place they always are. So help yourself."

"Great. We will."

Since Elwood had to be in his early to mid-eighties, Dade asked if he wanted a ride down to the boat slips. Though in the past, Elwood had always refused, this time he nodded.

"That might be helpful," he admitted. "These old knees aren't what they used to be."

"Let's get everyone's luggage in their cabins, and then we'll head down. You know the drill. I can go out with you, or you can fish on your own like you usually do."

"No offense, Dade. But you know we like our private family bonding time." Elwood laughed.

Once he had everyone's luggage in the right cabins, he drove the older group to the boat slips. The younger men had beat them to it. Dade hung around long enough to make sure everyone's boat started and watched as they motored out into the river. They'd be gone a couple of hours, and someone would text or call when they were back so he could meet them there. He'd clean their fish for them and pack it on ice.

Then he turned around to head back to the main house. He'd have to fill Maddie in on what to expect next. While he knew it would be too much to expect her to help with the fish cleaning, he figured she could get the lunch ready and serve it when the clients returned. Past experience told him they'd all be starving and ready to celebrate their first catches of the season.

The one thing Dade had not allowed himself to do was think about that kiss. That amazing and electrifying kiss. While he wasn't one hundred percent sure she'd felt the same jolt as he had, allowing himself to continue to think the kind of steamy thoughts that would keep him up at night was foolish. Beyond foolish. Now that things had returned to a sort of awkward normalcy between them, he sure as hell didn't want to mess that up. If Grady's Lodge—*their* lodge—were to have a successful season, neither of them could afford to take any chances.

Back at the house, he found Maddie in the kitchen, chopping celery and mixing something up in a large bowl. She looked up when he walked in and smiled.

"Salmon salad," she said. "Since you seemed to like it, I thought I'd serve it on toasted brioche along with home-made potato chips for lunch."

"What about the menu we planned?"

She shrugged. "I'll mostly stick to it, but for some reason, this just sounded good."

Relieved, he nodded. "I think that would go over well. They'll likely fish for the next couple of hours, and when they get back, they'll definitely want to eat."

"And then what?" she asked. "Do they go back to their cabins until dinner? Or do they fish more? Please tell me that we're not supposed to entertain them."

He suppressed a chuckle, aware she likely wouldn't appreciate it. Judging by the edge in her voice, her earlier nerves had returned full force. "Other than making sure they have anything they need, they're on their own. You saw the mini fridges? Those are for them to store their own beer or soft drinks, anything they might have brought with them. They know the drill."

She exhaled and allowed her shoulders to sag. "Oh, good. I've been trying to come up with activities in case that was required."

Now a snort of laughter escaped him. Her eyes widened, but then one corner of her mouth curled up, and she smiled.

"I would have warned you," he said, grinning. "There's no way I would have sprung something like that on you unannounced."

"I appreciate that."

For a few seconds, they stood smiling at each other like fools. Then, realizing how dangerously close he was to kissing her again, he took a step back. "Did you get any more of those text messages?"

His question wiped the smile from her face. "Honestly, I don't know. I deliberately left my phone on my nightstand. I didn't want any distractions from our guests' first day."

"Good thinking." Now he regretted bringing the subject up at all.

"I guess I should go look," she continued, her expression grim. "Though I really wish whoever is sending them would take a break."

Though she kept her tone light, he could tell the subject bothered her.

As she turned to go past, he reached out and grabbed her arm. "Wait."

She froze.

"Don't look at your phone. You can check it later if you have to. I don't think you should let anything spoil this day. It's the first of many, but one you'll always remember."

Her gaze searched his face. He held his breath until she exhaled and nodded.

"You're right," she said. "My phone can wait. I've got to figure out how to make what we have on the menu for their dinner, too. I'm not used to cooking so much, never mind cooking in bulk."

"Let me help you," he offered. The look of gratitude on her pretty face made him regret not offering sooner.

"I'd appreciate that." Gesturing toward the rack of cookbooks, she sighed. "Any suggestions would be welcome. It's their first night here, and I want to make something special."

"I get that," he said. "Grady had the meals down to a science. He rotated them, but basically every group got the same dinner on their first night. Want to guess what it is?"

The way she wrinkled her nose was cute. "I don't know."

"Salmon. It's plentiful, easy to prepare and reminds them why they're here and what they're fishing for."

"I got that. What did you serve for sides?" she asked.

Walking over to the large stand-alone freezer, he showed her all the giant bags of frozen vegetables. "Grady always did a bunch of baked potatoes—those are stored in the pantry—and a variety of different vegetables along with them. We also have large bags of dry beans, though I'd advise soaking them overnight before you cook them."

"Broccoli!" she said, rummaging through the supplies. "Or green beans. Any of those will go great with salmon and baked potatoes."

"Sounds good. Give the potatoes slightly over an hour to bake since there are so many. You can always do them ahead of time and keep them warm. I can help you get them ready when it's time."

Lunch went without a hitch. The fishermen trooped into the kitchen, still talking about their catches. Dade had put all of them on ice in a special freezer in the boat shed. Toward the end of this group's stay, some of the salmon would be sent to the smokehouse to be smoked. Most of it would be packed on dry ice and sent home with them.

Everyone in the group appeared to enjoy the salmon-salad sandwiches and homemade chips. One of the teenagers acted as if he might refuse to eat it. He sat and stared at his plate for a few minutes, but then hunger apparently got the best of him, and he dug in.

"Now what?" Maddie sidled up next to Dade. "What do they do after they've eaten?"

Elwood, who apparently had pretty sharp hearing for a man his age, laughed. "Some of us take a nap. The younger ones like to go hiking. But once the food has settled, we take the boats out again and fish. That's why we're here after all."

Dade nodded. "So true. I'm going to clean up in here, and then I'll be down at the boat slips later if anyone needs anything."

"I'll help," Maddie offered, clearly deciding to ignore their earlier agreement. She caught his sharp look and shrugged. "What can I say? I like keeping busy."

After all the guests had left, Dade and Maddie worked side by side, in a rhythm that had begun to feel familiar. He realized he liked having her here, which surprised him as he'd been so certain he would hate it.

"Now what should I do?" she asked, drying her hands on a dish towel. Again, he found himself suppressing the completely inappropriate urge to kiss her.

"This is your little bit of downtime," he told her, turning away in case he revealed some of what he felt in his expression. "Take a nap, read a book, do whatever you want in the few hours before you have to start preparing dinner."

She nodded. "Okay. But I will say, I'm looking forward to you doing all the cooking tomorrow."

This made him laugh. He swore, he'd laughed more since she'd been here than he had in all the time Grady had been sick. There'd been days when Dade wondered if he'd ever laugh again.

"I'll be back to help you with dinner preparations," he said, heading toward the door. "But whatever you do, don't check your phone."

Now she laughed. The pleasant sound of it followed him out the door.

Passing the cabins, he waved at some of the guests who'd chosen to sit outside on their porches. Since it was a beautiful afternoon, he couldn't blame them. Even the mosquitos hadn't gotten that bad yet.

Down at the boat slips, he started up each one, checking to make sure they had enough fuel. Years ago, Grady had installed a gas pump with an underground tank near the water, and every year at the end of the season, he had a truck come out and fill it.

Since all of the boats currently had close to three-quarters of a tank, Dade left them alone.

"Hey, Dade!" Braden, one of Elwood's sons headed toward him. "Do you have a minute?"

"Of course, I do," Dade replied. He jumped out of the boat and waited on the wood dock while the older man walked over. "Is there a problem?"

"Not a problem exactly." Braden jammed his hands into his pockets. "I'm just wondering what's up with the guy lurking around the property? The kids are making jokes about him, but I've got to tell you, he's making some of us uncomfortable."

"Guy?" Dade asked, searching the other man's face to ascertain whether or not he was serious. "What are you talking about?"

Now Braden stared. "Some guy has been watching us from up in the woods. Several of us saw him when we first took out the boats. And, again, he was there when we got back from fishing. I figured he must be a new neighbor or something because we've never noticed him before this trip."

"I had no idea. I've never seen him." Frowning, Dade glanced around. "I haven't heard of any new neighbors. But even if someone had bought some property nearby, all of the land around here belongs to the lodge."

"That's what I thought." Braden nodded. "I figured he might be trespassing. You really need to check it out."

Dade definitely agreed. He couldn't help but wonder

if this stranger had something to do with the texts Maddie had received. "I wish I could hang around in case he shows up again, but I'd better go check on Maddie."

Chapter 6

When Dade finally came back from the boat area, he seemed preoccupied. He went directly to his room, barely nodding at her as he passed by the couch where she'd been sitting with a book. She briefly considered calling after him to ask if something was wrong, but then decided he'd tell her if he wanted to. She'd started reading a thriller that everyone at her firm had been reading when she'd left, and she could see why the book was so popular. She could barely put it down.

Engrossed in the story, she'd barely read another chapter when Dade returned. He dropped down onto the armchair opposite of her and sat silently waiting until she looked up from her book.

"Are you all right?" she asked, beginning to feel a little concerned. Something in his expression seemed...off.

"I just heard something weird," he said, dragging his hand through his longish hair. "It may be nothing, but I think you need to know."

"Weird?" she asked, wondering if she'd inadvertently done something wrong. "Is all okay with the guests?"

"The guests are fine. I stayed to double check everything before they headed out on their last fishing expedition of the day," he said. "That's when one of Elwood's sons told me they'd noticed a strange man lurking around the woods watching them. I hung around awhile trying to catch a glimpse of him but didn't see anyone. I'll try again in the morning."

"Strange man?" she asked slowly. "Someone trespassing? Because my understanding is Grady's property extends a good bit in all directions."

"Yes, it does. Anyone lurking around the boat slips is definitely not supposed to be there."

Closing her book, she set it aside. "But why? Has he said anything to any of the guests?"

"No. My first thought is that someone might have gotten lost while hiking and stopped to watch them take the boat out. It's the most likely."

"Except you said it happened more than once," she said.

"Right. He was there when they left and again when they returned several hours later."

Now, she sat up straight. "That's weird."

"I know. I'm definitely going to try and confront him if he's there again in the morning. But I wanted to make you aware, just in case he has something to do with those texts you've been getting."

Startled, she instinctively reached for her phone, only to realize she'd never retrieved it from her nightstand. "I guess I'd better go see if he's messaged me again. While it's actually been really nice not dealing with it, I can't pretend it's not happening and hope he goes away."

His gaze never left hers. "I agree. Though it doesn't hurt to take a break once in a while."

Which meant she needed to go check for any new texts. "I'll be right back."

All the way to her bedroom, she found herself hoping

her stalker had decided to take the day off. Honestly, she dreaded checking her phone. Which was ironic, considering how attached she'd been to the device when she'd been living in Dallas. She'd always been one of the first in line to buy the latest version of her particular model. Now, she could barely stand to look at it.

Having limited access to social media didn't help, she had to admit. But the texts, the awful, anonymous texts, needed to stop. Heck, if the stranger in the woods had anything to do with sending them, she'd march up there and confront him herself.

Her phone sat right where she'd left it, on her nightstand. Bracing herself, she picked it up. Once facial recognition had logged her in, she saw she had twenty-three text messages. Twenty-three. "This can't be good," she said out loud, walking back into the living room without looking any further.

"Another text?" Dade asked, pushing to his feet.

"Yes." She tried to keep the dejection from her voice but failed. "More than one actually."

"Do you want to look at them together?" he asked.

Not bothering to try and hide her relief, she nodded. "Yes, I do."

He sat again, and she dropped down in the spot next to him. Sitting so close their hips touched felt comforting. She took a deep breath and opened her phone.

All of the text messages came from a single number. They started out innocuous enough, short and to the point. They followed the same pattern they had before, ordering her to leave and making threats about what would happen if she didn't.

But instead of sending one or two in a short time span, her stalker had seemed to grow more and more agitated.

"All caps," Dade mused. "I don't get why he's so angry. Do you usually reply? Is that why, because you didn't?"

"No, I never reply," she said, wondering if he too felt the heat generated where their bodies touched. "I usually delete the text and then block the number. Which doesn't matter because I'm guessing they just choose another one from the app."

She got to the very last text and sucked in her breath.

I'M WATCHING YOU! PREPARE TO PAY FOR WHAT YOU'VE DONE!

"What have I done?" she asked, swallowing hard. "I don't understand why this person hates me so much."

"I think you should try texting back and ask him."

At this point, she would have tried just about anything. "What should I say?"

"Just ask him why he's texting you and explain you have no idea why. Maybe you can get him to explain what the hell he wants," he said.

Figuring she had nothing to lose, she did exactly that.

Who are you and why are you saying all these things? I don't know what you think I've done to you, but you clearly have the wrong person.

Then she and Dade both sat staring at the screen, waiting to see if there would be a response.

When a reply finally came, it wasn't at all an answer, or even close to what she'd expected.

You're a liar as well as a thief. I wouldn't sleep too soundly if I were you. Because soon, you'll pay.

"Wow," she said, shaking her head. "Still no answers, just more vague threats."

"But the name calling, isn't that new?" Dade asked.

Distracted, she read the text again. "I think so. Obviously, he believes I know what the heck he means. But I honestly don't have any idea."

"Liar as well as a thief." Dade read the words out loud. "I wonder what he thinks you stole."

"Or she," she corrected. "This person could be male or female."

"True."

"And as far as me stealing anything, I haven't. I've never stolen a single thing in my entire life. Not even as a teenager." She shrugged. "I don't get the point of sending these texts. If you have something bad to say about me, say it to my face. Don't dance around the subject with random accusations."

"I agree," he said, surprising her. "I'm a fan of being direct, especially if you want to accomplish anything. And I guarantee you, if I see that guy who's been lurking around in the woods, I'll be very direct."

"I'd like to go with you," she said, putting her phone face down on the coffee table. "I'd like to ask him to his face if he's the one sending these texts."

Dade slowly shook his head. "Not this time. I don't want to risk it, in case he's armed or something."

Horrified, she stared. "You think he might *shoot* at you?"

Expression neutral, he stared right back. "There's always that possibility. I'm hoping he won't, since he didn't take any pot shots at the guests. But you never know."

She didn't like that. Not one bit. "I'm assuming you'll be armed, too?"

"Yes. I always am." He raised his shirt, letting her see his holstered pistol. "Around here, it pays to be careful."

"Of what?"

"Let's see." Letting his shirt fall back into place, he grimaced. "We're in a remote part of Alaska. Out here we have snakes, bears, wolves and various other dangerous animals. Not to mention the occasional drifter who finds his way to our neck of the woods. One thing Grady taught me as a young kid was to always be prepared."

He made sense. She might have lived all her life in the city, but she knew plenty of women who carried a small handgun inside their purses.

"Will you teach me?" she asked, surprising herself. "How to shoot, I mean? Since I'm going to be here for a while, I'd like to protect myself, too."

"Sure. We'll make time for that," he said. "But right now, we need to start getting dinner prepped. They'll be back and hungry before you know it."

"Let me put this phone back in the bedroom." She picked it up from the coffee table and turned the sound off. "It's easier if I don't have it around. I don't want to be jumping at every text message. Too distracting."

"I think that's a good idea," he agreed, holding her gaze a moment too long.

After she shoved the phone into the nightstand drawer, she returned to find him already gathering ingredients on the kitchen counter.

They worked side by side in the kitchen, Dade with a

graceful ease that seemed astonishing in such a large man. Though it was her turn to cook, she ended up letting him take over and simply imitating what he did. After all, he'd done this sort of thing numerous times before.

By the time the group trooped back into the dining room, everything was almost ready. Though Maddie had never cooked a meal on this large of a scale, Dade made it surprisingly easy.

Once everyone was seated, they began serving the food. The salmon had turned out perfectly, same with the baked potatoes. Dade had made a condiment tray with butter, bacon bits, sour cream, shredded cheese and green onions. And he'd shown her how to take a couple of large bags of frozen broccoli and turn them into a cheesy casserole. For dessert, they'd put a large, premade frozen peach cobbler into the oven, which they'd serve along with vanilla ice cream.

They also served a basket of still warm yeast rolls.

Only once every guest had been served did they retreat to the kitchen to scarf down their own meals.

"That was really good," Maddie marveled, pushing away her empty plate.

"It was." He smiled approvingly. "Now, we need to clear the table and serve dessert."

Everyone tucked into the cobbler, clearly appreciative. Once again, Maddie and Dade stepped back, staying in the background. They'd left just enough cobbler in the pan for themselves.

"Nice how that worked out," she told Dade, making him laugh.

"And it always will," he promised.

After everyone had eaten and wandered back to their

cabins, Maddie and Dade cleaned up, side by side. Since he'd helped her cook, she pitched in on the cleanup. "We make a pretty good partnership," she said, keeping her tone light.

"Yes, we do," he agreed. The warmth in his voice made her tingle all over.

Once the last dish had been put in the dishwasher and the machine turned on, she dried her hands on the dish towel and turned to look at him. "Now what?"

"We're done for the day, unless someone needs something. From now until breakfast, they'll amuse themselves. Even though it doesn't get dark until late, they won't be fishing anymore today."

She nodded. "Now that I'm off the clock, I'm going to get back to that book I was reading. What about you?"

"I'm going to do a brief patrol of the area," he said, his carefully blank expression not fooling her. "I want to make sure that guy isn't camping out somewhere nearby."

With that, he quietly let himself out the back door.

She went to get her book, but found she couldn't really concentrate. So she carried the book outside and dropped into one of the chairs there.

In the distance, she could hear the sound of laughter. Despite everything, she found herself on the path, headed down toward the cabins.

As she drew closer, the sight of flames leaping into the darkening sky stopped her in her tracks, an unfamiliar ache in her chest.

The guests had ended up seated around the bonfire in the pit, exactly as Dade had predicted. They'd broken out the beer, at least for the older ones, while the teenagers had moved to the open meadow to toss around a football.

Her first instinct was to reach into her pocket for her phone so she could snap a picture. Then she remembered she'd left it in her nightstand. Maybe another night she'd capture an image on her phone. Tonight, she'd have to keep this inside her heart.

And she missed Dade. Way more than she should have.

As she stood on the path staring, she wondered what it would be like to join them sitting around the fire pit. To be part of such a thing. Naturally, she wouldn't. Hosts didn't crowd their guests. Even Dade, who'd known them for years, gave them plenty of space.

Still, the idea of sitting around a fire as the night air cooled sounded inviting. She wondered if there would be any time between when this group left and the next arrived. If so, maybe she and Dade could do that. If he ever came back.

Her worry grew as the shadows lengthened and Dade didn't reappear. Several scenarios played out in her head. What if the intruder had taken Dade by surprise and captured him?

Turning around, she trudged back to the front porch. If he didn't show up soon, she'd have to go look for him.

Dade knew every inch of these woods like the back of his hand. After all, he'd been roaming them since he'd been a child. He searched every hollow log, downed tree and hidden grotto that he knew of, finding nothing. If that guy was camping on these lands, Dade saw no sign of it.

Circling the ridge above the boat slips, he also looked for clues that someone else had been here. While he didn't think the intruder would be foolish enough to try and build a fire, he had to have left traces of his presence.

From this vantage point, he could see the cabins and the group beginning to gather around the fire pit. Soon there'd be orange flames reaching into the night sky. As a youngster, this had always been his favorite time of the day. More than once, Grady had caught him hiding in the shadows watching the adults' merriment around the campfire.

These days, he knew they'd likely invite him to join them, welcoming him with the easy camaraderie of long acquaintance. But Grady had drummed into him the importance of keeping himself separate from the guests. They visited, sure. And during Grady's long drawn-out illness, some of the guests had wanted to spend time with Grady in the main house instead of fishing.

Grady, being himself, shooed them away. He'd told them they'd paid to fish, not shoot the breeze with an old man. Grady had never realized how much his guests loved him or that they'd considered themselves family.

He pushed aside the melancholy memories before turning and making his way back to the house. He knew a path that would skirt the group at the fire pit and would bring him to the main house from the south side.

When he made his way out of the woods, the sight of Maddie's slender figure standing on the front porch made his breath catch in his throat.

She turned toward him as he approached. With her face in shadow, he couldn't read her expression. "Any luck?" she asked.

The husky timbre of her voice sent a shiver up his spine.

"Nope," he replied, taking the steps up two at a time. By tacit agreement, they both dropped into the side-by-side rocking chairs.

He began slowly rocking back and forth, willing his heart rate to return to normal. Next to him, she sat motionless, staring out at the plume of smoke still visible below them.

"They seem to be having a good time," she mused.

"Yes. It's a nice close to a good first day."

Still, she didn't turn to look at him. "Did they catch a lot of fish?"

"Enough to keep them happy," he replied. "We have a large freezer down at the boat shed where we keep them on ice. Some of them will go to the cannery to be canned or smoked. Most will be packed on dry ice and taken home with them."

She nodded and began rocking.

They sat out on the front porch while the sky darkened. The crickets began to sing, warring with the sounds of merriment from the guests below.

"Sometime in between guests, could you and I sit around that fire?" she asked, her low voice wistful.

The yearning in her tone made his throat ache. He knew that feeling all too well.

"We will,' he replied, deliberately keeping his voice light. "That's tradition around here, too."

"It is?" Now she half turned, facing him. Then, without waiting for an answer, she sighed. "I've never experienced anything like this before. Sometimes I feel like a little kid who's been sent away to camp for the first time."

"I thought all you city kids went to summer camp," he teased. "You really never went?"

"No. We moved around a lot. My mother didn't like to stay too long in one place. I think she skipped out on rent most times. And we definitely couldn't afford summer camp."

Again, he felt that twinge of sympathy, of kinship. He'd never known his people or where he came from. If not for Grady stepping in and filling the void, he suspected he would have crashed and burned long ago.

It took every ounce of willpower he possessed not to pull her into his arms and offer comfort.

They sat outside for a long while, the darkness complete and absolute long before he finally stood and stretched. "I'm going to go in and start getting everything ready for the morning. The day will start early."

"Really?" She stood, too. "Even though they sound like they'll be up drinking until dawn?"

"Yep. Sure, some of them will have hangovers, but I guarantee not a single one of them will stay in bed. They're grown men."

She followed him inside the house. "I know that's true. What can I help with?"

Once again, he was working side by side with her. As partners went, Maddie wasn't half bad. He certainly hadn't been expecting this.

By the time they'd finished prepping for tomorrow, Maddie was swaying on her feet. Taking pity on her, he told her he'd see her at sunrise, reminding her they'd be starting early.

He went to bed shortly after. Instead of tossing and turning the way he'd been lately, he fell into a deep and dreamless sleep.

The next morning, he worked quickly, glad they'd done all the meal prep the night before. Maddie's bedroom door remained closed, but he imagined she'd be out shortly. She emerged just as he'd finished making a large sack of breakfast sandwiches for the group to take out on the water with them and a large thermos of black coffee. This had been a long-standing tradition for the second day for as long as Dade could remember.

"Good morning," Maddie said, stumbling over to the coffee maker. While her cup brewed, she apologized for not helping him assemble the sandwiches.

Once again he found himself resisting the urge to touch her. "You helped plenty last night. This didn't take me long at all."

He'd dug out an old coffee maker so he could make a large pot rather than the individual brewer they normally used. Maddie watched him fill up a thermos and offered to make a second thermos, but he told her they didn't need it. "The younger ones drink cola instead of coffee, so they'll have packed an ice chest."

"Oh." She brushed back a wayward lock of hair from her face. "Do you want me to go with you?"

"No. Just wait here," he said. "I'll be back once they're all out in the water."

She nodded sleepily and sipped her coffee. Looking at her, with her tousled dark hair and kissable lips, he once again battled that sharp stab of desire. He supposed he ought to be used to it by now, but the sheer intensity of his need for her never failed to surprise him. It only seemed to get worse day by day.

"I'll be looking for that intruder, too," he reminded her. "So it might be a bit before I get back."

"What are you going to do if you manage to catch the guy?" she wanted to know. "Does Blake even have a police department?"

"No, we don't," he answered. "We tend to call for the state police, who get here when they can. We do have a place we can hold criminals, if necessary. But as far as this intruder goes, it really depends on his intentions. He could be some harmless wanderer who strayed too far off the beaten path."

"True." She yawned, covering her mouth with her hand. "Or he could be the person who's been sending me those awful text messages."

Forcing himself to drag his gaze away from her, he slowly nodded. "That's what I'm hoping to find out. He likely has already moved on."

Except Dade wasn't sure he truly believed that. Grady's Lodge sat far off the beaten path. No one ever accidentally wandered out this way. Well, no one except Dade himself when he'd been a small child. And even then, despite the fact that he'd been far too young to have been left on his own, he suspected someone had dropped him off.

He shook his head, wondering why losing Grady had made him think so much about the past. Nothing he could do would change what had happened to him then. And Grady had been the one to change that for the better. Dade missed him so damn much.

And wanted Grady's granddaughter way more than he should. For an instant, he wondered if the old man had planned and hoped for this.

"Are you okay?" Maddie asked, her soft voice almost as appealing as her kissable mouth.

"Sure," he lied. "Just a little tired." With that, he turned to go.

The lights were on in all the cabins, but no one had yet emerged. Though the sun hadn't yet cleared the horizon, the sky had started to lighten enough to bathe everything in an early morning glow. He loved this time of the day the best. It had always felt borderline magical, which was something coming from a man who didn't believe in magic.

Pushing aside his fanciful thoughts, Dade saw nothing out of the ordinary, at least not around the cabins or the fire pit, with its still smoldering ashes.

On his way down to the boat slips, he scanned the tree line, keeping an eye out for any signs of an intruder. Nothing, not even any wildlife, which was unusual. Normally, he expected to see a bear or two fishing for their breakfast in the water.

As he tinkered around with the boats, making sure they all had enough gasoline, the guests started to make their way down from their cabins.

After greeting him, they immediately went for their breakfast sandwiches. Some devoured them right then and there, while others tucked them into pockets or backpacks to eat later.

Elwood's son Braden strode over to Dade. "Any sign of him?" he asked quietly.

"No," Dade answered. "Maybe that means he's moved on."

"I hope so." Exhaling a sigh of relief, Braden watched the youngest group of fishermen. "My wife would kill me if I let anything happen to our grandsons."

"I got you, man." Dade clapped the older man on the back. "I'm sure that guy was just some drifter who wound up in the wrong place. I walked the woods yesterday and didn't find anything indicating he might be camping out here. And no one has seen him this morning."

"You're probably right." Expression relieved, Braden

turned a complete circle, checking out the woods around them. "I appreciate you checking on this."

"No problem," Dade replied. "And if by any chance you happen to see him again, please let me know immediately. I'm going to hang around here until you all are out on the water."

Going from boat to boat as each group climbed aboard, Dade made sure no one needed anything. He untied each from the dock, helped push them out into the water, and watched as motors were started and the fishermen moved away. All the while, he kept watch but saw nothing unusual.

As the last boat turned the bend on the river and vanished from sight, a brown bear emerged from the woods slightly upstream. Dade eyed the familiar sight and wondered if the intruder had truly gone or had simply gone into hiding, waiting for a better moment to strike.

Then, chiding himself for his fanciful and uncharacteristic thoughts, he made his way back toward the main house. About halfway between the boat slips and the cabins, he caught a glimpse of movement. Was that a man watching from behind a large pine tree?

Heart rate in overdrive, Dade took off running. Not directly toward his target, but more to intercept him. If this intruder intended to make his way toward the main house, that meant Maddie could be in danger. Not if he could help it. No way would he let that happen. He needed to take this guy down once and for all and find out what he wanted.

Chapter 7

After Dade had left, Maddie had drifted around the small house, wondering how simply sharing space with him put her into a heightened state of awareness.

She'd never met anyone like him, and she suspected she never would again. Men like him didn't exist in the fast-paced life of the city. His large size wasn't the only reason he filled up a room. He'd been kind and patient as well, but to be honest, she hadn't been able to stop thinking about that kiss.

Though clearly, she hadn't had the same impact on him.

All for the best, she supposed. Because that knowledge, and the common sense that had always served her well, had been what kept her from going to his bedroom in the middle of the night to slake her constant yearning. Talk about a disaster waiting to happen. Just the thought made her want to hyperventilate. But then again, she'd never dealt with rejection well. And having to face a man who'd from that moment on look at her with nothing but pity… Her skin crawled at the thought.

That didn't mean she stopped wanting him. Ever present, desire simmered just under her skin. Hopefully, after they'd spent a few months together, that would go away. But for now, she had to figure out a way to deal with it.

And keeping herself in check didn't keep her from dreaming about him. Oh, she did, with achingly sensual detail. She might be able to turn her craving off during the daylight hours, but at night her subconscious got free reign.

Think of something else, she told herself, slugging back the rest of her coffee. Out of habit, she reached for her phone so she could scroll social media.

But then, she remembered. Last night, when she'd returned to her room, too exhausted to think clearly, she'd switched her phone off without even checking for text messages. She'd shoved it in her nightstand drawer.

Which was where it might have to stay. It had been ages since she'd been this unplugged, and while at first she'd found it uncomfortable, now she'd started to think she could easily begin to like it. There wasn't much that interested her on social media these days anyway, and without reliable internet, those feeds had trouble refreshing.

Not having to worry about some unknown person constantly threatening her turned out to be an additional bonus. Sometimes she thought she might never turn her phone on again.

After finishing her coffee, she made a second cup and then assembled herself a breakfast sandwich. She ate at the small kitchen table and tried to think about what she could do to help out. Though he hadn't mentioned gathering up towels or anything, she needed to ask if she should be swapping them out or doing loads of laundry.

For now, since she was alone and the camp was emptied, she planned on staying put. She'd even taken the extra precaution of locking the front and back doors to the main house, something that she'd never seen Dade do. Just in case.

A loud bang from outside made her jump. She was too afraid to open the door, so instead she hurried around from window to window, peering outside to see if she could see what had made the noise.

Finally, she spotted the culprit. A large raccoon had knocked over one of the metal garbage cans and was now rummaging through the spilled contents. Smiling, she watched for a moment, the intensity of her relief making her sway.

She hated feeling so paranoid. But learning about the intruder spotted on the property had been jarring, to say the least. The possibility that her phone stalker might have gone from text messages to showing up in person absolutely terrified her. Discovering that Dade at least carried a weapon helped some, but she'd never been one to rely on others for something she could do herself. As soon as possible, she wanted to learn how to handle a firearm and get one of her own.

The backdoor knob rattled, and she jumped. Someone started pounding on the wood. It startled her to the point where she froze. But then she heard Dade's voice calling her name.

After she hurried to let him in, her apology stuck in her throat when she took in his disheveled appearance. His color high, breathing ragged, with his mane of hair wild around his face, he looked as if he'd just taken on fighting a bear in one-on-one combat.

He also looked hot as hell. She tried not to stare.

"Good thinking," he growled, brushing past her. "From now on, always lock the door when you're here alone."

She nodded. "I will. But, Dade, are you all right?"

Slowly, he turned to face her. His eyes still were wild. "I'm fine. I thought I saw someone on the way back from the boat slips, but I couldn't catch him. And I'm not even sure it was a person, rather than a trick of light."

She managed to nod. "Did any of the guests see anything?"

"No. In fact, Braden appeared relieved. He's going to text me when they're on their way back in, so I can meet them down there. Until we clear this up, I don't want to take any chances with anyone's safety."

Knowing she needed to get her raging libido under control, she turned away and made a show out of looking out the kitchen window. "I get it, believe me. A few minutes ago, a raccoon got into one of the trash cans. The noise scared the heck out of me until I realized what it was."

"That must have been Clyde." He said that so matter-of-factly that she stared.

"Who must have been Clyde?" she asked, confused.

He gave her a sheepish smile. "The raccoon. He's been around here for years. Grady used to put out food for him. I've been meaning to do that, but I forgot. That's probably why he got into the trash. He's hungry."

Since he said this as if it was the most ordinary thing in the world, she decided to go along with it. "I see. What do raccoons eat?"

His smile widened. "A little bit of everything. They'll snack on fruit, veggies, nuts, fish, insects, frogs, even small rodents. We mostly feed them spoiled fruit and vegetables. And some of the leftover parts of fish. They really enjoy that."

"Really?" She started to make a face and then thought better of it. "Aren't raccoons considered a nuisance?"

"Sometimes. But Clyde's been around since he was a young, sickly one. We think his mother was killed. Grady was always one for taking in orphaned things. Clyde would have died if not for us."

She noticed the way he included himself. A sudden image of a younger Dade, nursing a tiny raccoon back to health, made her feel all warm and fuzzy inside. Who knew a man so big and tough could also be so soft and caring.

Nope. Thinking like that would be dangerous. She gave herself a mental slap and nodded. "I see. Well, I guess you'd better go back to feeding him. I suspect he made quite a mess out there when he knocked over that trash can."

"I'll clean it up." He checked his watch. "I'll need to start getting lunch put together soon. Since they had breakfast sandwiches, I wanted to do something a bit more filling for lunch."

"Like what?" she asked. "I'd be happy to help."

"I appreciate that. While we're still keeping meals simple except for dinner, in the past, they've really enjoyed hamburgers and hot dogs cooked on the grill. I made sure the propane tank is full, so I'm good to go. We'll just need to prep all the condiments. Onion, lettuce and tomato for the burgers, and chopped onion and pickle relish for the hot dogs."

While he was outside straightening up the trash cans, she located several packages of hamburger and hot-dog buns. Dade had also stocked up on industrial-size cans of baked beans, so she used the electric can opener and dumped them into the Crock-Pot, which she turned on high. That way, she wouldn't have to worry about them burning.

"That's exactly what we always serve as a side," Dade said, gesturing toward the beans. "Now we just need to get busy chopping."

Working side by side, him chopping onions, her slicing tomatoes, she felt content. In fact, she'd begun to realize this might not be a bad life after all.

They'd just finished up when Dade's phone buzzed, indicating a text. "They're heading back in," he said. "Apparently, they had quite a catch. I'm going to head down there to meet them."

"I'm going with you," she declared, hurrying to wash her hands in the sink. "I need to get out of the house."

Though he glanced at her sideways, he didn't argue. "Let me make sure the front door is locked. From now on, until we figure this out, we're locking up any time we leave the house."

Once outside, she waited while he dug out his key and locked the back door. "I take it this isn't something you normally do?"

"Locking up? No. We've never had a need." He glanced at her, and the hard edge to his gaze softened. "We will get this figured out."

Though she wanted to melt right there on the spot, she managed to nod instead. "I hope so. It's been a lot. Not only did I uproot myself and move thousands of miles away, totally changing my life, but then some random person decides to start stalking me. I still don't know why."

"Stay by my side," he ordered as they started off down the path. "I take it you got more text messages?"

Busy scanning the woods for anything out of the ordinary, it took her a moment to answer. "Honestly, I don't know. I haven't looked at my phone."

They continued on in silence for a few seconds. The cabins had just come into view when he spoke again. "I understand not wanting to deal with all of that. But I don't think ignoring the texts is the safest thing to do."

Startled, she stumbled and nearly fell. Dade reached out and grabbed her arm, keeping her upright. It took a moment for her heart rate and breathing to return to normal.

"Sorry," she finally said, shaking his hand off and moving forward again. "I'm not usually clumsy."

Instead, he grabbed her again. "Wait. Don't move."

His low, urgent tone got her attention. Instantly on alert, she moved closer to him. "Did you see something?"

"I don't know. Maybe." Though he stood still, he constantly scanned the woods around them. "We need to keep moving. Act casual, as if we're completely unaware anyone could be out there."

Could? Heart once again racing, she somehow managed to move forward.

"Keep looking straight ahead," he said. "I'm checking the woods. If someone is out there, they're likely watching you."

She wanted to ask him if he still had his pistol, but didn't. Instead, she reminded herself that they didn't truly know if anyone actually *was* watching them. And also, even if someone was, they might not be the same person who'd been sending those texts.

As she kept moving forward, every nerve ending on edge, she understood why she shouldn't have tried to ignore those texts. What if the sender had made more specific threats, in effect giving her a warning? What if he'd specifically mentioned he'd be out in the woods today waiting for her?

"It's going to be okay," Dade muttered, clearly understanding her nervousness. "We still don't know what this person wants. It might not even be related to the texts."

Though she nodded, she wanted to tell him her gut told her it was. But then again, she'd always had a vibrant imagination. The possibility did exist that she might be making too much out of nothing.

Riiiight.

She wanted this person caught, and she wanted him caught now. She needed to look him in the eye and ask him what she'd ever done to deserve all the hateful text messages. Because while Maddie knew she wasn't even close to being a saint, she'd always tried to treat other people the way she herself wanted to be treated.

Somehow, she and Dade continued to move forward. Though she worked hard to appear oblivious, she could no more keep herself from constantly scanning the woods around them than she could keep herself from breathing.

"There," Dade growled. "Keep moving and stay right next to me. I think I spotted him, near the meadow where we store our boat trailers."

Only the force of his arm linked through hers, propelling her forward, kept her going.

Was this it? Were they finally about to confront the faceless and nameless person who'd been stalking her?

"Hey! Good morning!" Two of the teenaged members of Elwood's party came running up. "We slept in, so we missed the fishing. Are you on your way to meet them at the boat docks when they come in?"

"Yes." Disengaging his arm from hers, Dade turned to

face them. "Will you two keep Maddie here company for a minute? I need to check on something up in the meadow."

"Sure," they replied, jostling each other for a chance to stand close to her.

Relieved and resigned, she smiled at them. They ended up on either side, flanking her.

"Good," Dade said, already making his way up the hill. "I'll see you in just a few minutes."

And then he disappeared into the trees.

Taking a back way to make it appear he'd doubled back toward the house, Dade made his way toward the meadow and the small group of trees where he swore he'd seen someone standing. Enough was enough.

The boats with their guests would be back soon. Hopefully, all that activity would be enough of a distraction that the intruder wouldn't realize Dade had circled around behind him until it was too late.

When he reached the meadow, he didn't see anyone. No footprints or crushed grass. Nothing but all the boat trailers, lined up in neat rows. Dade skirted around the edges, sticking close to the trees. If he continued on in this direction, he'd come out on top of the cliffs overlooking the river and the boat docks. That would be the best place for a trespasser to observe while remaining as invisible as possible.

But as the trees thinned and the soft earth gave way to rock, he still saw no sign of anyone else. From up here, he could see the boats coming in from a bit down the river. Below, Maddie and her two teenaged escorts had just reached the docks. Dade saw no signs of anyone else in the immediate vicinity.

Maybe, just maybe, the intruder had moved on. It now seemed entirely possible that, instead of being tied in with Maddie's threatening texts and the letter asking them to sell the lodge, this had been some hiker who'd taken a wrong turn.

Relieved, he turned to make his way down to the boat slips to join Maddie in greeting the returning guests. Halfway down the path, something exploded.

The force of the blast nearly knocked him off his feet, sending him staggering. It took him a few seconds to figure out what had just happened. A second blast, and then a third, shook the earth. Dade cursed, his heart pounding. And then he started to run, pressing 911 on his phone as he went. Luckily, the call went through. He managed to tell the operator his location and what had happened. "Send help," he pleaded, before ending the call.

By the time he reached Maddie, he realized the explosion had been behind them. The plume of black smoke and accompanying fire carried their own kind of danger. Though he hoped the foliage had remained damp enough from all the recent rain, a forest fire would be devastating.

"What was that?" Maddie gasped, when he reached her. She pointed to the smoke. "Did something blow up?"

"Judging by the area, I'm going to guess it was near the boat storage shed. We do keep extra gasoline there. Plus some propane tanks."

Both teenagers seemed nervous. Dade studied them. Had they done something to cause this? "Is there anything you two need to tell me?"

Immediately, they both shook their heads. "No, sir. We're just hoping that wasn't our cabin."

Dade nodded. "You two wait here for your family.

When they get here, tell them to hurry. I'll need everyone's help to make sure this fire doesn't spread." He glanced at Maddie. "Come with me. Let's get started."

Leaving the two boys behind, they raced back along the path. As they rounded the corner, the boat storage shed came into view. One side of the metal building had been blown out, and an inferno raged inside. Flames licked at the air, but hadn't spread beyond the building yet.

"Is anything else going to blow?" Maddie asked.

"Good question. But judging by the force of the first blast, and the fact that there were a couple smaller explosions after, I'm going to guess everything that could blow up, did."

Wide-eyed, she nodded. "Shouldn't we call someone?" Maddie bent over, trying to catch her breath. "I'm guessing Blake has some sort of volunteer fire department."

"We do, and I did." Satisfied that, for now, the fire appeared to be contained, he started for the tractor. "Just in case they don't get here in time, I want to be ready. If I have to, I'll knock the rest of the building down to keep the flames contained."

She went with him, clearly wanting to stay close. "How will they get the fire truck out here?" she wanted to know.

"We don't have a fire truck. They call it Project Code Red. Lots of small villages utilize it. We have a fire department in a box. It's two metal trailers with thirty-gallon solution tanks, a water pump and one-hundred-foot hose reels. It uses compressed air to produce firefighting foam with a small amount of water. They can be hooked up to pickup trucks, all-terrain vehicles, heck even snowmobiles in the winter. Works really well."

Inside the shed, something else popped. The flames

briefly reached higher. Dade was grateful for Grady's foresight in clearing the immediate area of trees and foliage and spreading gravel on all sides of the metal building. If left alone, there was a very real chance the fire would simply burn itself out.

When Maddie slipped her hand into his, he froze. But he didn't pull away, figuring all of this had terrified her, and she most likely needed comfort.

Plus, if he were honest with himself, he liked being the one to offer that to her.

"What could have caused this?" Maddie asked.

"That, I don't know. But it definitely wasn't an accident."

The group of returning fisherman all arrived, the younger ones first with their elders bringing up the rear. In the days before Blake had gotten the Fire Department in a Box, as it was called, Dade would have organized everyone into a bucket brigade, which wouldn't have been too useful at putting out a fire of this size.

The fire volunteers arrived a few minutes later, which meant they'd broken every speed limit to get there. Dade motioned his guests back while the firefighters got set up. Maddie, appearing remarkably calm, helped herd everyone out of the way.

Though Dade had seen the fire system work before, he still found it fascinating. He knew the crew had attended three days of training to learn how to use it, and their expertise showed. Working quickly, they began the process of spraying the foam. It didn't take too long to knock the flames down to a manageable size. They continued until the entire fire was covered in foam and extinguished.

The guests cheered. Grinning, the firefighters high-fived each other. "This never gets old," one said.

Another came over to Dade. "Any idea what caused this?" he asked. He stuck out his hand. "Mike McKenzie."

"Nope." Dade shook Mike's hand and kept smiling, aware he didn't want to alarm any of the guests. "We had propane tanks in there, which exploded. Beyond that, I don't have any idea."

"If you're planning on filing an insurance claim, they're going to want to know," Mike advised. "They'll probably want to send their own investigator out, but I can tell you up front, if he waits too long to get here, any evidence that's buried under all that foam will have disappeared."

Since Dade wasn't sure if Grady had insured any of the outbuildings beside the main house and the cabins, he simply nodded. "I'll keep that in mind," he said.

Mike went back to his crew and helped them finish packing everything up. "We're going to take off now," he said with a friendly wave

After a chorus of thank yous, Dade, Maddie and the entire group of guests watched as the firefighters loaded up and drove off. Once they'd gone, Dade turned and noticed the ice chests the guests had used to bring their catches up in. He realized he no longer had the huge stand-alone freezer in which to store the fish. That had been destroyed in the fire.

And though he had another large one at the main house, he'd packed that full since he'd be feeding various groups of guests for the next several months. For now, he'd see how much of the day's catches could be stored in there, even if he had to toss some frozen vegetables. Beyond that, dry ice might be an option. Taking the salmon to the cannery to be smoked or canned was another one.

Right now, he supposed he had to break it to the guests that anything they'd caught yesterday had been lost. He'd opened his mouth to do exactly that when Elwood shook his head and hobbled on over to him.

"They'll figure it out," he said quietly. "And if they don't, I'll tell them later tonight when we're sitting around the campfire. You've lost a lot more than some salmon."

Before Dade could reply, Elwood walked off, heading in the direction of the cabins. Noticing, Braden and the others immediately followed. Even the teenagers went, though they straggled behind the adults.

Dade turned to Maddie, who stood staring at what remained of the boat shed. Clearly lost in thought, she didn't appear to notice him watching her. Finally, he cleared his throat.

"Let's head back to the house," he said. "We've got to feed this crew lunch. I'm sure all of this made them work up an appetite."

"Really?" She shook her head. "I've completely lost mine."

"You'll get it back, once the shock fades."

Side by side, they made their way toward the main house. He fired up the grill, glad they'd done all the prep work earlier. The beans were still simmering in the Crock-Pot, so she stirred that and began setting out the meat for him to cook.

Soon the mouthwatering aroma of grilled burgers and hot dogs filled the air. Maddie put out all the buns and the vegetables they'd sliced, along with mustard, mayo, ketchup and relish.

The smell pulled the guests from their cabins. As Dade had predicted, they declared themselves to be starving. For the next thirty minutes, Dade manned the grill. By the time everyone had eaten, Dade's stomach had begun rumbling.

"Maddie?" he asked. "Do you want a burger or a hot dog?"

Despite her earlier declaration that she had no appetite, she chose a burger. He made himself one, too, and they scooped up the last of the baked beans.

Instead of joining the boisterous group at the main dining table inside, they sat down in two rickety outdoor chairs near the grill and balanced their plates in their laps.

Neither talked. Instead, they ate with a single-minded intensity.

When he'd finished his burger, Dade went and got another. Maddie grabbed a hot dog. He tried not to watch her eat, but failed miserably. Somehow, she managed to make eating look sexy.

Finally, with their bellies full, they sat back and groaned. "At least with paper plates, there won't be as much cleanup," she mused.

Right on cue, the back door opened, and the teenaged members of the Hilbarger family came barreling out. Acknowledging Dade and Maddie with a quick wave, they raced on past.

A moment later, the rest of the group emerged.

"That was really good," Elwood commented. "We've all decided to take a couple hours and nap before we do our afternoon fishing."

"Sound good," Dade replied. "Just let us know if there's anything you need."

Once the entire family was gone, Dade began cleaning the grill while Maddie put away everything else. They finished around the same time. He walked back inside to find she'd taken a seat at the smaller kitchen table and had gotten them both a tall glass of iced tea.

"What a weird day," she mused. "I certainly hope that explosion and fire was an accident."

"I doubt it was."

Eyeing him, she slowly nodded. "You're probably right."

"I think you need to get your phone and check the texts," he said. "Your stalker may have actually given us a heads up about his plans for today."

Eyes huge, she stared. "I thought of that. If he did text a warning, all of this might have been averted." The recrimination in her expression and voice tore at his heart.

Without thinking, he took her hand, marveling at the softness of her skin. "Maddie, I didn't mean for you to blame yourself. You have zero control over what this guy does."

"True. But if I'd kept up with the text messages, that might have given us a clue." She clung to his fingers as if they were a lifeline.

He wanted to kiss her. Instead, he gave her hand a squeeze and made himself let go. "How about you go get your phone, and we'll check? You might be bashing yourself for nothing."

With a nod, she hurried off into her bedroom. A moment later, she returned, cell phone in hand. "I'd turned it off. It'll take a minute to come back on."

"Okay," he responded.

"I'm dreading looking." Expression grim, she waited

a moment, then tapped on the screen and waited for the facial recognition.

"There are thirty-three text messages," she said, her voice faint. "All from the same person. And it's a different number than the one before. That's how that app works."

"Thirty-three?" Astounded, he waited for her to tell him what they said. Instead, she passed him her phone.

"You read them. Only tell me if there's something I need to know. If it's just more of that useless nonsense, then I really don't care."

He nodded and opened the message thread. The texts started out short and succinct. Scared yet? You should be. They continued on in a similar fashion for a bit. There were ten texts essentially saying the same thing.

And then the tone of the messages changed.

You think you're better than me, don't you? Both of you do, I can tell. But you're not. You're nothing better than thieves. The time has come to make you pay.

And this gem—Death would be too easy. You need to suffer.

Disgusted and worried, Dade shook his head. "Still vague. More threatening, but nothing specific."

"So, he didn't threaten to set something on fire or shoot at anyone?" she asked.

"No. Read it yourself." Passing the phone back to her, he waited while she scrolled through the thread.

"You're right," she said, once she'd finished reading. "But he seems to be coming more and more unhinged. I have to wonder what he thinks I stole."

"We," he corrected. "He's referencing both of us."

Glancing back at her phone, she read it again. "You're right. He is. Then why aren't you getting texts? Why just me?"

"I'm guessing because he somehow got your number. I barely use my cell phone, and all the calls to the lodge come on the landline. It's more reliable than cellular and is tied to an answering machine."

"I remember you telling me that. It seemed archaic then and still does. Somehow getting my number doesn't make sense," she said. "If he could obtain mine, then why not yours?"

Dade winced. "The last time you and your mother disappeared, Grady paid a private investigator a small fortune to find out everything he could about you. I'm guessing your cell phone number was one of the things he learned."

Appearing dazed, she dropped into a chair. "Wait. You're saying Grady had my phone number for *years*? Then why did he never call me?"

"Actually, he did." He kept his voice gentle. "Several times. You never answered, I'm guessing because you didn't recognize the number. He said he didn't feel comfortable leaving voicemails." He took a deep breath, wondering if she'd been aware of the rest. Somehow, he doubted it.

"Is there more?" Regarding him steadily, she waited. "I can tell there's something else. What are you not telling me?"

"Your mother answered the last time he tried. Apparently, she recognized Grady's number. She told him that he was dead to her and to never bother you again. That damn near broke him."

"What? You're saying my mother knew he was trying

to reach me? That's not possible." But something in her expression revealed she thought it might be.

Since he hadn't known her mother, he kept quiet to let her sort things out inside her mind. Who knew, but her stalker might be tied to something or someone in her past.

Chapter 8

Her grandfather had made numerous attempts to contact her, and her mother had turned him away. Learning this hurt. More than she'd have believed possible after all this time. Maddie shouldn't have been surprised. What was one more betrayal in a lifetime of them? But this one cut deep. Ever since she could remember, Maddie had expressed her longing for more family. Her classmates had siblings, plus aunts and uncles and cousins, while Maddie had only a mother who'd seemed disinterested at best.

When younger, Maddie had pressed for more information, aching with a childish longing for the joyous holidays, summer outings, that her friends enjoyed. Maddie's mother had scoffed at her questions. Instead, she'd reiterated that they were on their own. No one cared about them at all. Not even the endless string of men her mother constantly brought home.

In time, Maddie had given up and stopped asking. She'd managed to avoid the brittle bitterness that was her mom and accepted gratefully any of her friends' invitations to join them, whether at the holiday table or on short vacations. She'd managed to keep her home life secret, hiding her mother's increasing spiral and doing her best to live her own life.

Maddie had worked hard, graduating high school at the top of her class, and earned several scholarships to help pay for college. Instead of being proud, her mother had mocked her, claiming Maddie was too serious and had no idea how to enjoy life. Through all her adolescence, Maddie had steadfastly refused her mother's attempts to show her how to party. She'd said a hard no to the drugs, the alcohol, all of the things her mother felt made life bearable or fun. Early on, Maddie had determined that she would not be like her mother.

When her mother had died, too young, Maddie had mourned, but truthfully, she hadn't felt any more alone than she had before. She had her friends and her boyfriend and, as she had in school, focused on building her career.

Then, her life had been upended, and she'd wound up here.

Dade cleared his throat, making her realize she'd retreated into her thoughts. She blinked and met his gaze, surprised to realize he still had his hand on her shoulder.

"Are you all right?" he asked, expression concerned.

"I'm not sure," she answered truthfully. "It's shocking to have heard one thing all my life, only to find out it had been a lie. Learning my grandfather had cared, had even reached out more than once, is a hard truth to learn too late."

"I'm sorry." Dade placed his large hand on her shoulder. "Grady often wondered if he should have tried harder. He'd never stopped hoping to reconcile with his only daughter and to get to know you. Even though he never got the chance, please know he loved you from a distance."

Love. Her mother had scoffed at that word, claiming such a thing didn't exist. She'd actually forbidden Maddie from saying she loved her, which broke now-adult Maddie's heart.

Fighting the urge to lean into his touch, instead she shrugged and took a step away. Even so, she could still feel the lingering warmth where his fingers had been.

"Thanks for telling me all that," she said, trying for breezy. "But I think we need to focus on figuring out what this person who keeps texting me wants. Clearly, if he set that fire, he's getting more and more dangerous."

Gaze locked on hers, he slowly nodded. "You're right. I think the time has come to challenge him. I know you've asked and he hasn't responded, but maybe there's a way to do it to get him to say what he wants."

"Challenge him? But that goes against everything I've ever heard or read about how to react to a stalker. Wouldn't that make him angry.? You're supposed to ignore them, block them, and eventually they'll go away."

"Since that hasn't worked, I think you need to change up the plan," he pointed out. "Engage him. Find out what he thinks you—we—stole. Maybe we can get some insight. Or even better, help him realize he's bothering the wrong people."

The more she thought about it, the more the idea made sense. She took a deep breath and opened up the text thread. I think you have the wrong person, she wrote. I don't know what you want or what you think I've done.

"There," she said, hitting send. "We'll see how he responds."

Dade nodded and moved to take the chair across from her. Refusing to sit and stare at her phone while awaiting an answer, she placed it on the table. "What are you making for dinner?" she asked.

If her quick change of subject surprised him, he didn't show it. "Since we had such a big lunch, I'm going a bit lighter for the evening meal."

"More fish?"

Her question made him laugh. "Yes, but this time we're serving it as part of a big salad. Do you want to help me prep?"

"Sure." She glanced at her phone and decided to leave it face down on the table. If her stalker responded, she'd get the alert, though she already hated how jumpy she now felt. "I still wonder if engaging him was the right thing to do."

Dade grimaced. "Well, ignoring him only seemed to make him angrier. I guess it depends on if he responds or not. Maybe this will encourage some sort of a dialogue rather than a bunch of threats."

She could only hope. Except the phrase that kept going through her mind was something along the lines of *never negotiate with terrorists*.

The rest of the day passed uneventfully. To Maddie's surprise, dinner was a huge success. Everyone raved about the salad bar they'd set up in the kitchen and several of the younger members of the Hilbarger family went back for seconds and even thirds.

As they had the night before, while Dade and Maddie cleaned up, the group made their way back to their cabins.

"Will they have another bonfire tonight?" Maddie asked, a little wistful.

"Most likely. They've already picked up ingredients to make s'mores." He shook his head. "I figured maybe they'd have had enough fire for one day after what happened, but clearly not."

Unable to help herself, she glanced at her phone, still face down on the smaller kitchen table. "He hasn't responded," she said, picking up her phone to double check that she hadn't missed an alert. "But then, I'm not sure if that app he uses has already changed his number. If so, he might no longer be able to receive texts at that one."

"I didn't think about that." Dade shook his head. "Let me try sending a text from my phone."

"I don't think you should," she cautioned. "He doesn't have your number right now. If you text him, he will."

"I don't mind. Let's see if he's brave enough to threaten me." He picked up his phone. "What's the number?"

She read it off and watched as he typed it into his phone. "I'm creating a contact, too," he said. "Makes it easier."

"You know that number will change if it hasn't already." She opened the messages tab and scrolled. "So far he's used several different numbers to send me texts."

"I guess we'll see," Dade said. "I just texted him and asked him if he had anything to do with the fire."

"Bold move." She exhaled as she finished wiping off the counter. "Now we're good until breakfast."

"Yep. And it's your turn to cook tomorrow."

The teasing note in his voice made her smile. "I'm well aware. I've already been revamping my menus. Those old cookbooks of Grady's have been a lifesaver."

"Do you need any help with prep work?" he asked.

"Not tonight. I'm just making a traditional breakfast for tomorrow. Eggs, bacon, toast. Nothing fancy. But after that, I might need your help."

"You've got it," he promised.

They ended up outside again, sitting side by side in the

two chairs on the front porch. Dusk hadn't quite fallen, so their guests hadn't yet started gathering around the fire pit.

"It won't be long now," Dade mused. "When I was a little kid, I used to hide in the woods and watch them. That's why Grady bought these chairs. We'd sit here instead, listening to the guests laugh and party. Grady taught me how to whittle, and the two of us would compete to see who could make the most detailed carving."

The affection in his voice made her heart ache. Dade had clearly loved Grady, and this made her wish she'd had the chance to know her grandfather. Even just a little.

"Do you still have any of them?" she asked. "The carvings? I'd really like to see."

Dade went really still. "I still have every single one," he told her. "The ones Grady carved are important to me."

She waited, realizing this might not be something he wanted to share. After a moment, he got up and went inside. Though she wasn't sure if he'd be back, she stayed in her chair.

A moment later, he returned, carrying a large, brown wooden box. Sitting, he kept this on his lap. Slowly, almost reverently, he opened the lid.

Curious, Maddie leaned over to see what was inside.

Dade lifted out something small, wrapped in cloth. Gently unwrapping it, he held it up and studied it. "This was the first piece Grady made for me. I've had it since I was really small."

"May I see it?"

For a moment, she thought he might refuse.

"Sure." He handed it over. "It's not fragile or anything, but I've been careful to make sure it doesn't get scratched."

Accepting it, she turned it over in her hand. The small piece of carved wood had been polished to a high sheen.

"It's a bear," she said, amazed at the details.

"Not just any bear. Grady carved Old Smokey, the black bear that used to live near the boat shed."

"It's beautiful," she said, handing it back. "Will you let me see the others?"

One by one, he removed carved figurines from the box. Most of them were various animals and birds. One incredibly detailed bald eagle made her catch her breath. "This one looks so real," she said. "I think it's my favorite."

Dade ducked his head. "Thanks. I carved that one."

Sensing further praise would embarrass him, she simply nodded and passed it back to him. "I've been hoping to see a real bald eagle soon," she said. "I know they're all over the place out here in Alaska."

"They are." He finished wrapping all the carvings back up and put them back into the box. "Would you like something to drink?" he asked, pushing to his feet.

Though she wished they had wine, she asked for water.

With the box tucked close to his chest, he went inside. A moment later, he returned, carrying two tall glasses of ice water.

The light had begun to change, dusk finally settling over the sky. Below, they could hear the sounds of their guests, likely getting ready to light their bonfire. Someone turned on music, a wireless speaker, no doubt, streaming from their phone.

The music drifted through the quiet evening. Sultry, slow, it wasn't the music of the younger boys but that of the elders, men Elwood's age. The rawness of the singer's voice started an ache inside Maddie's chest.

"Grady used to love her," Dade said, his voice quiet.

Throat tight, Maddie nodded. "I've never heard her before. Who is that?"

"Etta James. Old-school stuff."

"I think it's beautiful." Realizing that, for whatever reason, she was perilously close to tears, Maddie stood, placing her water glass on the deck near her chair. With her back to him, she wrapped her arms around herself and swayed, drawn to both the music and the complicated swell of emotions it brought to life.

Behind her, she heard Dade stand up. "Would you like to dance?" he asked, his low voice matching the notes in the song.

Instead of answering, she turned and walked into his arms.

They fit together as if they'd always been a couple. Despite the difference between her frame and his height and breadth, she nestled herself against him. When he started to move, she followed his lead. Her pulse settled into a slow and steady beat, echoing the rhythm of the music. As the light faded, so did everything else except for the scent of this man and the feel of his muscular arms wrapped around her.

Then all at once, the music cut off, replaced by the sounds of laughter and good-natured shouting back and forth.

Dazed, Maddie moved away, wondering what the hell she'd been thinking.

"They're lighting the bonfire now," Dade said. He'd already turned away, looking out in the direction of the cabins and the fire pit. The steadiness to his voice told her she'd made too much of their dance. The intimacy she'd experienced had clearly been one-sided.

All for the better, she supposed. Still, needing some time to get her composure back, she excused herself and went inside.

After the door closed behind Maddie, Dade exhaled. It had taken every ounce of self-control he possessed to keep from kissing her. Worse, she appeared to have no idea of how she affected him. If he kept on like this, he'd be taking ice-cold showers every single day for the next year.

Watching as the sky turned dark, he dropped back into his chair. The scent of the smoke from the bonfire drifted his way. He had to figure something out. The more he got to know Maddie, the more he liked her. What had happened between her and Grady hadn't been her fault, as he'd earlier supposed. And while he suspected she might have her own plans for the lodge that he wouldn't agree with, he couldn't fault her work ethic or determination to help the place succeed.

He actually liked her. And not because of her smoking hot body or the way the corners of her eyes crinkled when she smiled. She'd come to a remote location in a state she'd never been, far from her home in Texas, and deserved so much more than a guy who found himself aroused every time they were in the same room.

Which meant Dade needed to simply...stop. He had to rid himself of his desire for her and make himself think of her as his partner, which she was.

And never, ever again ask her to dance.

The door opened, and Maddie emerged. She appeared

subdued, as if she'd also had second thoughts about their impromptu dance.

After sitting, she sighed. "I got a response to my text."

It took a moment for her words to register. Whatever he'd expected her to say, it wasn't that. He blinked. "Can I see?"

"Sure." She passed her phone over. "Basically, he seems to think we stole something from him, but when I asked what, he wouldn't say."

You're thieves of the worst kind, and you don't even care.

But you still can make this right, Dade read out loud. "Make what right? He doesn't ever come out and say?"

"I know." Sounding miserable, she made a face. "I think I'm going to ask him. All this vague nonsense and the fact that he's escalated his threats to cause an actual fire make me think it's likely all inside his own mind."

Slowly, he nodded. "I was about to ask what he's getting out of all this, but it's entirely possible that he's living with his own, made-up and distorted reality."

"Let's see." She held out her hand. Once he'd given back her phone, she began typing. "There," she said once she'd finished. "I asked him to tell me specifically what we've stolen and how. I told him up front that I have no idea what he's talking about."

"Good." He settled back into his chair, listening to the sounds of partying coming from the guests. "Other than the fire at the boat shed, I think it's safe to say they're having a great time."

"Have they caught a lot of fish?" she asked.

He appreciated the way she honed in on what would be

most important to them. "Yes. Some of it was lost in the fire, but I think by the time their stay is over, they will have caught more than enough to make up for it."

"That's good. I assume you're going to make sure we have a place to store it since that freezer was destroyed?"

"I am. I've already put in an order with Kip for a new freezer, but in the meantime, I've reorganized the one we have here at the house. I'm also going to talk to them about taking some in to be canned or smoked, or getting started on shipping it home."

Her phone pinged, making her start. "I'm almost scared to look," she said, wincing. "But here goes nothing. I'll read it out loud."

Leaning forward, he waited.

You have stolen my birthright. My identity. All that I am and all that I should have been. For that, you will have to pay.

She put her phone down. "A different number. And more nonsense."

"Well, you tried. If he wants something, he's going to need to spell it out. Otherwise, neither of us have any idea."

Slowly, she nodded. "When he talks about birthright, I wonder if he's someone who knew my mother. Or my father."

Since this was the first time she'd mentioned her father, he waited to see if she'd elaborate.

"Though I never knew my father's name," she finally said. "My mother always refused to even talk about him. After she died, I went through her things, but she must have destroyed anything related to him. Because I learned nothing."

Again, he felt that twinge of kinship. He kept his mouth shut, though, because the only person who'd ever known about his past had been Grady. The last thing he wanted from Maddie was her pity.

"This is surprisingly pleasant," Maddie mused, leaning back in her chair and closing her eyes.

"Surprisingly?"

"Yes." She didn't even move. "You have to understand, I've always been a Dallas girl. I've never lived anywhere like this before." She waved her hand vaguely. "Look at all the stars in the sky. At home, you can see only half of them."

They sat together in companionable silence. He appreciated once again the way she didn't feel the need to fill the silence with aimless chatter. His awareness of her, the prickling of his skin, his consciousness of her breathing, felt both amazing and scary as hell.

Until Maddie had arrived, Dade hadn't realized how badly his life had been lacking. Grady had teased him, especially toward the end, telling him man wasn't meant to live his life alone. Honestly, Dade hadn't thought the idea sounded that bad.

Now, with this woman who often seemed his complete opposite, Dade had to wonder if Grady had planned this all along.

That night, he tossed and turned, burning with desire for the last person he should crave.

With the sunrise, the final morning of the Hilbarger family's visit dawned. After breakfast, the unusually quiet group thanked Dade and Maddie before trooping back to their cabins to pack up. Though the posted checkout time was noon, neither Grady nor Dade had ever been particularly picky about enforcing that. After all, since they were a small operation, they'd always given themselves a couple of days in between fishing parties to get everything cleaned up and ready.

Nevertheless, the Hilbargers had everything loaded up in their vehicles by eleven.

On their way out, Elwood and Braden stopped off at the main house to say goodbye. Braden helped his father get out of the SUV, and the two of them came up to the porch where Dade and Maddie waited.

"We enjoyed it," Elwood said, his weathered face creased in a smile. "And our wives will soon be enjoying trying to figure out new ways to cook salmon."

"You say the same thing every year," Braden chided. "We just wanted to give you both a personal thank you. We'll see you again about this time next year."

"Make sure and reserve the dates," Dade responded, smiling. "I know how you all like to be the first group here once the season starts."

"We do and we will." Elwood moved forward, shaking first Dade's hand and then Maddie's. Braden did the same. And then both men got into their vehicles, and the caravan drove away.

"Whew." Exhaling, Maddie sat down. "How long do we have before the next group of guests arrives?"

He pulled out his phone to check the calendar. "The next group arrives on Friday. We get to take the rest of the day off if we want. That gives us Wednesday and Thursday to get everything cleaned and ready."

"That seems like a lot of lost revenue," she said, frowning. "Do you always have groups arrive on Friday and leave on Tuesday?"

"Pretty much. Sometimes, they might want to stay an extra day, which is fine. They have to book that up front, so we know. Since we're a small operation, we need at least a couple days to clean and restock."

"Hmmm." Finally, she nodded. "I guess that makes sense. I know I'll definitely appreciate time to recharge."

He managed to keep from laughing, just barely. "I don't know how much of that you'll be doing. We've got to clean the cabins, wash the bedding and towels, and after taking a quick inventory, make another run into town for supplies."

Though only their second time working together, they got busy and had all the cabins cleaned and the bedding stripped and washed in record time.

While the washer and dryer were going, they raided the backup stash of linens and remade the beds. Once that task had been completed, all the cabins were ready for the next occupants.

"Half a day," he mused. "That just might be some sort of record."

His comment made her laugh. "I'm guessing I move a bit faster than Grady did."

Though his first instinct was to be defensive, he realized she meant no offense. And she was absolutely correct. Even before his illness, Grady had been getting up there in years. As a result, he'd moved quite a bit more slowly.

Since they'd gotten so much done, he was able to spend the rest of the day taking inventory of their supplies. Together, he and Maddie made a menu for their respective cooking days and compiled a grocery list. They needed to keep as much of the house freezer empty as possible, so any fish the guests caught could be stored there. Fresh ingredients would mean a little more work, but would also provide a better dining experience. Since the next group were all businessmen who traveled quite a lot, he knew they'd definitely appreciate that.

"We'll head into town tomorrow after breakfast," he said.

Smiling, she nodded. "I'm looking forward to it. Now, I just need to figure out what we're going to eat for dinner tonight. Originally, I'd thought something light, but with all the work we've done today, I'm thinking maybe something heartier."

With her long hair up in a messy bun and her eyes glowing, she looked beautiful. More than her outward appearance, she appeared comfortable, as if she finally felt she belonged here. Eyeing her, he realized he could no longer imagine running this lodge without her.

"Sounds good." Grateful she couldn't read his thoughts since he ached to kiss her again, he managed to smile back. Turning away to distract himself, he went into his bedroom and closed the door.

What the hell? Chastising himself silently, he paced the confines of his room. Maddie hadn't even been here very long. Certainly not nearly enough time for him to like her so much.

However awful Dade's life might have been in the years before Grady took him in, after then he'd had a normal life. Better than average, as Grady made sure he was warm and fed, attended school, and most importantly, felt loved. Grady had thrown him his first ever birthday party for his eighth birthday, with a cake he'd made himself.

Growing up, Dade had dated a few girls from Blake.

One of them had even been semiserious, until she'd broken up with him to go away to the University of Alaska. Since then, he'd kept things extremely casual, going on a few dates here and there in the off-season. Since there were more men than women out here, these had become few and far between.

Clearly, it had been too long since he'd indulged in being physical with a woman. That had to be why being around Maddie had him in a near constant state of arousal.

He considered taking a cold shower, but ultimately decided to go for a walk. As he strode through the house for the back door, Maddie must have sensed his mood as she simply looked up and waved without asking a single question.

Outside, he breathed deeply of the fresh air and set off to patrol the grounds. He couldn't risk the intruder deciding to set something else on fire, so he planned to stay alert and watch for any signs of that man back on the property.

He found nothing, which was a relief. And all the walking and focusing on something other than his simmering desire had helped. When he returned to the house, he felt back to normal.

"You're just in time," Maddie said. "Dinner will be ready in just a few minutes."

"Let me wash up, and then I can help you," he said.

"No need. I've got it all handled." Her sweet smile made him catch his breath. When he headed to the bathroom to wash his hands, he splashed a little water on his face and tried to think about fishing.

She surprised him with dinner. Though she'd clearly gotten the idea from one of Grady's old cookbooks, the mini meatloaves had long been one of Dade's favorites. Grady had even made them, at Dade's request, for birthday dinners.

Watching him expectantly, Maddie placed everything on the table. She had no way of knowing what memories this particular meal held for him. Or that Grady had cooked with a special touch. Dade didn't think Maddie's could possibly taste as good.

But they did. Surprisingly, even better. "Did you tweak the recipe?" he asked as he went back for seconds.

"Yes. Do you like it?"

"I love it," he replied, meaning it. "This is really great." And then he told her about the memories the simple meal brought him.

She listened, her expression rapt. "I love when you tell stories about my grandfather. It makes me feel as if I'm finally getting to know him."

Luckily, they sat across from each other at the table. Otherwise, he might not have been able to keep himself from kissing her.

"I'll clean up," he said, his tone firm. "You go ahead and relax now. We'll be heading to town in the morning."

"Sounds good," she replied, and headed into the other room to turn on the TV. "By the way, I'm planning to talk to Kip tomorrow about the internet service provider. I'm hoping I can get everything set up within the next few weeks."

Since she'd used the same no-nonsense tone he had, he decided to simply nod and get busy doing the dishes.

He managed to make it through the rest of the night without problems, though he turned in early, claiming exhaustion.

The next morning, he rose before dawn and, after making coffee, got busy fixing them breakfast. Since she'd made such an effort the night before, he decided to make the most Southern thing he could think of, biscuits with sausage gravy. By the time she emerged from her room, he had the first batch ready.

She exclaimed over the meal, which had him grinning like a fool. They ate heartily, and when they'd finished, she shooed him out of the kitchen so she could clean up.

After they'd both showered—separately, though he'd been unable to keep from imagining them under the spray together—they piled into his Jeep and drove into town.

"As a bonus, no new texts," she said, showing him her phone.

At the general store, they shopped, sticking closely to their list. When they were done, Dade marveled at how smoothly everything had gone. His mood light, he found himself wishing he could treat Maddie to something special. Maybe a meal in town, even if Mikki's donut shop, restaurant and bar might not be up to her city-dweller standards. Since only a few hours had passed since they'd had breakfast, the timing wouldn't work today. Next time, he vowed, after this upcoming round of guests left.

On the drive back home, he turned the radio on to a classic rock station. To his amusement, Maddie sang along to a couple of songs. She had a pretty decent voice, he thought, smiling.

Even the trip from Blake to the lodge went quickly. He turned onto the driveway, happier than he'd been in a while.

But the instant he pulled up to the house, he knew

something was wrong. "Maddie," he warned, shifting into Park. "Stay in the Jeep."

"Why?" She sat up straight. "What's going on?"

"The front door is open. And I locked it when we left. Whoever broke in might still be inside."

Chapter 9

Maddie swallowed. "I refuse to stay by myself. I'd rather take my chances with you."

For a second, Dade's grim expression made her think he was going to refuse. Instead, he nodded and then lightly touched her arm. "Fine. Just stay right behind me."

She jumped out and did exactly that, staying close enough that she could reach out her hand and touch him.

When he pulled out his pistol, her breath caught. She wanted to ask him if that was really necessary, but realized in a place where they couldn't call the police, they only had themselves.

"It's likely the stalker," she whispered. "Right?"

Instead of answering, he shrugged. He didn't need to actually respond because who else would it be?

Keeping his weapon aimed in front of him, like she'd seen FBI agents do on numerous TV shows, they moved through the front door. Though absolutely terrified, she stayed right on his heels.

They went from living room, which appeared undisturbed, to kitchen. Again, everything seemed to be exactly as they'd left it. Still, Dade didn't lower his pistol.

"Our bedroom doors are closed," he pointed out, his voice low. "They were open when we left."

She bit back a curse word, suddenly terrified of what they might find when they opened the doors. Clearly, she'd watched too many horror movies.

"Mine first," he decided. "Get back behind me."

Realizing she'd moved too far away, she hurried to get closer. She marveled at how safe the sheer size of him made her feel.

Dade turned the knob and shoved open his bedroom door.

"Empty," he said. "But look."

She peered around him and gasped.

The room looked like a tornado had torn through it. Dresser drawers had been emptied, their contents thrown around the room. The bed linens appeared to have been slashed with a knife, tattered and shredded. She wondered if the mattress had also been destroyed.

Even the mirror above the dresser was shattered, glass shards all over the floor.

A muscle jumped in Dade's jaw, but he didn't speak. Instead, he turned and went next door to her room.

As he opened the door, she braced herself. Dade moved to block her view. "Maybe you shouldn't see this," he said.

Having none of that, she pushed herself past him. And gasped. "This is even worse than what they did to your room. I wouldn't have believed that was possible."

"At least you don't have a broken mirror," he drawled.

Which was true. Instead of shattering her mirror, the intruder had used Maddie's best red lipstick to write across the glass.

Go back to Texas! And take that fake son with you. Or you both will die.

She had to read it twice. "Fake son? What do you think that means? I don't have any children."

Dade's expression was somewhere between fierce and anguished. "I think he means me. Grady always told everyone that he loved me like a son." Despite his stony demeanor, his voice cracked a little at the end, which broke her heart.

Not sure how to respond, she focused again on surveying the damage. Like in Dade's room, all of the contents of her dresser drawers had been strewn around the room. Since she had fewer belongings than he did, her cleanup would be slightly easier.

Her bed had also been stripped, the sheets cut up into ribbons of tattered material. And her nightstand had been turned over, the antique lamp broken into three pieces.

The nightstand. Heart in her throat, she hurried to set it right side up. Then she realized all the little mementos she'd kept that had been Grady's were gone.

This bothered her more than anything else. She barely managed to bite back a cry.

Yet somehow, Dade appeared to know. "What's wrong?" he asked. "I mean, other than the obvious?"

When she told him what had been taken, he blanched. "How'd they know?" Then, without waiting for an answer, he spun around and headed back to his room. She followed right behind him.

He went directly to his own nightstand, which still stood upright with the drawers slightly open. When he looked inside, he cursed. "Son of a… He got everything Grady left for me, too."

A horrible thought occurred to her. "What about the wood carvings?"

Rushing to his closet, he reached into the back and

pulled out the large brown box. Even from several feet away, she could tell his hands were shaking as he opened it. "They're still here," he said. "He didn't find them."

The relief in his deep voice brought tears to her eyes. "That's good," she managed. "The bastard didn't take everything."

"Right." Jaw tight, he placed the box back inside his closet. "I can't believe I'm saying this, but I'm going to call Kip and see how long it would take him to get in some kind of camera system."

"You'll likely need internet for that," she pointed out.

He glared at her. "Then we'll get internet. Right now, we'd better get started cleaning this mess up. And once we're done, I want to file a police report mentioning the specific threat. We might as well get everything on record. There's no telling what this guy might do next."

Back in her room, she began refolding her clothing inside the dresser drawers. Since she didn't have a whole lot, putting her things away didn't take long.

Next, she snapped several pictures with her phone. She hoped Dade did the same thing to document what had been done in his room. What worried her was that she didn't know how long before things escalated again. First the boat shed, then the main house. What would be next? Unfortunately, she suspected it would be physical attacks upon them.

When she started shaking, she dropped down onto the edge of her bed. Wrapping her arms around herself, as if for comfort, she struggled with the urge to cry. Finally, she gave in, letting the tears roll down her cheek and stifling her sobs so Dade wouldn't hear.

Dade appeared in her bedroom doorway anyway, his

large body making the space seem much smaller. She glanced up, bit back a cry and swiped her hands across her face. "Sorry," she mumbled. "It's all just a bit much for me. I'll be fine in a minute."

Instead of leaving, he sat down next to her and pulled her into his arms. "Let it out," he told her, smoothing the hair away from her face.

So she did. All her life, she'd never been much of a crier. As a child, her mother hadn't allowed it. She'd learned to keep her emotions inside, which she knew wasn't healthy.

But now, with this big man holding her, his large body making her feel safe and wanted, she wept. Her body shook with the force of her sobs.

And through it all, he sat unmoving, a rock. As her tears dried, something shifted inside her. Anguish became... need. Her breath hitched as she turned in his arms. She buried her mouth at the base of his neck and inhaled his scent, that unique mixture of pine and outdoors.

When she raised her face to his, she saw her desire reflecting back at her, darkening his eyes. Without hesitation, she pressed her body against him. "I want you," she said. She'd never meant anything more.

"Are you sure?" he rasped, his gaze glittering, his mouth mere inches from hers.

"Positive."

Claiming her lips, he kissed her with a raw hunger, his tongue mating with hers. His hands hot upon her skin, he pushed her clothing away, lifting her shirt over her head. She helped, stepping out of her shorts and standing before him in her bra and panties.

When he reached for her bra, she chuckled and pushed his hand away. "You next," she said, tugging at his T-shirt.

While he removed that, she fumbled with his belt, aching to touch his swollen body. Once the belt had been undone, she helped him ease his jeans down, unable to suppress a gasp as she freed his massive arousal.

He reached for her. Meeting him halfway, she arched toward him, a moan escaping her. One hand tangled in her hair, he caressed her. She allowed herself to explore his skin, his muscles, him. Hard everywhere she was soft, passion roared through her, firing her blood.

To her amazed shock, he had a condom in hand. He managed to get it on before returning to kiss her again. They fell back onto her bed, locked together. Gasping with need, she welcomed him inside her with a kind of desperation she'd never experienced before.

He began to move, slowly at first. Craving more, she used her body to urge him faster. When he did, she bit down to muffle a shout of triumph. *This*, she thought, giving in to sensation. This was what a thousand books had been written in futile attempts to describe. Nothing she'd read or watched or heard about had prepared her for anything even close to this.

Dade cried out, seconds before she did. Waves of pleasure, pure and explosive, rocked her, making her entire body shudder with ecstasy. Deep inside of her, he did the same, before collapsing.

After, they held on to each other, waiting for both their heart rate and breathing to slow. While she lay there, secure in his arms, Maddie marveled at how perfect their lovemaking had been.

She also realized that they'd both made a huge, irrevocable mistake.

It would be best to clear the air. She didn't want the

two of them slinking around, trying to avoid each other for the next year.

Pushing herself up on one elbow, she rolled over to face him. His amazing brown eyes were open, and she once again felt a jolt as he met her gaze.

"This doesn't have to change things," she said, keeping her voice soft.

"Doesn't it?"

Since she couldn't tell from his tone if he was teasing or serious, she lifted one bare shoulder in a shrug. "Wouldn't things be easier that way?"

"Maybe," he conceded, his expression inscrutable. "But I've never been one to take the easy way out."

She didn't know how to respond to this, so she didn't. She knew for certain that the only thing she didn't want him to say was that they should never do this again.

If he said that, she thought she might shrivel up and die.

Dramatic, yes. But they were going to be sharing the same space for a year. Why deprive each other of the pleasure of this? They were both adults. They could handle it.

"Can we?" he asked, making her realize she'd spoken her thoughts out loud.

"Yes," she responded, her voice firm. To prove her point, she pressed a quick kiss on his lips. "Otherwise, we're going to spend the next twelve months tiptoeing around this thing between us. As long as we both agree there won't be any emotional entanglements, I don't see any reason why we can't continue to, um, enjoy each other."

He laughed out loud at this, the sound a combination of amusement and possibly an underlying thread of anger. "Damn, you're innocent."

Wondering if she'd imagined the anger, she decided

not to allow herself to feel insulted. Instead, she smiled. "Possibly so. But sometimes that's a good thing."

"Maybe it is." He kissed her again, nothing casual about the way he slanted his mouth across hers. He continued to kiss her until she couldn't think, couldn't breathe, until she'd melted into a puddle of desire.

When he lifted his head, she nearly begged him to make love to her again.

"Still think you're right?" he asked, the glint in his eyes telling her that, this time, he was teasing.

"I know I am," she replied.

"Good." With that, he pushed himself up off her bed. "I'm going to take a quick shower, and then you can if you want. After that, we'll eat. I don't know about you, but I've worked up quite an appetite."

Grinning, he turned around and left, giving her a great view of his naked backside.

Sated and comfortable, she dozed until she heard the shower cut off. A few minutes later, he returned, his hair damp and a towel wrapped around his waist. "Your turn."

"Great." She made a conscious choice to try and be as comfortable with her nakedness as he'd been. Pushing back the sheet, she swung her legs over and stood. Shoulders back, chin up, she strode from the room as if she felt perfectly normal parading around without any clothes.

In the bathroom, she closed the door and finally exhaled. While she'd had a couple of relationships since college, the only even remotely serious one had been her last boyfriend, the guy who'd dumped her after two years together. Everything about that relationship had been mundane, and once she'd gotten past the sting of rejection, she'd been glad to be free of it.

After showering, she felt fabulous. Energized and ready to tackle any problem that might come her way. As if on cue, her phone buzzed, indicating a text.

She really, really didn't want to check it. But as Dade had said, she couldn't simply ignore this person and hope he'd go away. He'd already proved that wasn't going to happen.

Like my handiwork? If you don't, it doesn't matter. Unless you leave Alaska and go back to Texas, things are only going to get worse.

Sighing, she left her hair damp and joined Dade in the kitchen, where he'd started preparing them large salads for lunch.

"He messaged me again," she said, handing over the phone.

Dade frowned as he read the text. "Again, he's wanting you to leave. Like he's refocused on you once more."

"What does this person hope to gain from all of this?" she asked. "Let's say I did listen to him and packed up and high-tailed it back to Texas. You'd get the lodge. It wouldn't be sold. How would that benefit him?"

"I don't know." Expression grave, Dade grimaced. "Unfortunately, I suspect he's mentally ill. Which means you can't expect to apply logic to any of his actions."

"Maybe not," she conceded. "However, there has to be a motive. What made him decide to target us? I take it no one bothered you before, right?"

"Right." Gaze steady, he regarded her for a moment. "The next question would be, what changed? You came here, true. But did anyone send you weird texts before you learned that Grady had died?"

"No. And since he referred to you as a fake son, does he believe we took something that should have been his? Like the lodge?"

Dade shrugged. "It seems likely."

"Then I have to ask, so please don't take offense. Did Grady father any other children that you know of?"

"None taken," he replied. "I don't believe so. Grady took me in as a young boy, out of the kindness of his heart. If he had any other kids, he definitely would have made sure they were part of his life."

She believed him. "I truly wish I'd known him. He sounds like he was a wonderful man."

"That's what really bothers me. It seems like if this stalker would just sit down and have an honest conversation with me, we could clear things up."

Getting out her phone, she pulled up the text thread, took a deep breath and hit the button to call the number. As she'd expected, a recording came on saying it wasn't a working number.

"What did you just do?" Dade asked.

"Tried to call him. I agree with you. It's high time we all just had a conversation. This harassment has got to stop. But he's not using that number any more. Like usual, the next text will come from a completely different one. And it won't allow calls either."

"Then we'll have to send a text right away," he said. "As soon as we get his. That's the only chance we have of reaching him."

That night, it took every ounce of willpower Dade possessed to remain in his own bed, in his own room. He would have thought that the amazing sex they'd had would be enough to satisfy him for a while. But instead, he craved more.

He tossed and turned, so aroused that he considered taking an icy shower or taking matters into his own hands. But somehow, he managed to drift off to sleep.

It rained during the night, the kind of heavy rain that left the air heavy and always created a lot of sticky mud. When Dade stepped out onto the front porch, the first thing he noticed were the paw prints a few feet away from the house.

Maddie, right behind him, almost crashed into him when he stopped short. Her coffee sloshed a little onto her hand.

"Look." He pointed.

Stepping past him to see, she frowned. "What the heck caused those?" she asked.

"Wolves. More than one. What's unusual is they came so close to the house. Bears will do that, but wolves usually keep their distance." Though he didn't say it out loud, he couldn't shake the feeling that something was wrong.

"That's not good, is it? My first thought is the cabins," she said. "Good thing we don't have the next batch of guests yet. I'd be worried about teenagers and wolves."

"The next group is a bunch of older businessmen," he said absently. "Mid-forties. They come every year. Luckily, we have one more day before they arrive." He started off the porch, feet slipping a little in the mud. Two steps and he turned back to look at her. "Wait here."

Naturally, she ignored that. Coffee cup in hand, she followed him. "Where are you going?"

"To see where the tracks lead. With so many wolves, they must have a fresh kill somewhere around."

That finally made her stop. "Like a dead animal?"

Somehow, he reined in his so far unfounded worry. "Yes. Probably something big. Maybe a deer, I don't know."

Eyes huge, she took a step backward. "I think I will wait here. I'll let you figure it out."

Which was probably for the best. She took a seat in her usual chair and sipped her coffee. Satisfied that he didn't have to worry about her, he began following the tracks into the woods.

In a few places, he lost them. Leaves and brush obscured their path. But he managed to pick them up again. They led to a small clearing off the beaten path, where at one point Grady had contemplating building another storage shed. Though he'd kept the area cleared of trees and brush, he never utilized it.

In the middle of the grassy area, Dade saw a fresh mound of dirt, as if wild animals had been digging for buried bones. Since other wildlife didn't bury their dead, this couldn't be a good thing.

With a sickening feeling in the pit of his gut, Dade moved closer. This was no deer. Though scattered around what appeared to be a fresh grave, the bones, with most of the flesh removed from them, were clearly human. The wolves had been feasting on human remains. Someone had been recently buried here. Had they been murdered here as well? And if so, by whom?

Suddenly, the unknown man who'd been lurking around the lodge became much more dangerous.

Knowing better than to disturb anything further, Dade backed away and hurried toward the house. Maddie stood when she saw him coming, as if some of his urgency had conveyed itself to her.

"What was it?" she asked.

Though he hated to destroy the peace of one of their last private mornings before more guests arrived, he had no choice.

"A body," he replied. "Human, from the looks of it. I've got to call the state police and report this. Then I've got to figure out how to protect the site until someone can get here."

She followed him inside, silent while he made the necessary phone calls. In addition to reporting what he'd found just now, he also relayed information about the explosion and resulting fire, plus the numerous sightings of a stranger lurking around in the woods.

The person he spoke with at the state police office took down everything, remarked that they'd just called about a break-in the day before, and promised to send someone out as soon as possible. From past experience, Dade knew this could be anywhere from a few days to longer. Hopefully, since there'd been a murder, it would be much quicker.

Once he'd ended the call, he turned to find Maddie staring at him. "You think my stalker killed someone?"

Since he didn't believe in sugarcoating the truth, he nodded. "If that man is the same person who's been texting you, it's a very real possibility. I imagine once the state police get here, they'll send for someone with a search-and-rescue cadaver dog. Just to make sure there aren't more unmarked graves out there."

She blanched. "If there are, that would mean he's what? A serial killer?"

Unable to help himself, he reached out and gently squeezed her shoulder. "Let's not go there yet. Until we find out for sure what else is out there, okay?"

Slowly, she nodded. "Either way, whether there's one body or five, he's a murderer. And since he has a major grudge against both of us and has broken into the house, I'd say we're in danger."

He couldn't fault her logic. "Yes. Which means we need to take precautions."

Briefly, she leaned into his touch before appearing to collect herself and moving away. Clearly restless, she went to the window and looked out. "Like what? I know you're armed, but I'm not. I don't have the faintest idea how to handle a gun. I need you to teach me."

Though with the next group of guests about to arrive, he had no idea when they'd find time to do such a thing, he nodded. Briefly, he wondered if they should consider cancelling, but not only did they have their reputation to uphold, they needed the money. "We'll try. But it's more than me simply showing you how to load and shoot," he said. "There's safety issues, target practice and learning how to clean the weapon. And since I don't want to do any of that around our guests, we'll have to work it in between groups."

Turning, she met his gaze. "I get it," she said. "I don't like it, but I totally understand how having daily target practice might be bad for business."

He shrugged. "Maybe we can time it for while they're all out fishing. Sound carries around here, but if they go far enough out…"

Her smile started a warmth inside his blood. "I'd like that," she said. "And thank you."

Aware he needed to focus on something else to keep himself from getting any more aroused, he swallowed and kept the conversation on track. "Also, I heard back from

Kip about the security cameras. He's ordered them, and while he can't say for sure when they'll be in, he's hoping it won't be more than a couple of weeks."

"I don't like being this worried about our safety," she told him, her voice soft, her expression vulnerable. "It was bad enough getting all those weird texts, and then the explosion and fire, but this? A body buried nearby? Maybe more? And there's a strong possibility we—or more specifically, I—might be next."

"Come here," he said gruffly, tugging her into his arms. He'd simply hold her, he told himself, nothing more. Offering comfort seemed like the least he could do.

Except his body clearly had other ideas. The instant their skin made contact, he went on red alert. And when she turned her face up to his, he could no more keep himself from kissing her than he could keep his heart from beating.

She kissed him back, making sweet little guttural sounds in the back of her throat. He tried like hell to maintain some semblance of control, but when she pressed her body up against his, he went wild.

They undressed quickly, managing not to tear their clothes off. He again managed to get a condom on. Then they fell upon each other, just like before. Hot, passionate and uniquely Maddie.

This time, instead of leaving her bed after, he fell asleep with her in his arms.

When he opened them again to sun streaming through the window, he realized Maddie had already gotten up. He found her in the kitchen, humming under her breath while she mixed something up.

"Good morning," she said, smiling.

He liked that she never acted awkward around him. Going up to her, he kissed the back of her neck. She shivered, which made him consider taking things a step further. But coffee beckoned. He made himself a cup, using the opportunity to get his act together before turning to face her again.

"What are you making?" he asked.

"Something else I found in one of Grady's cookbooks." Her eyes sparkled. "Have you ever had a baked Dutch baby pancake? It sounds amazing. I even found some lemon juice to put on it along with the confectionary sugar. I'm about to put it in the oven."

While the pancakes baked, they sat at the kitchen table drinking coffee. "I hope the police take my call seriously," he said. "Finding an actual dead body ramps all of the other stuff up to the next level."

"Surely, they will." She sounded certain. He didn't have the heart to tell her it all depended on who got assigned to the case and how much time that officer felt like spending on investigating it.

The baked pancake turned out amazing. Bursting with pride, Maddie commented that it turned out she enjoyed cooking far more than she'd ever thought she would.

"And you're really good at it, too," Dade told her, meaning it.

Between the two of them, they polished off the entire thing. "I think we should consider adding this to the breakfast menu for the guests," Dade suggested. "You'd have to make several, but unless they're labor intensive, I think they'd be a big hit."

Beaming, Maddie nodded. "I'll consider it."

Watching as she bustled around the kitchen, Dade realized they'd begun to feel like a true partnership, though it felt as if it had the potential to become something deeper and possibly more enduring than just business.

Because thoughts like that could be dangerous, Dade pushed them away. He got up, helped her clean up and then headed for the bathroom to shower. Again, he thought about asking her to join him, but decided against it.

When he'd finished and she'd gone in to take her own shower, he once again went over the guest list for the next group. Since they'd been to the lodge the year before, Dade checked his notes from that visit. Grady had taught him to always make notes, that way guests who returned could be taken care of in ways that enhanced their experience.

The Alaska State Trooper arrived shortly after Maddie finished showering, which was faster than Dade had ever known them to be. Dade had just gone outside, planning to head down and fuel up the boats, when the police car pulled up.

Dade stopped and waited. The police officer got out, his uniform freshly pressed, and smiled.

"I was in the area," he said, answering the question before Dade even had a chance to ask it. "I'm Officer Taggert."

"Dade Anson."

They shook hands, the other man sizing Dade up. While Taggert was tall, Dade still towered over him by at least half a foot.

When Maddie walked out onto the front porch, looking stunning, the police officer grinned. "Good morning, ma'am. You must be Mrs. Anson. I'm Officer Taggert, with the Alaska State Troopers."

"Maddie Pierce." She stayed on the porch. "I hope you

can figure out what's going on. Honestly, I just want this man caught so Dade and I can get on with running this fishing lodge."

"Yes, ma'am," Taggert replied, smiling. He never took his eyes off her as he moved on up to the porch. "Do you mind if we take a seat so you can tell me what's been happening?"

Maddie blinked. "Didn't Dade tell you already?"

"Yes, ma'am, he did. But I'd like to also hear it from you."

Dade nearly snorted out loud at the obvious flirting. For her part, Maddie seemed oblivious. Instead of commenting, he lifted his hand in a wave. "I'll be down at the boat docks. Officer Taggert, when you're finished, let me know. I'll take you up to where I found the shallow grave."

Taggert barely looked up. "Will do," he said, getting out a notepad and a pen. "Now, Maddie, why don't you start at the beginning."

Shaking his head, Dade took off. His flash of anger and—to be honest—jealousy, surprised him. Maddie wasn't his, she was her own person and could make her own choices. If she wanted to flirt with Taggert, that was none of Dade's business.

As long as the man did his job. Maybe that was why Dade felt so irritated. Finding a body in a shallow grave after having the house broken into and the boat shed set on fire seemed a pretty damn important reason to investigate.

Dade got to work refueling the boats, one by one. When Taggert strolled up less than fifteen minutes later, Dade motioned that he'd be right with him. Pleasantly surprised, since barely fifteen minutes had passed, Dade topped of the gas tank and drove the boat back to its slip.

Once he'd tied it up and killed the motor, he stepped out. "Follow me," he said, and took off for the meadow. "Wolves dug the body up, and I'm afraid they did a number on it."

"We've got a really good forensics team," Taggert replied. "I've already given them a call, and they're on their way to collect the remains."

Dade nodded. It looked like the state police were taking this case seriously after all.

Chapter 10

Though she'd been glad to send the flirtatious policeman away to do his job, now that she found herself alone in the house, Maddie felt more nervous than she'd expected. Which made sense because she had no idea what else her stalker might be capable of. Finding a body in a shallow grave on the property sent her anxiety into an entirely different realm. Though an official determination hadn't been made yet, she just knew the body had been a woman.

In the beginning, she'd treated the random texts like some kind of tasteless joke. They were annoying, but she hadn't truly viewed them as any kind of real threat. She'd even briefly considered the possibility that they were being sent to the wrong person.

The fire, then the break-in and the note on her mirror had stripped away any of her previous delusions. Whoever this man was, he seemed to enjoy the process of tormenting them. He hadn't made any demands, other than ordering her to leave. Since that was the one thing she couldn't and wouldn't do, and he refused to allow her to communicate with him, they were stuck in a weird limbo of his making.

Even living in downtown Dallas, she'd never felt as if her life might be in danger. These days, she did.

She briefly considered walking out to find Dade and Officer Taggert, but since doing that would make her more vulnerable, she decided to remain inside. As a precaution, she locked all the doors.

She kept busy putting together all the ingredients for dinner. She'd decided to make a pork roast, and she'd been able to find one small enough that two people could share it for a couple of days. Following one of Grady's recipes, she peeled potatoes and carrots, cut up onions and put everything in the Crock-Pot. After adding the seasonings, she closed the lid.

In the past, she'd never been much for cooking. She'd had a lot of food delivered and had rarely cooked anything more than instant oatmeal or frozen pizza.

Now look at her. She'd practically become a domestic goddess.

What next? She wanted to keep busy. Should she make some bread? Why not? She'd seen an older bread machine with the recipe book tucked inside. Smiling at her sudden culinary longings, she located the machine, found all the necessary ingredients and started a loaf of basic white bread.

Keeping busy worked. At least, provided a necessary distraction. Yet the entire time she bustled around the kitchen, she kept a lookout for any movement outside the windows and listened for any sound that might be out of the ordinary.

Finally, she caught a glimpse of Dade and Officer Taggert walking up toward the house. They appeared to be deep in conversation.

More relieved than she cared to admit, she unlocked the

front door and stepped out onto the porch. Neither man looked up as they went over to the police cruiser.

Opening the driver-side door, Taggert reached inside and then handed Dade what looked like a business card. After pocketing it, Dade stood and watched as the other man drove off before making his way back to the porch.

"What did he have to say?" she asked.

"He's got a forensic team on the way, so he wanted to know if there was any kind of motel in town. I told him he could stay in one of the cabins if he wanted, though not for long since we have guests due to arrive soon." He shrugged. "He told me he'd let me know, but for now, he wanted to check out the lodgings in Blake."

"That's weird. Is there a place to stay in town?"

"Sure. Kip's always got a room or two for rent. That's where I sent Taggert. If it doesn't work out, I'm sure he'll be back."

Dade lowered himself into a chair, his expression troubled. "What I'm worried about is the effect this police investigation will have on our guests."

"That's understandable. But since that meadow is off the beaten path, hopefully the two won't intersect. Especially since there won't be teenagers in this next group."

He looked up. "True. They're all middle-aged businessmen. All they're interested in is fishing. They tend to drink a lot around the bonfire at night, but beyond shoveling down whatever we serve them and sleeping, they want to be out on the water."

Placing her hand on his arm, she smiled. "It sounds like it will all work out."

"Will it?" He met her gaze, expressionless. "We still have to worry about the stalker. What will he try to do next? I don't want any of the guests hurt while they're on vacation here."

"Do you think he'll still hang around, once he realizes there's a police presence?"

"Who knows. I haven't yet figured out what this guy even wants." Dade grimaced. "And now we don't know if he's some sort of serial killer or if we're dealing with two different people."

Since *that* thought had never occurred to her, she took a moment to process it. "You don't really think that, do you?"

"No," Dade admitted. "I'll admit I'm struggling with this. It's difficult not to be angry. First, I lost Grady. Then…"

"You had me foisted on you," she supplied. "It's okay. I get it."

"Fine. I'll just say running the lodge for the next year with a total stranger wasn't something I'd planned on. But so far, I have to admit, we've been able to work it out. We are well on our way toward making a good team."

Touched, she nodded and waited to see what else he'd have to say.

"Then this guy inserts himself into our lives. This is our business, our home. He's got to be stopped, before anyone else gets hurt."

"I agree."

The landline rang, the sound carrying outside. Startled, they both looked at each other. Then Dade jumped to his feet and hurried inside to answer.

Maddie stayed where she was, trying to relax on the front porch. She could hear the occasional word from Dade's end of the conversation, but not enough to understand the entire call.

A moment later, Dade returned. If he'd looked serious before, now he appeared positively grim.

"That was our next group. They've had to cancel and are aware they'll be forfeiting their deposit."

Stunned, she stared at him. "Why? Did they hear about everything that's been going on here?"

He dragged his hand through his hair. "All he said was that something came up. He did apologize, for all it's worth. I can't believe this."

"Are we going to be okay without that booking?"

Dade sighed, dropping into the chair next to her. "I don't know. I'll have to run the numbers. They were a good-sized group and repeat guests. It's going to hurt us, for sure. Especially since we don't have another group coming for ten days."

"Does this happen very often?" she asked. "People cancelling their reservations at the last moment?"

"No. In fact, it's never happened as long as I've been here."

The bewilderment in his voice made her long to comfort him. But then she realized an awful possibility. "Dade, what if all these things are tied together? Do you think there's any chance that this stalker has somehow gained access to our guest reservations and is doing his best to turn them away?"

Instead of rejecting the idea outright, Dade considered her words. "If we did everything on the internet, I'd definitely think that might have happened. But since we still do everything the old-fashioned way with pen and paper, I don't see how."

About to remind him that the house had been broken in to, she saw the moment he came to the same realization.

"Damn it." Shoving himself up from the chair, he stormed into the house.

She hurried along right behind him, hoping she might be wrong.

The table that housed the landline phone sat next to a small, simple wooden desk. He opened the middle drawer and cursed. "It's gone," he said, his bleak voice matching his expression. "Our reservation book is gone."

Though she wanted to ask him if they had some sort of backup, she knew better. It would be too much like rubbing salt into an open wound.

"Damn it." He began rummaging through the desk, as if he thought it might merely have been moved or misplaced. "It has to be here somewhere. How would he even know where to look?"

"You have a point," she said. "Because even though you told me you have everything written down, I had no idea where you kept it. I should have asked."

"Help me look." Continuing his frantic search, he glanced at her. "Please. I'm trying to remember the last time I looked at it. I'm hoping I just forgot to put it back."

"I'll check the kitchen," she said. "I seem to remember you looking at something when we were planning our supply run for the upcoming visit."

"That's right!" His expression cleared, relief shining in his brown eyes. "I bet that's where it is."

But though they both searched every inch of the kitchen, they found no sign of the missing notebook.

"I'm going to check my bedroom. Would you mind checking yours?" he asked.

Even though she'd never handled the dang thing and had no idea what it looked like, she agreed. After all, when the break-in had happened, the house had been in such disarray that anything could have ended up in the wrong place.

She went through her dresser first, checking underneath all her clothes. She looked in her closet and on top of her bed, moving aside the pillows and even the sheets. As she'd expected, she found no notebook.

Right before leaving her room, she dropped down to check under her bed. That was when she saw it. A red spiral notebook, on the floor, right in the middle.

On her hands and knees, she couldn't quite reach it. She had to wiggle herself under the bed, arm outstretched, until she connected and dragged the notebook toward her.

Once back out, she called for Dade. "I think I found it!"

"Seriously?" He appeared in her doorway.

When she held out the notebook, he took it and began flipping through it. "This is it," he said. "I'm so relieved. Where was it?"

"Under the bed. I think it was shoved under there."

"Nothing appears to be missing." The relief in his voice made her smile. "Though he might have taken pics with his phone, at least he didn't destroy this. While I have a good memory, without these records, I'd really struggle remembering who was coming when."

"We need to make some sort of backup," she suggested. "Since you don't have anything set up online, how about we use our phones? We could simply take photos, just like you think he might have. That way we have something to refer back to."

"We'll do that." He pulled her to him and hugged her, fierce but quick. "How about I take you out to dinner tonight to celebrate?"

"Out to dinner?" Puzzled, she frowned. "I don't remember seeing any restaurants in Blake."

"There's only one. Mikki's."

"The donut shop?" She didn't even try to hide her disbelief. "You want to go out to eat donuts for dinner?"

"Mikki sells donuts in the morning," he said. "After that, she runs a restaurant and bar in the adjoining space. It's a great place to go have a drink and a bite to eat. In fact, it's the only place." He thought for a minute. "One of our newer residents, Brett Denyon, is a renowned chef from Anchorage. He married our doctor, Dr. Taylor. He's in the process of opening up another restaurant, but it's not ready yet. I think it's supposed to open Memorial Day weekend. So it's Mikki's, right now."

"That sounds...interesting." She thought for a moment. "Actually, I'd like that a lot. It'll be fun."

The slow smile that spread across his handsome face started a fire low in her belly. Flustered, she looked around her room. "Do I need to dress up or anything?"

"Not really. It's Blake," he replied, as if that explained everything. "Just be comfortable. It'll be nice to eat something that someone else prepared."

"Yes," she agreed. "It will."

"Let me know when you want to go. We can do lunch or go later, for dinner, if you'd rather."

She didn't even have to think about that one. "Dinner, please. I like the idea of relaxing out somewhere else at the end of the day."

He smiled, once again making her entire body tingle. "Sounds good. We'll leave here around seven."

Suddenly, absurdly tongue-tied, she settled on a nod.

* * *

While doing small chores around the property, Dade found himself really looking forward to their dinner out that evening. While he wouldn't go so far as to call it a date, in truth, it felt like one. Either way, both he and Maddie needed a break from all the drama that had been occurring lately.

Though he hadn't said as much to Maddie, until they'd found the body in the field, he'd truly believed the stalker had followed her here from Texas. He'd suspected it was someone who'd had a grudge against her. Maybe an old boyfriend or someone from her former job.

Now, with the possibility that someone had been murdered around here recently, he had to admit he might be wrong.

But a *local*? Dade had grown up here, at least since Grady had taken him in as a small child. He knew these people, loved them (or at least most of them), and knew he could depend on them if he ever needed help. The same way they knew they could depend on him.

Dade could not think of a single one of them who'd set his boat shed on fire or break into his house. Hell, he and Grady had never even locked the doors. There'd been no need.

And he still didn't know if the guests' unusual cancellation had something to do with the stalker or some other valid reason. Though he didn't want to appear too pushy, he decided to call the man who'd originally made the booking and find out. He'd been so stunned at the call cancelling everything, he'd forgotten to get the guy's name.

He flipped through the notebook and retrieved the guest's contact info. Using the landline, he called. When after several rings, he went to voicemail; he left his name and number, asking for a call back.

Satisfied with that, he took a peek ahead to the set of guests due to arrive the week after the ones who'd cancelled. This time, a smallish company had booked an employee retreat as a team-building exercise. There would be two women executives and four men. Maddie would definitely be an asset with that group.

Hell, so far, Maddie had been a great partner. And more, though the instant he thought about their sensual activities between the bedsheets, his body stirred.

Shaking his head at himself, he got busy power washing the boat docks. Usually, they kept this machine in the boat shed, but luckily Dade had moved it to the garage to tinker with it. Otherwise, they'd have lost that, too.

Thinking of all the fire damage made him scowl. Hopefully, this Officer Taggert would be on the ball. If they could just get the stalker and potential killer caught, he really thought he and Maddie could have a successful season.

Grady, he thought fondly, had truly known what he was doing. Dade's earlier anger and sense of betrayal when he'd learned what Grady had done had been misplaced.

He finished up power washing, and after he put the washer away, his phone pinged, indicating a text.

Officer Taggert had texted that he'd rented a room from Kip and would be staying in town. The forensics team was scheduled to arrive tomorrow and would be transporting the body back to the lab in Anchorage.

Dade texted back, offering the policeman one of the cabins since there'd be no guests. Having law enforcement on the premises could benefit them all, he thought.

Thanks, but I'd rather stay in town, Taggert replied quickly. It's interesting the nuggets of information I can pick up when I hang around with the locals. You never know when I might hear something that could help me with this case.

Since Dade couldn't argue with that, he let it go.

The unusual afternoon heat hadn't even started to lift around the time they were supposed to leave for Blake. Dade decided to remote start his Jeep right before they were ready to go in order to give the air conditioning time to cool off the interior. Even though he'd left the windows cracked open, he knew from experience it would still be hot.

He went inside to get his keys. Stepping into the house, he got distracted by Maddie puttering around the kitchen.

"What are you doing?" he asked. "You're not cooking, are you?"

"I am, but not dinner." Her bright smile had him aching again. "I decided to test out a recipe for banana bread since we had a few going bad. I thought we could have it later when we got back or even in the morning with breakfast."

Words briefly stuck in his throat. Though she had no way of knowing, Grady had always made Dade banana bread to celebrate special occasions. Birthdays, he'd made it the day before, calling it a pre-birthday cake since he always made a real one on Dade's special day.

"Thanks," he managed. "That sounds great."

Something in his voice must have revealed a hint of his inner turmoil. Eyeing him, she tilted her head. "Are you all right? Don't tell me you don't like banana bread?"

"I do," he assured her. "Grady used to make it a lot. It just brings back a lot of memories." Not wanting to discuss it any further, he checked his sports watch. "Are you still wanting to leave at seven? I want to let my Jeep run a few minutes so it will cool off."

"I will be. The bread will be done in about five minutes. I just need to brush my hair and change, and then I'll be good to go."

"Sounds good." Turning to go to his room, he knew later he'd have to eat that bread, so he needed to get a grip on his emotions. He didn't like the way things that had always been happy memories made him miss Grady so badly he ached.

Like he always did, he shoved his emotions back inside and grabbed his wallet. It had been a while since he'd had dinner at Mikki's. He checked out his appearance in the mirror and decided to change his T-shirt to a clean one. While he was at it, he changed out of his work boots into a better pair.

When he walked back into the living room, the freshly baked loaf of banana bread was cooling on the stove top. Maddie's bedroom door was closed, so he guessed she'd gone to get herself ready.

A moment later, the door opened, and she emerged. Instead of her usual jeans, T-shirt and sneakers, she'd changed into a bright red sundress with white polka dots. She wore sandals, and he saw that she'd painted her toenails the same color as her dress. She'd also put on lipstick and long, dangly earrings that showcased her beautiful neck.

He stopped in his tracks, his mouth dry. She looked… different. Stunning as usual, but in a big-city rather than rustic-fishing-lodge kind of way.

In that instant, he understood she'd likely never stay here. She didn't belong, and he chastised himself for ever thinking she would. Despite all that, he kept wanting her, the sharp fierceness of his desire roaring to life inside him.

Standing there staring at her, fully aroused, he wondered how he'd managed to let her get so far inside his heart.

Again, another thought he needed to shut down.

"What's wrong?" she asked, her hand going to her hair. "Is this dress too much? I just thought it would be fun to wear something different."

"No," he managed. "You look amazing."

"I'm glad you think so," she replied, lifting her chin. "Because I wasn't planning on changing. It's a hot day, and I like getting dressed up once in a while. Are you ready to go?"

Holding out his arm, he couldn't help but grin. Just like that, she'd managed to put things back to normal. "Let's do this."

When they reached the Jeep, he hurried over to open her door and help her up. The brief flash of leg as she climbed inside made his gut tighten. Mentally shaking his head at himself, he went around to the driver's side. As he'd hoped, the Jeep had cooled down comfortably.

"This is really nice," she said, buckling herself in.

"Remote start for the win. And I just started it a few minutes ago."

By the time they arrived in Blake, Dade felt like himself. Relaxed and happy to be sharing an evening out with Maddie. His business partner.

Mikki's seemed busy, the small parking lot behind the building at least three-quarters full. He found a spot and, after killing the ignition, jumped out and hurried over to help Maddie.

"Thanks," she said, taking his arm. "You're really a gentleman underneath all that wilderness-man exterior."

Again, he found himself grinning at her. With her arm in his, they walked into the bar and restaurant.

The first thing that struck him was the noise level. He hadn't been here during the evening rush in forever. Every seat at the long bar was occupied, and most of the tables were, too.

He found them a table close to the small dance floor, across from the makeshift raised stage. "They have live music sometimes," he said, pulling out a chair so Maddie could sit. "It's usually someone fairly local."

A waitress hurried over and gave them menus. "I'd love to take your drink order," she said. "The bar is a little backed up, so it might take a couple of minutes."

"I'd like to try a King Street hefeweizen," she said, surprising him. "Or a Glacier hefeweizen, whichever one you have."

He ordered a club soda with lime. After the waitress left, he leaned forward and looked at Maddie. "How'd you know about our local beers?"

"Like I said, when I knew I'd be helping run Grady's Lodge, I did a lot of research. I wanted to learn all I could about local brewing companies. Hefeweizen is my absolute favorite beer, so I memorized the two most popular ones that are brewed in this state."

Impressed, he nodded. "Once again, I see I underestimated you," he said.

"People tend to do that," she replied, smiling. "It's okay because I have a lot of confidence in my own abilities."

Once more, she made him laugh. "I like you, Maddie Pierce."

"I like you, too, Dade Anson."

They sat there grinning at each other like a pair of fools until the waitress arrived with their drinks.

"Here you are," she said. "Are you ready to order?"

Since neither of them had even taken a look at the menu, they shook their heads. "Give us just a few minutes, please," Dade requested.

After taking a sip of her beer, she made a hum of pleasure. The sound made his body tighten.

"This is good," she said. She picked up the menu and began scanning the offerings. "I assume you must have eaten here before. What's good?"

Since he figured she, like him, would be heartily sick of eating salmon by now, he told her to try one of the burgers. "They have several to choose from. I always get the blue cheese burger and fries."

"Interesting," she replied, taking another drink of her beer. "I've always been partial to a decent Swiss and mushroom burger myself."

Stunned, he stared. "That's what Grady always ordered," he told her, his throat aching. "With onion rings."

"That sounds perfect," she said cheerfully, putting the menu down. "Seems like Grady had great taste. Maybe I inherited it from him."

The waitress appeared to take their order, which gave Dade a moment to get his act together. Once she'd written down their burger choices, she hurried off toward the kitchen.

The ebb and flow of the conversations going on felt completely different than the peaceful nature sounds he'd grown accustomed to.

"This is nice," Maddie said, sipping her beer and looking around. "And it's actually the first time since I arrived that I've felt like part of a community."

Genuinely curious, he studied her. "What do you mean? You've been an integral part of Grady's Lodge."

"Thank you." Beaming, she gestured vaguely at the packed bar. "But this is different. We're in town, in Blake. And no one is staring at me, wondering what I'm doing here. This may sound silly, but I actually feel accepted."

He could have said several things, like point out that she'd been to town with him on supply runs on numerous occasions. Or point out that she was with him, and by now everyone in town knew that Grady's granddaughter had arrived to help run the lodge. But Dade could relate. He had never forgotten the feeling of being on the outside looking in and wanting so desperately to belong.

"You *are* accepted," he said gently, taking a long drink of soda to cover any emotion.

"Hey, Dade!" Samuel Quinton, a burly man with a bushy beard walked over. "And you must be Maddie."

After the introductions, Samuel pulled out a chair without asking. "Did you hear? Amy White is missing."

"What?" Immediately thinking about the shallow grave in the meadow, Dade frowned. "Since when?"

"Yesterday," Samuel replied. "She went out hiking on her own and didn't return home in time for dinner."

Dade exhaled. If she'd just gone missing the day before, that meant it wasn't her body they'd found torn up by wolves.

"On her own?" Maddie asked, looking from one man to the other. "Why would she do that? I'd think it wouldn't be safe."

"She grew up here," Samuel answered. "Most of the

kids who live in the area around Blake know these woods like the back of their hands. She's an amateur photographer, so she was always going off on her own and taking pictures. They found her car parked near that bridge by the river. Her phone and camera were inside. It's not like her to not check in. Her parents are really worried."

"I imagine they are," Dade glanced around the room. "I'm assuming they contacted the state police?"

"Yep. Did you know there's an officer staying in one of Kip's rooms above the general store?" Without waiting for an answer, Samuel continued. "Having him in town turned out to be handy. He's sent for a search and rescue team out of Anchorage. Meanwhile, the rest of us are meeting up in the morning to fan out and help look. Do you want to join us?"

"Definitely," Maddie said. "Where are we meeting?"

"The general store. Kip is helping organize the whole thing." Smiling with approval, Samuel clapped Dade on the back.

Their food arrived just then, so Samuel pushed to his feet and took his leave.

As usual, the burgers were large and meaty. They'd been cut in half to make them easier to manage. Maddie regarded hers. "Wow."

Though the mouthwatering aroma made his stomach growl, he found more pleasure watching her experience her first bite than chowing down himself.

She bit in, chewed, and her eyes went huge. "That's amazing," she said, going in for a second bite.

"Yes, they are," he agreed, finally picking up his and beginning to eat. He hadn't traveled outside of the state, but he could honestly say he believed Mikki's had the best burgers anywhere. Including his own home-grilled ones.

Only once she'd devoured the first half did she slow down long enough to try one of the large, perfectly crispy onion rings.

"I wonder what happened to the missing girl," she mused. "Do you know her?"

"Not really." He dipped one of his fries in ketchup and popped it into his mouth. "I went to school with one of her older brothers. She's pretty young. I think she might have just graduated high school."

"I have to say, when Samuel first mentioned someone was missing, I immediately thought of what you found in the field."

He appreciated the way she chose her words with care. Though none of the nearby tables appeared to be paying attention to them, he didn't want anyone to overhear. Spreading half-baked rumors could get out of control in a town as small as Blake.

"Me, too," he admitted. "That's why I asked when she went missing."

Maddie eyed the other half of her burger, making him wonder if she planned to get a to-go box. Instead, she picked it up and took a huge bite. Making a sound of pleasure that made his mind go elsewhere, she rolled her eyes and proceeded to demolish the rest of her food.

Since he'd already finished most of his, he ate his fries and watched her.

When she'd finished, she blotted her mouth with a napkin and drank the last of her beer. "That was amazing."

As if on cue, the waitress appeared. "Does anyone want dessert?"

Both Maddie and Dade shook their heads. The waitress dropped off the bill, told them she'd be their cashier and left.

"My treat," Dade said, grabbing it before Maddie could.

She thanked him, leaning back and patting her stomach. "I'm stuffed."

Once he'd paid, they walked outside.

"We'll have to do this again," he told her, taking his key fob out of his pocket and hitting the remote start button.

Instead, his truck exploded, the force of the blast knocking them both to the ground.

Chapter 11

Dazed, ears ringing, Maddie struggled to get up from the pavement. Knees and elbows bleeding, dress torn, it took her a few seconds to process what on earth had just happened.

"Maddie?" Dade's voice, raspy and interrupted by a bout of coughing, reached her through her stunned fog. "Maddie, are you all right?"

Somehow, she managed to stagger to her feet, still not able to see clearly. "I...think so. What about you?"

"I'm okay."

Since his voice seemed to be right beside her, she slowly turned, hand outstretched, trying to connect with him. She swayed, unsteady on her feet as she waited for her vision to clear. Smoke, there was so much smoke. She, too, began to cough.

Dade, still coughing, took her hand and pulled her close. "I'm right here. Lean on me."

She did. Supporting her with his arm, they moved away from the fire.

Dimly, she realized that people had spilled out of Mikki's when the Jeep had exploded.

"The volunteer fire department is on the way," someone said.

"Dade, Maddie. Are either of you injured?" Officer Taggert appeared, shepherding them both toward the bar.

"I don't think so," Maddie replied. "A few minor scrapes, that's all. Nothing serious, at least for me." She glanced at Dade, finally able to see him, and gasped. "Dade. Your face. It's all bloody."

Eyes narrow slits, he stared at her. "Head wounds bleed like a mother. I'm good."

Then his legs appeared to buckle, and he went down.

Taggert barely managed to get under Dade before he hit the ground. While Taggert was a large man, Dade was even bigger.

Slowly, Taggert eased Dade onto the pavement. "Can someone send for the doctor?" he shouted. "I know you have one. I saw the sign for the medical clinic."

"She's on her way," someone called back.

Uncaring of her bloody knees, Maddie knelt next to Dade. His eyes, while open, appeared dazed, the pupils dilated. She took his hand and squeezed. "Stay still," she murmured. "A doctor is on the way."

A moment later, a woman with long, red hair in a ponytail came running up. "I'm here," she gasped, slightly winded.

Maddie looked up, realized the doctor appeared to be pregnant, and then also saw another man hovering nearby who must be her significant other.

Meanwhile, the Jeep continued burning. Vehicles on both sides of it had now caught on fire.

"Everyone move away," Officer Taggert shouted. "Any of the others could blow at any moment, once that fire hits the gas tank."

"We need to move you to safety. I'm Dr. McKenzie Taylor," the doctor said. "Dade? Can you hear me?"

Dade blinked, clearly struggling to focus. "Yes. But it's like you're really far away." He swallowed hard. "No idea why."

"You hit your head," Dr. Taylor said. "Brett, can you help me lift him?"

The other man came over. Letting go of Dade's hand, Maddie stood. Watching the quickly spreading fire, she tried not to panic.

With Officer Taggert on one side and Brett on the other, they managed to get Dade back on his feet. Though he swayed slightly, the color slowly returned to his face.

"Let's get him into my car and take him to the clinic," the doctor ordered. "I need to take a good, thorough look at him."

As the two men walked Dade away, Maddie got a good look at the back of his head and gasped. "He's got a bad cut," she told the doctor. "He must have hit it when we were knocked to the ground."

Once Dade had been placed safely inside the doctor's vehicle, Taggert returned to the scene to do crowd control and clear the area. Maddie looked back. "Oh, thank goodness. The volunteer fire department is here."

"Come on," Dr. Taylor said. "If you're coming with us, we need to go."

Immediately, Maddie got into the back seat and closed the door, and they were off.

"What the heck happened back there?" Brett asked, turning around from the passenger seat to meet Maddie's gaze. "How'd those cars catch on fire?"

"We don't know." Maddie sighed, briefly closing her

eyes. "We'd had dinner at Mikki's and were leaving. Dade hit his remote start, and his Jeep blew up. Which means someone deliberately set some sort of bomb."

Brett narrowed his eyes. "Why would anyone want to do that?"

"It's a long story," Dade murmured. "For another time."

Understanding, Maddie took Dade's hand. Brett, too, appeared to get the hint, as he turned back around to face the front and didn't press the issue.

They reached the medical clinic. Maddie wondered how, if he still couldn't walk, they would get Dade inside. But Brett helped him out. After taking a moment to get his bearings, Dade waved the other man off and moved toward the entrance on his own. Maddie kept close to his side.

Dr. Taylor rushed past them and opened the door. While Brett held it open so Dade could enter, she began turning on the lights. "The exam room is this way," she said. "Brett, would you take Maddie to the break room and help her get those knees and elbows cleaned up? I've got some wipes on the counter back there."

Maddie didn't budge. "I want to go with Dade."

"I understand," the doctor said calmly. "But right now, I need to do a full examination and clean up his head wound. I'll call you as soon as you can come in."

"It's going to be all right," Brett told her. "McKenzie is an excellent physician. She'll take care of your boyfriend. Let's go get you fixed up."

Capitulating, Maddie didn't bother to correct his misconception. There was no need to explain she and Dade were partners. She followed him back to the kitchen, while the doctor took Dade into the exam room and closed the door.

"Have a seat." Brett gestured at a table with four wooden chairs. "Do you mind if I get some wipes and help you get cleaned up?"

She liked that he asked, at least. "I can do it myself," she replied. "They're just scrapes."

"No problem." Fetching the wipes, he handed them to her and took a seat. "I'm sorry this happened to you. Any idea who placed that bomb?"

Looking up from wiping the blood off her knees, she debated how much she should say. He had kind eyes, she thought, and the way he'd looked at Dr. Taylor had been like something out of a romance novel. "Someone has been threatening me, ever since I arrived here," she said. "A little before that, even."

As she told him the details, leaving nothing out, his pleasant expression darkened. By the time she'd finished, he looked absolutely furious.

"You know, when I came here, I had something similar happen to me. I was in an accident and had some temporary memory loss. There were some bad guys after me, too, and I had no idea why."

"That's why Officer Taggert is here," she said. "He actually came to investigate the body the wolves dug up. Now that he's heard about everything else, including the missing girl from town, he's likely going to have a lot more to look into."

"It sounds like he might be staying here awhile," Brett agreed. "Can I get you anything to drink? We have soft drinks or bottled water here in the break room fridge."

Before she could answer, the exam room door opened, and Dr. Taylor stepped out. She smiled at Brett before turning attention to Maddie. "He has a pretty nasty gash on the back of his head," she said, walking over. "I've cleaned it and put some stitches in. He also has a concussion, so when you take him home, you'll need to keep an eye on him. Keep him hydrated and moving every couple of hours. If you see any swelling or anything unusual, that could indicate something more serious. If that happens, give me a call."

More serious? Like a cracked skull? Maddie pushed back a sudden wave of fear. "Maybe we should take him to the hospital and have a CT scan or an MRI done, just in case," she said.

Both Dr. Taylor and Brett stared. Finally, the doctor's expression cleared, and she shook her head. "I forgot, you're new here. The nearest hospital is in Anchorage, over two hours away if you're lucky. For life-or-death urgent situations, they'll send a plane or a chopper. For everything else, we treat it ourselves."

Slowly, Maddie nodded. "Sorry, I'm still getting used to things out here."

Dr. Taylor smiled. "It's okay. When I arrived, I found I had to make a lot of adjustments. Practicing rural medicine is certainly a lot different."

"Will Dade be okay?" Maddie asked. "That's what really matters."

"Yes." Dr. Taylor's firm tone felt reassuring. "Just keep an eye on him. Dade's a strong man and—"

"I have a thick skull," Dade said, emerging from the exam room. Seeing the cuts and bruises on his handsome face, Maddie winced. His walk seemed a bit wobbly, and he had a large bandage on the back of his head. "Come on, Maddie. Let's get back to the lodge."

Relieved to see him, Maddie took a deep breath. "I'd love to, but how? We no longer have transportation."

Dade cursed and took a step forward. Apparently, he moved too fast. He had to grab a hold of the doorframe to steady himself. Blinking, he took a moment to collect himself. "You're right," he said. "My Jeep is gone. We have to be able to get into town and back."

He took a deep breath and dragged his hand across his battered face. "Grady has an old truck that I haven't started up in a while. I'll need to work on getting that running. We can use that. At least, until the insurance comes through, and I can buy another Jeep."

"In the meantime, we can take you both back to the lodge," Dr. Taylor offered. Brett nodded, agreeing.

"We'd appreciate that," Dade replied. "I can call Officer Taggert on the way and find out if he's learned anything." He took a deep breath. "Let me settle up with you, and then we'll go."

"I'll just send you a bill," the doctor said. "My assistant handles all of that sort of thing, and obviously, she's not here this late at night."

"Sounds good." Moving with clear difficulty, Dade turned toward the exit.

Maddie jumped up, aware he'd need some assistance. But Brett beat her to it, sliding his shoulder under Dade's arm. "I got you, big guy," Brett said.

Since Brett could clearly handle Dade better, Maddie turned and rushed to open the door instead.

When they were all outside, Dr. Taylor locked up. Blake helped Dade into the back seat, and Maddie climbed in next to him. Brett took the passenger seat, and the doctor got in behind the wheel.

Once they were all buckled in, Brett turned to look at Dade. "You'll need to direct us. While I've heard of your fishing lodge, I've never been out there."

"Me, neither," Dr. Taylor chimed in. "I have no idea how to get there."

Dade was leaning back in the seat with his eyes closed, but opened them long enough to give a few directions. "Beyond that, Maddie should be able to point out the way," he said. "She's been to town and back a few times."

Brett looked at Maddie. Slowly, she nodded. "Sure. I can do that."

To leave town, they had to drive down Main Street and right past Mikki's. From what Maddie could see as they went past, the fire appeared to have been extinguished and most of the crowd had dispersed. She couldn't see Officer Taggert, so she figured they'd have to wait until tomorrow to hear what he had to say about all of this.

Which likely was a good thing, since Maddie would have her hands full tonight taking care of Dade.

Sitting in the back seat next to Maddie, Dade kept fading in and out. He couldn't shake the strange lethargy that made him incapable of moving much. And his head felt like it had been split open with an axe, even if that sounded a bit dramatic.

Still, he'd a thousand times rather be the one who'd been hurt. As long as Maddie was all right, he'd be fine.

Maddie. Even with his inability to focus, he knew one thing. In the short period of time he'd spent with her, Maddie had come to mean more to him than she should. In fact, he'd begun to think he couldn't imagine life without her.

He shook his head at his inner thoughts but then winced. All this had to be due to his head injury. He'd never been a man given to fanciful thinking.

Somewhere between Blake and the lodge, he must have dozed off. Luckily, Maddie had apparently remembered how to get back to the lodge because when he opened his eyes again, they'd just pulled up to the house.

"Do you need help getting out?" Brett asked, turning around from the front seat.

Since Dade wasn't sure how to answer, he shrugged. Even that small movement sent jagged shards of pain shooting through his skull.

Briefly closing his eyes, when the door opened and Brett reached in, Dade grunted. "Give me a sec," he said. He managed to push himself up and grab hold of the other man's arm. Once out, he waited a moment to get his bearings. Then, shaking off Brett's attempt to help, he managed to make his way up the front steps and to the door.

Turning the knob, he cursed again. He'd forgotten that they'd locked it when they left. And the keys had been in his hand when the Jeep exploded. He had no idea what had happened to them.

"Let me unlock the door, please," Maddie requested, right behind him. "I picked up your keys after you fell."

Conscious of the doctor and Brett watching them, Dade shuffled aside. Once Maddie had opened the door and turned to help him inside, he tried to turn and wave to Dr. Taylor, but couldn't find the coordination or the energy. He settled for stepping over the threshold without stumbling.

"I hate this," he said, teeth clenched.

After she closed and locked the door, Maddie came over

and kissed his cheek. "I imagine you do. How about we get you settled on the couch with a pillow and a blanket?"

Any other time, Dade might have retorted that he didn't need to be coddled, but right now, having someone take care of him felt nice. He started to nod, but remembering the pain that came with sudden head movements, settled on a faint smile instead.

He lowered himself onto the couch, and she went to his bedroom, brought out his pillow and put it at one end of the couch. He managed to get his shoes off, and she helped him lie back.

"Would you like out of those jeans?" she asked. "They're pretty torn up."

"Sure." Though he really didn't care. All he wanted to do right now was get some sleep.

Any other time, the feeling of her small hands unfastening his belt and tugging down his zipper might have been arousing. Instead, he sighed with relief as she helped pull the jeans off, freeing each leg. Clad only in his boxers, he settled back onto the couch.

"I'll be right back," she said.

A moment later, she returned with an old throw blanket that she'd found somewhere.

"Here you go," she said, covering him as if he were a young child. "Let me get you a glass of water."

While he liked having her fuss over him, he'd much rather their positions were reversed. He'd always been the caregiver, never the vulnerable one in need of help. He'd taken care of Grady when the older man had fallen ill, and he'd done a damn good job of it. Dade simply needed to regain his strength, and he'd be back to his old self in no time.

He dozed off while waiting for her to return with the water.

When he next opened his eyes, all the lights had been turned off, and the house was dark. Gingerly, he raised himself up on his elbows and realized the pain in his head had subsided.

Swinging his legs off the sofa, he sat all the way up, holding himself still for a moment. He would get up, he thought, and go to his bed. But he wanted to wait until his eyes adjusted to the darkness. And a brief spurt of dizziness gave him pause.

"Are you okay?" Maddie's soft voice, from the chair on the other side of the couch.

Stunned, he attempted a nod. This time, the head movement didn't hurt nearly as much as before. "I'm better, I think," he replied. "Have you been there all night?"

"You've only been asleep for a couple of hours."

Sitting with her in the complete darkness felt like another kind of intimacy. His body stirred. It surprised him that he could want her so damn much, even while bruised and battered. "Go on to bed," he told her. "You don't need to sit with me. I'm fine."

"You're not fine. And the doctor told me to keep an eye on you due to your concussion. I was just about to wake you when you sat up on your own."

Since he couldn't dispute that logic, he sighed. "I never thought I'd say this, but I'm actually glad the next group cancelled. They would have been here the day after tomorrow."

"Me, too," she agreed. "Though I hate the lost revenue, at least this way you can heal up."

"True." Deciding he'd had enough of being disabled,

he tried to push himself up to his feet. He made it, but just barely. And he felt glad for the darkness because he felt more unsteady than he liked.

"Let me help you." Somehow, Maddie got right beside him. "Are you needing to go to the bathroom?"

"I'm not a child," he said crossly. Immediately, he felt bad. "Sorry. I'm not used to being hurt."

"I get that." Despite everything, she sounded cheerful. "But we're partners, remember? I'm here to help you. I know you'd do the same for me if our situations were reversed."

Partners. With a grunt, he acknowledged her point. "Thank you," he said. "I think I can walk on my own now."

"Great. I'm just going to stay close to you just in case."

And she did. He made it to the bathroom without incident and closed the door.

When he emerged, she was standing in the hall. "Do you want to go back to the couch or would you rather spend the rest of the night in your bed?" she asked.

In the dim lighting, he could see that at some point she'd changed into a large T-shirt that ended at her thigh. The soft, thin material did little to conceal the lush outline of her curves underneath.

Again, desire blazed to life. "My bed," he managed. Then, since walking would be even more of a challenge, he used the wall for balance.

Luckily, it wasn't far. Once they reached his room, Maddie turned on the lamp. Standing in front of it had the effect of turning her T-shirt translucent. He'd thought his arousal couldn't be any fiercer. Turned out, he was wrong.

Her eyes widened as she noticed. "You need to rest," she said, her voice firm.

Though he hated to admit it, he knew she was right. "Maybe in the morning," he said.

She turned back the sheets and gestured. "In bed you go."

Despite his still raging arousal, he managed to crawl between the sheets. "Will you lie here with me?" he asked. "Nothing else. Just hold me until I fall asleep?"

"I will." She got into bed with him, pushing him gently onto his side so that his back was to her. "But only if you face that way."

Then she wrapped her arms around him and held him until he fell asleep.

When he opened his eyes next, the sunlight streaming in through his window announcing the morning, to his astonishment, Maddie was still asleep next to him.

Instant desire slammed into him. He forced himself to keep still, trying to be content with watching her sleep.

Finally, when he had his body under control, he slipped from the bed and headed to take a shower. Once the next group of guests arrived, neither he nor Maddie would be able to sleep past sunrise, so Dade decided he wouldn't wake her. She'd worked hard and deserved her rest. Thanks to the last-minute cancellation, they'd have a lot more time in between groups of people. He'd figure out a way to make up for the lost revenue.

After showering, he headed to the kitchen. He made his usual cup of strong coffee and got to work preparing a hearty breakfast. Today would be a busy one, since he had to deal with the insurance, see if he could get Grady's old truck running and stop by Dr. Taylor's office so she could check him out again.

Now, he actually felt relieved that the next group had

cancelled. If they hadn't, it would have been difficult to get ready without a working vehicle. Though the cabins had already been cleaned and made ready, they still would have needed to shop and meal prep before the guests arrived.

Now, he could work on Grady's truck, and then they could simply focus on figuring out who was doing this to them and why.

Turning the bacon, he shook his head. This, the off days in between guests, had always been fun. In years past, he and Grady had thoroughly enjoyed themselves, making bets on who could do what the fastest. Grady had a way of making everything, even the most menial of chores, seem fun.

Dade missed him more than he could ever explain.

"Mornin'." Maddie appeared, her hair tousled, her eyes still sleepy. "That bacon smells delicious."

"Breakfast is just about done," he said, working to control his body's wham-slam reaction to her. "Grab yourself some coffee."

"Coffee," she breathed, moving toward the pot. "That's exactly what I need."

Unable to help himself, he watched while she got herself a mug and poured. She carried that over to the table and sat. "I take it you're feeling better this morning?"

"I am." He couldn't help but smile. Seeing that, she blushed, which made him want to kiss her. And more.

He set a plate down in front of her. "Here you go. Eat up."

Momentarily distracted, she eyed the meal he'd made. Fluffy scrambled eggs, thick pieces of toasted bread and perfectly cooked bacon.

He went back, got his own plate and took the seat across from her. "Is something wrong?" he asked.

"Not really," she said, picking up her fork. She took a bite, made a sound of pleasure and continued eating. After a moment, he grabbed his own fork and did the same.

Once she'd finished her breakfast, she sat back in her chair and looked at him. "Something is wrong," she admitted. "A lot is wrong, and you know it. Not only is someone stalking us, but I'm worried about the missing girl from town. What if the guy who killed and buried that woman on our land has her?"

He nodded. "I've thought the same thing. I'm hoping that's not the case, and she shows up home soon. And since they've organized a search for her, if our stalker does have her, he'll be running out of places to hide."

"Maybe so." She drained the last of her coffee and got up to get another cup. When she returned to her chair, she met his gaze. "I think it's time to go on the offensive."

"How so?"

Leaning forward, she grimaced. "It's just weird that this guy is texting, breaking into our home, setting things on fire, and we don't have any idea why. He's made no demand, other than insisting I go back to Texas. What does he actually want? Is there a way we can confront him and find out?"

"That might be dangerous, don't you think?" he pointed out. "Sometimes, unstable people with unresolved mental health issues don't have a valid reason. Since it seems like he's started ramping things up, I don't know."

"I want to talk to Officer Taggert and see what he thinks." She lifted her chin. "If this guy turns out to be a killer, then we're already in danger. I came out here ready to start a new life. I'm working hard and learning from you. I have plans. Big ones."

Swallowing, she took a long drink of her coffee while she visibly gathered her composure. "In the last several months, I've had a lot of losses. I'm not willing to endure any more. Inheriting half of this fishing lodge became a second chance for me. I moved far away from familiar places and people, and I refuse to let this person drive me off."

"I admire that," he said, meaning every word. "And you're doing great. We make a good team. As far as the stalker, I'd also like to know what he wants and why he's doing this to us. I have to think he has some sort of grudge against the lodge. Maybe he was a past guest or something. But he seems to be doing everything he can to shut us down."

"I hadn't thought of that." She sat back in her chair, expression dazed. "Until you just said that, I'd assumed his attacks were personal, directed at me, and you just got caught up in it due to proximity. I mean, he started texting me right after I learned of my inheritance, before I even left Texas."

"True. I honestly don't know. If he'd give us an opportunity to have an actual conversation, maybe we could finally find out what he wants."

The sound of multiple vehicles on gravel outside had him and Maddie looking at each other.

"What the...?" Dade asked, getting to his feet. "Stay put and let me check this out."

Eyes wide, Maddie nodded.

Before he went out, he grabbed his pistol, checked to make sure it was loaded and put on his holster.

Then he took a deep breath, opened the front door and stepped out onto the front porch.

Three large SUVs had parked in front of the house. As Dade stared, the doors opened and several men emerged.

"Dade, my man." A tall man with a trendy haircut and mirrored aviator sunglasses stepped forward, hand outstretched. "Bradley Hartfield. We're really looking forward to another few days of fishing here. We can't wait to get started."

It took a second before Dade realized who these people were. The guests who'd called and cancelled. Except obviously they hadn't. It appeared that their stalker had struck yet again.

Chapter 12

Heart pounding in her chest, Maddie waited. Once again, she felt frustration at her lack of control and inability to help Dade protect the lodge.

A moment later, he came barging back into the house, looking flustered and slightly out of breath. "The guests are here. You know, the ones who we thought called and cancelled."

Horrified, she stared. "But they didn't?"

"Obviously not. Which means someone else pretended to be them just to mess with us."

She didn't have to ask who. "Okay. We can deal with this. The cabins are all ready, and I'm sure we have enough food to cobble together some meals. How long are they staying?"

To her surprise, he hugged her. "Thank you. These guys have four nights and three days. It's our standard package."

She nodded. "What would you like me to do?"

"Come on outside and let me introduce you. Then we'll get them settled in their cabins, and we'll figure out a menu for their stay."

She took a deep breath and followed him outside.

A group of forty-something men, dressed in expensive casual wear, stood around three large, late-model

SUVs, all black. It looked like a presidential motorcade or something.

Exchanging a quick glance with Dade, Maddie pasted a bright smile on her face. "Your cabins are all ready for you," she said. Since this group seemed comprised of relatively fit men, she doubted she'd need to get out the golf cart. "If you all will follow me, I can take you there."

"We're doing the same ones as last time," one of the men said, a tall, lanky guy who wore mirrored sunglasses and had an air of inflated self-importance.

Maddie recognized the type. She'd certainly dealt with a lot of them at her old job back in Dallas. "Since I wasn't here last year, I'll just let you all pick and choose the cabins," she said. "Follow me, please."

No one moved.

"Last year, the guys got out a golf cart so we didn't have to carry our luggage," another man said. "We'd like that same service this time."

Several of the other guests agreed.

"I'll get it." Dade's smile came off as more fierce than welcoming.

Though Maddie's first impulse was to rush to help Dade, she didn't. Instead, she attempted to make small talk while they waited, asking about their flight or drive and where they were from.

Naturally, the guy with the sunglasses took over the conversation, talking about his important job in banking and how he'd wanted to vacation at a golf resort, but his buddies here had insisted on Grady's Lodge. "Which means I'd better catch a lot of fish," he concluded, managing to sound vaguely threatening. "I've never been much for wilderness type things. I get enough of that living in Anchorage."

A couple of the other guys laughed. "You live in a condo downtown," one said. "And you've been here before. Last year, you said you had a great time."

Grinning back at them, he shrugged. "Maybe I did. We drank so much last time, I can't really remember if we did or not."

This comment was greeted by cheers and more laughter.

Dade and the golf cart came around the corner, and the guests began piling their luggage inside. Once everything had been loaded, leaving barely enough room for Dade to drive, he pulled away. "Follow me, gentlemen," he ordered.

Immediately, all the men trooped after the golf cart, without a second look at Maddie.

Relieved, she watched them go. After they'd left, she realized that she actually felt apprehensive. This group of guests brought a completely different vibe than the last one. But she could handle them. After all, she'd worked around men like them before.

She went back inside and started cleaning up from breakfast. At least it was still early, which would give her enough time to figure out what to serve for lunch. She grabbed a notepad and pen and started taking inventory. If she could get a menu planned out based on what they actually had, all would work out fine.

By the time Dade returned, she had the week's menu all planned. She handed him the notebook. "I'd like your thoughts. I checked on our supplies, and I can make all of these meals. Do you think this would work for this group?"

Accepting the book, he looked it over. "This is amazing," he said. "Good job."

She smiled. "I'll do all the meal prep and the cooking. Why don't you concentrate on seeing if you can get that old truck running?"

To her surprise, he grabbed her, hauled her up against him and kissed her. When they finally broke apart, their breathing was ragged. "You're something else, Maddie Pierce," he said. "I wish Grady could have gotten to know you. He would have been so proud."

Swallowing hard, she turned away so he wouldn't see the sudden tears that sprung to her eyes.

A moment later, Dade cursed, which made her turn around. "All my tools were in the boat shed. Which means they're gone. I don't know how I'll be able to work on that truck now."

"Did Grady have a toolbox in his truck?" she asked, taking a guess. Working in property development, she'd been around more than one construction foreman with a pickup and one of those long, metal toolboxes bolted into the bed.

Dade nodded with relief. "He did." Grabbing her, he kissed her again, this time a quick press of his lips on hers. "I bet I can find what I need there." Glancing at his watch, he grimaced. "But first, I need to make sure these guys all get safely out on the water."

Once Dade raced off again, she got busy doing prep work in the kitchen. She'd make a simple but filling lunch. Shaved beef sandwiches with melted cheese and potato chips, which should go over well with this type of crowd.

For dinner, she got busy thawing several packages of bratwurst. She figured Dade could throw them on the grill, and she'd make a huge bowl of potato salad. While she got the water boiling for the potatoes, she opened an industrial-size can of beans and put them in the Crock-Pot, along with barbeque sauce, chopped onions and some green pepper. If she had to guess, she'd say this group would be hungry. Since she'd rather have too much food than not enough, she'd make a lot.

Several hours passed. Dade texted, letting her know the boats were coming back in, and they'd all be up there for lunch. Since she'd already gotten everything ready, she heated up the shaved beef, loaded the brioche buns and sprinkled shredded mozzarella cheese on top.

By the time the group trooped into the main dining area, she had everything ready.

As she'd expected, they fell upon the food like starving jackals. She watched from the doorway, not liking the way that Bradley guy stared at her. She couldn't tell what he was thinking.

Deciding it didn't matter, she retreated to the kitchen, where she'd kept back a couple sandwiches for herself and Dade. They ate together at the smaller kitchen table, listening to the good-natured joking and conversation from the other room.

"Did they catch a lot of fish?" she asked quietly.

"A few," Dade answered. "But that hotshot guy Bradley is mad that he didn't get any. Hopefully, he will when they go back out later."

After the guests finished their lunch, several of them declared they wanted to go back to their cabins and nap before the next fishing outing. Maddie waited for them to go, managing to hide her impatience.

Finally, only one man remained. Bradley. He remained

sitting, watching as Maddie and Dade gathered up the paper plates and plastic utensils. Anyone else might have offered to help or, at the very least, left and gotten out of the way.

"Do you make a large profit here?" he asked, his dismissive tone indicating he felt he already knew the answer.

Maddie glanced at Dade. He'd stopped what he'd been doing to turn and look at Bradley. "I'm sorry, but we are not in the habit of discussing our operation with our guests."

"Why not?" Bradley challenged. "That answer makes it sound like you have something to hide."

Ignoring him, Dade carried the condiments back into the kitchen.

"What about you?" Bradley asked, directing his attention to Maddie. "I'm assuming even though you're new, you must know something about this business. Is it profitable?"

"Why?" Facing him, Maddie stared. "Are you thinking of investing?"

"Of course not," Bradley huffed. "I'm just curious how a dump like this stays in business."

"If you think the lodge is so terrible, why don't you leave?" Hands on hips, Maddie challenged him. "We have plenty of guests who truly enjoy their stay here."

His mocking laugh made her see red. "I don't know why you and your boyfriend are so defensive. I just asked a simple question. Does this place turn a profit?"

Exasperated, Maddie bit back what she really wanted to say. "None of your business. Now if you wouldn't mind vacating the dining room, we've got some cleaning up to do."

He finally stood, making a show of stretching lazily.

Looking her up and down as if he could see through her clothes, he smiled. "I meant no offense," he said.

If he considered that an apology, he was wrong. She nodded, said nothing more and continued clearing the table. When she joined Dade in the kitchen, she heard the sound of the door opening and closing.

Depositing her tray of paper plates and plastic utensils in the trash, she went back to make sure the dining room had finally emptied.

"I don't like that Bradley guy," she said. "He's rude and entitled."

Dade looked up from the sink, where he'd been cleaning pans. "He was like that last year, if I remember. Just try not to let him bother you. He'll be gone soon enough."

Once he'd washed everything she'd used and stacked it in the dishwasher, he dried his hands on a dish towel. "I'm going to go down and refuel the boats. They'll be going back out in a couple of hours."

"I'll start doing prep work for dinner," she said. "That way, all I'll have to do is cook."

The rest of the afternoon passed uneventfully. Once the group of guests had left for the afternoon fishing trip, Dade went out to work some more on Grady's truck.

When dinner time arrived, the sunburned group filed in, exchanging jokes and teasing each other happily. Dade grilled bratwurst and once he'd delivered a heaping platter to the kitchen, he murmured to Maddie that he'd be back shortly. Nodding, Maddie served their guests without incident, and then, since Dade hadn't reappeared, she made two extra plates and set them aside. She'd wait to eat until Dade could.

Once they'd finished, everyone thanked her and filed

out of the room. Judging from the conversations she'd overheard, they were eager to get the campfire going and break out the beer.

About thirty minutes after the house cleared out, Dade appeared. While he washed up, she warmed their food.

Thanking her, he ate quickly. "I'm going back out there," he said. "I think I've found the problem. It's the carburetor. I'm hoping I can get it fixed tonight."

She nodded, careful to hide her disappointment. "I'm planning on parking myself in front of the TV for a while. Unless there's something I can do to help you?"

To her surprise, he kissed her cheek. "No, but thank you for offering. I'll be back as soon as it gets dark or I get the truck started, whichever comes first."

And then he was gone.

She stared at the door for a few seconds after he left. Odd how she, a woman who'd lived alone her entire adult life, could feel his absence so strongly.

After settling down in front of the TV, she must have dozed off. The next thing she knew, Dade came bursting into the house. "I did it!" he exclaimed. "I got the truck running!"

Sitting up, she blinked at him, trying to emerge from the fog of sleep. "That's awesome."

"It is." He came over and kissed the top of her head. "Go back to sleep if you want. I'm going to jump in the shower. I need to wash off all this sweat and grime." He held out his dirty hands and laughed. "I'll show you the truck in the morning. It's almost dark outside, but at least we have transportation again."

After he left, she checked the time on her phone. Almost nine thirty. She got up, stretched and padded into the kitchen to get a glass of water.

The house phone rang. Startled since it was kind of late, Maddie glanced at the thing, debated whether or not to answer and then snatched the receiver out of the cradle.

"Hello?"

"This is Bradley Hartfield, from cabin 2. We are in need of more clean towels. Right away."

Before she could even reply, he hung up the phone. She noticed he didn't even try to be polite.

Since Dade had jumped in the shower, if their guests were going to get clean towels, she'd have to bring them. She wondered what had happened, because each cabin had been fully stocked with all the necessities, including towels. And judging by the sounds occasionally drifting up from below, most of the other men were still sitting around the campfire, drinking and telling fish stories.

Unsure what to do, she considered poking her head in the shower and getting Dade's thoughts. They'd both worked hard all day, her cooking and cleaning up after serving their guests both lunch and dinner, and him popping in to help before going back to trying to get the old pickup truck running.

The last group of guests—her first—had seemed to understand unspoken boundaries regarding requests. Maddie really didn't understand how anyone could phone after nine thirty at night and expect towels. Or anything, honestly. It wasn't as if she considered that an emergency.

Maybe the towels could wait until morning.

Except she didn't want to give any guest, especially one with an entitled attitude, a single reason to complain. This was a simple, straightforward request. She went into the laundry room, grabbed a couple of fresh, folded towels from the basket and headed toward the door. On the way, she grabbed one of the flashlights they kept on the counter and scribbled Dade a quick note, just in case.

Outside, darkness had settled over the sky. Glancing up, she still marveled at the vast star-scape visible out here, so far away from city lights. The scent of smoke from the campfire below drifted on the air, and she could still hear the sound of men's laughter. Which meant they were still enjoying their evening. And why shouldn't they be? They were on vacation, and though fishermen were early risers, it wasn't that late yet.

Cabin number two had lights shining from the window, which meant at least one of the guests must be inside. Maybe Bradley had decided to turn in early and take a shower. She stepped up onto the small front porch and knocked.

"I have your towels," she said.

A moment later, the door opened. A man she didn't recognize stood in the doorway, clad only in a wet towel. "I'm Bradley," he said. Another man holding a bottle of whiskey stood behind him, leering drunkenly.

"Here," Maddie said, shoving the towels at Bradley. "Breakfast will be at six in the morning."

Instead of reaching for the towels, he grabbed her arm and yanked her inside, kicking the door shut behind her.

Enjoying the spray of hot water on his sore muscles, Dade wished he'd invited Maddie to join him in the shower. But he knew she'd been working hard to feed their unexpected guests. No doubt when he came out, she'd be sitting on the couch watching television and trying to relax.

He definitely could use some of that, too. In fact, he planned to join her in just a minute. Hopefully, he could convince her to join him in his bed later.

Wandering out into the living room, he looked around. Baffled to find the room empty, he took a quick peek into her bedroom. Not there.

In the kitchen, he found her note on the counter.

Taking towels to cabin 2. That Bradley guy wanted them right now.

Dade frowned. While he wasn't sure how long it'd been since she'd left, he didn't like this scenario at all.

He considered texting her, but decided he'd go down there and help her. After grabbing a flashlight, he made an abrupt turn and went back for his pistol.

Just as he opened the back door and stepped outside, a scream cut through the night air.

"Maddie!" he bellowed, taking off at a run.

By the time he reached cabin 2, all of the other guests had gotten there. The cabin door stood open and lopsided, telling Dade someone had likely kicked it in.

He sprinted up onto the small porch, pushed through the men and saw Maddie standing in the corner. Her eyes were wild, her clothing torn, and she clutched one of his flashlights like a weapon. The towels she'd brought were scattered around her feet.

Bradley sat on the floor, nursing a cut to his head. Another man sat on the edge of the bed, drinking from an open bottle of whiskey and clearly too drunk to register what was going on.

Though Dade wasn't sure what had happened, he had a pretty good idea.

He went to Maddie first. "Are you all right?"

It took a moment for her gaze to focus on his face. "I am now," she replied, her mouth tight. Her gaze flashed past him to Bradley. "That fool tried to mess with the wrong woman."

Tamping down his fury, Dade slowly turned to look at Bradley. "Are you sober?"

Slowly, the other man shook his head. "Not really."

By now, the rest of the group had crowded inside.

"How many of you are sober enough to drive?" Dade asked. "Or have all of you been drinking heavily?"

The group fell silent, shuffling their feet and looking at each other.

"Since I don't want to send impaired drivers out onto the road, you can pack up tonight and leave in the morning." Dade let his voice reflect his disgust. "Your time here at the lodge is over. And you are not welcome back."

Now all of them started talking at once. Most of them protested, a few of them openly chastising Bradley and his roommate.

Ignoring all of this, Dade took Maddie's arm. "Let's go," he said, leading her through the crowd and back toward the path to the main house.

No one followed.

Maddie held on to his arm with a death grip the entire way. Once they'd reached the house, he held open the door. She finally let go of him and stumbled inside.

He stayed close to her all the way into the living room,

where the TV was still on. Grabbing the remote, he turned it off. "Do you want to sit down?" he asked.

With a nod, she dropped onto the sofa.

Sitting down right beside her, he took her hand. "Do you want to tell me what happened?"

"Sure." Her mouth tightened. "I got a call demanding fresh towels right now. I took them, and when I knocked on the door, that drunk idiot yanked me inside and tried to assault me."

"How were you able to fight him off?" he asked.

"Luckily, since I worked with so many construction workers at the job I had in Dallas, I took a couple of self-defense classes. Just as a precaution. To be honest, I never had to use any of what I learned until tonight. That fool never saw it coming."

He squeezed her hand. "Do you want to press charges?"

"Charges?" Slowly, she shook her head. "I'm not sure. Right now, I just want him out of here." With a loud sigh, she made a visible attempt to relax, rolling her neck. "Thank you for telling them they have to leave."

"He's lucky I didn't beat him to a pulp," Dade said, meaning it. "But since you already did that, I didn't see a need."

For the first time since he'd found her, she cracked a smile. "True." She thought for a moment. "For a minute there, I even considered the idea that Bradley might be my stalker."

Since he had no idea where she might be going with this, he waited.

"But then I realized, no. He isn't. He's just an entitled jerk from Anchorage."

He put his arm around her and pulled her close. She

rested her head on his shoulder, taking long, deep breaths until some of the tension seemed to leave her.

They slept in the same bed that night, though they didn't make love. He simply held her, offering comfort and nothing more. She'd been through a lot, and he counted his blessings that it hadn't been worse.

Though his body needed sleep, he couldn't turn his mind off. Thank goodness she knew self-defense. He shuddered to think what might have happened to her if she hadn't.

With Maddie sleeping soundly, snuggled close, he finally dozed off. He knew she'd let him know if she wanted anything more than comfort.

When he woke in the morning before dawn fully aroused, he slipped from the bed while she still slept. Careful not to wake her, he took a quick shower. By the time he went into the kitchen and made himself his first cup of coffee, he felt relatively normal.

Meanwhile, Maddie continued to sleep. Dade stood there a moment in the doorway to the bedroom and watched her. He hoped when she did wake, she'd feel at least refreshed. Having the guests, especially Bradley, gone would no doubt help, too. He knew it would be better for him since if he saw that Bradley guy again, he'd have to fight to keep from punching him in the face.

Pushing away a surge of anger, Dade sipped his coffee and took several deep breaths. As he often did these days, he thought of Grady. Picturing the older man's reaction to someone laying hands on his granddaughter made Dade realize Bradley better consider himself lucky that he'd only been asked to leave. Maddie could press charges.

Even though she'd said she wasn't sure, she might still change her mind and decide to. Dade hoped she would.

When he walked outside shortly after sunrise, he saw the three black SUVs were still there. Fine, since he figured the guests likely weren't even awake yet. He'd simply walk around the place, do what needed to be done and basically stick around to make sure they left as soon as possible.

Right now, he wanted to check on the boats and make sure they were all tied up properly. More than once, he'd had to go out and retrieve a boat that hadn't been secured.

As he walked past the fire pit, the embers from last night's blaze still glowed. Beer cans and bottles littered the ground all around it, along with pieces of trash from snacks. Since he figured the boats would likely be in a similar state, he went back to the house and got several large trash bags. Maddie still slept, so he took care to be extra quiet.

Then he began cleaning everything up.

Just as he'd filled the first trash bag, the door to cabin one opened. One of the guests, a short, quiet man named Robert, emerged. When he caught sight of Dade, he walked over, his expression apologetic.

"I just wanted to let you know that the rest of us don't condone Bradley's actions," he said, shoving his hands into his jeans pockets. "I barely even know him, but in the short time I've spent with him, I dislike him immensely."

Dade nodded, pretty sure he knew what the man was going to say.

"That said, I'd like you to reconsider making the rest of us leave. Bradley and his buddy, yes. What he did was wrong. Beyond wrong. But most of us were simply enjoying ourselves around the fire. We had no idea what he planned to do. And as soon as we found out, we tried to stop him."

Since his anger from the night before still simmered deep inside him, Dade had to force himself to consider Robert's words. The other man had a point. Except for the mess they'd left, the rest of the group hadn't done anything wrong.

"Fine. The rest of you can finish out your stay. Only the two guys in cabin 2 need to go. Can I trust you to make sure that happens?"

"Of course." Robert nodded. "We're all pretty pissed off about it, so it will be our pleasure."

Robert's unusually formal way of talking made Dade smile. "One more thing," he said. "Can I ask you to talk to everyone about not littering? I've been picking up trash from this entire area."

"My apologies." Robert looked down. "I will definitely speak to them about that."

"Great." Dade picked up the last two beer bottles and straightened. "I'd appreciate it."

Robert nodded. "Consider it done. And thank you so much. I have to say, I'm really glad you agreed. I haven't caught my big fish yet. That's the entire reason I came on this trip." He took a deep breath. "It's my first time here. I never expected anything to happen like this."

Hearing this, Dade felt a little better about his decision to let the rest of the group stay. "I hope you catch that fish," he said, clapping Robert on the back. "Just make sure Bradley and his buddy get in their SUV and leave, okay?"

"Will do. I'll tell the others once they wake up. I thought I'd go for a hike and try to clear some of the cobwebs from my head." Robert gave a sheepish smile. "I'm not used to drinking that much beer."

"You got your bear spray?" Dade asked.

"Yep." Robert pulled it from his shirt pocket. "I wouldn't go out into the woods without it."

"Good deal," Dade turned away. "Be careful out there, man."

Once the other man had walked away, Dade made his way down to the boat slips. As he'd expected, while the boats had all been securely tied, the guests left a mess inside them. He went from one to another, picking up litter. By the time he reached the last boat, his trash bags were full. Now he'd just need to haul them back to the house. By the time he did that, he hoped everyone would be awake. He couldn't wait to evict Bradley and his friend.

As he made his way back up the path, Robert came charging from the woods. "Dade," he shouted, his complexion red. "You've got to come quickly. I found a body in the woods!"

Chapter 13

Snuggling down deep into her pillow, Maddie took her time opening her eyes. When she did and realized Dade had already risen, she sighed. Disappointed but not surprised, she glanced at the clock. Nearly seven, which meant she'd overslept a little. But since the guests would be going home, she planned to enjoy as much of the day as possible.

The sounds of someone shouting outside had her jumping to her feet. She dressed hurriedly and rushed to the back door.

Halfway down the path to the cabins, Dade stood talking to one of the guests. The man was gesturing wildly, clearly upset. Other guests were emerging from their cabins, likely because of the noise.

Maddie hurried down, glancing quickly over at cabin 2 as she didn't want to see either of those men's faces again. That door remained closed.

"What's going on?" she asked as she reached Dade and the guest.

Expression grim, Dade shook his head. "I've got a call in to Officer Taggert. Robert here found a woman's body in the woods. I went up there with him to take a look, and I'm afraid it's the missing girl from town."

For a quick second, Maddie couldn't catch her breath. "Is she dead?"

"Unfortunately, yes." Dade took her arm. "From the looks of it, she was murdered. It's not anything you need to see."

Straightening, she pulled herself free. "I appreciate you wanting to protect me," she said, choosing her words with care. "But if I'm going to survive whatever this is, I have to be able to know exactly what's going on."

Gaze locked on hers, Dade slowly nodded. "When Officer Taggert gets here, you're definitely welcome to accompany us to the body, if that's what you want."

Robert looked from one to the other. "I really would prefer to stay and catch my big fish. But this scenario changes things. I find I need your assurances that it will be safe."

"I don't know what to tell you," Dade replied. "Both victims, if they were killed by the same person, were women. Since you're not…"

"My gender gives me better odds," Robert finished. "Though, I will say that finding a dead body while out for a morning stroll is disconcerting, to say the least."

Just then, something caught Robert's eye, and he grimaced. "It looks like the occupants of the second cabin are emerging. Let me go on over there and make sure they leave right away."

Both she and Dade watched as Robert hurried away. Since Maddie didn't want to see Bradley's face ever again, she kept her attention on Dade. "What did he mean by saying he wanted to stay? I thought they were all leaving this morning."

"He pointed out that he and the others had nothing to do with Bradley's actions and that they all rushed over as soon as they figured out what was going on to try and stop it. So I agreed the rest of them could stay as long as Bradley and his roommate leave."

"That makes sense." She touched Dade's arm. "Does it look like they're leaving? I'm sorry, but I really don't want to look."

"Right now, they appear to be in discussion. I'm keeping an eye on things."

"Robert has an interesting way of talking," she commented, desperately needing a distraction. "Very formal. Like an older person. I kind of like it."

"He seems like a nice guy." Dade kept his attention fixed on whatever was going on over at cabin 2. "I'm hoping those other two don't give him any trouble."

"Me, too."

"Wait here," Dade ordered. "It looks like they're arguing. I'll be right back."

Suddenly, Maddie realized she hated allowing herself to feel as if she'd done something wrong. She spun around and marched herself back to where both Dade and Robert were arguing with a clearly furious Bradley.

"Is there a problem?" she asked, her voice icy. "Because if there is, since Officer Taggert with the Alaska State Troopers is already on his way, I'm thinking I might just go ahead and press charges."

"For what?" Bradley asked, sneering. "Nothing happened."

She kept her head up and held his gaze. "For assault, to begin with. You put your hands on me, which definitely wasn't welcomed."

Bradley opened his mouth, likely to argue, but his friend grabbed his arm and steered him back toward the cabin.

"We're going to pack," the friend said, glancing back over his shoulder at Maddie. "We'll be out of here in just a few minutes."

As promised, they'd vacated the cabin, loaded up their black SUV with their luggage and driven away all before Officer Taggert pulled up.

Lucky for them, Maddie thought darkly. But she had to admit, just having them gone made her feel lighter.

"Good morning," the police officer greeted them. He got out a pad of paper and a pen and looked at them expectantly. "Why don't you tell me what's happened. Start at the beginning."

"There's been a lot going on," Dade said slowly. "Starting with Maddie getting a bunch of vaguely threatening text messages."

"Threatening how?" Taggert asked.

Maddie shook her head. "That's just it, they're intentionally vague. He's using an app to disguise his actual phone number. He clearly wants me to go back to Texas, but hasn't actually said why. We don't know why he feels this would be to his benefit."

"The last group of guests spotted a stranger trespassing on lodge property," Dade said. "He was watching them. I went looking, but other than finding the remains of a small campfire, I never was able to catch him. The guests didn't like having him lurking."

"I didn't appreciate that either," Maddie added.

"And then he set the fire at the boat shed and blew up my Jeep," Dade continued, his large arms crossed. "He's escalating and is now an actual danger, but we still have no idea what he wants."

"But no actual proof he did any of that." Taggert looked

from one to the other. "Do you feel this is the same individual who murdered the two women?"

"We don't know," Maddie answered. "But it seems
likely."

"I see." Grim-faced, the police office considered everything for a moment. "I think you should try to get him to
tell you what he wants." He took a deep breath. "My forensic team is expected to arrive this afternoon. Now they have
two bodies to examine. We need to try and keep wildlife
away from this new one. But first, I've asked the parents
of the missing girl to come out here. If it's her, they can
give us a positive ID."

Maddie closed her eyes. Her heart ached for the family. She couldn't imagine the anguish of having to identify the body of a beloved child.

"I'd better get back up to the house and make these
guests some breakfast," she said. "It'll be something simple, like pancakes with bacon and sausage."

After the group had eaten, Dade went down to the boat
slips with them to see them off. When he returned, he
helped her do some meal prep for the lunch and dinner. "I
promise I'll be cooking tonight," he said. "Steaks on the
grill along with baked potatoes. It'll be a welcome break
from salmon all the time."

This made her smile. He had a point.

The family of the missing girl arrived right after they'd
finished getting the food ready. Office Taggert pulled up
right behind them.

Dade went out to meet them, with Maddie following
right behind. "I'm so sorry," she murmured, meaning it.

The woman nodded, her eyes red and swollen from crying. Her husband kept his arm around her, supporting her even though he appeared on the verge of collapse himself.

"This way, folks." Taggert gestured that they should follow him. Silently, they all trooped after him, on a hiking path that any other time might have sparked exclamations of beauty.

Though she'd insisted on going, Maddie hung back. She realized she had no desire to see the body, and she didn't feel right being a witness to these people's private grief.

Noticing, Dade slowed his steps and then backed up to her. "Are you all right?" he asked.

"I'm fine," she replied, even though she wasn't certain she was. "I'm worried about those folks." She gestured, even though the others were no longer in sight.

"Me, too." He took her hand, just as the dead girl's mother let out an awful, anguished cry.

Tears in her eyes, Maddie stood and bowed her head. When she raised it again, she met Dade's gaze. "We have to stop this," she said. "Before anyone else gets killed or hurt."

Later, while Officer Taggert spoke with the family, Maddie and Dade returned to the house. They had lunch to prepare because soon the remaining guests would be looking for a meal to carry them through their afternoon fishing session.

Once everyone had been fed and they returned to their cabins, Dade and Maddie cleaned up. They'd barely finished when the police forensics van arrived. Officer Taggert, having finished with the family, had joined the guests for lunch. He ate with a quiet, determined air and didn't interact with anyone else.

After the meal, when all the guests had drifted back

to their cabins, Taggert took his leave. "I'll be back later to meet the forensics team," he promised. "Thanks for the grub."

Since Dade had already started washing the dishes, he didn't respond. Maddie walked the officer to the door and thanked him for coming. Then she went back to the kitchen and helped Dade finish cleaning up.

"What do you think about Taggert?" Dade asked.

"I like him," she replied. "He seems focused on doing his job."

"I agree." Dade put the last pan into the dishwasher, added soap and turned the machine on. "Is it just me, or is today dragging?"

"It's been a long day," she said and sighed. One of the remaining guests had gifted her a bottle of white wine as a gesture of good will. She'd stuck it in the refrigerator, and now that it had gotten cold, she poured herself a glass. "Would you like some?" she asked Dade.

"No thanks." He lifted up his glass of iced tea. "I'm good."

"Sorry." She sat. "I forgot you told me you didn't drink." She glanced at her wine glass and frowned. "Is it okay if I do around you?"

"It's fine," he replied. "I used to have a problem, so I quit. Being around alcohol doesn't bother me."

"Okay, good. I'm going to go sit outside, if you want to join me." Taking a sip of her wine, she exhaled. "I really just need to try and relax and clear my head."

He followed her out to the front porch. The fishermen were still in their cabins, no doubt resting up before another night sitting around the bonfire.

"You know, Taggert made sense," Dade said, sitting

down in the rocking chair next to her. "We need to figure out a way to get this guy to tell us what the hell he wants."

"Maybe." She shrugged, taking another sip of her wine.

"Though, at this point," Dade continued, "I think it'd be better if we could just trick him into letting us capture him."

"Us? Wouldn't that be something the police need to handle? This guy is guilty of several crimes."

"If we could prove he's the one who did all of this." Dade's expression echoed the frustration in his voice. "Right now, we have nothing to go on other than some texts and spotting a stranger trespassing. None of that would hold up in a court of law."

"Unless the forensic people find DNA on the murder victims. That would clinch it, right?" she asked.

"It would be enough to charge him, once they figure out who he actually is."

She sighed. "I hate to seem like I'm avoiding reality, but I really need to decompress. Do you mind if we change the subject?"

Just then, in some kind of ironic twist, her phone pinged. Immediately, she tensed.

Dade sat up straighter. "It's been a while since we've heard from him."

"True." Instead of looking at her screen, she passed the phone over to him. "Here. You deal with it."

You should be dead, he read out loud. Immediately, he typed something and sent it. "I asked him how that would benefit him, if he killed us both."

No response. In fact, her phone sat silent for so long she figured the stalker would do like he always did and ghost them until his next text from yet a different number.

Then, as Dade appeared ready to hand it back to her, it pinged again. "Vengeance, he says. He feels we stole something from him and should pay with our lives."

"Ask him what," she prompted. "What did we steal?"

But before Dade could text it, another ping sounded.

Grady's Lodge should have been mine. Grady owed me that much.

Looking up from the phone, Dade frowned. "Who is this guy?"

"I don't know," she replied. "Since you've lived here for years, I wonder if you know him."

Shrugging, Dade sent another text. "I asked him if he's willing to meet in person to discuss this."

Her heart skipped a beat. "I'm not sure how I feel about that."

"I doubt he'll agree, but I have to try. We need to end this, once and for all."

Though they both waited, the stalker didn't text again.

The next morning, Dade woke up alone in his bed and reached for Maddie. It took him a few seconds before he remembered they'd each slept in their own rooms. The guests would be here until tomorrow, so they had one more day of fishing left. Thus far, Robert's big fish had eluded him, though he remained ever hopeful.

Padding into the kitchen for a much-needed cup of coffee, he noticed Maddie's bedroom door remained closed. Since the sun had just started to rise, he tried to be as quiet as possible.

Nevertheless, he'd just taken his first sip of coffee when

Maddie emerged, looking tousled and sleepy and absolutely gorgeous.

For a heartbeat or two, he froze, simply staring. Luckily, she didn't appear to notice.

Only once she'd made her coffee and taken a drink did she look at him. "What's on the agenda for today?" she asked.

"Once the guests go fishing, I'm going to go look up one of Grady's oldest friends," Dade announced. "I'm hoping she might know who this person is claiming he should have inherited Grady's Lodge."

"She? Did Grady have a girlfriend?"

Dade smiled. "You might call her that. They had an arrangement. Interesting woman. I always liked her."

"I'd like to go with you," Maddie said. "I'm willing to try anything that gets us a step closer to identifying this person."

First, they needed to make breakfast. Since Dade hadn't cooked in a few days, it would be his turn. He decided to make a bunch of scrambled eggs, hash brown patties, toast and bacon. While he cooked, Maddie poured several glasses of orange and tomato juice and set the table.

Right on time, the guests trooped in. Since today would be their last day, they were ready to get out onto the water.

As soon as they finished eating, they headed to their cabins to grab their things.

"I'll meet you down at the boat slips," Dade said. He helped Maddie clear the table.

"Go ahead and go," she told him. "I'll clean up."

Grateful, he kissed her cheek. She froze, before turning to smile at him. "Come here, you," she said, pulling him close and pressing her mouth against his. "If you're going to kiss me, you might as well do it right."

Laughing, he kissed her one more time, lingering a little longer. Then he took off, mood jubilant despite all that they had going on. Maddie brought out the best in him, somehow. He couldn't help but wonder if he affected her the same way.

When he reached the boat slips, Robert and one other guest were already there, stowing their supplies.

"Today's the day," Robert exclaimed, smiling broadly. "I'm going to catch the big one. I can feel it in my bones."

"I hope you do," Dade replied, meaning it.

Over the next fifteen minutes, the rest of the group showed up, chose their boats and headed out. Dade waited until every last one had gone around the bend in the river before returning to the main house.

When he arrived, he found Maddie sitting on the front porch, reading. She looked up as he approached and smiled. The warmth in her eyes made his breath catch.

"Hey," she greeted him. "What's up?"

"We've got a few hours to look up one of Grady's old friends. Are you still in?"

"Yes." She put down her book and jumped up. "Let's go."

Taking her arm, he led the way to Grady's old truck. Proud of the work he'd done to get it running, he helped her up. Then he climbed in the driver's side and turned the key. Instantly, the engine rumbled to life.

"First try," Maddie said. "I'm impressed."

"Thanks." He waited until she'd fastened her seat belt before shifting into Drive. "Brace yourself. This thing rides rough."

Which turned out to be the understatement of the year. And the ancient truck didn't even have power steering, so turning became more of a chore than usual.

"Grady didn't have any other relatives in the area?" she asked.

"Not that I know of," Dade answered. "Grady and I did just about everything together. He mentioned one distant cousin, but that guy lived in California."

"So you're thinking this stalker might be a friend?"

Dade shrugged. "Anything is possible. I know Grady kept his relationships low-key and quiet, but I'm also wondering if this is related to his former girlfriend."

Turning her head, she stared. "You mean it might be possible that the person who's been texting me and doing all of these horrible things might be female?"

"Doubtful. Angela wouldn't do anything like that. I know her too well. As far as any other woman, it's unlikely, but you never know. Officer Taggert says females are rarely, if ever, serial killers. And with two dead bodies, he's inclined to think the murderer is a male."

Maddie went quiet, clearly considering his words. "What about a team? One man, one woman. Like maybe the woman has a brother or a boyfriend who's helping her get what she feels she should have."

"That's another strong possibility. The only thing is, Grady was pretty old, and all of his friends are, too."

"And whoever killed those two women had to be stronger than them," she added. "Which would rule out most seventy-five-to-eighty-year-olds."

"Right. That's what I'm thinking, too. But we won't know until we have a few conversations. The first place we're going is Angela Bishop's house. That's the woman

I told you about. She and Grady had an arrangement for years. I think she might have even known your mother. She was always kind to me. I want to get her take on all of this and see if she can think of anyone."

Maddie nodded. With the sun shining in her long black hair and her blue eyes glowing, she looked stunningly beautiful. And he swore he could see some of Grady in her features.

Pushing the thought and the feelings that accompanied it away, he drove from memory to the little frame house where Angela Bishop lived. He'd been there many times growing up, though he hadn't gone back after Grady had gotten so sick. Angela had visited once or twice in the beginning, but he hadn't seen her again until she'd attended the funeral.

Parking in front, he killed the engine and turned to Maddie. "I hate to show up here unannounced, but I don't have her phone number."

Maddie eyed the overgrown lawn and out-of-control shrubs. "It almost looks like the house is empty."

"It does," he agreed. "But Blake is a small town. If anything happened to Angela, I would have heard about it."

He led the way up the front porch, noting the rickety condition of the wood. "I need to come back out here and make some repairs," he said. "I feel bad. I got so caught up in taking care of Grady and then keeping the lodge going that I never checked in on her. Clearly, she could have used some help."

"She doesn't have any family that live close?" Maddie asked.

"Not that I know of." Dade pressed the doorbell, waited and then tried it again. Nothing. Glancing at Maddie, he tried knocking. Three sharp raps on the wooden door. Loud enough even for an elderly woman with poor hearing.

But the door never opened, and as far as he could tell, there were no signs of movement inside of the house. Just in case, Dade tried the handle, but the door was locked.

"I guess she's not home," he finally said, looking around. "I'm not sure if she's still driving, but there's no car here."

"Unless it's in the garage." Maddie pointed to a rickety frame building with a single garage door. There were no windows, so he had no way of knowing if there might be a vehicle inside.

"I'll ask around in town," Dade decided. "Before he got sick, Grady used to meet up with a couple of guys at the donut shop once a week. They'd sit around, drink coffee and shoot the breeze."

"I guess we'd better go." Maddie turned to make her way back toward the truck. As she did, a beat-up four-door Toyota careened around the corner and pulled into the driveway.

Dade grabbed Maddie's arm. "That looks like Angela's car."

But instead of a petite woman with long, wavy white hair, a slender man with wire-rimmed glasses and a goatee got out. "Can I help you folks?" he asked, his tone friendly.

"We're looking for Angela Bishop," Dade said, keeping Maddie's arm tucked into his. "Do you happen to know where we might find her?"

"She's in a memory care facility in Anchorage," the man said, smiling easily as he made his way toward them. "I'm Chet Bishop, her nephew. I'm about the only family she has left."

Introducing himself and Maddie, Dade shook his hand. Then Maddie did the same. Chet had a firm, steady grip, which made Dade inclined to like him.

"I can get you the address if you'd like," Chet offered. "I'm sure she'd love to have visitors, even if she can't always recognize people she knows."

"That'd be great, thank you."

Chet pulled out his phone. "What's your number? I'll text it to you."

Since Dade had expected the man to jot something down, he hesitated. Then, with Chet eyeing him expectantly, Dade rattled off the number.

Typing quickly, Chet looked up from his phone, still smiling. "There you go."

Dade's phone pinged. There was Chet's text, with the name of the memory care facility and the address. "Thanks," Dade said. "Have you been in town long?"

Chet looked from Dade to Maddie and back again. "Not really. Why do you ask?"

The last thing Dade wanted to do was make the other man aware of his suspicions. "No reason. Blake is a small town, and people talk. Since I haven't heard anything at all about you or about Angela, I was just curious."

"I keep to myself," Chet responded, the flatness of his tone no doubt meant to discourage any further questions.

Nevertheless, Dade continued to press. "Are you staying here at Angela's house or are you selling it?"

"I'm just visiting for now," Chet answered, his narrow gaze revealing his annoyance. "And yes, I'm staying here and getting a few things taken care of for my aunt. She hasn't decided yet if she wants to sell the place or hang on to it."

With a patently bored expression, he glanced at his watch. "Well, it was awfully nice meeting you. I'm sure I'll see you around."

"I'm sure you will," Dade replied. "Nice to meet you, too."

Maddie murmured something similar as they turned away.

Chet stood on the porch watching as they got in their truck.

Once they were out of sight of the house, Dade shook his head. "I'm really sorry to hear about Angela. But I'm glad she has family looking out for her."

"Me, too." Maddie half turned in her seat, looking back toward the house even though they couldn't see it. "Was it just me or did that guy seem a little defensive?"

Dade considered. "He did," he conceded. "Maybe because placing a relative in a facility is a difficult decision. If Anchorage wasn't so far, I'd definitely make the trip and pay her a visit. Right now, I plan to call and check on her."

She nodded. "This might sound like a weird question, but do you think there's a chance that Chet might be the stalker?"

"There's always a chance," Dade answered bluntly. "And since he's the only new person around here, I plan to pass his name on to Officer Taggert. It can't hurt to have him run an investigation on Chet."

"I agree. Do we have time to stop in town?"

"Not now. We'd better get back to the lodge in case that group comes back with a boatload of fish. Plus, those old men that Grady used to hang out with only meet up in the mornings. We'll have to try and catch them another time, after our guests leave."

She nodded. "This sounds odd, but I'm glad we at least have a suspect. Even if he's the only one, it's better than nothing."

"True. I'd really just like this to be over so we can get on with our lives." He glanced at her, struck by a thought. "You haven't even gone fishing yet, and we're on our second set of guests."

"That's fine." Her quick response made him smile. "I don't really need to actually fish, do I? So far, everything has worked out just fine."

He decided to take pity on her. "You don't have to if you don't want to. But someday, I think you and I should go just for fun. It's relaxing."

"For everyone except the fish," she quipped. "Seriously, I'm good. Also, don't ever expect me to hunt either. It's just not my thing."

If he hadn't been driving, he would have pulled her in for a thorough kiss. Instead, he laughed and told himself he'd kiss her later, once they were back home. Together.

When they pulled back into the driveway, they saw the state police forensics van had gone. Officer Taggert's cruiser sat in front of the house, and he'd apparently been waiting for them, since he got out as soon as they pulled up.

"We've got everything we need," he said. "The body is on the way to the lab so they can determine cause of death. We were able to pull some DNA samples, so hopefully we can get a match."

Dade nodded. "There's someone I'd like you to look into," he said. "He says he's Angela Bishop's nephew and is staying at her place. His name is Chet, and here's his phone number and the address."

Taggert scribbled down the information. "I'll check

him out. Meanwhile, you two watch your backs. If you see anything out of the ordinary, call me. I'll be hanging around town until after Memorial Day."

Startled, Dade checked the date on his phone. "I hadn't realized it's this close to the end of the month," he said. "There's always a cookout and a parade, though on a smaller scale than the Fourth of July."

Taggert grinned. "Yes, I've heard. I'll see you there."

With that, he got into his car and drove away.

Dade watched him go, unable to shake a sense of foreboding. He didn't know why, but he felt like all this would be coming to a head soon. He'd have to make sure to keep Maddie safe if it did. No matter what it cost him.

Chapter 14

The guests came back an hour later, which gave Maddie enough time to help Dade with dinner prep and to make a quick dessert. Robert had caught his big fish, and his jubilant mood had everyone smiling. Since it was their last night, Dade grilled brats. They served them up with sauerkraut, a giant pot of barbequed beans and buns.

Declaring themselves ravenous, the guests ate and laughed and ate some more, until they said they were stuffed. That was when Maddie brought out the strawberry shortcake she'd whipped together. Everyone oohed and awed, and then they fell upon the dessert like a pack of starving wolves. She barely managed to rescue a couple of small slices for her and Dade. They ate them quickly in the kitchen before returning to the big dining table and starting to clear it.

As the group began to make their way back to their cabins, Robert lingered. "I wanted to thank you both," he said, looking from Dade to Maddie and back again. "I wasn't even in the original group slated to come, but one of the others dropped out, so I was able to step into their place. I really enjoyed this vacation, and I can't wait to show off my fish."

"I'm glad you had fun," Dade replied, slipping his arm

around Maddie's shoulders and pulling her close. "And I've got everyone's fish packed in dry ice, ready to take with you. I'll see you again in the morning."

"Roger that." For a second, Robert's smile slipped. But then Maddie told herself she must have imagined it because when she looked again, it was back in place.

After he left, she looked at Dade. "I have to say, I'll be glad when we have the place to ourselves again. How long do we have before the next bunch arrives?"

"The usual three days. Memorial Day is Monday, and a lot of people take advantage of the long weekend. The next group arrives on Friday. We have enough time to clean up and get everything ready."

"Then that will have to do," she replied. "Want to join me out on the front porch? It'll be nice to just sit and relax for a little bit."

"Sure." He poured two glasses of iced tea and handed one to her. "Let's go."

Outside, the afternoon's heat lingered in the air. As they settled into the rocking chairs, Maddie sighed. "This is my favorite part of the day."

His answering smile started a warmth deep inside her. "Me, too."

When her cell phone rang, she actually jumped. It had been so long since she'd received an actual call. Picking it up, she stared at the name displayed on her screen.

Mighty DFW Property Management Company

Her old job. For a heartbeat or two, she considered whether or not to answer. The parting had been less than amicable, and she couldn't imagine any conversation after the fact improving on that.

Dade looked at her, frowning. "Are you going to take that?"

She sighed and pressed the button to decline the call. "No. It's my former employer. I have nothing to say to them."

"Are you okay?" he asked, his gentle tone reflecting his concern.

"You know what?" she replied. "I definitely am okay."

When he reached for her hand, she slipped hers into his willingly. She liked touching him. The contact always made her feel as if she could draw upon his gentle strength. She'd never known anyone like him.

In fact, she thought she might love him. No, she corrected herself. She did love him. With all of her heart. She could only hope that someday he might feel the same way.

At any other point in her life, a thought like that would have shocked and dismayed her. Now though, it only felt right. She'd come to this place, to this new life, for a reason. And since she suspected her grandfather had done a bit of matchmaking with his bequest, she wished she could thank him. He'd given her a new life.

As she took a long drink of her iced tea, her phone chimed, letting her know she had a voicemail.

Curious, she played it back on speaker.

"We'd like to apologize for how the events leading up to your termination played out. We've always regarded you as one of our best employees. In fact, we'd like to offer you your old position back, with a twenty-five percent raise in salary and a new title to go with it. Please contact me immediately to discuss. My name is Grant Resinor, the new director of human resources. I'm at extension 5567."

Stunned, she stared at her phone. "Wow," she said, glancing up at Dade. "I definitely didn't expect that. Especially since I was told my position had been discontinued, and I was no longer needed."

Expressionless, he nodded. "What do you want to do?"

What did she want to do? Odd question, but she liked that he bothered to ask. Even though, judging by his shuttered gaze, he thought he already knew the answer.

She sighed. "None of that matters anyway. By the terms of the will, I have to stay here for one entire year."

Instead of agreeing, he turned in his seat to stare at her. "True. But the attorney seemed to think there's a way to circumvent that clause, if we both agree. So what do you actually want, Maddie Pierce? If you want your old life, there's got to be a way you can have it. That way we both get what we want."

What the...? Was he trying to get rid of her? She shook her head and looked away. "I'm turning it down," she said flatly. "I made a decision to honor Grady's wishes, and that's what I plan to do."

Finally, he looked away. "Up to you." His dismissive tone grated on her.

"You know what?" she shot back. "I do have plans, though. For the lodge. There's a reason my old employer wanted me back. I'm really good at what I do. I've done a ton of research, checking out the other, really profitable fishing lodges in this part of Alaska."

At first, he didn't respond. Since she figured he'd shoot down her ideas without even listening, she simply stopped talking.

"And?" he finally asked, when the silence had stretched into minutes. "I know some of the larger ones have amenities we don't. They have more staff and other facilities to entertain the guests. And they attract a completely different sort of clientele than we do."

Impressed despite herself, she nodded.

"I've done the same research," he admitted. "When Grady first made me a partner, and I thought I had things to prove. I pitched those same ideas to him several years ago."

"And what happened? Was he receptive or totally unwilling to consider any changes?"

"He agreed to let me implement a few things," he said, his expression rueful.

Surprised, she stared. "And?"

"But first, I had to come up with the money. Those kinds of changes—additions, more employees, upgrades—all cost money. While we do make a profit now, there's not enough to make any kind of meaningful changes. And we have to live on the excess once the tourist fishing season is over. Running out of funds during the winter months would be disastrous."

She shrugged, thinking of how things were done in the world she'd recently left. "Then take out a loan. Once your profits increase, you can pay it back quickly."

"Grady's number one rule is no debt. And I do agree with that," he said. "We own everything outright. As long as we pay our taxes, no one can take anything away from us."

"I can't disagree with you there," she admitted. "But sometimes you have to take risks."

"Not with this," he said firmly. "This lodge is my entire life. Yours now, too. And I have to say, I now see the beauty of Grady's vision. The simplicity and rustic experience is what brings our guests back year after year. People wanting a more luxurious vacation can go to one of the other lodges. It all works out."

"But there's so much money being left on the table," she protested. "It takes money to make money."

"Truth." He looked at her, and the warmth she saw in his gaze took her breath away. "You haven't been here very long, Maddie. Give it a bit longer. You've been fitting in really well, I think. You might be surprised at how fulfilling this life can be."

She thought about his words for a few minutes. To her surprise, she realized he might be right. She'd been so focused on her vision of how things should be that she hadn't allowed herself to appreciate how awesome they actually were. Changing things might ruin the charm.

Finally, Dade cleared his throat. "Are you going to call them back?" he asked. "Because if you really want your old job back, maybe we can reach some sort of agreement."

Hearing him say that hurt more than she could believe possible. Lifting her chin, she looked him right in the face and smiled. "We already have an agreement, remember? That's the only one I'm willing to concentrate on. You're not getting rid of me so easily, Dade Anson."

She pushed up from her chair and headed back into the house. Whether or not she called Grant Resinor back didn't matter. The only thing she cared about at this moment was Grady. Had she imagined their growing closeness, the partnership that seemed so amazing? Was he actually secretly wanting to get rid of her, so he could have the lodge to himself?

Once inside the house, she felt restless in a way she

hadn't since arriving here. Before, receiving a job offer and an apology from what she'd considered her dream employer would have sent her over the moon. Now, she realized she had absolutely zero desire to ever go back to that environment. She wanted to stay here, with Dade, and run the fishing lodge she'd inherited.

Even if he really hoped she wouldn't.

The rest of the evening, she managed to avoid Dade. Though she really wanted to take a long walk, with a potential serial killer still on the loose, she couldn't risk it. Luckily for her, Dade made himself scarce, claiming he needed to check on the boats and make sure the guests didn't need anything before they left in the morning.

While he was gone, Maddie shut herself up in her room with a good book and read. She'd definitely be sleeping alone tonight.

The next morning, she rose early and headed to the kitchen, hoping to get her coffee before Dade woke. Instead, she found him already there, sitting at the kitchen table as if he'd been waiting for her.

"Good morning," he said.

She managed to mumble something back. Busying herself making her coffee, she knew she couldn't tiptoe around the subject forever. But she thought if she gave herself more time to process everything, maybe it wouldn't hurt so much. Only then did she think she could go back to acting relatively normal.

For now, polite and distant would have to do.

Dade was about to ask Maddie if she was okay when a loud banging from outside sent him up out of his chair and out the back door.

He skidded to a stop as soon as he realized what was causing the noise. A large black bear had gotten into the metal trash cans, knocked them over and was vigorously searching for food.

Glad the guests were still in their cabins, Dade went and grabbed the air horn that Grady had kept handy for such occasions. If anyone was still sleeping, they'd be wide-awake soon.

He blew the horn, and the bear took off. When he returned to the kitchen, Maddie had taken her coffee and disappeared into the bathroom. A moment later, he heard the shower start up. He knew she was avoiding him, and he couldn't really blame her. She thought he wanted her gone so he could have the lodge to himself.

But the truth of the matter was more complicated. He liked the way their arrangement had been working. Over the course of a few weeks, he realized he didn't want to even consider running the lodge alone. He wanted Maddie, his friend, his lover, his partner, by his side. But only if she wanted that, too. That was the reason he'd tried to give her a way out. If she wanted to go, he'd move heaven and earth to help her. He preferred to remain debt free. But if Maddie decided this wasn't the life for her, then he'd take out a loan if he had to so he could buy her out.

And though he knew he needed to explain why he'd said what he'd said, he wouldn't do that yet. She needed to make up her mind without any prompting from him.

Later that morning, the usual flurry of getting the guests checked out to go home kept them both busy. Dade hated the way Maddie would barely look at him, and he fought the urge to offer up the reasons for what he'd said.

As the group finally drove off, Robert beaming since

he'd texted all of his friends photos of him finally catching his big fish, Maddie and Dade stood side by side and waved until the SUVs disappeared from sight. Then she dropped into one of the porch rocking chairs. Dade sighed and did the same. He didn't know how long he could take her giving him the cold shoulder.

"Do you want to talk?" he finally offered. "I can explain—"

"No need." She cut him off, her breezy smile not reaching her eyes. "I understand more than you know. It's all good. We have to work together and get along. But you should know that I have no plans to go anywhere. I chose this life, and I'm going to see my decision through."

He took a moment to let her words sink in. Then, his heart lighter than it had been in ages, he nodded. "I'm glad to hear that," he said, meaning it. "I just wanted to make sure."

Then, while she stared at him, her expression confused, he grinned. "I kind of like having you around."

She started to shake her head and then sighed. "That's good, because we're stuck with each other for a year. You're going to have to get used to it."

Changing the subject, he told her about Blake's annual Memorial Day festivities in a few days. "We might be a small town, but we do it up right. This isn't as big of a celebration as the Fourth of July, but it's a lot of fun. The guests like to attend, but not always. Would you like to go?"

"With you?"

Slowly, he nodded. "Yes. With me."

"I'd like that."

Her soft answer brought his grin back. He'd make sure she had a great time.

Getting the cabins ready for the next set of guests, they fell into an easy routine. It didn't take long before the rooms were done, with clean sheets and towels. They'd settled on a simple menu and did the prep work quickly. By the time the new group arrived, they were ready.

"We make a good team," Dade said, complimenting her.

Chin up, she nodded. "We definitely do."

Memorial Day morning, Dade woke up feeling as excited as a little kid. Until Grady's illness turned severe, the two of them had always gone into town for the various holiday celebrations. Blake might be small, but they enjoyed a strong sense of community. Parades, cookouts, the ice cream social on the Fourth of July. Everyone knew everyone else, and Dade looked forward to sharing all of that with Maddie. Not for the first time, he felt grateful that Grady had stipulated she had to stay an entire year. And the fact that she actually wanted to, well, that was the icing on the cake.

They drove into town right after breakfast, arriving early enough to stake out a great spot along Main Street.

"The parade starts at nine," he told her. "And after that, they do a cookout with hot dogs and hamburgers in the empty lot across from Mikki's. There's a big, open, grassy area near the medical clinic, and people set up booths, selling their wares. Everyone walks around and catches up. It's a lot of fun."

His enthusiasm made her smile. When she reached for his hand, he thought his heart might just explode out of his chest.

By the time the parade started, people lined both sides

of Main Street. The mood felt celebratory, as most considered this holiday the unofficial start to an all-too-short Alaskan summer.

"Here they come," he told Maddie. And sure enough, the bright yellow 1955 Cadillac Eldorado convertible carrying Mayor Gregory Norman and his wife, Jane, led the procession. With his white hair and beard, Greg resembled Santa Claus, and he enjoyed that role in the winter months. Today, however, he wore a bright Hawaiian shirt decorated with palm trees and pineapples. Next to him, Jane donned huge red sunglasses. Together, they smiled and waved to the citizens of their town.

Various floats, some having seen better days, followed. The Blake 4-H club kids rode their horses and mules, beaming as they pranced past.

A couple more classic cars, the small high-school marching band, one more float, and the parade was over. Laughing and joking, everyone made their way to the cookout area. Most people had brought their own coolers, with drinks and snacks and maybe even an occasional adult beverage.

Long rows of picnic tables had been set out. The four older guys who made up a Beatles tribute band had set up on a makeshift stage and were warming up. Kip had propped the door open to the general store, and a quick glance showed Mikki's had done the same.

"Where'd you say the outdoor market is?" Maddie asked. "I love that kind of thing."

"They'll be setting up after we eat."

"You didn't tell me it's a potluck." She pointed to where several people were setting out dishes and desserts on a banquet table. "I should have brought something."

"It's not. Those were sides donated by Mikki's and Chef Brett Denyon, Dr. Taylor's husband. I heard he's wanting everyone to sample some of the offerings at his new restaurant."

"Which opens this week," Dr. Taylor said, grinning. "Can you tell I'm a little bit proud of my man?"

Maddie laughed. "I can't blame you. We'll be sure to try it, once our current set of guests leave."

Mayor Norman stepped up on the stage with the band and tapped the microphone. "Thank you all for coming," he said. "Now let's eat, shop and mingle. And never forget the reason for this holiday—remembering those who gave their lives in service to our great country."

Everyone clapped and cheered. Hamburgers and hot dogs were thrown on the grills, and people grabbed plates and lined up for food. Several people stopped to talk to Dade and meet Maddie.

"Everyone is so friendly," she mused, and then stuffed the last bit of her hot dog and bun into her mouth.

After the meal, hand in hand, they meandered over to the outdoor market, along with most everyone else. Maddie bought a necklace and a jar of homemade blackberry preserves. Dade couldn't remember the last time he'd had such a perfect day.

They ended up back at the picnic area, where several other couples were dancing to the music. Dade sat down on one of the benches and pulled Maddie into his lap.

"It was a good day." Head on his shoulder, Maddie leaned back into him. They shared a leisurely kiss, neither caring who might see.

"I like having you around," Dade murmured, tightening his arms around her.

For a second, she stiffened, making him wonder if he should have kept quiet. No doubt, she was remembering him asking her if she wanted to leave. He considered explaining but decided such a serious discussion would be for another day and time.

Finally, Maddie sighed and relaxed again. "I like being here. This town, these people, are amazing. At least today we got a bit of a break from everything."

All around them, groups of people were drifting away. Some returned to their vehicles to drive off. Others went inside Mikki's to have a few drinks and prolong the fun.

"Are you ready to head home?" he asked, catching her covering her mouth to hide a yawn.

"Sure."

He helped her get up, and then, keeping his arm around her waist, they headed toward where he'd parked the old truck.

The lot had mostly emptied, though there were still a couple of small groups standing around talking. When they reached the truck, Dade stopped short and swore.

Someone had slashed all four of the tires.

Maddie sagged against him. "Looks like I spoke too soon. Even on a holiday, our stalker won't leave us alone."

Tamping down his anger, Dade made his way toward the closest cluster of people. "Did any of you happen to notice anyone suspicious?" he asked. "All my tires have been slashed."

But no one had. And Dade had no idea how they were going to get back home.

"Let's go into Mikki's and see if we can talk someone into taking us home," he said.

"This is the one time I wish we had Uber or Lyft,"

Maddie joked, her smile looking forced. He hated to see that look of worry on her pretty face.

"True." He took her hand. "But Blake is full of good people. Someone will help us out. I'll have to get one of the guys from Eddie's to replace all of the tires tomorrow. Luckily, he carries recaps, so it won't be as expensive."

She nodded. "I have no idea what that means, but as long as you can get it fixed, I'm glad."

As they stepped into the crowded bar, Dade led her over to an empty table. "You might as well sit while I see if I can find someone willing to drive all the way to the lodge," he said. "Would you like a beer?"

Her gaze searched his face. "Is that okay? I know you don't drink."

"They know me here," he told her. "Club soda on the rocks with a twist of lime. What would you like?"

"I'll have a beer," she decided. "A hefeweizen, I don't care what brand."

Dade went up to the bar to place their order. A few minutes later, he returned with their drinks. He took a seat across from her, scanning the room while he sipped his drink.

The door opened, and Chet walked in. He smiled when he spotted Dade and Maddie and headed over toward their table.

"Nice to see you two again," he said. "You don't happen to know who drives an older model Chevy pickup, dark green, do you? Someone slashed all four of their tires. I figured I'd let them know."

"That's my truck." Grimacing, Dade took a sip of his club soda. "No way we're going to be able to drive it home tonight. That's why we came in here. To see if we could find someone willing to give us a ride."

"I can do that," Chet offered. "I was just going to have a beer and head home anyway. Where exactly do you live?"

"That's just it." Dade told him the location. "It's a fair way out of town and pretty much the opposite direction from your aunt's house."

"Oh." Chet shrugged and dropped into a chair. "It's all good. I seriously don't mind. It's not like I have anything else planned, anyway. How about you buy me a beer, and then after that, we can get going?"

Before Dade could reply, Maddie spoke up. "I'll get it. You two talk. I'll be right back."

Watching her walk through the crowded room to the bar, Dade sighed.

"She's something else," Chet commented. "Are you two a couple or…?"

Tearing his gaze away from Maddie to focus on the other man, Dade smiled. "It's complicated," he said. He took another drink and changed the subject. "What about you? Did you enjoy the Memorial Day celebrations here in Blake?"

"Sure. I like this town. I used to come here all the time as a kid and visit my aunt."

Which seemed odd. Because Dade didn't remember Angela Bishop ever even mentioning a nephew, never mind having one hanging around. While Dade might be a few years older, he would have thought Angela would have wanted the two to play as young boys.

"When was this?" he asked. "My grandfather took me to visit Angela a lot when I was a kid. I'm surprised we haven't met."

A weird, wary expression crossed Chet's face. "Yeah, I don't know. Maybe the timing just wasn't right."

Maddie returned just then with the beer, which she placed in front of Chet. She slid back into her seat, looking from one man to the other. "What's up?" she asked, picking up her own glass and taking a sip.

Chet took a long drink of his beer and smiled. "We were just talking about how strange it is that we never ran into each other as kids."

Something in Chet's smile didn't sit right with Dade. Right then and there, he decided there was no way he would allow this man to take them home. He'd find somebody else.

A large, boisterous table of guys caught his attention. He'd gone to school with most of them. Surely, one of them would be willing to drive, especially if Dade offered gas money.

He caught Maddie's eye. "Excuse me," he said, picking up his drink to take with him. "I'll be right back."

All his old friends greeted him loudly. Dade chatted for a few minutes, discussing the parade and next year's high-school reunion. Once, Dade glanced back over at Maddie and Chet, saw they appeared to be in deep conversation, and returned his attention to his old friends.

One of the guys noticed. "Is that your girlfriend?" he asked.

At this point, Dade decided he wasn't taking any chances. "She's my everything," he replied, meaning every word. He braced himself, certain they'd all tease him. Instead, they mostly appeared envious.

"She's beautiful," Tim Ragan said. "You're a lucky man."

Dade thanked him, before telling the group about his

tires getting slashed and him and Maddie being stuck here in Blake. Immediately, a couple of them vied for the opportunity to give Dade a ride home. "A great chance to catch up," Johnny Everitt said. "And to meet your lady." Since he and Tim had ridden to town together, Tim agreed.

Relieved, Dade told them he'd be right back.

When he turned, ready to tell Chet he wouldn't need a ride after all, the table was empty. Both Chet and Maddie were gone.

What the hell? Both drinks remained, Chet's beer virtually untouched, Maddie's almost empty. Dade scanned the bar, thinking maybe Maddie had gone to the restroom or something, and maybe Chet had spotted a friend he wanted to catch up with.

But he didn't see either of them, anywhere.

"What's wrong?" Tim asked.

"Did you happen to see where they went?" Dade asked, gesturing toward the empty table. "Since you're facing that way?" He refused to panic. Not yet.

"The skinny dude?" Johnny asked. "I think your girlfriend mustn't have been feeling well because she looked like she could barely stand. He helped her outside. Check there. They likely went out for some air."

No longer caring what anyone thought, Dade rushed outside.

Johnny had said Maddie had trouble standing. But she'd been fine a few minutes ago. Had Chet dropped something into her drink? How quickly does a roofie work?

Two women had been murdered. If he didn't find her soon, Dade had a feeling Maddie would be next. Which meant Chet had to be the stalker, the one who'd been sending all the text messages, started fires, blown up the

Jeep and broken into the house. And now, slashed the truck's tires.

Johnny and Tim appeared, having followed Dade outside.

"Any sign of her?"

"No." Dade took a deep breath and told them a rushed, abbreviated version of what had been going on. "We've got to find her."

"Call her cell phone," Tim suggested. "If she has it on her, and she's anywhere nearby, we could hear it ringing."

Since at this point, Dade would try anything, he pulled out his phone to do exactly that. As he went to call her, his phone rang.

"It's her," he said, relief flooding him. But when he answered, no one was there.

"Look!" Johnny pointed. "Something's going on in that part of the parking lot. Those people are circling something. And they're hollering."

Seeing the commotion, Dade took off running. Johnny and Tim were right behind him. When they reached the group, which had grown to several people deep, Dade pushed his way through. He spotted Chet crouching protectively over a woman sprawled unconscious on the pavement.

"Maddie!" Dade shouted. Then, when Chet made to block him from reaching her, Dade swung. His fist connected squarely with Chet's jaw, sending the smaller man flying backward.

Dade paid him no mind. All of his attention on Maddie, he dropped to the pavement and lifted her in his arms. For one awful second, he couldn't tell if she was alive, but then she moaned and shifted in his arms.

Holding her close, he looked up to find Tim and Johnny restraining Chet. "What did you give her?" Dade demanded.

Chet looked away without answering.

"A state trooper named Taggert is staying above the general store," Dade said. "Can someone please go get him? This man needs to be arrested."

"I've called Dr. Taylor," someone else said. "She's on her way."

Chet turned and glared at Dade. "I have as much right to the lodge as you do. More, even."

"How so?" Dade asked, keeping his voice level.

"I'm Grady's son."

Stunned, Dade wasn't sure how to respond. "If you are, then Grady didn't know. He wasn't the type of man to abandon his responsibilities."

Chet spat. "Looks like he did. That's why I wanted to take what should have been mine."

Later, after Taggert had arrived and taken Chet into custody, Dade helped get a still unconscious Maddie into a vehicle so they could transport her to the Medical Clinic.

"We'll get some fluids into her," the doctor said. "And we'll take some blood so we can find out what she was given. Most importantly, we'll need to monitor her."

"I can do that," Dade said, settling into the seat next to Maddie. Unwilling to let go of her, he took her limp hand and held it in his. "Is she going to be all right?"

Though Dr. Taylor looked grim, she met his gaze. "It depends what she ingested and how much. Do you know what she was drinking?"

"She just had one beer," he replied. "But I have no idea what Chet might have put into it when she wasn't looking."

"We'll get her fixed up," the doctor promised.

At the clinic, Dade stayed by Maddie's side. Her eyelids fluttered, and she moved her head restlessly from side to side. She appeared to be trying to wake up.

Watching her, Dade tried to bottle up the simmering fury he felt. It was a good thing Officer Taggert had taken Chet into custody because if Dade were to get his hands on him right now, it wouldn't be good.

As if Dade's thoughts had summoned him, Taggert called. "This guy wants to talk to you," he said. "He's admitted to drugging Maddie. Also to sending the texts, the fire and explosion and the murders, but he keeps saying you owe him."

"He's going to have to wait," Dade replied. "I'm at the medical clinic with Maddie. I'm not leaving her until the drugs are out of her system. Please keep him locked up, and I'll let you know when she's better."

After ending the call, Dade watched while Dr. Taylor took Maddie's vitals. She started an IV and took some blood, saying she hoped to run a few preliminary tests on it. "Though we don't have as fancy of a lab as an emergency department, we make do."

"Thank you," he said. "I'm staying with her."

Since it wasn't a question, she nodded. "I'm staying, too. I'll be checking in periodically."

Sometime in the middle of the night, Maddie groaned and cried out. She began gagging and retching. Instantly awake, Dade barely got a plastic bedpan under her before she threw up.

Dade looked up to see the doctor standing in the doorway. "Vomiting will clear out her system. Why don't you go home and get some rest? I'll keep an eye on her and call you if anything changes."

"I'm not leaving her."

Something in his voice, perhaps, or possibly the way he looked at Maddie made the doctor smile softly. "I know that feeling," she murmured. "I'm glad she has you."

With that, she left the room, closing what must have been her office door behind her.

"Dade?" Maddie's voice, raspy and dry. "What happened to me?"

Then, before he could answer, she began to cry. "Chet drugged me. He was going to kill me."

Pulling her into his arms, he smoothed the hair away from her face. "Shhh, it's all right. I've got you. You're safe here with me. Officer Taggert took Chet into custody."

Wiping away her tears, she sighed. "It's over? It's finally over?"

"Yes, it's finally over. Chet believes he's Grady's son. I have my doubts. But a simple DNA test should tell the truth."

"His son?" Maddie frowned. "That explains why he felt entitled to the lodge."

"It does. And if he hadn't done all the horrible things that he did, if the DNA test says he is, I would have made sure he got part of the lodge. Now, no matter what the results, I want him to go to prison."

"Me too."

He held her close, feeling as if he never wanted to let her go. That part of her life might be over, but something else, something better, had just begun.

"Why are you smiling?" she asked, looking up at him. Then, before he could answer, she took a deep breath and continued. "What you said the other day, about taking my old employer up on their offer. Do you really want me to leave?"

There were several things he could have said. Excuses, explanations, and none of them real. "I do not." Heart in his throat, he met her gaze. "I want nothing more than to have you stay. But it has to be your choice. Not because of some terms in a will. But because this—our life, our partnership—is what you want."

Slowly, she nodded. "It is. But what about you, Dade? What do you want?"

"You," he answered, his voice raw. "I like what we're making together. I think we have a real chance at a future."

Then, thinking about how he'd felt when he thought he'd lost her, he realized he was still holding a bit of himself back. Going all in, he decided. "Maddie, I think I might love you."

Her beautiful blue eyes filled with tears. Still holding his gaze, she swallowed. "I feel the same way about you."

He gathered her into his arms, taking care to be gentle.

"Hey, there," Doc Taylor said from the doorway. "She needs her rest. You've got the rest of your lives to cuddle. Right now, she needs to sleep."

With that proclamation, Dr. Taylor left the room.

Dade chuckled. "She's right. And I like the sound of that. We do have the rest of our lives."

Settling back against her pillow, Maddie's eyes already drifted closed. "All of our todays and our tomorrows," she murmured.

Her words filled his heart. As he settled in to try and get some shut eye in the chair by her bed, he wished he could somehow thank Grady. The man who'd raised him and loved him and taught him right from wrong had gone and given him one final gift. Dade would forever be grateful. All his todays and tomorrows, indeed.

* * * * *

Safe In Her
Bodyguard's Arms

Katherine Garbera

MILLS & BOON

Katherine Garbera is the *USA TODAY* bestselling author of more than one hundred and twenty-five novels. She's a small-town Florida girl whose imagination was fired up by long hours spent outside sitting underneath orange trees. She grew up to travel the world and makes her home in the UK with her husband. Her books have garnered numerous awards and are sold around the world. Connect with her at katherinegarbera.com and on Facebook, Instagram and Twitter.

Visit the Author Profile page
at millsandboon.com.au for more titles.

Dear Reader,

I'm so excited to bring you the second book in my Price Security series. This book features Xander Quentin, who isn't exactly thrilled when his estranged brother asks for a favour. When Xander arrives in Florida, he encounters Obie Keller, whom Xander's brother also asked for help, and they are driven into the swamp and marshes near the Everglades to escape the criminal gang that's at the heart of his brother's problems.

I'm a Florida girl, born in South Florida and raised in Central Florida. I grew up on the Green Swamp, which is something I had a chance to revisit with my heroine Obie. She too grew up in the swamp and like me she got out, but there is a part of her that misses the savage beauty of it. Obie likes the woman she is now, but that swamp girl is still inside her. When she and Xander are forced deeper into the swamp, it's her knowledge of it that helps save them from nature while Xander battles the men searching for them.

I hope you enjoy this book and getting to see the Price Security team again.

Happy reading,

Katherine

DEDICATION

For Rob. So glad to be sharing this journey through life with you, falling deeper in love every day and finding the joy in the moment.

ACKNOWLEDGMENTS

Growing up in the swamp and in Florida gave me such a rich setting to draw from, but my memories were that of a child/young adult. I want to thank the men in my family who helped me out with research on Key Largo and the bays that surround it.

The conversations we had in Mississippi about the unique tropical wetlands that make up the area around the Everglades were very helpful in pointing me in the right direction for research. Any mistakes are my own, of course, but thank you to Rob, Dad, Uncle Pat and Scott.

Chapter 1

Obie Keller had a soft spot for lovable losers. She didn't need to go to a therapist to know it was partially because she was still trying to save her brother, Gator, who'd run away when he was seventeen and she was sixteen. Aaron Quentin, the long-haired, tattooed dishwasher with the crisp British accent she'd hired, fit the bill of sad-luck cases. He hadn't worked for her long at the coffee shop she managed in Miami, but she liked him.

The coffee shop was owned by a Cuban American couple and was a small place in a strip mall close to Obie's house. She drove to work but could have walked if it wasn't so hot in Florida.

When Aaron had first called her from jail and asked her to get in touch with his brother and tell him Aaron needed to call in a favor, she'd agreed. But the number he'd given her was an undisclosed service that had simply allowed her to leave a message with her return number. That had been three days ago.

She hadn't heard back, and she was very afraid that Aaron was on his own. Which wasn't supposed to be her problem. He was her dishwasher, she reminded herself as she put on her good skirt and blazer so she'd look more professional. Obie was preparing to go down to visit Aaron and offer him the services of Adam Montel, a pro bono lawyer who she'd gone to school with.

After that, he'd be on his own.

Which of course she hated.

Aaron, with his bright blue eyes and British accent, couldn't have been further from her own brother, Gator, who'd had average brown hair and brown eyes like herself and spoke with that slow Southern accent they'd inherited from their Georgia-born mother.

Their pa had died when she'd been fourteen and Gator had been fifteen along with Mama in an airboat incident that had been ruled an accident. Something that had never felt right to Obie or her brother. Their parents had been adept at piloting airboats and at staying alive in the swamp. But the investigators said it had been due to operator error, that their parents had crashed and the airboat caught on fire, leaving them both dead.

Neither Obie nor Gator believed that. Their father had been the sheriff of their rural community near the Green Swamp in central Florida. He had been cracking down on drug traffickers using the swamp to move their product right before his death. Gator had done research once they'd been sent to live with their aunt Karen in Miami, and he was sure that La Familia Sanchez cartel had been behind their parents' deaths.

Aunt Karen hadn't been too happy to have been saddled with Obie and her brother. She'd told them to drop the drug cartel speculation and concentrate on moving on so they didn't end up dead like their parents. Obie stopped trying to convince their aunt and transformed—straightened her long, curly hair and became a clone of her cousins, who were popular at the school they attended.

But Gator couldn't. He'd become more rebellious, and when he'd turned seventeen he'd disappeared. Obie had been alone since that day. Survival must have been bred into her because it was what she'd done in response. She'd graduated high school and then gone to college using the Pell Grant, receiving a degree in hospitality management. What else was she going to do living in Florida?

Outwardly, she might have looked like her aunt and cousins, but inside she was still that wild swamp girl who missed her parents.

Her aunt had since tried fixing her up with several men with good jobs. But Obie wasn't ready for marriage. She still hadn't figured herself out and didn't want to bring someone else into her bland, haunted life until she did.

She knew that the swamp girl inside couldn't survive in the real world and had resigned to leave that part of herself behind. Until Aaron Quentin showed up, reminding her so keenly of her brother that she'd wasted a few nights on internet searches trying to find him again. But there was no record of her brother.

Aunt Karen believed he must be deceased, but Obie had never allowed herself to think that. Instead, she'd always imagined he had found a better life out of Florida. She hoped he had.

For herself, she was content running the coffee shop and living in her condo a few blocks from the beach. Normally she rode her bike to work in her A-line skirt and tank top because the heat in Florida was unrelentless. But because of Aaron she was dressed up today. She drove to the jail and waited to see him.

There was something about being around police officers that always stirred memories of her dad.

She pushed them aside as she waited on one side of a glass window for Aaron to be brought in.

It was odd, but Aaron didn't seem quiet or bowed by being held. His eyes were direct when they met hers, and he seemed for a moment as if he was surprised to see her. He must have been expecting his brother.

Aaron sat down across the table from her. He was in the same clothes he'd been wearing when he'd been arrested. He had been held in the jailhouse while waiting for his bail hearing.

"Wasn't expecting to see you."

She smiled over at him. In his voice and on his face was that disappointment that she'd seen on so many faces before. Gator when he'd asked her to leave. Her aunt when she'd tried and failed to set Obie up with another guy. And now her dishwasher.

Sometimes it felt like she wasn't enough for anyone. That she always let the people around her down.

"Sorry. I haven't heard back from your brother and I think you're meant to have bail set today." Which was why she was here. She wasn't sure if she could make whatever bail that was posted for Aaron, but if she could, she'd do it immediately.

"I am," he said. "Thanks for trying."

"Oh, also I have the name of a really good pro bono lawyer. We went to school together. I wrote his name and number down for you. Maybe he can help at your bail hearing."

She pushed the paper toward him and he looked down at it, tapping it with his finger. His pinkie ring with the signet flashed before he balled his hand into a fist. "I'm good with the lawyer."

"Are you sure? You don't have to take the one they give you," she said. She had no real idea how familiar he was the criminal justice system, but she had some knowledge from her father's work.

"Yeah, Obie. Don't sweat it. I have a good attorney," he said.

"I'm glad. If you need anything at all, let me know," she said sincerely.

"Actually…" he said, pausing for a moment. "I have some information that would exonerate me, and the district attorney's office is willing to take a look at it. But I obviously can't go get it."

She wanted to believe him but didn't. He'd been arrested on drug-dealing charges, and while she'd never seen any sign of him using or selling while he'd been working for her…it was for an entire two weeks. She knew nothing about him.

That last part sounded like Aunt Karen in her mind.

"Yeah, like what evidence?" she asked. "You probably won't have to serve that much time for dealing."

"I wasn't dealing, Obie. I was gathering information on La Familia Sanchez cartel. That's the evidence I have. It's on a SD card at my place in Key Largo. If you get it for me we can show it to the district attorney."

"I'd have to talk to the district attorney's office first," she said, not sure she wanted to go out to Key Largo anytime, but certainly not in the hot summer months and not on a wild-goose chase.

"I'm meeting with them later today," he said. "Call the office and ask for Crispin Tallman."

There was an edge to Aaron's voice. But he also had a surprisingly sincere look, and she found herself nodding and agreeing to call the DA's office.

"You got a message from the service," Giovanni "Van" Price said as Xander Quentin entered the briefing room at Price Security.

Xander had been having a pretty good day. He beat Kenji in Halo, his latest client sent him a thank-you basket with his favorite protein bars and after three days off he was ready to get his next assignment and get back to work. He arrived for their daily briefing and the rest of the team was already assembled.

Price Security were an elite team of bodyguards who provided services to A-listers, diplomats and celebrities. The team was comprised of members from diverse backgrounds. Xander was the only Brit on the team and former SAS. Kenji Wada was former CIA and scary and lethal with any weapon. Rick Stone, ex-DEA agent, always looked like he needed a cigarette and was stoned or hungover, but once he was on a case, he was alert and one of the best in the business.

Lee Oscar was a seasoned intel operative for a secret organization in her past. She was cagey about admitting who it was. She was a youngish-looking forty-year-old who was their eye-in-the-sky when they were on assignment, tracking all members of Price Security and keeping them all connected when they were out. Luna Urban—currently engaged to hotshot billionaire Nicholas DeVere—was a top-notch bodyguard who'd been a MMA and street fighter before she'd joined them.

Giovanni Price was the boss of the organization and handed out the team assignments. He was short—but then everyone was compared to Xander—bald and had tattooed angel wings on the back of his neck. He went by Van and considered them all family, taking on a fatherly role, though Xander assumed Van wasn't much older than his own thirty-five years.

"I did?" Xander asked. He never got any calls. His parents sent him a card on his birthday and on Christmas and his brothers never contacted him.

They all had been changed by the accident that had paralyzed one of his older brothers, Tony, when they were young. Each remaining person in the family had taken on the blame for themselves. Xander still wasn't sure who was actually to blame. If it was him alone or all of them. Or the environment that had pitted them against each other and left them feeling like only the strongest would survive.

"Yeah. A woman named Obie Keller was calling to ask for a favor for your brother Aaron."

Hell.

Aaron was the last brother he expected to hear from. Not that he heard from any of his brothers in the last decade or so. It was just Aaron and he had the most beef with each other. The two of them had been in the SAS together, and after a particularly brutal mission they'd had a fight that had resulted in them both being discharged. But fighting was what the Quentin brothers did. They fought with each other, the world and anyone unlucky enough to cross their paths.

Aaron was eighteen months older than Xander. They had grown up rough and wild. Running all over the council estate where their family had lived. Their father was a taxi driver and amateur boxer and their mother did her best to keep them in line, changing the wallpaper and the carpet every time they were too stained with blood from the fights between him and his brothers, to be cleaned again.

Since joining Price Security, Xander had dialed that rage back by protecting those around him. He'd found his center by working closely with the other members of the team. He'd channeled some of Rick's chill, Kenji's calm and Luna's observation. They all had taught him to look outside of himself instead of dwelling on the beast inside. When he had a focus, the violence that had ruled him in the past took a back seat. "Thanks, boss."

"No problem. You're on paid leave for the next two

weeks. Think that will be long enough to take care of the favor?"

Paid leave. He really didn't want to go and see Aaron. He was still mad at his brother, and even just thinking of seeing the other man made Xander's fist ball up in his lap.

"Xander?"

"Sorry, boss. I have no idea. We're not close so… Let me check this out before you put me on paid leave."

"We'll discuss it at the end of the meeting," Van said.

Van handed out assignments to everyone but him. So he wasn't getting a job until he found out what his brother wanted. He waited until the conference room was empty of just him and his boss.

Just get up and walk out. But he couldn't. He needed an assignment. He needed something more than this shove from the universe forcing him to face his family and his past. He needed to stay busy.

Already he felt the beast inside of him stirring. Just hearing Aaron's name did that to him. Brought back the old rage and need to prove he wasn't weak.

"I'm sure the favor won't take two weeks," Xander said. "You got a job for me in Miami?"

"No."

"Why?" It wasn't like his boss to be this hard-nosed about time off. Van knew better than any of them that sometimes work was the only thing that kept them sane.

"Why what?"

"You know my history with Aaron."

"I do. I also know that you both have had time to

cool down. You're not the same man who I hired nearly ten years ago."

"I don't think he's changed."

"You won't know until you go and see him. I had Lee run a search on the woman who called and your brother. He's currently in jail in Miami/Dade and she manages a coffee shop where he'd been working as a dishwasher until his arrest."

"Fu—"

"Language."

"For *fudge's* sake, seriously?"

"Yeah. Lee's sent you an information packet on the situation and all the intel we could gather. The jet is gassed and ready to go. Ping when you land and check in with Lee as you go."

"Van, this isn't a job."

"No, this is family. You know what that means," Van said as he stood and came around the table, clapping Xander's shoulder with his hand.

Van was tight-lipped about his own biological family, but Xander knew how hard the other man had worked to make all of them feel like they were one. How could he explain to Van that this found family was the only one that wanted him? That a long-ago mistake had cost him his place in the Quentin clan? And that Xander was okay with it? Because he knew that if he went back, there was a chance that he'd turn back into the rage monster he'd used to be.

Obie left the jail, driving through the midday traffic to the district attorney's office. She'd called ahead and been told that if she was willing to wait, there might be a paralegal who could speak to her sometime that afternoon. Having already called in her assistant to cover her shift, Obie had the afternoon off.

She could have gone home and spent some quality time playing Dreamlight Valley on her Switch, pretending this never happened, but that would be selfish, and if there was the slightest chance she could help Aaron…well, she had to try.

Lost causes and all that.

Truth was, she liked trying. She just wished that one time her efforts would be rewarded. Though to be fair she had saved herself by adapting and leaving the swamp girl she'd been when her parents had died behind. Most days she didn't even remember that her hair had a tendency to curl. She used a lot of product in it and had even splurged on that Dyson hair dryer that worked miracles.

So yeah, she was the heroine of her own story…*ha*. If changing everything about herself and making herself into a bland copy of everyone else was winning, then she was definitely a champion. Maybe that was why she was trying so hard with Aaron. Gator had asked her to come with him. To take a chance on the two of them making it. And she'd been too scared to leave.

Too scared to trust him, or herself, on their own.

Even though secretly she hated everything about her new life back then, it had still been secure. She'd needed that more than she would have ever admitted to Gator. He'd gotten pissed and said a lot of mean things, called her a coward and left.

She pulled her car into the parking lot of the building where the district attorney offices were. The address that Aaron had given her was on Key Largo as he said, but on the southern part of the long narrow Key. All the houses on Key Largo were pricey, not something that he could afford on the salary she paid him as a dishwasher.

Maybe the looming sense that Aaron had been keeping something from her was why she was reluctant to help.

But the moment the words *La Familia Sanchez cartel* had left his mouth, she was in. She didn't have to be Junie B. Jones girl detective to see that something wasn't right here.

It was scorching when she opened her door and the heat seemed to wrap around her. For a moment she was pulled back into the past and those hot, muggy summer days when she and Gator would run barefoot through the citrus grove that used to dot the landscape in central Florida. Fighting to find shade before darting into the Green Swamp and the playhouse their father had built for them up in a live oak tree.

She closed her eyes, and the longing and pain in her heart told her that unless the DA confirmed that Aaron hadn't spoken to him, Obie was going to retrieve his evidence. It might not be worth anything and might not set him free, but she would bring it to him all the same.

She pulled the strap of her large purse up on her shoulder as she headed inside. The air-conditioning brought goose bumps up her arms and legs and she almost shivered at the coolness of it as she pushed her sunglasses up onto the top of her head.

The receptionist looked up when she came in and signaled her to wait. Obie realized the woman was on the phone. When she hung up, the woman asked who she was there to see.

"I spoke to Crispin Tallman's office. They told me a paralegal might be free to speak to me this afternoon."

"Okay, what's your name?" the woman asked.

"Obie Keller."

"Okay, Ms. Keller, have a seat and I'll let them know you are here."

The office was like many of the buildings in this area, kind of comfortable but worn down from years of use. It was clear any money in the budget for updating the interior design was being spent on prosecuting cases.

Obie sat down, holding her bag on her lap because the floor looked dirty. She took out her phone but she didn't have any messages, and her socials were silent, just her looking at other people. So she put it back in her bag, noticing that the nail polish was chipped on her forefinger.

Ugh. Not going to make a very good impression with that.

But she didn't need to make a good impression, she reminded herself, though Aunt Karen said a lady always needed to.

"Ms. Keller? I'm Crispin Tallman. I was free and had some time if you'll follow me," he said.

Crispin held himself tall and with confidence. She

could tell he commanded authority. She smiled at him. He had a pleasing face and an easy grin. His hair had been slicked back and the suit he wore was slim fitting.

"Thank you for seeing me," she said once they were in his office. They'd walked past desks with people working on files and on the computer and into an office that wasn't huge but not too small either.

"No problem. I am the assistant district attorney working the Quentin case. If he has the evidence he's hinted that he does, then I am interested in it."

"Oh, that's good. He gave me an address to go and retrieve it, but I wanted to find out what I was getting myself into."

"How well do you know him?"

"He works at a coffee shop I manage as a dishwasher," she said. "I wasn't aware about the drug dealing and I have to tell you, I never saw any of that behavior at the coffee shop."

"I'm sure you wouldn't. He's not a street dealer. Our investigation revealed he was more midlevel in the cartel. In fact, that's the only reason I'm willing to offer him a deal. If he has the information on the higher-ups, then we can talk," Crispin said.

"So what do I need to do? Get the files from his home and bring them to you?" she asked.

"Yes. The cops searched his place and didn't find anything, so I'm not entirely sure what you are going to find, but maybe you'll see something we didn't," Crispin said.

"Do you think this is a waste of time?"

Crispin shrugged. "In my experience most people will say anything to get out of going to trial."

"Okay. Thanks. I'll be in touch if I find anything."

Obie left Crispin's office not confident that Aaron was going to get out of a trial…or jail time.

Chapter 2

Obie double-checked the address several times but this seemed to match the one that Aaron had given her. The houses in this neighborhood were spendy like she'd expected. But this one looked somewhat homey. Not at all what she expected someone who worked for a drug cartel to live in. In her head they were all living in a lux mansion like on the TV show *Bloodline*.

She parked her car under the car park. It was early in the afternoon and quiet. She had gone home and changed into a pair of shorts and tank top since the summer Florida heat was rising. Plus there was no one to impress on this errand she'd given herself.

What did she think she was going to find in Aaron's files? Someone who could potentially confess to having her father and mother killed, or at least being involved at the time? She knew that was unrealistic but had spent the drive down rehearsing what she'd ask Aaron if this worked out. Surely he'd have the connections to find out if the cartel had been involved in her parents' deaths.

Each of the properties was waterfront and all of them had docks behind the houses with boats in the back, including Aaron's. Having grown up in the swamp, Obie was at home on water and a part of her envied Aaron that he had this place. How *could* her dishwasher afford this place?

Crispin had said that Aaron was a drug dealer and pretty high up in the organization. She was still dealing with that reality. Her gut had been so wrong about Aaron. He wasn't a lost soul. Not at all. In fact he might be the one tempting people to leave behind their lives.

And he worked for La Familia Sanchez cartel. That was the only way he'd have evidence to get an indictment against the crime family that been notoriously hard to make convictions stick. Maybe she would get some answers about the cartel's involvement in her parents' deaths. She'd just tell Aaron that, if he wanted her to turn his evidence over, he had to tell her what he knew about her parents' deaths.

Which even in her head sounded impossible. It was a long shot, but she was definitely going to ask. She had to.

There were some lush hibiscus bushes growing on either side of the carport. The smell of the flower was so familiar. Like the heat, it wrapped around her and she was feeling nostalgic for the family she'd lost today.

This might have started out because she'd thought that Aaron reminded her of Gator, but Obie had the feeling this was more than wanting to help her brother. It felt like she was stuck in the shell of a Miami urbanite for too long—doing the right things, looking the right way but not feeling anything.

She shifted her bag from one shoulder to the other, feeling like someone was watching her. She glanced around. The road was empty.

Probably just her imagination.

She entered the house. Though Aaron had been in jail for a few days, the house was cool so he must have an automated air-conditioning system. Aaron had told her he'd hidden the files on an SD card that he'd taped under the wooden knife block in the kitchen.

She walked on the tile floors trying not to be envious and a little resentful that a drug dealer was living better than she was. Not exactly a huge surprise. But she worked hard to make ends meet and tried to bring something happy and good into people's lives...

She shook her head, trying not to get caught up in her assumptions. Aaron had made her laugh more than once. Maybe he was just as caught up in playing a role as she was.

The kitchen, like all the living spaces in this house, was on the second floor. This part of Florida was prone to flooding during hurricane season.

Aaron wasn't a bad man. Maybe he was lost, she thought, then shook her head. It would be nice to think he needed her help, that she could fix him with this one errand. But the truth was he'd probably be back to his old ways of making money. He'd probably taken the dishwasher job as a cover.

Who cared, right?

She entered the kitchen disgusted with her own conflicted feelings where he was concerned. The kitchen led directly into the open-plan living area, and there were floor-to-ceiling doors that overlooked the pool in the backyard and the dock with a boat on the waters of whatever bay was behind his house.

She set her bag on the counter, glancing around for the knife block but didn't see it at first. Walking around the kitchen she finally noticed a butcher block cutting board and saw the knife block next to it. Pulling it toward her, she held her breath as she took the knives out and then flipped it over.

Taped to the bottom was a small micro SD card.

That was what she'd come for. She removed it.

She heard a heavy footstep and pivoted, taking the large chef's knife in her hand as she did so. There was a huge man running toward her. She dropped the knife as she freaked out, turning to run, moving toward the door she'd come in from. She shoved the SD card into her pocket so she'd have both hands free to fight him. She didn't get very far before she was tackled to the floor.

The breath was knocked out of her by the fall, the man supporting most of his weight with his arms. He was big and hot pressing against her back. The forearm braced next to her head was thick, corded with muscles.

"Don't move if you want to live."

Her heart was racing so hard, all she could hear was the pounding of her own pulse in her ears.

"Fuck that."

She started to squirm underneath him just as a bullet hit the glass door, shattering it. The man above her wrapped his body around hers and rolled her farther from the door behind the kitchen island. He moved off of her. "Stay low."

Her hands were shaking as she watched him pull out a gun and then leaned around the island for a better position.

"Who are you?"

"Xander Quentin."

"Aaron's brother?"

"Yes. This is a fine mess. Did you get what you needed here?"

"I did," she said. "Are they shooting at me or you?"

"Well, no one saw me come in here, so I'm guessing you, Ms....?"

"Obie Keller."

"The woman who left the message for me. What kind of mess did Aaron get you into?"

Another shot was fired. He'd get to the bottom of what was going on later. First he had a job to do: protect Obie Keller and get her out of the line of fire. If he was on his own he might try to track down whoever was shooting at them. But with her at his side that wasn't an option.

He reached up to grab her bag off countertop to see if they were being watched from the back of the house. A shot hit right as he drew her bag down. She flinched.

He handed her bag to her. "Can you run in those shoes?"

She glanced down at her feet and just slipped off the flip-flops, putting them in her bag. Then she tugged the bag over her shoulder and across her body, and nodded at him.

"Which way are we going?"

"We have to get out of here—we are sitting ducks. Go to the door but keep low. I'll go first and tell you when to come. Move fast and get behind me."

She went low on her belly. For a split second the masculine part of him noted the curve of her hips and remembered how she'd felt underneath him, but he immediately shoved that aside. Now wasn't the time.

Moving cautiously, he got on his stomach, inching his way toward the door, but another shot went a little high and wide, hitting the wall next to his head, sending debris into his face and eyes. He hurried into the entryway not visible from the back of the house, rolling to pull himself out of view as more shots were fired.

He visually scanned the entire hallway. It was clear. Was there just one sniper outside? Or was he working with someone else closer to the house?

Xander estimated that the sniper to be within three thousand feet of them. And probably on a boat since all that was in the direction the shots had come from was open water, uninhabited Keys and then mangroves and the swamp. The sniper was accurate and must be well trained.

The house was quiet.

"Obie, when I tell you, run toward me," he said.

"Aren't they going to fire at me?" she asked.

"I'm going to give them a bigger target," he said dryly. He wished he had on a Kevlar vest, but honestly, coming to his brother's last known address, he hadn't anticipated being shot at.

"Be careful."

"You too," he said. "Go now."

She darted out and moved quickly toward him. Her shoulder-length brown hair swinging around her face as she did so. She concentrated, her face tight with tension as she slid around him and into the hallway without a shot being fired.

"Maybe they left," she said with a hopeful note in her voice.

Doubtful. But he didn't want to scare her. He was pretty sure, given the fact that there was a trained sniper firing at them, that whoever was out there meant business.

"Or they are moving closer. Let's get out of here. I parked my rental car down the street," he said.

"My car is out front," she said, opening her big bag and digging around in it for her keys. She looked scared but game to do whatever was needed. She had on a pair of shorts that ended at the top of her thighs and a halter neck tank top that was in a bright yellow color. Not the best for blending into the environment but he'd keep her covered.

"Stay close to me. When I do this—" he held up a closed fist "—that means stop."

"Yeah, I've seen movies with that in it," she said.

"Good, then you know what to do."

He started moving down the stairs, and outside the heat wrapped around him, reminding him how much he hated it. There was a scatter of shots as two men came up the drive from the street.

Xander grabbed Obie's arm and pulled her with him as he ran around the back of the house. There was a large pool with one of those underwater pool cleaners working in it. Xander quickly ruled out making a run for another house as he heard someone approaching behind them. Xander had cased the place before he'd gone inside. He knew there was a high-powered speedboat on the dock. He had even put the key in the engine and checked that it had gas.

Xander never went into a situation without having a backup plan and it was paying off. Part of the reason why he had been reluctant to come and see Aaron was that one backup plan where his brother was concerned was never enough.

For this woman's sake, he hoped it would be today.

It was one thing for Aaron to drop him in this shit, but it was something else for him to put an innocent civilian in danger.

"We're going to take the boat and get out of here," he said. "Run toward the dock as fast as you can."

He suspected the sniper would need time to set up for another shot now that they were on ground level. The sniper was now the secondary threat, the men on foot were a more immediate danger. Everything settled around him as he focused on his mission. Protect the woman, get her to safety. That was all he would allow himself to dwell on. Later he and Aaron were going to have words.

* * *

Obie was scared out of her mind as she ran full out behind the big behemoth in front of her. Her heart was racing and she was pretty sure she was going to die. This was exactly what she deserved for stirring up the past and coming here.

The stranger might be Aaron's brother but she wasn't sure she could trust him to keep her safe. At least he was the better of the two options right now. She heard gunshots behind her and flinched as one hit the ground near her feet. She stumbled and Xander turned, scooping her up under his arm as he ran full out.

Even wearing a backpack, carrying her and returning fire didn't seem to shake him. She felt a hand on her ankle and screamed as she was jerked from Xander's arms and hit the ground hard. Her head hurt and she kicked out at the man who had her ankle.

Xander turned and dropped to one knee, firing first at the man who lunged at her, his face a mask of rage as he took aim. She heard the sound of Xander's gun and a moment later her assailant flinched and blood exploded from his chest, hitting her face and chest. Then he collapsed toward her and she pulled her leg free.

"Run to the boat—start it."

She was on the edge of panicking and completely losing it. She felt the hot tears running down her face and her hands were shaking. Xander fired another shot and then as he looked up at her, their eyes met. "I won't let them hurt you. Go now."

His words were firm and forceful. But also reassuring in a way like he'd done this before. She ran toward the boat dock. The wood was rough from exposure to the elements and she got a splinter in her heel as she ran but didn't stop.

She felt something wet on her neck and reached up to wipe it away, flinching again as she realized it was blood. For a moment the face of the man who had been attacking her flashed in her mind before she mentally shoved it away. She jumped onto the boat, which was an older-model fishing boat with a shallow bottom ideal for navigating the waters in this area. She found the key in the ignition and turned it on.

Obie pushed her hand into her pocket, double-checking she still had the SD card. Once she brushed it with her fingertips, she went and untied the mooring at the back of the boat while Xander was only a few feet away.

"Can you drive the boat?"

"Yes, just need to get that last mooring," she said, going to undo the slip knot that was used to hold it.

She hurried back to the wheel. Normally she was a slow boater observing all the no-wake zones, but with two more men running toward them and Xander providing some cover fire, she maneuvered the boat away from the dock and hit the full throttle.

The boat lurched and then got up to speed, powering them away from the men firing at them. Her heart was racing, her hair was whipping around her head and she just kept them heading north from Key Largo. She knew there were some small, uninhabited Keys but didn't think they were large enough to provide any kind of cover.

But if she got them to Madeira Bay, Obie knew she could lose the men in the mangroves that bordered it. The boat had GPS, which she looked at to make sure she was heading in the right direction. Not that she needed it in a pinch. She might have become a city girl over the last ten years of her life, but at heart it was the swamps of Florida that she knew best.

"Keep away from other craft and the islands if you can. They had a sniper out here somewhere," Xander said.

He kept scanning the horizon, so she knew he was alert.

"I'm going to head toward the mangroves. We can ditch the boat and lose them in there."

"I'm not familiar with the terrain," he said.

"I am," she said. Aunt Karen had been clear that the backwoods rural girl Obie'd been needed to disappear if she was going to make a new life for herself. But now, Obie knew that it was only the swamp girl with the skills she'd learned from both her parents that would be able to save them.

She should have known better than to get entangled in this as soon as she heard that La Familia Sanchez cartel was involved. That cartel had been responsible for driving her from her home in the swamp, and the irony wasn't lost on her that Aaron's association with them was sending her back. She'd missed her parents, her old life and had been nostalgic all day, but *this* was different. She wasn't going to just be swimming in memories but wading in the brackish water of the mangroves and swamp just like she and Gator had done has children.

"Are we being followed?" she asked.

"Probably. I don't see anyone at the moment," he said.

Time seemed to turn into this unending thing, and she had no idea if it was ten minutes or forty-five before she saw the shoreline in Madeira Bay. Xander kept watch on their back trail as she got the boat as close as she could before killing the engine.

Xander held his hand up in the stop signal he'd showed her earlier and she crouched low as he did so in case the sniper he'd mentioned was back. He took in the open water around them and then lowered his arm.

"Looks clear, but move quickly and try to present the smallest target you can," he said.

Whatever that meant. "Sure." Before she moved, she thought about the SD card in her pocket. Was it waterproof? "Uh, I have SD card with Aaron's info on it. Will it be okay if it gets wet?"

"Not sure. Watch the horizon and let me know if you see anything," he said, taking one shoulder of his backpack off and opening it. A moment later he handed her a drybag she took the SD card out of her pocket, putting it and her phone inside the drybag and then placing it in her purse.

He just watched her without saying anything. She shrugged. He said he was Aaron's brother and he had saved her, but someone was trying to kill her to get what was on that card, so she wasn't going to let it out of her sight. Her parents and even Aunt Karen hadn't raised her to blindly trust anyone.

Sure, he'd protected her from being shot, but that didn't mean she was going to simply hand over evidence that someone else was willing to murder for. She'd keep her guard up until she was safely back in her condo. Then she'd figure out what to do. If she survived that long.

She hopped over the side of the boat, feeling the warmth of the seawater on her legs up to her thighs, moving as quickly as she could until they were into the mangroves. It would be easier to swim-walk than just plain walk. She started to do some, swimming through the deeper areas, noticing that Xander did the same. She put her face in the water, exhaling, hoping it would wash away the blood and maybe when she lifted her head, she'd be at the beach in Miami and not paddling for her life near the Everglades.

Chapter 3

Once they got farther inland and out of the water, Xander looked around. The ground was sort of marshy. There was still tidal water that flowed through the roots of the mangroves. They weren't especially tall near the edge of the open water and their roots were knotted together in a kind of weave that didn't always allow for human passage between them.

Somehow Obie inherently knew which roots were pliable and moved them expertly into the mangroves, creating cover from anyone approaching from behind them. The water at his feet was getting shallower. It seemed to him that the tide was going out. He glanced up and found a spot that looked as if it might provide adequate shelter for them.

"Let's stop up ahead next to that large tree."

Obie stopped, looking over his shoulder behind him. No one was following them and they were safe for the moment.

"Should we call the police?" she asked. "I'm not even sure what to tell them. Surely the neighbors would have heard the shots by now."

"I agree. I want to check in with my boss first,"

Xander said. "We are going to need some backup if I'm going to keep you safe."

Her hands were shaking as she pushed a strand of hair behind her ear and he noticed her flinch as she looked at them. There was blood on her fingers. He could tell she was scared but she must have a core of steel. She'd done what was needed to get them away from the house and through the mangroves to relative safety. While bleeding as an innocent civilian.

Damn.

"Let's get you cleaned up," he said.

She just nodded again. Was she going into shock? He wouldn't blame her. He had some mental health training because of his line of work, but his skill set was more to defend and protect someone than to counsel them after an incident. But he had to do something. If she lost it then his swamp expert was gone, and they were both good as dead.

One of the things Van always said was *When you don't know what to do, do what you know.* She knew this area so maybe talking about it would give her something to concentrate on. "So you said you know the swamp?"

He shrugged out of his pack and pulled out some wet wipes that Lee insisted they all carry in their go bags. He stood up and held it out to her. She took it and cleaned the blood from her arms just as he noticed a cut near her temple. She must have gotten hit by some shrapnel when the sniper had nicked the counter near them.

Using an antiseptic wipe this time, he cleaned around

the wound. She tipped her head toward him as he treated her. He had some antiseptic strips that he put on the wound to close it and hopefully protect her from infection.

"The swamp?" he asked again.

She licked her lips and chewed on her bottom one for a moment. He couldn't help noticing that she had full lips and a very kissable mouth.

Not that it mattered, as he definitely wasn't going to be kissing her. She was a client now. And they were still on the run.

"Yeah, until I was fourteen, almost fifteen, I lived in the swamp with my parents," she said. "So I know how to navigate it. I mean I grew up in central Florida, and the Green Swamp has a different ecosystems than the Everglades, but hopefully I have enough knowledge to keep us safe. I've read some stuff on the Everglades after moving here."

"You're doing great," he said, putting on the bandage. She was calmer now. Talking was helping.

He was also intrigued by her story. Why had she left the swamp? What was she doing in Miami if she was from central Florida? Mostly he liked the sound of her voice and realized her talking was calming him down as well.

Of course conversation and small talk weren't his thing, and right now he was dealing with keeping his anger at his brother in check, trying to figure out the situation they were in. He took Van's advice for himself. Focus on the mission and not on his stupid AF brother. "Catch me up on everything that Aaron told you?"

"Don't you know?" she asked, flinching back away from him. "How else did you know to come to the house?"

"Your message just said he was in jail and needed a favor. I figured I should start with his place to gather intel."

She shook her head. "Can I see some ID? I mean, you saved me from being killed and you have a British accent, but I'm still not sure…"

He got it. Her questions were logical. Xander knew his brother, and the kind of trouble Aaron was in would attract many enemies and require elite training. He pulled out his wallet, handing it over to her. He had nothing to hide and honestly, seeing her still shaking and scared and looking at him with suspicion made him want to do everything he could to reassure her.

He was going to punch Aaron in the face when he saw his brother for putting a civilian in the middle of this mess.

She took his wallet and pulled out his ID and the photo he'd forgotten he'd wedged behind it. She shifted the two things in her hand and her eyes went to the picture. He turned away knowing what it would show. Himself and Aaron in the middle, Abe and Tony on either side. It was taken the day of the accident that had changed all of their lives. They were all standing tall, posturing to show which was the biggest and strongest. Turned out none of them were.

"Okay, sorry about that, you're definitely Aaron's brother." She put the ID and picture back into his wallet before handing it back to him.

"I think we should call the cops," she said again. "But you wanted to call your boss. What is it you do?"

"I work for Price Security. We're a private body-guard firm."

"That explains the gun and your skill with it," she said. "Call your boss if you want, but I'm going to try the police."

She pulled her phone out of the drybag he'd given her, scowling as she realized there wasn't a cell signal. "My phone's useless."

"Mine won't be. It's a satellite one. Let me call my boss and *then* we can call the cops," he said, admiring the face that she was take charge. He shouldn't have been surprised based on how she'd behaved since the moment they met. The cops couldn't do much to help them, but he knew that it would make her feel better to call them.

Unless they were in on it too. The cartel's influence was clearly wide, and corrupting local law enforcement was a common tactic.

He turned on his phone and put his earpiece in. He hit the Price Security button and Lee was in his ear in a moment.

"What's up? Enjoying the sun and sand?"

"Not exactly. Someone just shot up Aaron's place. I'm with Obie Keller," he said.

He heard Lee's fingers moving on her keyboard; she was already locating him and doing a search on Obie.

"Gunfire was reported in Key Largo at your brother's last known address. Police dispatched. An alert is out for a man matching your description and a woman with brown hair, slender build. They want you for questioning. An eyewitness IDed you as the shooter of the deceased," Lee said.

"Fu—"

"Language," Lee said with a smile in her voice. "But yeah. I think you should get some cover. I'll dig and find out a safe place for you two to turn yourself in for questioning."

"Obie's been speaking to someone in the district attorney's office. They would be a good contact. Aaron has information that is going to be used in a case against La Familia Sanchez cartel. That means she has a target on her back now."

"She does, and so do you. That information is good to know. What do you need from me to keep her safe?" Lee asked.

"We are going to need extraction. We had to abandon the boat and we are hiding in some mangroves," he said concisely. Getting to a safe house would be the easiest thing at this point.

"I'll start working on it," she said, and he heard her fingers moving on her keyboard. "What's the contact's name?"

"Who were you talking to at the district attorney's office?" he asked Obie.

"Crispin Tallman. He is an assistant district attorney working Aaron's case, and he's willing to cut a deal depending on the quality of the information," Obie said to him.

He nodded and relayed the information to Lee. "I'll check in with him. If you head west, northwest you should hit Cuthbert Lake. I'd stay south and go around it. Just past it is West Lake and on the far west side there is a marina. Head that way and I'll dig up info, check in when you are there."

"Will do. Bye."

"Bye, X. Stay safe."

Obie arched one eyebrow at him. "What is going on?"

He caught her up on what Lee had told him as he dug out his first aid kit. A bullet had grazed his left bicep, and now that Obie was safe, Xander was ready to clean it.

"The cops want to talk to us?"

"According to what Lee heard. You said you got an SD card and that Tallman and Aaron were the only two who knew you'd be there?"

She gave a short nod and licked her full, rosy lips. She pushed her sunglasses up to the top of her head. "Let me help you with that wound."

She bandaged him up and then turned away, going around the side of the tree. Her breath came out in a ragged sigh as she sank to the ground, pulling her knees up to her chest.

Xander stood there unsure how to help. Protecting her from an assailant with a gun or knife he could handle, but managing emotions and a creeping attraction to his charge…not so much.

Her arms wrapped around her body, Obie held herself tightly. She'd been on her own since Gator had left, but the world that he'd abandoned her in had been one that was easy to adapt to. It had been boring, but safe. It wasn't that she had wanted to be on her own, but the promise of safety…she hadn't felt safe after her parents' deaths.

This was something else.

She hadn't heard gunfire since they'd left the swamp. Hadn't been shot at ever, and she was freaking out. They couldn't go to the cops, according to the behemoth, and she was putting her faith in the brother of her jailed dishwasher. She truly had no idea who that man was. She couldn't even remember his first name, though she'd knew he'd given it to her when they'd been crouched behind the desk.

God, that felt like a lifetime ago.

"You okay?" he asked.

"Yeah." No. She wasn't ever going to be okay again. But a part of her knew that was a lie. She had felt the same when her parents had been killed and she and Gator had been sent to live with Aunt Karen. She'd adapted and she'd learned to survive. Now she was going to have to dig deep and push past emotions she'd repressed for so long, telling herself she was fine. But fine wasn't going to cut it in the swamp. She was going to have to be her true self and she wasn't sure she was ready for that.

She had this, she told herself. Except someone had freaking shot at her and she could still feel that man's hand wrapping around her ankle. Her entire body ached from hitting the ground and she felt like…well, she'd never be safe again.

Her breath started to become more rapid and she felt her heart racing. She was having a panic attack.

Damn. She hadn't had one since she'd first come to live with Aunt Karen.

"Hey, you're okay. I'm not going to let anyone or anything get to you," the behemoth said.

"Yeah."

"Why are you doing this?" he asked.

"Doing what? Also what's your name? Sorry, I've forgotten it. I mean I know I just read it on your ID and everything."

"It's okay. I'm Xander. I'm a bodyguard," he reminded her with a gentle smile.

Bodyguard. Well, that explained his muscled frame and why he had put himself between her and the men firing at them so many times. Also he had a calm surety about him that made her feel like he'd be able to handle anything that came at them. He had carried her and taken down a man attacking her at the same time, so she wasn't even exaggerating that.

"I'm not sure either of us is safe. Do you think that the men were with La Familia Sanchez?"

"Yes. I'm more concerned about how they got our descriptions to law enforcement so quickly. I think we need to try to read whatever is on the SD card you picked up. What did Aaron say the evidence was?"

"He didn't. But Crispin—that's the assistant district attorney—said something about evidence to convict people higher up in the cartel."

"That's right. Evidence that has put your life in danger. Aaron never should have sent you to collect it," Xander said.

"I think he was hoping his brother would show up and he wouldn't have to ask me," she said pointedly.

"Yeah, I'm sure he was," he said in a biting way, and then he glanced at her and something changed in him. He scrubbed his hand over his face and shook his head. "I am sorry you were caught in the middle of this."

He pulled a bottle of Gatorade from his pack and twisted off the cap, offering it to her. She took it and, even though she wasn't a fan of the beverage, took a long swallow. She didn't want to chance getting dehydrated. He took another bottle and drained it one long gulp.

She looked at him, really *looked* at him, for the first time, noticing that he was an attractive man. She had seen the photo of him with his brothers and there was a similarity between him and Aaron, but they were also very different. They both had that same thick hair that tended to curl, but where Aaron's was brown, Xander's was black. They both had blue eyes, but Aaron's always seemed to hold a hint of laughter and Xander's... well, didn't.

There was a seriousness to him and a calmness that made her feel safe. Guess that was something he'd had to cultivate as a bodyguard. As he put the empty bottle back in his pack, her eyes drifted lower, to his lips. He had a full mouth, and she couldn't help staring at it for longer than she should.

He arched one eyebrow at her and she shook her head. "Why didn't you call me back?"

Something like anger, or maybe just annoyance, seemed to pass over his face. She was pretty sure he wasn't interested in discussing this with her. But if she didn't keep talking, she was either going to throw herself at Xander and kiss that tempting mouth of his, or she was going to let go of the control she was barely holding on to and completely freak out.

"If you had, we might not be standing here in the mangroves with the cops wanting to talk to us," she pointed out.

God, she sounded like Aunt Karen. Carefully assigning blame with a side of guilt to get what she wanted. She didn't like that side of herself.

"Fair enough. Things are complicated with Aaron. We aren't close and haven't really been in touch for years," Xander said.

He turned to face the water in front of him and she confronted the cut on his face again. He seemed invincible, and she'd cleaned the bullet wound on his arm so she *knew* he wasn't, but seeing the cut on his face was another reminder. Even this larger-than-life man was human and fragile, just like her. "I'm sorry to hear that."

"Are you close to my brother?" he asked.

She felt close to most people she worked with. Probably because they all had to have each other's back during the morning and lunch rush. She had to rely on her staff to get things done and they all bonded over working hard together. It wasn't something she could explain. Aaron had made her laugh during their downtimes while he washed the dishes and they'd reset for the next rush.

She'd thought…that she knew him. Never guessed

that he was hiding anything. Which was her bad, really. She spent most of her time pretending to be someone she'd had to become, so it was silly that she wouldn't have recognized the same qualities in him. But she hadn't. Part of assimilating into a clone of her cousins and aunt was expecting that everyone was normal. In her job she took people at face value. Clearly she shouldn't have done that with Aaron. She'd let her guard down and look where it had gotten her.

"He started working for me a few weeks ago," she said at last. "So no. Not close at all."

"Yet you risked your life for him."

When he put it like that, he must suspect she had another reason for helping Aaron. She just didn't know him well enough to really understand what he was thinking and what he might believe of her. Did she want to mention her own muddy past with La Familia Sanchez cartel? No. And she didn't know Xander well enough to trust him with that. Not yet.

"I mean I thought I was picking up a file and driving it back to Miami, which isn't really risky."

Xander gave her a half smile. "Guess today wasn't what you planned."

"Nope."

"Nothing with Aaron ever is."

"Really?"

"Yeah. I mean maybe that's the way it is with all siblings. I'm not really sure. Me and my brothers have a very difficult way of dealing with each other," he said. "You have any?"

"Um, I have a brother. That relationship is complicated too," she said. "Actually, Aaron reminds me of my brother."

Something rustled in the underbrush behind them. Xander pulled her to him, maneuvering her so that her back was against the tree and his body was pressed against her front. He was so close that she felt his exhalation against her cheek. Her lips parted and her body was once again making her very aware of Xander.

She felt her lips slightly tingle. This was a bad idea. She glanced over his shoulder and saw a small opossum scurrying from one bush to another. She should definitely not be checking out Xander while they were in the swamp with the cartel after them.

But it seemed being in the heat and the isolating swamp was stirring up all of her instincts, including the feminine ones she always ignored. She wanted to shake herself. Now wasn't the time to finally be attracted to a man.

Xander noticed it too and relaxed his grip on her, stepping back and shoving his hand through his hair. She missed his touch for a moment before she mentally gave herself a smack. *Snap out of it!*

"Aaron's an idiot. He knew I'd come. He just was impatient like always. He had no business putting you in danger."

"Thanks," she said. "But I volunteered."

"You said he reminds you of your brother. How?"

"Just lost. Like he needed someone to look out for him," she said. Not really sure why she was admitting this to a stranger. But the truth was she no longer was sure of anything. Being shot at, being in a boat traveling at high speeds across the Florida Keys. It stirred that long-ago girl she'd been, the one that craved adventure. Made her question all the changes she'd made to fit into a world that had never been her own.

Plus she still wasn't sure of Xander's motivations. He hadn't responded when his brother had first reached out and now he was here. Something must have changed his mind.

"Does it help with your brother?" he asked. "Because I've taken the opposite tack with Aaron and it's not really working."

"Well, I haven't seen Gator since I was sixteen. I didn't look out for him back then."

She heard the sadness in her own voice. This afternoon had made a mess of all the control she'd normally used to get through her day.

She looked up, and her eyes met Xander's blue ones. She was tempted to tell him about her parents and the information she was hoping to get from Aaron, to see how far trust could go, but instead she just wrapped one arm around her waist. "A part of me is trying to correct the scales and bring some balance. Maybe by helping your brother I can make up for not helping mine."

He put his hand on her shoulder and squeezed. A tingle of sensual awareness went through her.

"You've made up for it," he said.

"I don't think you get to decide that," she said. "I haven't really done much."

"Except drive a long way to get some info that may keep Aaron from jail. I'm not sure what you didn't do for your own brother but I think that counts. Plus you were shot at and you got us to safety."

"You make it seem like I saved the day when we both know it was you."

He put his hand under her chin. "You did a lot more than you realize."

Their eyes met and something passed between them. That awareness that had been stirring between them earlier was back. She let her eyes drift down to his mouth and then half closed them as he brought his mouth down toward hers.

Chapter 4

Xander wanted to blame the heat, or the adrenaline, or the fact that he was in party-centric Miami for almost kissing Obie, but he knew that the cause was the woman herself.

She tempted him. There was something about her resilience and the way she'd handled herself under pressure that got to him. Being so big, everyone just let him take control, but with Obie he could tell she was used to relying on herself, keeping control. He lifted his head and saw the same confusion coursing through him on her face.

He wanted to say something, knew that he should, but he had no words. Talking about anything had never made things better for him. He screwed up when he spoke.

Instead he leaned into what he did best—protecting her. He heard the sound of a boat motor coming toward the area where they'd ditched their boat earlier.

Damn. Had someone been watching them the entire time? They weren't exactly in deep cover, but even a seasoned tracker would have had trouble spotting them in the clutter of mangrove roots.

"We need to hide," he said. He wasn't sure how many men were in the boat that was following them or even if the boat was after them.

She gave him a tight nod. "I think if we go further into the mangroves until they pass it might give us the advantage."

"You know the swamp better than me," he said.

Her hair had started to curl as they stood in the humidity of the Florida summer day.

He regretted not kissing her for two reasons: one, he could see that she'd needed some kind of human touch. After being shot at and chased he totally understood where she was coming from. Adrenaline and fear had a comedown and human contact was the easiest way to manage it.

The second was that he needed it too.

She gestured for him to follow her. Before he did, he pulled her close and gave her a rough hug. He wasn't a physical person except for sex, which to him was a physical need, not something involving emotions. So comforting her wasn't something that felt natural, and the hug probably wasn't the best. But she gave a ragged sigh and then half smiled up at him.

That smile went straight to his groin...and something deeper. But he didn't want to be reacting to her emotions while he was turned on and they were fighting for their lives. The two weren't meant to go together. At least not for him.

"We're going to get wet again," she said.

"As much as I'm sweating I won't mind it," he said dryly.

She lead them farther away from the open water and the tree they'd taken shelter behind. The ground turned marshy and then it deepened into the brackish mangroves. She led them to the relative shelter of a large mangrove and then slipped under the branches, bringing him with her.

They heard the other boat slow, riding the edge of the mangroves. From his position it was hard to make out the features of the three occupants on the boat. They had guns and were using binoculars to scan the shoreline.

"Can you hold your breath?" he asked.

"Yes."

"Big breath and then under when I tell you," he said.

Her eyes went wide and then she nodded. He waited until the boat got closer to where they were. "Now."

She took a deep breath, as did Xander, and they both ducked under the water. The SAS training he'd had was a bit like the US Navy SEAL training, so he could hold his breath for almost three minutes. But he hoped it wouldn't be that long. He couldn't expect her to do this for hours on end; she was a civilian.

Obie put her hand on his arm and he turned toward her. Due to the sunlight he had a partial view of her face. Her eyes widened and she pointed behind him. He glanced over his shoulder to see an American crocodile swimming toward them.

Of course it was.

There was something in the cold eyes of the crocodile as it moved through the water. The predator in him recognized the same in the animal.

God damn his brother straight to hell. He'd known. Known the moment that he'd heard Aaron's name that this was all going to go to shit.

Xander had never confronted a croc. His training in the mountains of Wales strangely hadn't gone into detail on crocodiles. Somehow the idea of actually facing one on a mission seemed too ridiculous to be real.

Obie just squeezed his wrist, bringing his attention back to her.

Stay still, she mouthed to him.

He gave a quick nod of his head.

He had almost forgotten about the threat from the men following them as the crocodile got closer. It crept slowly toward him, its eyes moving over them. The closer it got, Xander could clearly see the teeth. He'd read once that crocodiles submerged their prey and took them into a death roll, suffocating them. Or was that an alligator. Hell, he couldn't remember.

But the crocodile slowly swam right on past them. As soon as it departed, Obie gestured for them to surface.

Slowly, she mouthed again.

He moved as carefully as he could, keeping one eye on the retreating croc, and then as his head broke the surface, he emerged only to his nose. The sound of the boat was gone but he wasn't taking any risks.

He scanned the edge of the mangrove swamp and noticed that the craft was gone. Obie had surfaced next to him. She was watching the direction the crocodile had swum in.

"Can we move?" she asked, her voice pitched low.

Given that they were facing danger on two fronts, he knew she didn't mean for the low timbre of her voice to be sexy. But it was. It was hard not to be attracted to a woman who'd kept her cool the way that Obie had. She surprised him. Something that rarely happened.

"Yes. Slowly. Stay low," he said.

"Get back on land," she said. "Crocs are fast on land so we don't want to catch his attention."

"Got it."

He led them from the shelter of the mangrove branches back the way they came. As they got back on the marshy land, he checked his compass and went in the direction that Lee had suggested. Obie was moving quietly behind him. She touched his waist at one point and he paused, glancing over his shoulder.

"I think we're clear now. From the croc anyway."

"That's good. I think the men chasing us are gone for now too," he said.

"Yeah? That's a relief. Do you think they'll be back?" she asked.

"Probably. I mean they were gunning hard for you. And I killed one of them…so yeah, I don't think they are going to just walk away."

"I was afraid of that," she said, tucking a strand of hair that had escaped her ponytail back behind her ear. "I wonder if I should use your phone to call the district attorney. Maybe if we get the SD card to them… But how are they going to stop La Familia Cartel from coming after us? If that even was them, but given that they have eyes and ears everywhere…"

Xander couldn't help smiling at the way she listed

options and then ruled them out. Strength was something he was drawn to. Obie had been thrust into this situation and she wasn't cowering and waiting for him to take the lead. "Exactly. The company I work for has a lot of connections. I think if we go to this marina they suggested, that will give them time to get some intel and us some time to recoup from being shot at. It's not my favorite thing."

She looked back over her shoulder at him. "I'd be worried about you if it were."

He cracked a smile and shook his head. "Me too."

"Why are you and Aaron in the US instead of still in jolly old England?"

She attempted a bit of a British accent on the jolly-old-England bit but sounded more like Paul Rudd in the movie *Forgetting Sarah Marshall* than like a true Brit. "Can't speak for Aaron as I didn't realize he'd come over here. But I was recruited by Van Price to join his security team after I left the SAS."

"What's the SAS?"

"Special Air Service. Sort of like your Navy SEALs." He'd needed to find a reason, a purpose for the big muscles and the strength that had always been a part of him. A way to try to make sense of his desire for strength instead of succumbing to the insecure destructive side that had led to one of his brothers being paralyzed. Joining the SAS suited him.

"Did you have to do a bunch of extreme stuff to prove yourself before you become one?" she asked.

"Yeah, some. Aaron was actually in my class."

"Really? I wouldn't have guess that about Aaron.

He's so chill and laid-back, but then I didn't know him the way I thought I did," she said, chewing her lower lip between her teeth and taking a deep breath.

"We both changed after the SAS. We had a falling-out and he went his own way. The man you know might be the result of the last ten years." He didn't let himself dwell on the emotions he still hadn't dealt with from that last fight with Aaron. It was past time to try to make amends, but he hadn't known how.

She wrapped one arm around her waist as a tepid breeze blew around her, making her ponytail sway. "Has it been that long since you've seen him?"

"Yeah."

He wanted to reassure her that Aaron wasn't using her, but that was more down to the woman Obie was. He wanted her to keep her faith in people. From Xander's experience, he didn't think he would be able to trust his brother. Aaron had gone rogue from life. Xander had seen it firsthand.

"Is that why you hesitated to come and help him?"

He shrugged. As much as he wanted to reassure Obie, he really wasn't into disclosing any part of his past. Partially because he was now thinking of himself as her bodyguard and he didn't want to blur the lines between personal and professional. Their attraction was already threatening that carefully made boundary. "It's complicated."

"Yeah, whatever, you said, but since we have a long walk and I don't want to keep reliving the memory of that guy who grabbed me…maybe you can talk to me about something sort of normal."

She turned away from him. The sun was hot and he felt that heat all the way to his bones.

Something primitive stirred deep inside of him and he was seconds away from just letting loose, relinquishing his control. He couldn't close his eyes and meditate, not while they were walking and the cartel was on their back trail.

He looked back at her. She had said *whatever*, like she thought he was copping out of admitting the truth.

"Things between me and Aaron are complicated and neither of us has ever talked about it. I'm not sure I can put it into words. But he was once my best friend and then everything changed. I blame myself and him for what happened but we don't talk to each other."

She barely nodded. "Why not?"

"Why not what?"

"Why don't you talk?" she asked. "Not that it's my business. I shouldn't be pushing you."

"I suspect you are trying to figure out what Aaron got you into and if he's worth it."

He paused to see if he was right. He wouldn't blame her for staying focused on getting out of the swamp and not really caring too much about Aaron or himself. She chewed her lower lip again and gave a half nod.

"*I don't know* is the short answer. The brother I knew was a man of honor and had a strong moral code. But it's been ten years—that might have changed," Xander said.

"Have you changed in the last ten years?" she asked.

"I have."

"And?"

"That's why I'm not sure. Life had required sacrifices from me that shifted the man I used to be. I haven't compromised or done the easy thing to stay comfortable, but that's not my way."

She shook her head. "This isn't helping."

"I know. I'm sorry. I hate getting into my feelings."

They continued walking. This situation wasn't what he'd expected and frankly he'd been expecting it to be pretty damned complicated and difficult from the beginning. Confronting the ghosts of the past was something he'd never thought to do in this situation, at least not with a beautiful stranger while his wayward brother was in prison.

He wanted to protect Obie. Maybe if he made her his job then he could get them both through this without having to deal with too much fallout from Aaron and his involvement with La Familia Sanchez cartel.

"What's next?"

"We've got about thirty more minutes until we reach the first lake. I have a pack-raft in my bag that we can use when he get there. It self-inflates so we'll take another little break. But going across Cuthbert Lake instead of around it should save us a lot of time."

Because if he didn't think of Obie as a client, as someone he needed to protect, he was very afraid he'd open that tight control he'd always kept on himself.

The one thing he tried to never do was lie to himself.

It was her. She was making things complicated for him. Complicated in a way that he wasn't sure he could control.

* * *

Obie wasn't entirely sure why she'd almost kissed him. She could say it was from relief, and of course it *was* the first time she'd been shot at. She'd been around guns all her life—all her early life. Living in the swamp necessitated knowing how to shoot a rifle to keep snakes away from their house. But she'd never been shot at, never faced the barrel of a gun head-on… It was still freaking her out.

Being on the water had always been something that soothed her, but walking through the swamp was stirring so much anxiety. She was having a bit of a panic attack just remembering Xander running toward her, then the bullet hitting the glass in the room.

The sun continued to blaze and she thought about the croc they'd seen. She'd been anything but chill when she first noticed it, but then she heard her daddy's voice in her head telling her most swamp creatures weren't out to attack. Just sort of inhabited a live-and-let-live attitude. It had been years since she'd allowed herself to think of her parents, much less hear their voices.

But walking through the swamp was something they'd done together so many times, it was almost as if she could feel them walking beside her.

She'd shut out so much when she'd landed at Aunt Karen's and had to figure out how to survive in a world that wasn't her own. But today she realized how much she'd lost when she'd done that. This was life-and-death and she had no choice but to use her swamp skills.

The shocking thing was that she still liked it. Loved

it. And she didn't have to hide her knowledge from Xander.

"You okay?" he asked after about fifteen minutes of walking.

No.

She was pretty sure she wasn't going to be okay until she got rid of the SD Card that Aaron had sent her to retrieve. But Obie forced a smile and nodded. "Yeah. Just hot."

The man was big and built. His shoulders were large, like Captain America when he was trying to keep Bucky from taking off in the chopper in *Captain America: Civil War*. She had no business checking him out but it was hard not to notice. He was also *tall*. Much bigger than Aaron, probably by about three inches in height and maybe twenty pounds in muscle.

Xander glanced over his shoulder at her and behind her dark sunglasses she felt safe letting her gaze move over that big body of his. She felt safe with him. Having him by her side with skills that she, as a basic manager of a coffeehouse, didn't have was reassuring.

"You probably want to put on some sunscreen," she said, realizing he was starting to turn a little bit red. She dug around in her purse until she found the small container she always carried.

He arched one eyebrow at her but took the container she handed him.

"Thanks."

Smiling at him, she had a moment where she felt like she was living someone else's life. "This is just so weird."

"Yeah, it is. I don't know how my brother got mixed up with a huge drug cartel."

"It's so hard to really know someone. Even when you live with them all the time," she said. "I guess ten years would make you more like strangers."

Xander didn't say anything as he poured the sunscreen into his hand and rubbed into his arms and then his neck and face. "We were strangers long before that."

She thought about her own relationship with Gator. She knew exactly what it was like to have that distance with a sibling. The only thing she wasn't sure about with Xander and Aaron was if one of them had regretted it. The way Xander was acting, she was pretty sure there was unfinished business between them. She'd regretted the distance between herself and Gator but she had never been sure if he regretted it too.

A part of her had reignited hope for an answer since the moment she'd heard La Familia Sanchez had wanted to find answers about her parents' deaths. As if in some way that would bring Gator back into her life or fix that broken past.

Xander didn't want to talk about his estrangement with Aaron in the middle of hiding from killers in a swamp. But it wasn't only Obie making him think of his brother. He'd been inundated with memories since Van had brought his name up in the staff meeting.

Why now?

And what exactly was this mess Aaron was in? Seeing his brother as a midlevel drug dealer made no sense. The house he'd gone to wasn't something a low-level dealer or dishwasher in a coffeehouse could afford. Also given the fact that the cartel had been watching the house, he believed the information that Aaron had was very valuable.

He looked over at Obie. She'd pulled her hair back into a ponytail but a few wisps still flew around her head. He had the coordinates on the map on his satellite phone but the geography here was foreign. He was drowning in this assignment. Which wasn't even an official assignment. Lee had sent him a list of bars and clubs to check out so he could relax when he was in Miami prior to landing, thinking bailing Aaron out of jail and getting to the bottom of things would take no time at all.

Now Lee'd updated his phone with information on poisonous snakes and plants to watch for as well as the coordinates to the area she wanted him to head to.

No one had anticipated this. But Xander should have. He knew Aaron; his brother wouldn't have reached out unless he was out of options. But Xander also inherently believed his brother was still a good person. So that meant he needed to read whatever was on that SD card and get more information about what exactly his brother had been up to.

"You said Aaron hadn't been working for long…" He sort of tossed it out as a question.

"Yeah, almost three weeks," she said.

"Did you notice anything about him?" he asked.

She licked her lips. "Nothing unusual. He got to work early, was a very efficient dishwasher and liked to flirt with everyone who came into the shop. He didn't hesitate to jump in and do any task that needed doing. Honestly I thought he was a really good worker. He seemed a little too educated to just be washing dishes," she said.

"In what way?"

"Just that I could tell he'd done higher level work," she responded.

"Why did you hire him?"

She took a deep breath. "Everyone needs a second chance. He was vague about his references and what he'd been doing previously but it seemed to me that he needed work. So I took a chance. And until today I didn't have any second thoughts about him."

Sounded like the brother he'd known. All of the Quentins had been raised to work hard. Everyone pulled their own weight and there was no job that was too small for any of them. A part of Xander was glad to hear his brother still had that work ethic.

He wanted to ask her more questions but before he could, she spoke.

"You said you're a bodyguard. What's that like?" she asked.

He shrugged. "I don't know. It's a job. I get a mission brief, I protect my client for the duration of the contract and then I go back to LA until my next assignment."

She shook her head. "I have a job. What you do is something you chose. A vocation or a lifestyle or something."

"Or maybe it chose me," he said without really think-

ing. After his brother's accident Xander had to tame
his own strength and learn to use it to keep others safe.
The path stretched in front of him before he could know
anything else.

"You always wanted to protect others?"

Shielding people from harm hadn't been on his
mind until the accident. It was Obie who was stirring
up all of his instincts in that department, and probably
more than a little residual anger toward Aaron that was
making him so protective of her.

The rage and the violence inside of him was once
out of control. All of the Quentins were used to fighting; punching, blood and gore was a part of their everyday life. And being the best was what they'd all
been striving for, until that moment when…everything
had changed.

He knew that protection was a means to the only
end he could live with. He had to protect because that
was the way his strength could serve others and control that beast deep inside of him. He was disciplined
not because he liked order but because if he wasn't
then no one was safe.

"Yeah, I guess so. I mean my dad was in the military so we grew up roughhousing." Even as the prac-
ticed words came out of his mouth he regretted them.
He'd heard his mom use that excuse about the violence
in their home and it had become his pat answer. But
the truth was they'd been allowed to run wild and no
one had ever tried to stop them.

Obie was making him very aware of the man he'd
been and the man he was trying to be. She'd put her

life in his hands whether she knew it or not. And the fact that Aaron had put her in danger made this more personal than Obie would ever know. But he wasn't going to let anyone hurt her, not the men who were after them and not the beast inside of him.

"You look very intense," she said.

Well, hell. He didn't know any other way to be, he guessed. "Yeah that's my resting face."

"Yeah? Mine is sort of bitchy so I have to remind myself to smile all the time. You should do that too."

He looked at her, not sure but…he thought she was teasing him. No one ever did that. He always thought it was his intimidating size. Some people called him a giant or goliath and he shrugged it off. He was sort of a half giant. He gave her a fake half smile, half smirk.

God, he felt so weird and awkward. Why was he trying to smile?

A genuine grin flashed across her face and she laughed. "Ya need practice."

"Ya think?"

"I do."

He was tired of being in his head and in the past. He wanted to know more about this woman who'd taken a big risk even if that hadn't been her intent when she'd come to help out his brother. She fascinated him. Even though she really shouldn't, given they were in the swamp and bad guys were chasing them. But nothing about today was normal.

"So Obie… That's an interesting name…" He just left that statement there. Wanting to talk about her and not his brother or the mess they were in.

"It's different, isn't it? It's a nickname. My parents named me Orange Blossom but always just called me Obie."

"Ah, I'm Alexander," he said. "Not sure why." Orange Blossom. It was something he associated with Florida and actually looking at her. She was very much a Florida woman. At ease in the sun and on the water.

Her name suited it because it was distinctly unique just as she was. Reminding her that she was in danger should have been his priority, but instead he couldn't help watching her move through the swamp with a natural grace and instinct. All he could think was that he'd gotten lucky Aaron had asked her to contact him.

Chapter 5

Xander had packed a few snacks in his bag, mainly dried nuts and fruit, and offered some to Obie, which she declined. The landscape hadn't changed much, except it was wetter in some spots as the tide completely receded.

Obie had been quiet for the last thirty minutes, which suited him. But he had a feeling it didn't suit her.

She'd been talking and chatting most of the time they'd been walking and while he wouldn't say he knew her, clearly something was up.

"You okay?" he asked. He'd asked her earlier but didn't mind repeating himself.

"No. I mean I know I said yes before but honestly who's okay after a day like we've had?" she said. Then she shook her head, her hands shaking as she tried to push her hair behind her ear. He was used to long endurance hikes from his time in the SAS and hiking up near Mt. Wilson in LA, but she clearly was reaching the end of her rope.

"I'm rambling. Sorry."

He stopped walking and turned to face her. "It's okay. You're okay. Everything you're feeling is normal."

"Nothing's normal," she said under her breath.

He took a gamble on the fact that she wasn't used to being chased or in life-threatening danger. She needed a distraction again. "That's life with Aaron."

"Is it?" she asked. "I know you haven't seen him in ten years but was he always...? How was he?"

God, the one thing he really didn't want to do was unpack the past, but right now that was what she needed. What his client needed, he reminded himself. And talking to her made it easier to keep his temper in check. He was mad at his brother, really pissed at the men who'd shot at them, and it was taking every bit of training he'd had to keep himself in that null zone. The one where emotions had no sway.

It didn't help that Obie was hot as hell. His body was noticing and his mind was tempting him with images of that kiss he'd denied himself earlier. Getting physical with her *would* work to kind of get him to that Zen headspace he needed to keep moving. But sleeping with a client was a big no-no. Not that Van had ever explicitly said it, but Van would never be impersonal with someone he'd hooked up with, would never risk hurting someone purely because of attraction. He just wasn't one of those people who was casual about sex.

Most of the time Xander limited himself to masturbating or some sort of no-strings exchange with one of the few women he felt like he could walk away from.

Obie was already different. This Florida woman with her quiet strength and resilience.

"Xander?"

"Sorry. I'm not going to say it's complicated again

but Aaron, my brothers and I have always been jumbled together. I think that's why I didn't call you back when I got the message. I just needed time to figure out if I was going to come here."

She licked her lips again and his eyes tracked the movement behind the dark lens of his sunglasses. His cock jumped and his skin felt too tight for his body.

His mind was busy listing all the reasons why he couldn't have her, but his body wasn't really paying attention. Instead some part of him was conjuring up images of her naked in his arms, his mouth moving over hers and then down the side of her neck, following the path that a bead of sweat was taking.

He jerked his thoughts away from that.

"Why did you come?" she asked.

He stopped and fumbled in his backpack, very aware that he needed a few moments to get himself back under control. He took a deep breath and pulled out his reusable water bottle, taking a long swallow before offering it to her. Their fingers brushed as she took it and all of the calm he'd forced on his body was gone. His pulse raced as a shiver of sensual awareness went up his arm and then straight to his cock.

She'd asked him something, but for the life of him he couldn't recall what it was. Something about why he was here.

"My boss is big on family. So I tried to weasel out of coming and Van said, 'He's your brother. Go.' And here I am."

"Does Van know your brother?" she asked, handing the water bottle back to him, and this time he was careful not to allow their fingers to touch.

"No. But he knows me. Our team... It feels more like real family than Aaron does to me. But Aaron and my brothers, they were...are a big part of the man I've become and I think... Well, not to get too deep but Van knew I'd regret not coming before I did."

That was one of the things he liked about his boss even if sometimes he resented it. Van always put the team members' best interests at the heart of everything. They worked hard and the job came first, but Van made them all feel as if what they were doing made the world a better place.

They were his found family. It was odd because the Price Security team wasn't like what he'd believed family was growing up. There was no fighting or yelling and everyone just had each other's back. He hadn't known that kind of group existed.

"So here I am," he said. "Sorry I didn't call you. If I had maybe...maybe you'd be safe at your coffee shop instead of in the swamp."

"Maybe."

"Just maybe?"

"Well. The thing is...once I found out that Aaron was involved with La Familia Sanchez cartel I had to find out more."

"Why?"

"It's complicated," she said with a wink at him. But her expression was closed and her mouth had tightened. As much as she was trying to keep things light, she couldn't. It was just a guess, but based on what he'd learned so far, she built her toughness up herself and she didn't want to let him see any cracks.

"Isn't everything?"

"Yeah."

He put the bottle back in his backpack. In a few more kilometers they'd reach the lake and he'd already decided they'd use the inflatable pack-raft he had in his bag to traverse it. They started walking again and she fell into step beside him.

"The cartel?"

"It's not really anything solid. But my dad was the sheriff and was investigating their movements through central Florida when he and my mom were killed."

"And the cartel was suspected?" he asked.

"By me and my brother. But the cops said it was an accident."

That was a lot to unpack. But it wasn't really that uncommon; many cartels and shady organizations had plugs within law enforcement. Corruption happened everywhere. "Why did you think it wasn't?"

Obie blamed the swamp and this wild day for why she was bringing up her parents. But also there had been a hint of honesty in the way Xander opened up about Aaron. Something that she always felt like she had to reciprocate.

Also, if she was being brutally honest with herself, she wanted him to tell her she was grasping at straws, and maybe make her give up on her idea of asking Aaron to find out more about her parents' deaths.

Something that every logical part of her being was sure would lead to nothing.

But her heart was hoping. Her sixteen-year-old self needed answers. Needed to know their deaths were something other than a random accident. Obie truly wanted to believe that her life hadn't changed so drastically, that she'd lost her parents and brother in the span of a year, for something random.

She wanted that loss to have a meaning. At the time grief had been overwhelming, and then with Gator's departure she'd struggled just to survive, but today mired in the swamp she wanted the truth for herself and justice for her parents.

If it didn't reveal anything, if it was just random… Well, she didn't want to dwell on that either.

So why didn't she believe her parents' deaths were an accident? As a kid she'd trusted the cops and didn't want to believe someone who worked for her dad was also in with the cartel. "They died in the swamp. That's the first thing. Daddy grew up in the Green Swamp. And Mama was from Georgia and knew how to survive in the bayou and had learned our swamp as well."

"Were they out walking in it?" he asked.

Though he'd said he was a bodyguard, the way he was asking questions and listening told her that he must have done some investigation in the past. She was so tempted to leave off talking about her parents and steer the conversation back to him. But she wanted answers, and Xander was making her view the situation differently.

"No. They'd taken the airboat."

"It broke down?"

She shook her head. "If it had Daddy would have fixed it. He was always fixing it and knew that airboat like the back of his hand. They hit a tree and the airboat exploded."

He raised both eyebrows, seeming surprised by her revelation. "Having seen your skills behind the wheel of the boat and in the swamp...that does raise a few questions. What did the medical examiner find?"

"The bodies were charred from the fire," she said, her voice cracked as she relived the grief and pain she'd felt back then. She'd never seen the bodies; Deputy Wade had made sure she and Gator hadn't. "They said that Daddy had a heart attack and lost control."

Logical. It was the only explanation that would make sense for two people as savvy about boats and the swamp as her parents had been. But her father had been in excellent health on his previous checkup only a year earlier. Deputy Wade had pushed for further investigations but it had been shut down by someone higher than him. Obie and Gator had believed that Wade was right to ask them to continue and resented the fact that he'd given up so easily.

As an adult, she almost got it. Sometimes in order to keep a job, rules had to be followed. But Wade had been friends with her parents and had been Gator's godfather. In Obie's opinion he never should have stopped looking into it.

"You don't think he did?" Xander asked, pulling her back into the present.

"He was healthy and he'd been close to arresting

someone in the cartel. Daddy believed that someone had been using routes through the swamp to smuggle something. Not being vague but he wasn't sure if it was just drugs or drugs and guns and maybe people. He saw a small hunting hut that looked as if it had been used as a shelter. He cleaned the trash out of it and when he checked in a few days later he could tell someone had been sleeping there again.

"He found the trail of the persons staying there and found some stuff—I'm not sure exactly what—but it made him suspicious and he brought it to his superiors, who told him it was nothing. He and Mama had gone to check it out the night they died."

She hadn't realized how much she'd been holding on to until the words spilled out of her. It had been such a long time since she'd allowed herself to think of them and even longer since she'd spoken of that night.

"So...you think the cartel killed them?" he asked.

She heard the questions in his voice. She had no proof, and even to her own ears it sounded like a string of circumstantial incidents. But she wasn't going to back down from her beliefs. "Yes."

"You think Aaron was involved?" he asked.

She hadn't even considered that. "They died ten years ago."

"Just about the time that Aaron and I lost touch. But I'm not sure that he would have been in the cartel then."

She let out another ragged breath. "I really don't think he's responsible. I just hoped maybe he could get some information for me."

Which sounded impossible to her. Xander seemed as if he wasn't sure what to say and she got that. "Yeah. So that's why I came to Key Largo this afternoon. I don't know what info Aaron has on the cartel or if it's all bullshit to keep himself out of prison, but I thought maybe there's something that will lead to some answers for my parents' deaths. Maybe something to connect the cartel to the deaths of other sheriffs. I'm not really sure what I want to find."

She'd never been sure if the cops had shut down her and Gator's concerns because they knew her dad's death had been the key to something bigger and more dangerous. In her heart she knew her parents would never have been involved in anything shady. But he could have been a target for trying to stop it.

"You want answers," he said.

"I do."

"I get that. I'm not sure what Aaron knows but I can ask my boss to look into it."

She appreciated him saying that and figured he was just being nice until she looked up and their eyes met. He was sincere. His blue gaze held hers. He put his hand on her shoulder and she knew he had her back. It had been a long time since she'd talked about this and even longer since she'd thought someone would be at her side. "Okay."

"So I guess even if I'd shown up we might still have met," he said.

"Probably. Would you have seen the threat before they shot at us?"

He shrugged. "Who knows? I mean I saw you enter and I was watching the house and didn't notice them."

"Should you have?"

"Maybe. I think I was in my head. Aaron and I have a lot of history. I mostly hate being told what to do. I didn't want to be ordered to come to Miami."

"I'd be pissed if my boss forced me to do anything," she said. But Helen wouldn't have had to force Obie to go if Gator called. In fact if Obie as much as heard a rumor about her brother she would follow it. "But I would drop everything if Gator reached out. Family is blood, and you don't go against blood."

Obie would do whatever she could to help her family. There was a well of caring inside of her that was obvious. She'd handled everything the day had thrown at her but her emotions were clearly deep given the way she talked about them.

Part of Xander wanted to open up to her. He wasn't that guy. Never had been. That was his secret shame. He just couldn't feel the things that others did. Instead of feeling empathy when someone was devastated, he got angry and enraged. Not helpful, as his mom had pointed more than once.

At Price Security there were protocols in place that made it so he didn't fail. There were always backups. Right now he'd give his right arm to have his best friend, Kenji Wada, by his side. Kenji saw things that Xander didn't but he was also very good with people. He could do the small-talk stuff that Xander didn't want to.

But Kenji wasn't here.

Xander had never felt more like he was failing than he did at this moment. Meanwhile Obie watched him in that quiet way of hers. What was she trying to find in him?

Probably some reassurance that he'd keep her alive. She'd been shot at and forced to go deeper into the swamp and it was clear she wasn't prepared for this. She'd brought up the cartel. He really didn't know anything about them but sent the information to Lee so she could pull up everything the internet and dark web had on them.

"I know you would do anything for your family," he said at last. "But I'm not that guy."

"Why not?" she asked.

He started to shrug but she just sort of rolled her eyes. "Don't lie. It's okay to just not answer."

As empathetic as she was, it didn't translate to her being a pushover. She'd probably shared more than she'd meant to about her parents' deaths and now she wanted to even things up. At least, that was his guess.

"I didn't make you tell me about your parents," he pointed out.

"Did I say you had? Listen, we are stuck in the swamp for the rest of the day at the very least and someone is after the both of us. I probably shouldn't have overshared and the conversation sort of naturally went to your relationship with Aaron. I didn't ask any deep, probing questions. You're the one throwing up barriers and acting defensive. I don't know you or Aaron well enough to be judgy about your relationship. That's all coming from you."

He rocked back on his heels. He felt so seen right now. He didn't at all blame her for what she'd said. "Truce."

"Sorry, I just am not someone who is going to be all like sorry you are getting into your feelings. That's not who I am."

Steel ran through her. Why he was surprised was beyond him. He'd seen flashes of it at the house and then in the boat and when she'd been so cool with the croc. Some of the people he'd worked with in dangerous situations would have lost it when confronted with a predatory animal. No amount of training could make someone immune to fear.

"How'd you know how to deal with the croc?"

"I like animals. In another life I might have been a marine biologist. I still like them so I spend a lot of time reading books on the ecosystem of the different swamps and have been studying the Everglades and surrounding areas for the last few years. There are a lot of dangers in the swamp."

"Do you miss living in the swamp?" he asked. He was piecing together the woman before him. She had been so polished and very much like all the women he'd seen in Key Largo and before that in Miami when he'd flown in. She had looked urbane and sophisticated. Now sweat had dissolved her makeup, leaving her skin fresh and tanned looking. Her hair had lost that board straightness, curling and escaping the ponytail holder she'd caught it up in.

She seemed at home here. Learning about her up-bringing in the swamp helped it make sense. But why had she left and changed so much? And having done so, why was she still keeping her knowledge of the swamp? Plus if she was talking then she wasn't asking him uncomfortable questions.

"I didn't think so," she said. "Should we get going?"

"Yes. When we get to Cuthbert Lake I'll inflate the pack-raft. I think it will be easy to cross and quicker than walking all the way around it," he said.

"You have a pack-raft?"

"Yeah. I mean it's Aaron so I sort of prepared for everything," he said.

"What's everything?"

"Land, water and air escape," he said.

"Air?" she asked, eyeing his huge backpack with its 120-liter-capacity tag on full display. "Really?"

"I'd call Van for a chopper if needed."

"And we don't need one now?"

"It's for emergency use only. It's expensive and in-volves a lot of paperwork," he said.

"So are you some sort of British Boy Scout? Do the Brits even have Boy Scouts?" she asked.

"Yeah. But I wasn't one. I simply do better when I have a plan for every outcome," he said. Some things he knew couldn't be anticipated. His brother's acci-dent, for one thing. Aaron sending his hot coffee shop boss into a dangerous situation for another.

Reacting to her like he was.

He still wanted her. And no matter what he did to distract himself, she reeled him back in.

It made his skin feel too hot and his concentration harder to hold. But it was the truth. He was pretty damned sure that was a truth she wasn't looking to hear from him.

But he couldn't deny it or ignore it any longer.

Ah, hell.

He didn't want to tell her the truth about himself because he didn't want to disappoint her. And women never really reacted well to a guy saying hey, I don't do feelings but let's hook up. Or at least not a woman like Obie, with her big brown eyes full of unspoken feelings, staring right into his core.

Chapter 6

The mangroves they'd ditched the boat near gave way to a saltwater swamp that would lead them to the Everglades, about a couple of days' walk to the northwest. The swamp was different from the one she'd grown up in but she'd come to love these southern swamp areas. The mud flats and sand were thinly covered by seawater during high tide, but because the tide was out, it was just wet as they walked across it.

Most of the plants that thrived in the area were able to tolerate tidal flooding, such as their saviors the mangrove trees, which grew and formed thickets of roots and branches. Their thin, tall roots anchored them to the sand. Providing the perfect cover for Obie and Xander as they moved farther away from Madeira Bay.

She smiled as she noticed some crabs and other shellfish feeding on the fallen leaves and other materials from the decaying roots of the mangroves. She loved seeing this side of nature. And though she limited herself to visits to the Miami Seaquariam these days, she missed being in the water and the swamp, the feeling of being at home.

Birds flew overhead circling and looking for their

lunch, making Obie aware that she hadn't put any snacks in her purse before heading out to Aaron's house. She hadn't been prepared for any of this. Which was probably a good thing. Who wanted to be prepared to be attacked by a vengeful drug cartel, right?

"I had no idea the swamp would be so…alive," Xander said.

"Marine biologists call this area the nursery of the ocean because so many species thrive here and come here to spawn. Fish who lay their eggs in the salt marshes ensure their young have plenty of food and some protection in the swamp grass as they grow," she said. She'd spent a lot of time reading up on the swamp. As much as Aunt Karen wanted her to forget, a part of her had never been able to.

"I can see why. In my head I was thinking of the bayou in Louisiana when I thought of the swamp. But this area isn't what I was expecting," he admitted.

"Florida usually isn't," she said. "I mean my Florida. Not the theme parks or condos on the beaches but the quiet, natural Florida."

"You live in the swamp?"

She shook her head. She didn't want to get into the messier parts of her past. But being here again, feeling her hair adapt to the humidity and the heat wrapping around her in a comforting way reminded her of being with her parents before they'd died.

They moved farther inland, and while the ground wasn't as wet it also wasn't totally dry. The swamp was a dense ecosystem that sort of worked as a filter between the sea and the land. And the land in Florida was very porous. She wanted to take a moment to dig her feet into the sand like she had as a girl. But she knew her swamp reunion wasn't really a happy one.

They had a lead on the men following them, but eventually their pursuers would find their discarded boat and be on their trail again.

"Which direction should we go?"

"We need to get to Cuthbert Lake," he said. "I have the coordinates in the map on my satellite phone so I can check it in a few minutes but if we stick to heading west, northwest for now we should be good."

She trusted him. She had no choice. Her phone had Google Maps but wasn't really getting much of a signal out here. Plus, when she mentally listed her skills, the ones she had didn't come close to his. He'd literally shot a man who was trying to kill her.

Obie focused, watching the swamp creatures and birds flying overhead, trying as much as she could to pretend this was a normal day. But the swamp had ceased being normal to her a long time ago. The time away created a much needed distance, but also some uncertainty if she could survive there again. Being chased by gun-toting thugs wasn't helping either. "Tell me about your team."

"What do you want to know?" he asked.

She glanced back over her shoulder at him. "Well, is it a big team? You mentioned Lee and Van."

"There are six of us. Van's the leader. He put the team together and once he recruits you to work for him... Well, he says we're family and I guess we are. We all live in a condo tower in LA that Price owns when we aren't out on assignment."

That sounded…interesting. Was that the right word? It was unconventional to say the least. "Why?"

He rubbed the back of his neck and looked down at his watch. She glanced over at it and saw a compass on it, but she was pretty sure he'd done that to distract himself rather than check for their direction.

"Not sure. We all work a lot so the apartments are a nice perk. It doesn't make sense to own a home when I'm on the road most of the time."

"Sounds like my place. It's not really home but just more a place to crash."

"Why is that?"

Now it was her turn to look for a distraction. "Just is. So the rest of the team?"

"Not letting that go, are you?"

"It's a long walk to Cuthbert Lake, figured we might as well chat more," she said.

"Fair enough. You can tell me about your coworkers at the coffee shop, deal?"

"Deal," she said.

Her coworkers were fun and funky and made the job she took after college seem like it wasn't really her giving up on her dreams. But she knew in her heart she'd gotten her degree in hospitality management to please Aunt Karen. A part of her still regretted not following her own path and going into marine biology.

At the time she'd thought the only life for her had been the one that she could copy from the other people around her. She'd been afraid to let herself continue to be a part of the world she'd left behind, even if it caused problems. To her there had only been the new life in Miami or her old life as a swamp girl, no in between.

Aaron had unintentionally given her a new perspective with this adventure.

Maybe she could have both.

His team. He missed them. If Kenji were here he'd be miserable in the heat but probably wouldn't show it, sticking to his slim-fitting black suits and dark glasses. His Japanese American friend wore his glossy black hair long in the front with a huge fall of bangs and short in the back. Kenji was lethal with any weapon, but then all of the team were. It was the trust they'd developed as friends that made them such good partners in missions like these.

"I'm probably closest to Kenji. He's damned smart and lethal. We spar a lot. Then there's Rick. He used to be a DEA agent and frankly would probably be better in this terrain than I am. He's really good at blending in and finding paths out of any situations. Then there's Luna. She looks kind of unassuming, but she's fast and smart and puts things together faster than the rest of us. Lee is sort of tactical and stays in the tower— that's the offices and apartment building. She keeps us all connected to each other, she's going in the field more often now. Her skills are legendary. She used to be with a secret government agency. So she tends to give very little away."

Obie stopped walking, turning her face up to the

sun and watching a seagull flying overhead. "I like the sound of your team and that you listed their skills."

He glanced at her. Was she teasing him?

He was pretty sure she was. But he still wasn't used to it, being treated like he's not too scary to joke with. He'd been this big and bulky since birth. His mother told him to smile and people would think he was friendly, but based on his last attempt with Obie it clearly wasn't so easy.

Somehow his early-childhood memories, the positive ones, had been obscured by that one horrific teenage incident. Sixteen had changed him and made him into the mess he'd been when Van found him. He had read enough psychology books to know that he'd grown past that experience and he'd made peace with his part in the accident. Something that had been a long time coming.

But he hadn't been able to forgive Aaron for his part. Was he holding on to that lack of forgiveness because he knew that it had been chance that Aaron knocked their brother Tony to the ground where he'd hit his neck on a rock and taken the spinal cord injury that had paralyzed him? Xander could easily have done the same thing to their other brother, Abe, or even Aaron. It could have been *any* of them, but it had been Aaron and Tony, all because Tony asked a girl out that Aaron liked.

So juvenile. And the impact of that day changed them all forever.

"You okay?"

"What?"

"You look scary and angry."

He shook his head and closed his eyes. Of course he did. Thinking about the past always brought him back to the man he used to be. "Sorry."

"Was it the teasing?" she asked. "I was just trying to make things feel a bit more…normal."

"I liked it," he said. "Keep doing that."

"Do you work with your team often? You mentioned you were closest to Kenji."

He remembered the first time they'd met. Neither of them was keen on being on a team. Kenji was so polished and Xander had sort of hulked into the room in sweats and a plain T-shirt. On the outside they were complete opposites, but when they hit the mat to spar it was clear they were two sides of the same coin.

Over the years they'd grown closer and Xander had learned a lot from Kenji through playing games, sparring and observing his way with others.

"We don't always work together but there are times when the entire team is needed for a job. We all have a different skill set."

"Do you prefer working on your own or with the team?" she asked as they continued walking toward the lake.

"Both," he said. "It's nice to be a part of a group on assignment but I can't do it all the time."

She nodded her head. "Same. I like when my entire crew is in the coffee shop during the rush and we are all doing our part but then I need some alone time and usually escape to my office and close the door."

"You seem pretty outgoing so I wouldn't have thought that."

"I can be. I mean I do like being around people most of the time. But after the rush we all need a break. Aaron was good about making everyone laugh. He seemed like such a nice guy...not saying he isn't but learning he was dealing was a shock."

What had led his brother into the drug cartel? Being booted from the SAS changed him, and it changed Aaron as well. His brother had been in the wind for longer than anyone in the family liked to acknowledge. Part of the reason why he'd been reluctant to come and see Aaron. Their mom had tried several times to reach Aaron but she never got in touch.

Perhaps what he was doing for a living had kept him away. Xander wanted to believe that was the case. That his brother had been trying to protect them all. But there was another part of him that wasn't entirely sure.

Maybe Aaron completely separated himself from the family because he no longer felt anything for them.

Xander wasn't going to get any answers until they were out of the swamp and he had a chance to talk to Aaron. He was definitely going to discover the truth—not just for their family, but also for Obie, who Aaron shouldn't have used.

The things she liked about the swamp were coming back to her, but she didn't necessarily love all of it. She'd learned to live under Aunt Karen's roof and found things to appreciate there. The swamp girl she'd been had no real place in the life that Obie had carved for herself.

Working with other people and enjoying being around them was all a product of her life with Aunt Karen. She'd been encouraged to socialize. Aunt Karen even signed Obie up for all sorts of clubs in high school and they had helped to transform her.

Aunt Karen had done the same thing for Gator but her brother just hadn't settled into it. He didn't want to be on the baseball team or in the math club, even though he was really good at both. He'd just wanted to be back in the swamp. Back home, he'd said.

But home for Obie had been tainted by their parents' deaths and the questions around it. Home was a distant memory and not a place. It had become something inside of herself. And if Gator had been able to stay with her at Aunt Karen's she might have been happier in her new life.

After Gator had left, she'd had a fight with Aunt Karen and it had taken Obie about a day to regret not going with him. So she'd swiped Aunt Karen's debit card and gotten enough cash for a bus ticket back to Winter Haven.

Dumb.

So she skipped school the next day and went to the bus station, which had scared her. She'd only ever been in her small town near the swamp or in the suburbs with Aunt Karen. The bus station had been in the city and it had been frightening.

She'd almost turned back but she knew if she had even the smallest chance of catching up to Gator she'd have to get to Winter Haven and then get a ride out to their home between Lake Alfred and Haines City and then get in the swamp and search.

The bus ride had been long and she'd deliberately turned her cell phone off so she wouldn't have to lie if Aunt Karen called. She'd pretended to read a book on the bus so that the person sitting next to her wouldn't talk to her. She'd had her iPod and her headphones in the entire time listening to Green Day because they'd been her mom's favorite band and trying not to cry.

She'd hated that feeling and never wanted to experience anything like it again. When she got off the bus in Winter Haven she had been shocked to see Aunt Karen waiting. The older woman was pale and her hands were shaking.

She gave Obie a lecture but then told her to get into the car and they'd drive out to her parents' old place. At the time Obie had been pissed that one of her cousins might have ratted her out, but now she appreciated that Aunt Karen had been worried about her and the fact that she'd taken her to the house had meant a lot.

Gator hadn't been there. In fact, no one had been at the place in months. Aunt Karen had been trying to sell it so Obie and Gator would have the money to pay for college. Eventually the house did sell and Aunt Karen gave Obie the leftover money after paying for her community college courses.

She shook her head. Why was she thinking about the past? Why was the swamp showing her not the perfection of her childhood but a greater understanding of what brought her here as an adult? Maybe the truth of her life was somewhere between the swamp girl she was deep inside and the sleek urbanite that her aunt had helped her become.

As much as she felt she was forced to change, another part of her knew she had wanted to. At least a little.

She saw a snake slithering toward them, jerking her away from her thoughts, and she put her hand on Xander's arm to stop him. They watched the colorful snake until it slithered past them.

"I can never tell the king snake from the coral snake," Xander said.

"That was a king snake," she said. "They are bigger than the coral and of course not poisonous. The color pattern is so similar. I had to wait until it was closer. The king snake's red and black bands touch each other. Coral always touches yellow."

"I think I'll just keep trying to avoid them both."

"Good idea," she said. "I'm pretty much that way with everything in the swamp. Most creatures are dangerous if pushed but if you let them be you're okay."

"Aren't we all?" he asked.

She thought he might be teasing her now. "Some of us more so than others. Why do you think those men tried to kill us?"

"It's easier than taking you hostage and killing you later. They can just search the bodies, find the information they are looking for and dump the bodies. Now that they aren't sure if we've read the SD card and/or contacted anyone, they will probably try to take us alive."

Great. "Do you think they'll stop if we get rid of the card?"

"No."

She stopped walking and put her hands on her hips as she shook her head at him. "You could at least pretend to think about it. Give me a little bit of hope that I can stop them from following me by doing something."

"Yeah, I'm not like that. The truth is until that information is used in some way they aren't going to stop coming after you. I know that's not easy to hear but that's the truth."

She had suspected that was the situation they were in. "And you think your team and Crispin can help?"

He didn't answer, which wasn't reassuring. As much as she'd have wished for some platitudes, his silence told her what she needed to know. He wasn't sure if anyone could help them. Which meant they had to escape with their lives on their own. And even if she got out this time, the next…

She dropped her arms and turned to start walking again but he stopped her with his hand on her shoulder.

"I'm not leaving your side until you're safe. That's my promise to you," he said.

Gratitude washed over her. He was a stranger still, despite what they'd been through together. But she knew that he'd keep her safe. That was one thing she was sure of in this day where nothing seemed right anymore.

The moment Aaron had been arrested, normality had gone out the window. Her life was swirling around her and she felt like that scared sixteen-year-old again.

But this wasn't the start of something else. This was some weird in-between thing that, at this moment, Obie couldn't see a way out of. She wanted to tell him that she appreciated having him by her side but he was the reason she was here. If he'd come to Miami when she'd first called, maybe she wouldn't have had to go to Key Largo.

But then she wouldn't have known that Aaron was connected to La Familia Sanchez cartel. She wouldn't have this chance to maybe find out what had actually happened to her parents and if the cartel had been involved. That chance at closure was too tempting to keep her away from Xander. She needed to see where his investigation led.

It wasn't exactly a fair trade-off. Her safety for answers about her parents. Answers she wasn't sure she'd ever really get.

"You okay?" he asked.

"No. I'm not okay. There is a part of me that feels like this is going to go on forever and I'm not getting out of the swamp or out of survival mode. And I left that behind a long time ago. I don't want to be back in that situation."

"We will get out of this. In fact when we get to the marina at West Lake I'll have my team take you to a safe house. I can set a trap for the cartel and get to the bottom of Aaron's involvement with them."

"Flush them out? How?"

"I'll set a trap," he said.

"I'd like to help with that."

"Uh, no way. You're a civilian and you need to stay safe," he said.

She hated it when someone told her what to do. She knew she wasn't trained like he was. He had a point, but if he was staying in the Everglades then he needed her expertise. "Would you set a trap in the swamp?"

"Yes," he said.

"Then you need me. I'm your best chance at catching them and not getting killed or injured in the process."

"I need you?"

"Yes."

Chapter 7

"Someone's coming," Xander said, drawing Obie off the rough path toward the surrounding marshier area. Lush vegetation and brackish water deepened as they moved toward the large cypress trees with their knobbly roots.

Not exactly an ideal place to hide.

Obie grabbed his wrist and pointed toward the mangroves, which were thicker and lower to the ground, providing more coverage.

He nudged her to go first and then followed her as she sank back into the water as it deepened and found a way to get under the branches of the mangrove tree, using their tangled roots as shelter.

His pack was large and didn't enable him the maneuvering that Obie had done. She mimed taking his pack off and held her hand out to him. He handed it to her and she pulled the waterproof hiking sack toward her, shoving it under the water and dragging it into the shelter she'd found. He ducked into it just as the first person came into their view.

Two men wearing Army green utility pants and matching T-shirts appeared. They had on dark sunglasses and from their build Xander guessed they had to be security of some kind.

He noticed that they had on shoulder holsters and both men had earpieces in. They looked like military and he waited to see what they were going to do next. Had Van sent the military to find them? Seemed unlikely since Van knew that Xander would get the two of them to safety, and more players could sabotage their mission.

One of them put his hand to his ear and then spoke in Spanish, which Xander didn't speak so he couldn't understand.

He glanced at Obie, who shrugged, which he took to mean she didn't understand them either.

They spoke quickly but he heard the words "gringos" and "Quentin."

Making a logical assumption, he was pretty sure they were working with the cartel. But these guys were in a different league than the men he and Obie had encountered at the house in Key Largo. These guys were trained to track them down through difficult terrain. Only someone with knowledge of this area would be able to keep finding them so quickly. If he ruled out military they'd have to be mercenaries. And so far he'd seen no indication that there were any government agencies involved in this.

Which begged the question what the hell was on that SD card of Aaron's that had the cartel sending guys like this after them?

He knew he was going to have to get the card from Obie at some point and read it.

As they moved closer, Xander leaned toward Obie

and whispered in her ear, "Try to form a good impression of the men so we can give their description to the authorities."

She nodded; her face was very serious as she turned back to look at them. They stayed still and Xander concentrated on the men, and not the snake they'd seen a few minutes earlier, or the crocodiles in these waters. Right now the threat from humans was the only one he could focus on.

The men were both tall, but the left one was slightly taller. Both had identical tattoos on their arms.

Maybe a cartel symbol?

He took particular attention to those details, which he'd relay to Van and the team for further research.

The person closest to them seemed uneasy and kept watching the path in front of them more than looking in the vegetation. But the other one was carefully skimming each of the bushes and roots of the trees. Xander pulled his knife from his belt—his gun was in the sack and useless once it got wet. He was confident he could take both men by hand if he needed to.

As they got closer, he took a deep breath and coiled his body so that he was ready to attack. Obie touched his shoulder and he ignored her. He was in fight-and-protect mode. Whatever she had to say could wait.

She squeezed; he tilted his head toward her so she could speak into his ear but didn't take his eyes from the men, who had stopped walking.

She leaned in, but then didn't speak, as the men were now looking toward their hiding place.

He hand tightened again, but he heard her hold her

breath and knew it was fear and not trying to communicate with him that had caused the squeeze. Something moved out of the water in front of them. A small American crocodile, probably about four feet long. Perhaps their friend from earlier. The men froze and the crocodile ambled past them into the marshy area and then into the water near the mangroves on the other side of the path.

Both of the men waited until it was gone and then started walking farther down the path. Once they were out of sight Obie let go of his shoulder. "I was going to warn you about the croc."

"Thanks. The men were the bigger threat," he said, pushing his knife back into the sheath. "Do you think we're safe here for a few more minutes?"

"I don't know. The croc sort of swam up while we were waiting. The swamp is a living ecosystem."

"I know that. I just want to let them put more space between us," he said.

"Do you think they know where we're heading?"

He had no real idea. It was concerning that their stalkers came from the direction of the marina they were trying to get to. But it was a day or so hike from here, and there were two lakes they had to cross before they got to it.

"We'll stick to the mangrove swamp until we can't," he said. "I'm going to have to rely on you to watch the swamp and I'll watch the path."

"I can do that. Do you want your gun?"

"Yes. But I have to keep it dry," he said. "Right now it's better in the sack. I can handle a few guys with just a knife."

"I'm glad to hear that," she said, but there was a ragged note to her voice.

He wasn't sure how much more she could take before she reached her breaking point.

Obie searched for the calmness she'd once had in the swamp, but it had been a long time since she'd had rely on her skills for survival, and back then it had been just a game between her and Gator. Other than that one scary bus ride and a few times she'd walked alone to her car in a dimly lit parking lot, she hadn't really had to rely on her own skills. She also wasn't a fan of staying in the low water while the tide was out, but then when it started to come in she didn't prefer the rising water encroaching on her either.

She focused on it though. She didn't want to let her mind wander to the two scary guys who'd been looking for her and Xander. She begrudgingly reminded herself that Aunt Karen might have been right when she'd encouraged Obie to take Spanish in high school and college. Not that those lessons had been helpful at all when listening to the two men talking. She hadn't really understood anything.

They'd looked scary, and that had been about where her mind had settled. Her heart raced, and then she'd felt the current in the water stir around her and saw the croc. She'd almost let herself panic before recognizing that panicking was going to get her killed either by man or beast.

Xander was a calming presence at least. He was just so *big*, and there was something reassuring in that. She remembered the way he'd looked when he'd tackled her to the floor at Aaron's house, and every moment after that when he'd kept her alive. A stranger, but one that she was coming to rely on.

She knew her limits and what she was capable of. But Xander had skills that she'd never considered acquiring, and maybe it was time to sign up for kickboxing or some martial arts class at the strip mall where her coffee shop was.

Though a part of her thought that might have the same real-world applications as the Spanish she'd taken in college. Which wasn't reassuring considering how little she had understood from the cartel members.

Her mind was starting to wind into a place where anxiety would take control. She had to find something else to think about. Really she wanted to keep talking. Just open her mouth and let all the wild thoughts and fears in her head out. But talking would give them away.

She also didn't know if those two guys were the only ones looking for them.

Xander was close behind her. He'd taken his pack and put it back on, and he wore his sunglasses again as the sun was bright. The water reflected the rays back into their faces.

She was *hot*, and even though she tanned easily, she could feel her shoulders getting sunburned. She wished she'd put on the linen button-down she'd left in her car before running in to check out Aaron's place. But she hadn't. Hadn't known where all of this would go. She was stuck with what she was wearing.

Again her anxiety started to tug at her. She closed her eyes and stopped walking. Just took some deep breaths and did box breathing to calm herself. Xander stopped.

"What is it?"

"Just need to catch my breath," she said.

He put his hand on her shoulder, his thumb rubbing against the side of her neck in a very comforting and reassuring pattern. Her breathing settled and his touch teased her. Her mind thought about him standing behind her. If she closed her eyes she could almost—almost!—pretend he was a guy she'd met in a sweaty club and maybe they were pressed together waiting for drinks.

Except the tide was rising around her feet, almost up to her calves, and a crab scuttled over her foot.

Yeah, this wasn't the distraction she wanted it to be.

"Thanks," she said.

"Want me to go first?" he asked. "Are you worried about what's ahead of us?"

She felt some laughter welling up inside of her and swallowed it because she recognized it as more of the same panic she was trying to manage. "I'm just scared."

"You'd be foolish if you weren't. That's perfectly normal."

"Are you scared?"

"I'm cautious," he said. "I don't know the terrain so that worries me, but those men back there don't bother me at all. I've fought men like them all of my adult life. So if they worry you, you can relax on that front."

She shook her head. "Everything is bothering me. I

can't shut my mind off and I know I need to stay quiet but here I am talking to you."

"I'm glad you are talking to me. What's one thing that you are concerned about?"

"If there are more men looking for us," she said.

"I'm sure they are moving in a grid pattern and the two we saw are the only ones in this area right now. We might move into the next part of the grid they are searching and encounter different people."

"What will we do?"

"What we did last time, and if they spot us I will take them down," he said.

There was so much confidence in him. This entire thing was outside of her comfort zone, but he was settled into it. More at ease here in the swamp with men chasing them than he had been in the boat as they'd crossed Madeira Bay.

This was what he did; he'd said that to her. But her mind hadn't been able to comprehend what being a bodyguard meant until this moment. He was in his element putting himself in danger and keeping her safe.

She appreciated it more than she thought she would. Knowing that he was with her was all the reassurance she needed. He'd asked her to keep an eye out for swamp dangers and she couldn't let him down. Wouldn't let him down.

After an hour they hadn't seen anyone else on the trail. It seemed they were alone for now. Which suited him. The tide had been steadily rising and was up to his thighs, almost to Obie's waist. "Let's move back on higher ground."

It had been a long time since he'd had to survive in the outdoors. He forgot how much he hated wet socks and shoes. As soon as they were on the trail he wanted to ditch them, but the path looked rough, and Obie was walking it in a pair of flip-flops. He wasn't sure he wanted to chance it.

Her legs looked long and lean under the hem of her shorts and she took a moment to wipe her hands down them. "I always feel so odd when I'm half-soaking-wet."

"Does it happen that often?"

"No, thank goodness. But I was tossed into my friend's pool on Memorial Day weekend and managed to only get the bottom half of my body wet."

It was odd to hear about her life outside of Aaron and the coffee shop. He didn't have a complete picture of her despite her talkative nature, and maybe that hadn't mattered when they were initially staying still around snakes and other swamp creatures.

But now it did.

They were relying on each other to survive, and neither could do it without the other, but there was more to it than that. He liked her. He could no longer deny that fact. He wanted to know her better. For the first time he felt comfortable opening up to someone and he was already wondering if he'd be able to see her after this was over.

"The last time I experienced anything close to this was SAS training. We were on a three-day survival hike on Snowdon in Wales. Hated it then, not really loving it now."

She smiled and it went straight to his groin. She was pretty when she relaxed and wasn't worrying. Not that she wasn't pretty at the other times, but a stressed-out woman needed comforting, not lust.

"So a survival hike... You signed up for that, right?" she asked. "Sort of seems like you might have been to blame for your experience."

"Too right. Aaron signed up first and so then I had to because I wanted to prove I could do anything he could."

"Are you older or younger?"

"Younger by eighteen months."

"That explains it. And you both made it to the end?"

"We sure did. I got there first but only by a few minutes," Xander said. That boy-man he'd been seemed like a different person to who he was today. Back then, winning and proving he was the faster and strongest had been the most important thing. He hoped he'd changed.

But honestly, he wasn't sure.

His line of work was different. There was no competing in bodyguarding. His objective was keeping his client safe and alive. So he had a lot of wins in that case. But there were also days when he needed to win in a real situation, not just keeping a client safe. That's when he and Kenji sparred hard. Kenji liked to win as well.

"Were you close growing up or was it always a rivalry?" she asked in that innocent way that people did when they learned he had a sibling so close in age.

His childhood was two parts, before and after the tragedy. But the young years... "Yeah, we were close with Abe and Tony as well. But we were always fighting to be the alpha. Abe is four years older than me and then Tony is three. They always had the jump on us because of that, but that just made me hungrier to one-up him."

"Did you ever succeed?"

Yeah. But he didn't like to remember that moment. Or what came after. "Not really. I figured out that type of winning isn't satisfying. Now that we are out of the water I want to try to sync the map again and make sure we are still on course."

"Okay."

He pulled his phone out and saw they'd drifted a little bit east on the last part of the trek. So he made an adjustment to the direction they were heading. "Did you see that tattoo on their arms?"

"There were a lot of them," she said. "I could only see the one closest to us."

Xander opened the drawing app on his phone and used his finger to make a rough sketch of the tattoo he was talking about. It was a snake wearing a three-pointed crown.

"I've seen that before."

She was pale and her hand had gone to her mouth. "Where?"

"On Aaron," she said. "Do you think he told those men to come and find us?"

From jail and the holding cell he was in, Aaron wouldn't be able to do that. All of the doubts he'd been trying to create, to tell himself his brother wasn't in the cartel, were gone. "I'm not sure. I don't believe Aaron would send you into a trap. Okay, so that tattoo might be for the cartel. I'm going to send it to my team so they can research it. Do you remember any other details?"

"Well the one on Aaron is on his left forearm and it has the letters in a Latin script under it. The letters are *LFS*."

La Familia Sanchez. That made sense. This connection was confirming that his brother had taken a dark path after they'd both left England.

He was the younger brother but he had always been the one to look out for Aaron, who was smaller than him. Was this his fault? Everything since Tony's accident had taken them on a path that Xander wouldn't have believed possible when they'd been boys. Whatever information they found on that SD card was probably going to show him a picture of his brother that he didn't want to know.

One question remained in Xander's mind right now. Was his brother so much a cartel man that he would send an innocent woman to her death to retrieve information for him? Because there was no way Aaron hadn't known the task he'd given Obie was dangerous. That was why he'd called Xander first.

Chapter 8

Her phone pinged as Xander was inflating the pack-raft. She pulled it from the drybag. A message from Crispin Tallman, the assistant district attorney. She unlocked her phone and started to call him back.

Xander still wanted to wait for his team before they called the cops. She knew he was right that they needed someone to facilitate turning themselves in, but at the same time, not calling the cops seemed wrong. Maybe the DA could help.

Xander said they were persons of interest in the shoot-out at Aaron's, which of course she knew they'd been involved in. In her entire life she'd never broken the law or committed a crime. She was a stickler about those things.

"What are you doing?" Xander asked.

"I'm fixing to call the district attorney. He left a message for me," Obie said.

Xander walked over to her and she was struck again by what a big man he was. She stood there for a moment, the phone in her hand. "Let's hear the message."

"Sure," she said.

She dialed her voice mail and put it on speaker.

"Ms. Keller, I heard there was some trouble at Aaron's house. Are you okay? The cops said there was gunfire. Call me and let me know you are okay, please."

She smiled. "I think he can help us with the cops. I'll call him and let him know what happened."

Xander crossed his arms over his chest. "How well do you know the assistant district attorney?"

"Just met him today before going to the house on Key Largo. Why?"

"Just trying to get as much intel as we can. Okay, call him but keep it on speaker."

"Why?"

"Only my brother and this guy knew you were going to Key Largo," he pointed out. "Aaron's in jail and asked you to get the SD card, so only one other person knew you were going to be there."

"The man who is trying to cut a deal with your brother and to get some hard evidence against the cartel," she said. "He's on our side."

"He might be. My job is to keep you alive and I don't know him."

"Are you always this…?"

"Thorough? Yes."

"I was going to say paranoid," she said smartly. Her dad had been a cop, and as a result Obie always trusted law enforcement and government officials. That didn't mean they were always right—after all, she still wasn't sure Officer Wade had acted in their best interests, but it was hard for her to believe that Crispin would have set her up. He'd seemed to want the information that

Aaron had for himself. Obie was one sure way of him getting it, wasn't she?

"Call it whatever you want. Until I talk to him I won't know."

"He said his men had already searched the house and found nothing," she pointed out. "He was skeptical I'd find anything."

"But still encouraged you to go," he said.

"Stop that." But his words made a certain sense. She just couldn't imagine someone from the district attorney's office would have been involved in that incident at the house. "I trust him."

"Then let's call him," Xander said. "I'm new to the situation. All I had before I landed was your name and Aaron's. We have no idea who the men were who shot at us. They could have been waiting for an associate of Aaron's to show up and you triggered them when you did."

"Associate? Does that mean they think I work for him?"

He shrugged. "Who knows. More likely they think you're his girlfriend."

Obie felt her anxiety flaring up and she wanted to just throw the phone and the SD card in the water and turn and walk deeper into the swamp, until she was completely cut off from everyone and everything. She was tired of this.

She wanted to go back to her old life. As much as she'd felt like she was playing a part working in the coffee shop and going back to her apartment every night, at least she knew what to expect. Not like this. Where everything felt out of control.

Xander put his hand on her shoulder and squeezed. "Sorry. I shouldn't have been grilling you. It's my job to keep you safe and to do that I act like everyone else is a threat. Doesn't mean they are."

"Why is it your job?"

"Because I didn't call you back," he said. "If I had maybe you wouldn't have come to Key Largo."

Maybe.

She licked her lips, which felt like they were getting sunburned, and then hit Crispin's number. The phone rang three times before going to voice mail. She looked over at Xander, who just sort of nodded at her. She took that to mean she should leave a message.

"It's Obie Keller. Wanted to let you know I'm okay. I'm with Aaron's brother and we are trying to get to a marina. Men followed us from Aaron's house."

Xander tapped her shoulder and made a cut-it-off motion.

"I'll try to call again later. Bye."

She hung up and glared at him.

"What?"

She could tell he wanted to say something else about not trusting Crispin but instead he just looked at his watch. "It's getting later and I want to get to the marina so we can get out of here."

"Me too," she admitted. As soon as she could, she was going to give the SD card to the assistant district attorney. She wanted this entire thing far behind her. Talking to Xander about her parents' deaths and say-

ing out loud the things her sixteen-year-old self had believed made her realize that she would probably never
find the answers she wanted.

And if it meant not getting shot at she'd be okay
with that.

"Hey, would you humor me and do something?"
Xander asked.

"What?"

"Take the SIM card out of your phone. I know you
trust the man you called but your phone can be traced.
Someone might have a tap on his phone," Xander said.
"Until we know that the cartel didn't follow you there
I think it would be the safest option."

She didn't mind doing that and handed her phone to
him. He removed the SIM card and returned both to
her. She put them back in the drybag with the SD card.

"Let's go."

Xander had to wonder if he was just getting too
paranoid or not. Obie's reaction to his suspicion of the
district attorney's office wasn't out of line. Of course
since it was Aaron who'd sent them into this mess,
Xander's objectivity was shot. Nothing had gone right
since the moment he'd seen Obie enter Aaron's house.

He pushed the pack-raft into the water and held it
steady while Obie got in. It was a two-seater, which
was a necessity with his six-five and two-hundred-
fifty-pound frame. He normally needed the extra
space. They both fit, but it was tight. She was sitting
between his spread legs, her back against his chest.

She shifted around to get the oars, her butt rubbing

against his groin, and he once again remembered that moment he'd been trying so damned hard to forget. That millisecond when he'd let his control slip and almost kissed her.

He stared down at the top of her head and then the back of her neck. A bead of sweat was there, slowly inching its way toward the fabric of her tank top, and he inwardly groaned. Then realized he'd made the noise out loud when she turned to look over her shoulder.

"Sorry if you're cramped. Let me try to shift forward and give you more room."

She put her hand on his thigh, lifting herself up, and her hips rubbed against him. He started to harden and put his hands on her waist. "You're fine. Just stay still."

His voice was gruff and harsh to his own ears. But she settled back against him...and he noticed the moment she felt his erection against her back. Her posture went stiff as she realized she'd turned him on. "Sorry."

"Stop apologizing. I'm sorry I can't help my body's reaction," he said.

She just took the oar he'd given her. "Okay. Tell me when to row."

He did, and as they moved farther into the water and found a rhythm, he was able to uncover some calmness. His body got used to the feeling of her against him, and he was able to rein in the thread of sensual awareness that had slipped from his grasp. He'd never struggled to control himself before, especially when he was working, but Obie had somehow gotten under his skin.

"Can we trust your people?" she asked after about ten minutes had passed.

"Yes. Why do you ask?"

She kept rowing. "You said only Aaron and Crispin knew I'd be there, but your people knew you'd be there."

She had a point and he almost smiled at the way she was analyzing the situation. "You're right. But they sent me to help Aaron and wouldn't have sent gunmen to prevent me from leaving."

"Are you sure? You're bossy," she said with a note of teasing to it.

"I am. But they know that about me."

"Were you particularly annoying before you left?"

"Surlier but that's my MO when I'm not working," he said dryly. "We can keep that as a possibility but I'm putting Price Security at the bottom of the threat list."

Price Security wasn't just his workplace; they were a family and they were way too close for there to be a mole in the organization. But he respected Obie for not ruling anyone out. He liked the way her mind worked.

"Who's at the top?"

"I'm not sure. I'll have a better idea after we talk to Lee later but I think the cartel have someone on the inside. It's not too farfetched to think they have someone in jail who keeps them informed."

"To that point, they know Aaron was arrested and might have been watching his place."

He had thought of that possibility after she'd defended the assistant district attorney. Probably because of how he was, Xander tended to always think that anyone not at his side was against him. Time and time again that had been proved true, and as much as he didn't want Aaron to be a potential accomplice, Xander knew he couldn't rule him out. Yet. "That's probably how they found us. Sorry if I sounded—"

"As you said it's your job to keep us alive. I think everyone is a suspect until we can rule them out," she said.

"Agreed."

She rowed a bit more. "Alligator to the left."

He glanced over at the object he thought was a piece of wood and then realized it was a gator sunning itself on the top of the water. "I thought gators and crocs weren't in the same ecosystem."

She tipped her head to the side and he could see her smiling. "The Everglades is unique and has a diverse landscape. Gators stick to the fresh water. American crocodiles are mainly in coastal area and rivers. They prefer salty water and tend to congregate in brackish lakes, mangroves and the like. The American crocodile is the only species other than the saltwater crocodile to thrive in saltwater. They are always fighting for survival down here and their population is monitored because of development and the degradation of their habitat."

When she talked about Florida, there was affection in her voice. There was a beauty to her when she forgot to be whoever it was she wanted him to see and just relaxed. She seemed at home here in this wild part of Florida. She tipped her head back up toward the sun and the breeze stirred around them as she continued to row.

She was in her element here. He knew what had made her leave. But he wondered if she regretted it, and if this errand that she'd gone on to help a friend would make her want to return.

There were so many questions he wanted to ask her. But given his body's reaction to her earlier he kept silent.

He felt on edge and irritated not just at the situation but at his past and his brother. He hated that they were in a place where he had to rely on the woman he was trying to protect. He did better when he was the one in charge—and the one to blame.

Obie wasn't used to keeping people safe, not in this type of situation. She deserved him at this best, but she was getting a man who was too busy trying to keep his emotions in check.

Xander knew that was one thing he tended to fail at. Damn Aaron. Why hadn't he stayed clean and kept Obie out of this?

He needed a distraction. Not Obie talking about the swamp or her curvy hips pressed against his groin. He needed someone to come out of the dense tree coverage on the lake, armed and ready. He needed the kind of threat he could observe and then face and defeat.

Xander fascinated her. He had clearly been turned on by her but he kept a tight leash on himself. She had to be honest—there was a part of her that wanted to push him and see what it would take for him to let go. She knew he wanted her the way she desired him. He'd almost kissed her and then of course there was his surprise boner, but he wasn't doing anything sexual when they were alone.

He also kept their conversations bland. Safe. He wasn't one to give anything away, so it had been nice when she'd gotten a reaction from him when she'd called him bossy. Aunt Karen wouldn't approve of her behavior, poking a man who wanted to keep his peace. But for the first time in years that didn't matter.

The deeper they got into this wild, untamed land, the more she felt the old Obie returning. She had shut away her memories of living in the swamp because they'd been too painful. Hearing the cicadas singing in the heat of the late afternoon made her remember the feel of the hot gray sand of the swamp under her bare feet, until she dug into it with her toes and felt that cool wet layer lying just below.

Florida was complex, both savage and beautiful at her heart. The cities had clawed out their existence along the coast and paved over so much making roads and malls and restaurants on the rest. But the real Florida couldn't be tamed or kept at bay forever. The bugs and the gators and the verdant trees and bushes that grew wild and out of control were constantly fighting to reclaim the land.

As she rowed across the lake seeing snakes and gators swim past them, she accepted that the savage beauty of the swamp was starting to reclaim her as well. When she'd left the swamp she'd been lost and damaged. What child could lose their parents and not be? And the only way to survive at Aunt Karen's house was to become more like her. That was the way to a place she'd found she could enjoy some peace.

It was also a cop-out. That was probably what Gator

had been saying when he claimed that he no longer recognized her. He had been trying to tell her that she was hiding from who she truly was.

But that girl…that swamp girl who was more at home in bare feet and cutoff shorts had no place in Aunt Karen's gated subdivision or her fancy private school.

She hadn't missed that girl. That girl had been sad and scared and angry. Shedding her had been the only way that Obie had been able to survive. But after a decade she was ready to look back at her past with some maturity and maybe…figure out a way to be the woman she'd always thought she would be.

She heard the low rumble of thunder and looked up, realizing that storm clouds were gathering behind them as the wind started to pick up. They were halfway across the lake. Damn. There wasn't really a chance of them making it across before the storm got to them.

"We need to find shelter. I think we can make it to the shoreline over there," she said, pointing to the right.

Xander glanced behind them, saw the blackening sky and nodded. "Let's do it."

For the first time in a while she felt Xander's strength as he dug deeper with each stroke of the oar and propelled the boat forward faster than before. Her strokes weren't really helping anymore and she took her oar out of the water. He could move them more quickly without her.

The first fat raindrops hit them as they got close enough to land that they could step out of the pack-raft and pull it to shore. He got out and lifted her out behind him, he handed her his pack and her shoulder bag while she waded to shore, then maneuvered the pack-raft behind her.

She scanned the trees at the shoreline and moved farther into the dense swamp area. There wasn't going to be any real shelter but if she could find a tree with some large branches... Except lightning was still a threat. She stopped and waited for Xander.

"I'm not sure what's safest. Rain is a pain but can't kill us, lightning can so I don't want to be too close to a tree," she said.

"Good idea. Just move us away from the lake. Maybe some of those mangroves that are lower to the ground. I have a tarp we can use to protect ourselves if you want to stay in the middle of the path."

She looked around. It had been a long time and she had been a girl the last time she'd been outside in this kind of storm. With her daddy and Gator. They'd found shelter together on a log and Daddy had used his big rain slicker to keep them dry.

She looked around and saw a spot that would work. She pointed to it and Xander moved with her. They sat down on the log, which was lower than the trees and shrubs around them. He lifted the pack-raft up over their heads and used his pack on one side and a bush on the other keep it suspended over them.

The rain increased, falling hard on the bottom of the pack-raft. Thunder rolled and they saw cracks of lightning as the storm grew in intensity, raging around them. Xander put his arm around her as the wind increased and water blew up under their makeshift shelter.

She leaned into him, stealing a bit of his warmth as she shivered. She looked up to check on him and make sure he was okay. He was smiling as the storm raged. And then he looked down at her. His eyes met hers.

She put her hand on the side of his face and smiled back at him. There was something about being alive while this wild storm cascaded around them. She shifted and leaned up until her lips brushed his and he opened his mouth, taking the kiss that she'd been craving.

Chapter 9

The rain was heavy, drowning out all the sounds around them, and her mouth was warm on his under the intimate shelter of the pack-raft. The kind of heat that he didn't mind. For the first time since he'd seen her pull under the carport at Aaron's house, he relaxed. Her mouth was firm and she tasted so damned good.

He didn't kiss many women on the mouth, and he tried not to let this be special but it undeniably was. She had kissed him. He probably wanted it more than she did.

In the past, he wouldn't have allowed himself to have this. Partially because he had rarely felt anything like this before and partially because he was on the job. But this wasn't a regular job anymore, no matter that he'd told her it was. He was here for a very personal reason and it was hard to keep those lines from blurring. Harder than he'd realized it would be when he'd first grabbed her in his arms and run with her earlier that day.

He put his hand on her shoulder. She was small but strong; he'd seen her strength enough to know it would be foolish to underestimate her. But she was still in over her head.

His mind was trying to keep processing and making a contingency plan, but her tongue rubbed against his and every base instinct he possessed roared to life. He put his hand on the small of her back and drew her closer to him as he deepened the kiss.

He felt the brush of her fingers against his neck as she held his face with just that one hand. Her mouth opened under his and she seemed to lean the slightest bit closer to him. The world outside the pack-raft had disappeared. It was all rain and thunder and lightning.

She lifted her head and he felt the brush of her breath against his lips. She licked hers and his body sort of clenched everywhere.

"If I was out of line, I'm sorry," she said.

He didn't know how to respond to that. He was pretty sure she was teasing him but he wasn't usually jokey with women. Maybe that was why he didn't have many women friends... Lee and Luna were sort of friends, more like family. And they weren't Obie. He had no freaking idea how to handle this.

"Technically I'm not being paid to protect you so I guess it's okay," he said.

Immediately, he knew he'd said the wrong thing.

She pulled back, wrapping her arms around her waist, canting her body away from his. "Glad to hear that."

"Hell, Obie. I suck at this. Want to know why Aaron I aren't close? We don't do relationships. We do fighting and one-upmanship and proving ourselves but we don't talk and sometimes there are things that need to be said. And as you've just witnessed I suck at saying the right thing."

She looked back at him. Taking in all he'd said. "That's a lot to drop on a girl. First of all, did you want to kiss me?"

"Hell yeah, I did. I know that I need to stay focused to keep you safe," he admitted. "I promised I wouldn't let anything happen to you."

Her arms dropped from her waist and she swiveled slightly back toward him. "Do you always keep your promises?"

"Definitely."

"You're a very serious man. But Aaron isn't despite how similar you say you are."

"I know. We all deal with life in different ways."

"Fair enough. My aunt does it through her rules," she said.

He assumed that comment was meant for herself and not really for him. "How do you do it? Deal with life without losing it?"

"By pretending to be someone who fits in. It's easier if you are just like everyone else. For a few moments it seems like you belong," she said. "You?"

The raw honesty in her once again struck him. How did he deal? "Rules like your aunt, I guess."

"Why?" she asked. She pulled her knees up to her chest. It was still pouring down rain but not as heavily as it had been.

"It's safer that way."

She reached up and took the ponytail holder out of her hair, running her fingers through it. "Safer how?"

How to explain without revealing how out of control he always was. Van said that part of Xander's strength was that he had all of that fear and rage inside of him and that he channeled it. But Xander wasn't channeling it at all. He'd caged it inside of him. Occasionally something escaped, and it enabled him to be ruthless when he protected his clients.

But it always felt like he was one moment away from a nuclear meltdown. From everything being shot to hell. From him ruining everything again.

She looked over at him, her eyes clear and seemingly safe.

"I'm one big rage ball inside. Rules are the thing that keep me in check," he said.

She tipped her head to the side. The humidity made her hair shorter and curlier, and one of the curls fell over her forehead. He reached out and pushed it back behind her ear like he'd seen her do earlier. Any excuse to touch her because now that he'd kissed her, he wasn't going to be satisfied until he had her under him or over him.

In his arms, naked, both of them taking and giving everything they had.

But how did that fit into the rules he'd made for himself?

It didn't.

"I don't see that," she said. "You've been calm under pressure and haven't hulked out one time."

"I'm at my best when I have to get someone out of danger," he said. "Bullets and bad guys fit into my rules for the world. I know how to dodge and outmaneuver them."

"What doesn't fit, then?" she asked.

"You."

"Oh." She gave him a sad smile then. "That kiss didn't mean I want to be with you forever."

"Maybe not to you. But to me…"

What was he going to say? That he craved her more than anyone he'd met before. He knew forever didn't exist, not the way she probably meant it. Marriage. Family. Those were words he had always felt weren't for him. But when he kissed her, he tasted something that made him crave a different life. One where he was a different man who might be able to fit into a family and have what he'd denied himself for so long.

Why had she kissed him? That was the main question running through her head as the rain started to lessen. And what the heck had he meant?

This day was stirring up too much baggage that she would have preferred to keep hidden for the rest of her life.

She'd been shot at, which wasn't helping things, and kissing him had almost made it so she didn't have to keep reliving that moment she'd been yanked from Xander's arms. The intent on his face had been intense and she had no doubt that man would have killed and then searched her dead body for Aaron's SD card.

Maybe she should focus on that instead of on the kiss she'd taken from Xander and his oblique statement.

"What do you think is on the SD card?" she asked.

"My guess either drop houses or names of people

in the organization. Whatever it is... Well, seems like Aaron has something important in the right hands to stop the cartel and hamper their operation," Xander said.

"Do you think we could read it? I mean they are going to kill us whether we know what's on it or not."

"They definitely are going to try but I'm not going to let them succeed," he said.

Once they were talking about the men chasing them and the SD card, Xander fell into a sense of calmness that hadn't been there when he'd been kissing her. Which was a good thing, right? She wanted this man to be hot and bothered by her.

She just also needed the capable version of him to make sure they got out of the swamp alive. Then take down the cartel and help her find out if there was any connection to her parents' deaths.

But it made her want to know more about him, to see him after this chaos was done. She hadn't been making small talk when she mentioned Xander's personality was very different from his brother's. Aaron was always flirting and chattering and making everyone laugh. There was a temporary quality that Xander didn't possess.

Xander was solid and sure of himself—oh, Aaron had confidence but it was draped behind his carefree image. With Xander's build and the way he held himself with that military stance, tall, shoulders back— nothing was getting through him.

Was that why she'd kissed him? Why she couldn't get him out of her head?

"You will put up a fight and that is reassuring. What do you think about reading the card?" she asked.

Trying to force the conversation back on the card since that was the safest thing for her at the moment. She started to laugh and realized that exhaustion and the stress of the day was getting to her. She laughed until she started to cry and the tears did that screwed-up thing of turning from mirth to fear in a moment. Then she was for real sobbing and pushed herself out from under the pack-raft, standing in the pouring rain so maybe he wouldn't notice.

Yeah, right.

Like this was any better. But at least she wasn't under the pack-raft anymore contemplating how knowing the details of a drug cartel's operation was the safest option for her at the moment.

She wrapped her arms around her waist and then felt Xander next to her. He didn't say a word, just pulled her into his body. Those big muscly arms of his wrapping around her. She put her face into his chest as she kept crying. He didn't say a word, just held her and honestly that was the only thing she could have handled at this moment.

Slowly the tears stopped and she knew she should step back but he smelled good, sort of a mix between expensive cologne and man. Like him. The other guys she'd dated and had sex with over the last few years all smelled of the same generic, artificial Prada cologne. Xander smelled and felt real.

Like swamp real. Not sophisticated Miami real.

In her head that made sense.

The rain started to lessen and she moved to step back but he held her. "Just a minute longer."

She stayed there, putting her own arms around his middle and hugging him back. He had been honest to a point about Aaron, but coming to help his brother out and finding himself on the run with a strange woman had to be jarring even to a man like Xander, who was used to protecting people.

Was he protecting people because he couldn't protect himself, or had he failed to protect someone else?

The rain nearly stopped and she stepped back from his embrace again. This time he let her go. "We should get back on the water if we are going to make the meeting point before dark."

"Affirmative," he said.

She smiled. He went full-on protector mode after he let his mask fall and his emotions were present. "I'll get the packs again."

"I want to check the map and I'll grab the pack-raft after that. I think I might have something to read the SD card in my bag. Lee always has a tech pouch she insists I carry."

His voice softened when he talked about the members of his team in a way it didn't when he talked about Aaron. She got it; she felt the same way about her family at the coffee shop. They all cared about each other, and it was so much easier than her relationship with her blood relatives. Aunt Karen was still demanding and Gator…he was in the wind. But she couldn't help hoping that maybe this would bring them back together.

* * *

The rawness of Obie's tears was hard to shake. She'd moved on in a way that he appreciated, admired. Accepting her feelings, then focusing on the task at hand. He had always felt like his anger set him apart from everyone else, but without saying a word Obie had shown him that they weren't that different despite the unique emotional storms they had weathered.

He checked the map and for messages from Lee. There weren't any new ones but that didn't surprise him. She wouldn't send word unless she had news.

He let her know the name of the assistant district attorney that Obie had talked to and suggested she coordinate with him in their teams messaging service. She thumbs-upped it.

"Lee is going to reach out to that assistant district attorney and let him know what's going on," Xander said.

"Thanks. Could she also let my boss at the coffee shop know I won't be stopping by later?" Obie asked.

He relayed that information for her and synched the map coordinates to his smart watch and put his phone back in his drybag. Obie wore her pack and had his slung over her left shoulder.

As she stood there, no sign of the tears or the fear that had been present earlier, his body stirred again. It was hard not to be impressed by her resilience. Everyone had a core of inner strength whether they realized it or not.

"Ready?"

"Of course," she said. Her stomach rumbled as she

said it and she looked a bit embarrassed as she put her hand over it. "Sorry, I'm used to eating a bunch of little meals during the day."

"Totally cool. I do that too. I have two protein bars—want one?" he asked.

She handed him his pack and he opened it, finding the bars and tossing one to her. She took it, opening it carefully. "Thanks for this. I'm pretty good at fishing. But we'd have to build a fire and hopefully we won't be in the swamp for that long."

"Hopefully. But if we are I have a camp stove," he said. "According to the map it's about another two hours to the marina where we are going to try to check in with the team. If I know Van he'll have transport waiting for us."

"Van's your boss?"

"Yeah," he said, shouldering his own pack before lifting the pack-raft. Obie took the oars as they started walking. He followed the trail they'd taken to the shelter and she fell into step beside him.

"You like him?" she asked. "You talk about him and Lee like they are family."

She wasn't wrong; they were family to him. Probably the only people who knew the man he'd become, and Van in particular was very aware of Xander's past, having bailed him out of jail after a drunken fight that had left another man in the hospital. Van, with his angel-wings tattoo on the back of his neck and his intense calmness, had come to visit him in jail.

"He offered me a chance to change my life. Told me if I wanted to learn to control the rage that I kept directing out to the world then he'd show me. Or I could spend the rest of my life getting locked up for fights until I took it too far and ended up in prison for killing someone."

Telling her about his past wasn't what he intended. He should be focused on the task at hand. But he had realized when he'd held her in the rain that nothing with Obie was as he intended.

"Wow. How did you do that? Because I'm not going to lie, you don't seem like the kind of man who would do those things," she said.

He thought about the last ten years. None of it had been easy. He started doing other things rather than fighting. He worked out twice a day, and the assignments that Van gave him at Price Security were usually physically demanding. Even the ones that weren't required a lot of concentration. Van kept him busy and Xander had found that by using his mind to solve puzzles, his hands to repair things or to play chess against Kenji—who probably could be grand master if he put his mind to it—helped him a lot.

He just always kept *busy*. That was probably why he was talking to her. There was a lot of downtime in the swamp as they were making their way through it.

But both of them were still on high alert, Obie listening for deadly creatures, him on the lookout for gun-toting cartel members. Their skills were keeping them one step ahead of danger.

The danger he couldn't avoid came from the woman she was. Adept at adapting to this environment, showing him her strength and intelligence and he wanted her. He had to keep talking about the stuff that he didn't normally address because it helped to put up a barrier between them in his mind. A barrier that he was going to use for as long as he could to keep from reaching out and pulling her back into his arms.

"I am that man. I've just learned how to control myself."

That was a hard thing to admit. He had been trained by the British military and his fighting instincts... Well, he'd been born with them, but the military had honed them. He'd never thought about reining any of that in until Van. Van had shown him that his true strength didn't come from hitting as hard as he could or his endurance. It came from marrying his mind and his body together. Something that he was really leaning into on this trek through the swamp with Obie.

Chapter 10

The fact that Aaron wasn't the man she thought he was had been driven home so many times today that she wasn't sure why having another acknowledgment of his connection to the cartel was giving her chills. He'd told her he had intel on them, asked her to go and retrieve it. But a part of her had been hoping he wasn't as involved as he must be to have that tattoo. It frightened her that her instincts, which she'd always prided herself on, had been so wrong.

"Are you okay?"

"Yeah," she said because talking smack about his brother wasn't going to make her feel better. The person she was really disappointed in was herself. Why did she let first impressions sway her? But she had and beating herself up about it now wasn't going to help.

Xander sent the rough sketch he'd drawn as well as a description of both of the men to his team and then shut his phone down, putting it back in his drybag. "We are a bit off course so we need to head more to the west to get back on track."

He acted so normal about this. Seeing men with guns searching for him was just an everyday thing.

Was there any way she could tap into his attitude and maybe make it her own? Maybe find a way to just be chill. Like, *Yeah, guys with guns are tracking me but I'm cool.*

Not in this lifetime.

She longed to be back at her little apartment right now, getting ready to go in and do some unpaid work ordering supplies or double-checking the receipts for the last week. Anything mundane and away from the swamp and the two Quentin brothers.

Xander was doing his level best to keep her calm and be reassuring. But she didn't know him well enough to relinquish her power like that. Probably even less than she'd known Aaron, who'd worked at the coffee shop for over a month.

But now she doubted that. She hadn't known Aaron at all. She'd seen something in him that had reminded her of Gator and blindly thought he was the same as her brother. Someone who needed her help.

Someone she didn't want to let down.

Someone who'd led her into a world she'd never thought to return to.

"I've never really liked coffee. I mean give me a lot of sugar and some cream and then I can tolerate it but not coffee on its own," Xander said.

The comment was so out of left field it threw her for a second. She looked over at him and saw a hint of concern on his face. He was trying to give her something else to think of other than the gang tattoo that had been on Aaron's arm.

And it was definitely *just* Aaron's tattoo and not the two men who'd been tracking her that bothered her.

Coffee?

He wanted to talk about *coffee*?

She was half-tempted to give in to the manic panic that was trying to dominate in her mind, but she shook her head hard. "I love it. I think it's because my mama used to give it to me and Gator when we were little."

"With sugar?"

"Oh, yeah. You'd have loved it. She served it to us in these demitasse mugs that had been her grandmother's. She'd put in a big teaspoon of sugar and fill the mug halfway with milk and then add in the coffee. Each morning we'd sit on the back porch watching the swamp come to life, drinking our coffees with her and she'd tell us tales of the swamp."

In her mind she saw her mama with the thick brown hair they shared, curling around her head as she talked in that deep Southern accent of hers. Some mornings they'd been chatty; other mornings the swamp had been. The animals and birds who woke up and started moving about. They'd just enjoyed being present, something she'd forgotten in the last decade.

"Do you still drink it that way?"

"No. Once I moved to my aunt Karen's I stopped having sugar. She also wasn't a fan of dairy products like milk and cheese. Too many calories."

"I need as many calories as I can get. I burn a lot," he said.

"I imagine you do." She couldn't help glancing over at him, trying to be surreptitious as she let her gaze move over his big, muscular body. She liked his large biceps and really appreciated his strength. His body was a testament to his own ability to survive.

"So now you take it black?"

He kept distracting her and in that moment she thought she really liked this guy. This man who'd shown up out of nowhere and now was saddled with keeping her safe. He could have just been stoic, dragging her along behind him through the swamp, but he was aware of her next to him. She felt seen by him in a way that made her feel unique, special and safe.

"Yes. Though sometimes Hilda, who owns the coffee shop, comes in and makes this Cuban coffee. It's really strong espresso and she puts in condensed milk. Oh my God, it's so sweet and strong. It's delicious. You might like it. Lots of calories."

"You can make it for me when we get out of here," he said.

"Will we?" The words just slipped out. In the back of her mind, she didn't see that happening. The last time she'd been in the swamp her parents had died. It was almost as if she was afraid that...she might not make it out either.

Sure, they were walking and he had his satellite phone, but the truth was that the men following them were dangerous, and no matter how many nice distractions Xander offered her, she was scared and unsure.

It was nice having him by her side, but that didn't mean he'd be able to save her. The only sure thing was herself.

* * *

Xander wasn't the best at small talk, and coffee had been the only thing he could think of to discuss. He wasn't entirely sure it had been helpful, but Obie wasn't as pale under her tan as she had been since the moment he'd drawn that tattoo on his phone. She had history with the cartel, and his brother hadn't exactly been forthcoming with all that his "favor" from her would entail.

He was tempted to ask Van to get her out of the situation so he could go hunting and find a man they could get information from. Except that course of action was a slippery path that he hadn't allowed himself to get back on in a long time.

It would be easy to blame his brother for the rage that was building inside of him. He was very tempted to just forget the training and the past ten years of the man he'd become and go back into eliminating any threat.

If he'd been alone, he might have killed one of the two men following them on sight and then pressed the other one for information. He didn't like to harm anyone, but sometimes that was the only option if it meant rescuing others, and if it came down to keeping Obie safe he'd do whatever was necessary. A part of him regretted that he hadn't done it even with Obie here. But then maybe the fear in her eyes would be directed at him and not at the cartel.

That shouldn't matter. Most of the time Xander didn't really give a crap what anyone thought of him. But somehow he wanted Obie to see the best side of him. The noble bodyguard. The brother who was somehow better…hah. He wasn't better than Aaron. He just had gotten lucky when Van had found him and offered him this job.

He had to remind himself that.

The Quentin boys were dangerous, and that hadn't changed just because they'd all left home and hadn't been in the same spot for too many years. They were still a threat to anyone who crossed them.

"You are getting out of this, Obie Keller," he promised. "Don't doubt it. And when you do I hope you'll make me that coffee."

"If—"

"When."

"Sure I'll make it for you. But Hilda's is better. She also makes the best black beans and rice. Have you had that?"

"No, I don't think I have," he said. "I have had beans on toast. One of my favorites."

"Gross."

"Excuse me? I think I'm offended by that," he said. She seemed lighter now and he'd do anything to keep her from drifting back to that scared spot she'd been in a short while back.

"I'm offended by beans on toast… Actually what is it?"

He laughed. "It's what it sounds like. Toast and then you open a can of Heinz baked beans and put it on the toast."

"Heinz? I thought they were catsup people."

"Over here maybe but in the UK they have the best beans."

"Hmm... When we get back to Miami you can make it for me."

He looked over at her, saw that she watched the trail in front of them, occasionally glancing back to check and see if they were being followed. "Deal."

They walked in silence for another twenty minutes before she stopped. "I need a break. And maybe a moment alone."

He suspected she might need the toilet. He did too. He looked around and then back at her. "Do you see a spot that would be safe for us to use?"

She took a moment to walk along the marshy mangroves and then nodded. "Over there should be safe."

"Okay, go first, I'll keep watch."

She didn't hesitate as she moved into the underbrush and behind some trees and bushes. He shrugged out of his pack and took out his Glock 22 handgun. Unless things went wrong, they should be able to stay on the dry part of the path until they reached the lake. He checked his weapon, and the clip he had in it before putting on the safety.

Obie came back and smiled at him until she noticed the weapon in his hand. "What's that for?"

"You. I figured you'd feel safer with it while I dash into the bushes."

"I don't know how to shoot a handgun. My dad had a rifle to scare snakes and other critters away but it's been years since I've used it."

He gave her a quick lesson. "The safety is on. So

you'll have to flip this switch before you fire. If you hear someone other than me, take the safety off. Those men we saw earlier will kill you."

Her hand shook as she took the Glock 22 from him. But she looked determined. "Does it kick? Should I use two hands?"

"If you want to you can," he said, showing her how to hold the gun with two hands and how to aim. "I doubt you'll have to use it but better safe than sorry."

"Yeah. Okay go fast," she said.

"I will," he reassured her. He dashed into the underbrush where she'd gone and quickly did his business.

He hurried back to where she waited. She handed the gun back to him as soon as he was within arm's reach. "I'm glad you're back."

"Me too," he said.

Her hair now framed her face now in a riot of curls instead of the smooth strands she'd had when he'd first seen her in Aaron's house. The swamp was changing them both. It was clawing away at Xander's controlled facade, and it was changing Obie from the urbanite she'd been in Key Largo to this woman who seemed to belong here.

Holding a gun wasn't her favorite thing, but she appreciated that he'd thought to try to make her feel safe. Honestly she wasn't as scared as she'd been earlier. There was something about Xander...he radiated an assuredness that she hadn't allowed herself to feel in a long time.

"That sounds good. Do you have anything to cook with in there?"

She'd seen quite a few crabs. And in the briny water, clams flourished. She could gather some stuff while he inflated the boat.

"I have a small camp stove."

"Great. I'll get some fresh seafood and we can cook it in the salt water. That way we can eat. I'm getting hungry."

"Me too," he admitted. "I do have some more protein bars as well."

"Good to know." Of course he did. He seemed to have thought of everything.

They continued walking and she glanced over at him. "Does anything surprise you?"

"You did," he said. "I mean I knew you'd called but I assumed that once I didn't call back that would be the end of things for you with Aaron."

"I'm not that kind of person," she said. She wasn't. She couldn't just walk away from anyone. That's probably why she was still hoping to find some sign of her brother and the truth about what had happened to her parents. But she also kept in touch with everyone she'd met in college and considered a friend.

Maybe it was because of how alone she'd been after Gator left. Sure, she'd had her new life, but she'd missed having someone to talk to. Someone sort of like Xander, who had just made silly conversation about coffee to distract her from the reality of the situation. She needed that.

She thought maybe everyone did. For herself she

needed people not interactions on social media. She stayed after her shift was over at the coffee shop and talked to Bea or Hilda or whoever had the next shift.

"No, you're not. You really care about Aaron? I mean…was there anything…?"

"Anything…?" *Oh.* He wanted to know if they'd hooked up or were dating.

"No. He was too into himself, doing his own thing. And he worked for me too. I mean that's just asking for trouble when you date a coworker."

"Yeah, today there are all kinds of rules about that," he said. It was clear the idea of her dating Aaron bothered him—but she couldn't help but tease it out a bit more.

"Even if there weren't rules, it's awkward AF if you date someone and then it doesn't work out. That happened to me in at my first job. We were both working at McDonald's and it was fun at first but then after we broke up, I hated when we had the same shift."

Even as a teen, dating had felt like a minefield. She was expected to act a certain way, talk a certain way… and then the few men she'd let into her life broke her trust anyway.

"When was this?"

"High school. So maybe there was some of that teenage angst going on too. I mean Rand was a bit of a player and dated everyone who worked there. So it wasn't him, it was me. I hated that I hadn't realized he was just dating his way through the restaurant."

"I'd hate it too," Xander said.

"Sure, you would. You don't seem like the type of person that would happen to," she said.

"You're right. But that's because I really don't date," he said.

"Why not?"

"The job mostly. My assignments are usually for a few months to a year. That's a long time to be away from a partner. And I also am not really good at opening up. I have heard from more than one of my exes that I suck at sharing my feelings."

She laughed. "I have the opposite problem, or did. Like you I haven't been dating a lot lately."

"Not because of your job, right?"

"No. Just me. In my twenties I was like, never say never. I can change a guy to be a man I want to spend more time with. But once I turned thirty I was like, maybe saying never to some losers isn't a bad idea."

He laughed, making her smile. Aunt Karen had been pushing her to find a trust-fund guy to get engaged to from her social circle, and she'd dated a few, but it was hard work. She had to look a certain way. Dress all preppy and go to the club on the weekends. It had taken a lot of time and she had been twisting herself more and more into someone she didn't really like. Finally she'd said no. Told Aunt Karen she was going to be single until she was eighty and stopped dating.

She had to like herself alone before she was going to be able to like herself in a relationship.

"So now you say never."

"Hell, yes. In fact if Aaron asks for another favor it's going to be a never again from me."

He nodded and smiled, making his eyes crinkle and his face relax. She wished she could stop noticing how good-looking he was. Maybe it was just the fact that he'd saved her from being killed that made him so attractive. Whatever it was, it didn't feel that shallow or simple, and that might be scarier than the situation they were both in.

Chapter 11

"I'm not sure we're going to make it to the marina before nightfall. I don't know the terrain like you do," he said. "Should we try to cross West Lake in the dark or find shelter and do it tomorrow?" He'd heard nothing from Van or Lee, which worried him. Was this situation even more untenable than it seemed?

More than once he'd seen Obie look behind them in fear. There was no way she was going to feel safe until the SD card was handed over to the district attorney's office and the men following them were arrested. He wanted that too. But it seemed like it wasn't going to happen soon.

"Probably find shelter while there's still some light. We should try to get up if we can. I had a cousin who got bit by a moccasin when he was sleeping on the ground. Do you have something we can use as a shelter in your pack?"

"I do. I have a critter- and element-proof tent," he said. "We can both fit in it."

It would be tight, and after that kiss under the raft he wasn't sure that sleeping close to her was a good idea, but there weren't a lot of options.

Hell, something kept biting him and it was sweltering hot even as the sun started to set. He hadn't felt like this ever before, unsure of the terrain and what awaited them. There was no way out of the swamp unless someone was in a body bag. And if they weren't careful, that someone would be one—or both—of them.

But that wasn't a scenario he'd ever accept.

He was relying on Obie, in a way that he normally only did with the Price Security team.

"Good. I saw some larger cypress trees, which would provide some cover but the roots are in water, so they might not hold both of our weights. Or we can go further away from the lake where the trees are a little stronger. We'd also have less threat from the snakes."

"Away," he said. "Let me deflate the raft first."

"Okay. Can I check in with the district attorney's office?"

"I'd rather we wait to hear from my team."

She turned away from him without another word, walking to the edge of the forest area to find a path or trying not to curse him.

He rolled up the pack-raft and returned it to his backpack before following her. "I'm not trying to be controlling. I just don't know what we are dealing with. You saw the gang sign same as me. Logically it makes no sense for Aaron to have sent them. The only other people who knew you'd be there was the district attorney's office."

"And your team."

"My team didn't know about Aaron's house. They knew Miami and if Van wanted me dead he wouldn't send me to Miami to kill me," Xander pointed out. He was hanging on to his temper by a thread.

Now she was making him feel like he was being unreasonable even though logic clearly showed he wasn't.

"Why do I have to just trust your people?"

"You don't. I am the one who trusts them. If you want to call the district attorney then do it. We'll see what happens."

"You're being an asshole."

"I'm trying to keep you alive and I'm sorry but taking a risk that we don't have to makes no sense. I'm hot, bug bites are now covering my legs and I feel damp in every part of my body. So if you want to call do it. I don't really think I'm going to be getting a lot of sleep tonight so staying awake to see if the men we saw earlier come back is fine."

She shook her head. "Sorry. I'm short-tempered too. I'm hungry and scared and you've been great but I still don't know you."

"I get it." He truly did. He looked around. There wasn't anyone else around as far as he could see. "Why don't you gather some seafood?"

"We're too far inland for the crabs now. We could try fishing but we don't have any bait."

"Protein bars it is," he said. He was feeling like they needed to be moving more quickly through the swamp but there was no way that the two of them on foot could. "Sorry."

"The bars are fine. They will definitely give us some energy."

"Not for that. For being a jerk. I know you are worried too and want to get help. I just… I have a hard time trusting anyone I don't know."

She gave him a slight smile, something she did more and more frequently. "I get it. But you should try trusting me."

"I do," he said. She had no idea how much he was relying on her because she was the expert. She was the only way they were safely making it across this marshy land and to the relative safety of the marina on the other side of West Lake.

"As much as I do you."

He arched both eyebrows. "How much is that?"

"A lot," she said. "Should we start walking around the lake?"

"Yeah. We'll have to find a place to pitch the tent. I have a feeling like everything else in the swamp its not going to be as easy as finding a safe place to put the tent for the night."

"I'm starting to feel a bit like Katniss did in the *Hunger Games*."

"Does this feel like that to you?"

"Yes. I feel like I was ripped from my world and dropped into this survival fest and I don't like it. But hearing that out loud I sound like a brat. I'm just tired like you."

"It's okay to complain," he said.

"Yeah, but you're not."

"Uh, I think I had a meltdown a few minutes ago," he pointed out.

"You were hangry. And I get it. You were thrown into this too."

He was, but he had been prepared for it in a way that Obie hadn't been. She had no idea what kind of trouble Aaron always brought with him.

It was nice to see a more human side to her bodyguard. He'd seemed unflappable when they were being shot at or hiding from crocs and cartel gunmen in the swamp. So she'd been a bit surprised to hear about the heat and bugs bothering him. But it was nice to see that he was more than some kind of sexy, hot robot guard that just kept functioning no matter what.

The protein bars were okay as fuel, but they were almost out of water and had been rationing it. She wished they'd captured some of the rainwater to drink. Not that it was totally clean but it would be better than lake water. She'd always thought of herself as a survivor but suddenly that was taking on a different kind of meaning. This kind of survival was pushing her to her limits and stirring fears that she hadn't realized she'd hung on to.

At first it had been sort of fun being in the swamp. Down by the coast with the mangroves and tidal water was so different than the swamp she'd grown up in but this...this part was more familiar. Bringing buried memories to the surface. Grieving for her parents' deaths and of course losing Gator the way she had.

But hearing the cicadas singing, smelling the rotting vegetation and seeing the sun setting through the branches of the live oak was different. This was every summer evening she'd experienced as a kid and early teenager. All the stuff that she'd forgotten.

Meanwhile her needlessly expensive flip-flops were wearing into the top of her feet. She knew her mama would have said to take them off. Shoes like that weren't meant for the swamp.

But she didn't want to let another layer of the woman she'd become slip away.

"What about here?"

Torn back into the present, she glanced at the area he was pointing to. It was high enough that they'd be safe from ground animals and probably from being spotted by any of the cartel members.

"Yeah, that looks good. Want me to check it out and clear some of the area so we have enough room to pitch the tent?"

"Go for it. I'm going to scout around down here and make sure that we haven't left any obvious tracks."

She heard him move away. That was one thing she really liked about Xander: he respected her enough to trust her skills and not keep watch over her at all times.

Walking around, she found the right place. She cleared a pretty large area but tried to make it look organic. She tried to move a log that was sort of in the clearing she made, but it was too heavy for her. God, she was really out of shape.

Well, she was definitely going to start working out when she got home. But then she almost laughed at the ridiculousness of that statement. It was as if she anticipated she'd be on the run like this again.

But, what if she was?

What kind of survivor wasn't prepared for every situation?

Be easy, girl.

Her daddy's voice seemed to whisper to her on the humid breeze that blew through the trees. *Be easy.* Daddy said that all the time when one of them had gotten wound up. Just be easy. It was a simple order. It meant calm down and take a breath. But she'd been breathing herself into a coma in her real life in Miami, and being here, being the opposite of easy made her feel something again.

Alive, for sure.

It had been a long time since she'd snapped at someone or allowed herself to just be. Not to carefully filter every single feeling she had through some kind of strainer so that all that was left was someone who was bland and boring. A woman who tried to look like everyone else and blend in.

"Will it work?"

She glanced over at him. Xander stood at the base of the clearing, scratching a bite on his neck and waiting. "Yes."

"I couldn't move that log but maybe you can?" she asked.

Shrugging out of his pack, he put it in the center of the clearing and then moved toward the log. Her breath caught in her throat and her heart beat faster, watching him move. He was so physical. It was impossible not to look at him. His muscles bulged in his arms, and she knew his strength and wanted to feel them around her. She was staring at him but couldn't stop.

Their eyes met and that heat that had been between them under the pack-raft was back. The irritation and fear and memories disappeared, and all she could do was stare at his mouth. Wish that he'd kiss her again.

And more.

Everything in her was starting to awaken, the needs and desires she'd been denying suddenly demanding attention. And the fact that she had no idea what was going to happen to them tonight or tomorrow just fed the urgency in her. She reached out to touch his upper arm.

He flexed his muscle as he put his hand on her waist.

"Are you okay? I'll get the tent set up and then you can climb in and get some rest."

After a lifetime of what felt like rest that was the last thing she wanted. She wanted the excitement and even the danger that she felt around Xander because at last she felt alive.

Xander wasn't entirely sure that the was going to be make it through the entire night in the tent with Obie without taking her in his arms again. His control was legendary when he was on the job. Kenji always teased him that he was an iron man when it came to keeping his emotions safely locked up. It was a good thing his friend wasn't here now.

Whenever he touched her, his mind went blank and his body took over.

He dropped his hand as she nodded.

He made quick work of setting up the tent in the area she'd found, which offered them a lot of cover. Once he had it set up, he put some of the branches back around it to help it blend in better. It was getting dark now and the noise of the swamp was louder.

"Is the swamp like the forest where the animals go quiet if another threat shows up?" he asked her as he pushed his pack into the tent. She bent and put her purse inside of the tent and then he motioned for her to climb in.

"Yes, animals go quiet when they sense a threat."

She made no move to enter the tent, just stood there for a long moment. Looking down into her face, he saw the effects of the day, slight reddish from too much sun and wind, the fatigue around her eyes, but she was still so damned beautiful everything masculine in him went on alert. Normally he made himself into someone less sexual when he was working, ignoring his baser demands and the attraction he sometimes felt toward his clients.

And maybe it was the bugs, heat and swamp or at least he wanted it to be, but he was struggling to do that with Obie.

He wanted to check his phone but after telling her she couldn't contact her district attorney friend, he wasn't sure how she'd take that. "I'm going to check in with my team. They should have some information for us. I know I asked you not to—"

"It's fine," she said. "For now it's fine. And you did say you might have something to read the SD card."

"Let's get into the tent."

She climbed in first. He forced his eyes away from her backside as she crawled in, but it was too late. He'd already seen the sweet curve of her ass and couldn't get that image out of his mind. He took an extra moment to check their surroundings before he followed her into the tent.

She had her purse next to her and she sat cross-legged on the floor with her arms around herself. Her shorts and tank top were suited to the day, but now that it was nightfall, a slight chill crept around them. "Want my shirt?"

"Why?"

"You seem cold. I've got a button-down in my bag that you could put on to keep yourself warm," he said.

"Thanks."

He dug it out and handed it to her, then turned on his phone to see if Lee or Van had gotten back to them.

He had a text from Van.

You really stepped in it. Situation is in flux. Stay low. Will see you at the marina when you get there. Not sure who to trust. Cartel dangerous.

He texted his boss back.

Assistant district attorney Crispin Tallman is working with Aaron to clear his name. Have the SD card. More cartel members were on our trail earlier this afternoon. Should be at the marina midday tomorrow.

Van answered immediately.

That's good news. Will reach out to the assistant district attorney. You good for the night?

Xander sent a thumbs-up back to his boss.

"Van's going to get in touch with Tallman. He said the situation is in flux."

"What's that mean?"

"That there are moving parts and he can't read them all," Xander said. He didn't like the sound of that any more than Obie's facial expression said she did. Aaron's information was the key to all of this. He pulled out his tech bag and looked around for the dongle he could attach to his phone and then insert the SD card in the other side.

"Let me see the SD card."

She opened her purse and pulled out the drybag he'd given her what felt like days ago instead of merely hours. She took the card out of the bag and handed it to him.

He shifted his bag around and then sat down.

"I'm nervous."

He glanced over at her.

She shrugged. She looked small with his big shirt draped around her body. Her arms were still around her waist; she was keeping it together and had been since that moment in the rain. That one moment he was trying his damnedest not to dwell on, but it was hard not to.

He wanted to pull her back against his body. Take her mouth under his again and kiss her until they both no longer remembered they were in the swamp and running for their lives.

He wanted to give them both something to think about that wasn't a drug cartel, family and death. But he also knew if he did that, if he compromised himself, he might screw things up and put her in danger. That wasn't something he was willing to do. He was the only one keeping her safe and he didn't take that duty lightly.

No matter how much he burned to pleasure her.

No matter how much his body demanded that he touch her.

He was having the hardest time not pushing that one silky-looking curl that kept falling forward against her cheek back behind her ear.

He literally balled his hand into a fist so he wouldn't touch her.

"The card," she said, holding it out to him.

Crap.

He opened his hand palm up, and her small finger rested against his palm, sending chills up his arm and heat spreading down his torso to his groin. The SD card dropped into the center of his hand but he was afraid to try to take it and put it in the card reader while he was touching her. He might drop it. He wanted to drop it and just turn his hand over and tug her off balance and against him.

But he didn't. He reached for the iron control he'd been lauded for and pulled it around him. Wrapping himself away from this woman.

Chapter 12

The closeness of the shelter made her feel safe. His critter-proof tent was surprisingly comfy. He had pulled out a packing cube of his clothes that he offered for her to use as a pillow. She set it to one side waiting while he held the SD card in one hand.

She was afraid to see what was on it. Afraid of what it would mean once she had that knowledge. He took the card, putting it into the reader while setting his phone aside. Their eyes met and then he just shook his head.

"Why did you have to agree to help Aaron?"

"I told you. Family," she said.

He cursed under his breath and then took her hand in his, lifting it to his mouth and kissing her palm. A shiver of awareness went through her, making her breasts feel full and her nipples tighten. This was what she needed, maybe more than whatever information was on that card. The information that the cartel was willing to kill for. She shifted up on her knees and leaned forward, willing away the fear that had been chasing her all day.

Xander had been reluctant to kiss each of the times

they had. She felt like she'd been the one driving that. But this time, he tugged on her wrist and pulled her off balance until she fell into his arms. Those powerful arms that she'd been admiring as she watched him building the shelter for them, making sure they were safe.

He held her, his body smelling of the swamp and summer and sweat. It was a heady combination that turned her on like nothing else had. No one else had in a long time. She put her hands on his shoulders and tipped her head back until she could see his eyes. He watched her mouth. She saw a wildness in him for the first time.

It was exciting to see her calm, cool, self-appointed bodyguard enthralled by her. She started to say something. To tell him that she wanted this too. But his mouth came down on hers. Hard and demanding. She opened her mouth under his, his tongue sweeping over hers and thrusting deep into her mouth.

She held on to his shoulders, and he kept her close with one hand on her back and the other one slipped under the button-down shirt he'd given her earlier. His touch moved to the hem of her tank top where it had ridden up from the waistband of her shorts. She felt his fingers moving over her skin, rubbing against the exposed flesh, as the intensity of the kiss changed.

He took his time, his tongue moving more leisurely against her, his finger following the same movement. Her skin felt so sensitized by his touch that chill bumps spread up her chest to her neck. His hand on her back shifted around, balling the fabric of the shift he'd given her until she felt his hand on her back. He pushed her tank top up and then the heat of his palm was on her bare skin.

She shivered and for a moment just let herself enjoy being touched by this man. His hands and his mouth held her. She opened her eyes, moving her fingers against the side of his throat and up to his jawline. He lifted his head and their eyes met.

She felt like he wanted to say something, but maybe he wasn't sure what to say. She got to her knees and straddled him. Letting her thighs slide along the outside of his legs and keeping her hands where they were framing his face. She lowered her body until the center of her rubbed against his erection.

Maybe he was going to say they should stop out of caution, but she didn't want to. The reasons why she wanted him didn't need repeating to herself. She knew what she needed. She needed to feel alive and to forget for a little while why they were together in this intimate little cocoon he'd created for them.

He started to speak but she brought her mouth down on his, caught his lower lip between her teeth and bit gently, sucking his lower lip into her mouth as she rocked her hips over his erection.

He groaned and the hand on her back moved lower to her butt, grasping at it and driving her harder against him as his hips moved up into her body.

She tossed her head back as he thrust against her and he felt his mouth on her neck, sucking against her skin and driving her mad. She rocked harder against him and he continued to drive up against her. His hand on her butt tightened and he brought his other hand to her waist, driving her harder and harder against him as he continued to thrust up against her.

Her orgasm washed over her, making her shudder and shake his arms as he brought her mouth down on his so she could taste more of him as she climaxed.

He cursed and pulled back from her, but she kept moving against him, until he buried his face in her neck, encouraging her to continue rocking against him. Sated for the moment, she collapsed against him for a minute. She lay there in his arms for a few more moments before he lifted his head.

"Well, that was unexpected."

She gave a soft laugh. "Understatement of the year. I'm not going to say I'm sorry. I wanted you and I would have liked you inside of me."

But she knew he wouldn't have done that.

"Obie."

That was all he said, just her name. He lifted her off his lap and turned away, busying himself with something in his pack.

What was it about her that made him regret every physical touch?

Xander was rock-hard. Hearing Obie say she wanted him inside of her made him even stiffer. But he'd already decided that wasn't happening. He was trying to keep every bit of his control, but each moment in her presence made it so much tougher.

She just wasn't someone he could resist. He had met a lot of women he admired and he hadn't been like this.

She was different. Which was why he was trying not to give in to his base temptations.

He knew she watched him. And there were only so many things he could shuffle around in his pack. He was stalling. His hand touched a deck of cards and he pulled them out as he turned to face her.

"What is going on with you?"

"I'm trying to be sensible."

"I thought we had gone past sensible. We've shared so much today…"

They had; he didn't need her to remind him all they'd been through together. But he felt like today might end up being the easiest day they had. Van's text was worrying. Was Aaron in deeper than he'd let on, or was someone Aaron trusted betraying him?

At least it wasn't Obie. It seemed far-fetched that she'd be involved with the cartel she thought had killed her parents.

Or had she just said that to throw him off? He thought about the SD card, which they hadn't read yet because he'd been distracted by their make-out session.

Was she trying to keep him from seeing something on it?

The moment that thought entered his mind he knew it was ridiculous. Who sets themselves up to get shot at? Especially a civilian who clearly had no training. He put the pack of cards on the floor of the tent. He pulled his phone back to him. "Let's find out what's on here."

He opened the reader on his phone and noticed there were several files on the card. Obie came closer, but not too close, which immediately confirmed he'd hurt her by making out with her and then putting up walls. He was going to have to talk to her about it, but right now the card had information that they both needed to see.

There were two photo albums with file names that were all numbers—dates were his best guess. The dates were from the last two weeks. He opened the first one and it looked like a strip mall of some sort.

"That's the coffee shop," Obie said.

She leaned over him, careful not to touch him when she was normally such a tactile person. He turned and started to say something, but she shook her head.

"Later. See if there are more photos of the coffee shop. Do you think this means he was dealing out of the shop?"

He had no idea. And wouldn't until they had a fuller picture of what was on the card. He opened more photos and saw that there was one of Obie laughing while she talked to a customer. She looked very different than she did right now. It was a photo of a beautiful woman with straight black hair, red lipstick, still gorgeous as she was now...but different.

"Why are all these photos of the shop on there?" she asked, more to herself.

They kept moving through the photos and eventually a car pulled up and the next photo was of Aaron.

Xander's breath caught. He hadn't seen his brother in ten years. He'd filled out from the twenty-four-year-old young adult he'd been. His hair was long, not too dissimilar to Xander's own style, and he was beefy but still a few inches shorter than Xander. In the photo, Aaron was in the process of taking off his sunglasses and seemed to be looking toward the photographer.

"I'm confused," Obie said. "Is he trying to get this back because it shows the coffee shop? I haven't seen anything that Aaron can use to cut a deal."

"Me either. But we haven't seen everything," Xander said. "I wonder if Aaron swiped this because it had photos of you and the shop on there."

"To protect us?" That note of worry was back in her voice and he knew that it wasn't just her picture being on the SD card that made her nervous.

He had done his own share of making scared.

"Maybe," he said, then turned to her. "I'm sorry."

She shook her head. "Don't be nice to me right now. Just be the bodyguard," she said.

She needed more from him than just being a bodyguard. They had gotten closer, and once he'd completely given in to temptation and taken her in his arms, she'd seen that as a bond between them. This woman shared her knowledge and skills of the swamp as well as her fears that someone had murdered her parents. She expected more from the people she shared her past with.

She deserved more too. He owed her the truth and he would give it to her, find a way to assuage her fears and make her trust him again. The files and the cartel's response meant that Obie might know more than she realized, and the danger to her might have been there all along, not just when she'd walked into Aaron's house on Key Largo to retrieve this card.

"You deserve—"

"To see more photos," she said. "Just show me what else is on there. I'm going to need to let Hilda know. I don't want anyone else to be in danger."

"Me either," he said, respecting her wishes and moving through the rest of the photos in the first album, which showed Aaron talking to another man in the alley behind the coffee shop. The man's back was to them and he had a tattoo on the back of his neck that was hard to make out.

She thought nothing would take her mind off what had just happened between them, but seeing the pictures of the coffee shop as well as Bea, Hilda and herself worried her. Aaron in particular looked different in the photos that had captured him. That carefree dishwasher she normally saw looked pensive and tense as he'd gotten out of his car.

"Do you think he knew he was being watched?"

"Probably or at least was taking some precautions. Do you recognize this guy?" He pointed to the last photo in the file, which showed the back of another man. The man wore a dark gray suit and had a tattoo that showed just above the collar on the left-hand side.

"No one dressed like that came into the coffee shop while I was working. And I can't really see the tattoo. Can you zoom in on it?"

He tried but the lines weren't any clearer; the collar on the man's suit jacket hid most of it.

Xander zoomed back out and opened the data file next, which was encrypted. He closed it and went to the next file, which had more photos from the file extensions, but these were encrypted too.

"So all we can see are pictures of the coffee shop and Aaron. Aaron must know the key to unlock the files," Obie said.

"That would be my guess. I'm going to send the files to my team. I'll ask Van to send someone to your coffee shop to watch the people who work there."

Van, his boss. The one he thought was going to be able to help them once they got to the marina. She was putting a lot of trust in this man who kept putting up barriers despite the fire that raged between them, and she was tired, hungry and hurt. Not a good combo.

For a minute, just the barest of one, she thought of Aunt Karen, who would tell her to keep her opinions to herself and go to sleep. But then she shoved them away. Aunt Karen wasn't here. She was in the freaking swamp. Obie wasn't the civilized, ordinary woman in those surveillance photos right now. She was the wild swamp girl again.

"Great. I'm glad your boss will watch out for them," she said.

"Yeah."

He put the reader and his phone back in the drybag and handed her the SD card, which she took and turned to put it away as well.

When she turned back around he had a deck of cards in his hands and was opening it. "I think I mentioned that I suck at personal relationships."

"Yeah, but I hadn't realized how that would impact me," she said. "I am really close to losing my temper."

"I can see that. You're like that lightning that flashed across the sky earlier. I can feel you singeing the hair on my arms."

"That's not all I'm going to singe."

"I had a feeling. How about we high-card and I'll answer any question you have for me no matter how personal?"

"And what will I do?" She liked the idea of him having to answer her.

"The same. I have a feeling there are things you still haven't told me."

"Fine. Let's go."

He shuffled the cards and then offered the deck to her. "Ladies first."

Obie took a small stack and held it next to her legs. Xander pulled another small stack and lifted his toward her.

"King of spades."

She lifted her card: three of clubs.

"So you lose. Why did you stop when we were making out? Do you just not want to be with me? Were you doing it to be nice?" All of the questions sort of fell out of her mouth and she knew she should have asked him about Aaron and the photos or something else. Anything else.

"Ah well, because I shouldn't have let it get started. I want to be with you, Obie, but we're in danger, and a man making love to a woman while being chased by a deadly drug cartel is a shitty bodyguard. You distract me and tempt me more than you realize. Keeping you safe and alive is my number-one priority. I'm sorry I let things get out of hand."

"That sounds... I'm not sure if I can trust you."

"You can," he said and it sounded like a promise.

She wasn't sure if she wanted to.

"Next," he said. He won the next round of High Card.

"The man with his back to the camera reminds you of someone. Who?"

She thought he hadn't noticed but shouldn't have been surprised that he had. The man looked like her father. A man she knew was dead. But his height and his shoulders weren't the same, nor were his military buzz cut and that small mark that she thought was a tattoo. It was how he carried himself, a sense of alertness and confidence that harkened back to her dad. When they'd zoomed in she'd realized it might be a birthmark.

"It's nothing."

"We said honesty."

"Yeah, we did. He looks like my dad from the back, but he's definitely dead because Gator and I had to identify the bodies when they were brought in," she said. "So I know that's not him."

"Does he have any brothers?"

"No. And I don't honestly think that's my dad. He just holds himself the same way. Like a cop," she said. "I think if I had to guess...that man is a cop."

Chapter 13

Xander wasn't sure what it meant that Aaron had been talking to someone that looked like a cop. Rick, who worked on his team, was a former DEA agent. Given the cartel's involvement, maybe he should ask Rick to reach out and see if he could find anything.

"I think you're right about it being a cop," Xander said.

"Does that mean Aaron is working with the cops or is that how they got the information to arrest him? I mean that guy isn't pretending to be a buyer," she said. "He sticks out in our neighborhood and like I said I never saw him."

"One of our team used to work with the DEA. I'm going to reach out to him and ask him to do some digging," Xander said.

He pulled his phone out and texted Rick, who answered back immediately.

On it. Also heads-up the entire team is heading your way. I will check in at the local DEA office when we land.

The entire team.

He just thumbs-upped Rick's message and then opened his chat with Van.

Why is the entire team coming here?

Shit is getting real. That encrypted file is hard to break and we are working on it. But the photos of the girl and your brother. The meta data shows they weren't taken by your brother. So someone was watching him and the shop. You stay focused on keeping the girl safe. The team is going to find out what the heck is going on.

Xander tossed his phone down. He didn't want the team involved in this. But he knew there was no stopping Van once he made up his mind.

I'll pay for the team to investigate.

Not happening.

Why not?

It's family.

Family.

Not yours.

You are. Not arguing. See you tomorrow.

"Everything okay?" Obie asked.
"Yeah. Rick's going to check in with the local DEA

office and see what he can find. My entire team is en route to us."

"Why?"

"Those encrypted files. I guess they are hard to crack or something worrying is on them," he said.

He had nothing more to add to it. He was relieved that Rick was checking the DEA angle.

"Could Aaron be working for them?" she asked.

"Maybe. The DEA could have been in touch to try to turn him—maybe that's what happened."

"And someone found out, that's why they staked out the shop?" she asked.

He glanced over at her; she still held herself stiff with him but she was relaxing more and more as they talked about what was going on with the card and the cartel chasing them.

"Maybe."

"In TV shows that's always the case," she said. "That would be nice. Then I wouldn't have been wrong about Aaron being a nice guy."

Nice wasn't something that Xander ever gave any thought to but he got what she was saying. "Aaron can be a nice guy to you and still be a criminal. Doesn't mean you read him wrong."

She shrugged, chewing her lower lip between her teeth, reminding him of the way those teeth had felt on his own lip when she'd sucked it into his mouth. He turned his head away and looked down at his phone for a distraction.

"Seems that as the daughter of a sheriff I should be able to recognize the bad guys," she said.

She sounded a little bit surly and he hid a smile. "Yeah, but it doesn't work that way."

"How does it work?" she asked. "Plus how do you know?"

"I read a book on it."

He had read many books on psychology and interpersonal relationships, as well as family dynamics and how they affected people as they became adults and entered the workplace. He couldn't be a bodyguard if he didn't know how to analyze the people close to his charges. Everyone had something complicated simmering under the surface.

"What did it say?"

"Just that we sometimes see what we want to see. That's how magicians and illusionists are successful. When Aaron came to you for work, he presented himself like a down-on-his-luck guy who needed a gig. That's what you saw. There's no fault in you."

She crossed her arms over her chest again and shook her head. "I don't like it. I've always thought I was a good judge of character."

She probably was. In her daily life he'd guess not many people were trying to deceive her. "That's why Aaron was able to fool you, you're used to relying on your instincts and they have always been right or right most of the time. So when someone who is used to deceiving shows up you see only what they are showing you."

"I don't like it. Makes me feel gullible."

She was naive in a way because she believed so strongly that doing the right thing would get her the results she wanted. And in her daily life that was all she needed to do. But in this world, the one where cartels and drug dealers and the DEA crossed, it was going to take a lot more than doing the right thing.

He didn't tell her that because he knew that wouldn't make her feel better. And he had her back. He had one objective since he'd scooped her up and ran for the boat. That was to keep her safe and alive.

But she was still worried.

"How long did you say Aaron work for you?"

"Three weeks," she said. "Why?"

"I bet if he'd worked for you longer you would have seen signs of things that didn't add up. As you said earlier he was more of an acquaintance than a good friend," Xander pointed out. "I wouldn't rule out your gut just yet."

She shifted around, curling her legs underneath her. He had a small camp blanket, which he dug out of his pack and tossed over her. "Try to get some rest."

"Are you going to?"

"Not yet," he said. He didn't really need a lot of sleep. Probably a sign of his profession, but he had to be on alert when he was on a job. A threat to his clients didn't stick to a schedule and a certain bedtime. The cartel would be the same. He wasn't going to rest until he got to the bottom of this and Obie was safe.

He'd said to sleep and she was pretending to, but she wasn't sure she actually could. Everything about the day was rushing through her head. She regretted that she'd given in to that need for closeness and kissed Xander.

It made her feel the way she had the first time she'd had sex. She'd been seventeen. Gator had been gone for a few months and Aunt Karen had been demanding things Obie wasn't sure she wanted to give. Obie had felt alone and scared and had thought that she'd find the connection she'd been missing in her boyfriend's arms.

But she hadn't. The sex had been okay. Fair enough, they'd both been new to it and hadn't really known what they were meant to do. But when it was over, even though Bo had held her, she hadn't felt that closeness.

If only she'd remembered that before she'd allowed herself to give in to her instincts and kiss Xander. You'd think that at thirty she'd have more sense than she did at seventeen.

Sex had just created another ripple in her self-confidence. That same confidence that had taken a hit when Aaron had called her from jail. The Quentin men were really pushing her to examine the way she looked at men around her.

She couldn't blame Xander for the way he'd reacted. Either during their making out or after. Well after… She shook her head and rolled onto her back. He'd turned the light out and was sitting quietly near the zippered opening of the tent. She could see the stiffness of his back.

She wished he'd magically turn into someone who would take her away from this nightmare she found herself in. Not realistic at all, she knew that. Didn't mean she wasn't still hoping to wake up at home in her own bed.

"Why did you kiss me?"

Startled, she hadn't realized he knew she was awake.

A part of her wanted to say something that would hurt him. But that was petty and below her. He hadn't asked for any of this either.

"I like you," she said. "You make me feel safe and I don't know, I just did. Why did you kiss me back?"

He turned around, still cross-legged on the floor but now facing her. "I want you."

"I wasn't exactly saying no."

"Yeah. I know. That made it even harder to stop. But I'm not so out of control yet that I don't know what's right."

"And sex with me wouldn't be?"

"I didn't say that."

"I know. I just… I'm feeling odd. I should have pretended to be asleep when you spoke to me."

He moved over to where she was and sat down next to her. "I'm glad you didn't. And *odd* sounds about right for the day you've had."

She nodded, not sure why he'd come closer. He smelled of bug spray now, along with the heady mix of their surroundings. But it wasn't an unpleasant odor. Part of her liked it.

"I don't want to add to the burden of this day," he said.

She understood what he was saying. Her trying to have sex with him had been a reaction to so many things. She liked the way he was so contained and then he'd shared little tidbits of himself with her.

But in reality would they see each other after they got out of the swamp?

Probably not.

His life was miles away and he had no time for relationships. She wasn't entirely sure she would want to be with him after they got out of here anyway. Wasn't sure if she could trust her own judgment. "I'm sorry. Let's put the kiss down to just being happy we were alive and not having to walk any more today."

"That would be sensible," he said.

She hated that word. Every decision that Aunt Karen had urged her to make since she'd come to live with her had been *sensible*. Or *logical*. The *right thing to do*. And the right thing hadn't healed her or solved her problems the way she'd hoped.

"Sensible sucks."

"It does. Seems like a compromise between two shitty choices."

"Exactly. When does anyone say *Do this thing that makes you happy*?" she asked.

"That's not what life is about," he said. "Or at least that's my impression."

"Yeah. I know. I guess almost dying today is making me reframe my life. That might seem melodramatic but maybe that's where I am."

He lay down next to her, stretching out and putting his hands behind his head. "I don't think it's OTT. Days like today force us to grow and change in a way that nothing else will."

"But you must be used to it," she said.

"To being shot at?"

"Mmm-hmm."

"As much as anyone can be used to that. But I meant unexpected accidents that force you off the path you thought you were on."

"Sounds like we aren't talking about me anymore," she said.

She wondered what had happened to him to make him a bodyguard. He'd told her about his brush with the law and about the SAS, but how did the kind man in the picture he'd shown her turn into this hardened warrior?

How did any of us become who we are?

He should have left well enough alone. Let Obie sleep, or pretend to, but he hadn't been able to stop thinking of her. He screwed up when he'd kissed her the way he had, knowing he couldn't let it go any further. The fact that they were being pursued by the cartel should have been enough of a boner-killer to keep him from touching her.

Even now, when he should be sitting by the tent opening on alert. Instead he was stretched out next to her. Talking. But he knew he wanted more. Wanted her under him. So that he could pretend for a few hours in the middle of this strange night that he didn't have regrets.

Regrets about Obie of course and how he'd kissed her and then pushed her away but also regrets about Aaron. The cop in the picture had thrown him. He knew better than to make snap judgments but some-how it had seemed easier to assume Aaron had become a midlevel drug dealer than to look beyond his old anger and pettiness toward his brother and be logical.

Sensible like Obie had said was some kind of double-edged sword that left him feeling unsatisfied.

"So?"

He'd said too much, which was why he usually kept his mouth shut. Perhaps his subconscious wanted to tell her about his brothers and what happened to Tony. Not just Aaron, but the other two as well. His part in the incident that had changed all of their lives.

Helping Aaron was never going to be just a favor from him. Coming here was always going to involve more than he wanted to give. Maybe if he had contacted Aaron sooner, his brother wouldn't have gotten into this mess.

"You must really be keeping something deep down. I get it. That's how I felt for the last decade or so about the swamp. But today when we were in that boat and there was nowhere else to go... I just had no choice but to face the past and the memories I'd buried there."

"You think I'm hiding?"

"I know you are," she said. "That picture you showed me to confirm you were Aaron's brother is old, and the four boys in that picture looked like they'd do anything for each other. Something happened to change that, Xander. You don't have to tell me what it is, but I think that's what you're hiding from."

She wasn't wrong. He didn't want to talk about it.

But the past was suddenly there in the forefront of his mind as it hadn't been when he was working. "Maybe I work so much so I don't slow down and have to face the past."

"That's what I do. I take extra shifts, volunteer at the homeless kitchen two blocks from the shop and just keep myself running until I collapse. I was where you are yesterday."

"Today really didn't leave you many choices, did it?"

"It didn't," she said, rolling to her side, and he turned his head in his hands to look at her. There wasn't really any light or even ambient light in the tent.

His vision was pretty good and his eyes had adjusted to the darkness so he could make out her shape. He had memorized her face earlier so he knew what she looked like even now. But what she felt, how to respond... Not even full-on light would help with that.

Today though he'd felt like he was starting to know Obie. Not that it made it easier for him to open up and talk to her.

"Do you wish you'd said no when Aaron asked you to retrieve the card?" he asked.

"Yes and no. I mean I couldn't have said no once he mentioned the cartel. I wish... I sort of wish I hadn't hired him. If he'd gone to work someplace else then I wouldn't be here."

"So once you hired him this path was inevitable."

"Yeah. I don't know if I said but Aaron reminds me of my brother, Gator. And I have lost him. I thought...

maybe I could save Gator by helping Aaron. Not in real life but in…"

She trailed off and he got it. She was trying to get rid of regret. Trying not to be haunted by it like him.

"Is it working? Do you feel less regret about Gator?" he asked. Somehow it was easier to have this conversation in the dark. He wouldn't have pushed her this way while they'd been walking. In part because of being followed and the threat from the swamp. But here in the dark it felt almost okay to ask.

"I wish I could say yes. But I don't think so. Aaron isn't Gator and he's also not the man I thought he was. I guess that's a pretty solid no."

He rolled toward her. "You didn't do this for Aaron— you did it for yourself. You made a different choice than you did with Gator…or at least that's what I'm guessing. Doesn't mean the outcome is different for either Gator or Aaron but is it something you can live with? Isn't that something to be proud of?"

She reached out and touched his hand. Just her cold fingers against the back of his. "I hadn't thought of it that way. But now that you've mentioned it I do feel better. Last time… I let my aunt influence me and my decision. This time… Well, from the moment I saw Aaron I had to hire him. Mainly because I don't know what happened to Gator and maybe if I hired this broken, lost man someone who ran across Gator might help him."

She rolled onto her back again. "God, I know how that sounds. Sort of woo-woo and like there is some big karmic ledger book that someone is keeping track of and my deeds will help my brother. Nuts, right?"

"Nah. Sounds exactly right for someone who has a complicated relationship with their sibling," he said.

Chapter 14

Obie drifted off to sleep and Xander watched over her through the night. When the first hints of dawn started to light the interior of the tent he shook her awake, taking her in as she stretched before sitting upright.

"I'm surprised I slept."

He wasn't. She had been exhausted and wrung out from the day. "Hopefully tonight you'll be in your own bed."

"Hopefully."

They got out of the tent and Obie went first to have some privacy in the bushes. Xander was on alert as he collapsed the tent and rolled it back up. Obie had folded his shirt up neatly and had taken the spare undershirt he'd packed to change out of her tank top from the day before.

She returned the clearing with his shirt knotted to the left side of her waist. "Thanks for the shirt. I wish I'd worn better shoes. Next time…"

She trailed off and sort of laughed. "I hope there won't be anything like this again, but in the back of my mind I have a list of things I'm going to start carrying in my purse. And I definitely won't leave the house wearing just flip-flops again."

"That's why I'm lugging this thing around."

She glanced over at his pack. "I like the idea of all that stuff, but it's a bit much for me to carry every day. I'd settle for some toothpaste and maybe coffee."

"I have some instant and we could use the camp stove if you want to make some," he said. "You're sort of the expert."

"Okay. Do we have water?"

"My filtration bottle is full. We can fill it up when we get down to the lake and let the filter do its thing. If you don't want to have coffee that's okay too." He wanted to get them moving and away from the camp now that it was daylight. But he knew that sometimes in a situation like this, the little things helped to make it easier for someone like Obie.

"I'm good for now. When we get to the marina hopefully they'll have some."

"It might not be until later this afternoon," he warned her.

"That's fine. Go and get changed. I'm slightly jealous that you have an entire change of clothes," she said teasingly.

"The gun is on the top of pack. Same as last time, there's a round in the chamber and the safety is on. Just click off the safety, point and shoot."

Her face got tight with tension but she nodded. He left her a moment later. He moved quickly. There wasn't really a place to wash up despite being the swamp. The parts they'd been in hadn't been the clean, clear springs that ran through different sections of the Everglades. He used the wipes he'd had in his pack to refresh himself and put on some deodorant before donning his fresh clothes and starting back toward the camp.

He stopped when he heard voices. He reached for his knife, which he kept in a sheath in the pocket of his utility shorts. He pulled it out, moving quickly back to Obie so she wasn't alone when the hikers got to her.

The voices made it seem as if the people weren't too far away. He entered the camp and Obie had the gun held loosely by her side and was turned to face the sound of the talking he'd heard. He came up beside her.

"Thank God you're back. Here," she said, handing him the gun.

He took it from her. "Want the knife?"

"No. I'd probably just hurt myself with it."

"Fair enough. Get ready to go. I'm not sure if they are with the cartel or not but if we move we can put some distance between us."

She nodded. "They are back toward West Lake."

"I know—we'll have to go around. Can you navigate us into the swamp and away from them and then we can double back?"

"I'll try," she said. "Good thing we decided to skip coffee."

"Yup. Let's go."

She put her purse across her body again and he shrugged into his backpack. Obie led the way deeper into the underbrush they'd used the night before to hide their tent. She kept walking until they were obscured by the dense roots of cypress trees. He put his hand on her shoulder to stop her.

The voices were getting closer and he wanted a look at whoever it was. Obie seemed to be on the same page. She turned toward them as well. She had the drybag with her phone in her hand.

"Should I try to get a picture of them?" she whispered to him.

"If you can," he said.

She took her phone from the drybag, quietly stowing the bag. He noticed her screen saver was a painting of an orange blossom. She used her face to unlock the phone and then tapped the camera app. She zoomed in so that their campsite was in focus. They both waited, and a few minutes later a man and a woman entered the trail, looked around and then stepped into their campsite from the night before.

They sat on the log he'd moved and took out a thermos of coffee and both drank from it. Obie had snapped a few photos of them.

He still had no idea if they were just hikers or if they were with the cartel or another party. Though Xander was tempted to rule out a third party. Thus far they hadn't seen anything to make him think there were players looking for the SD card.

The couple finished their coffee and then stood and looked carefully around at the ground. Xander knew he'd wiped all trace of the presence from the area before he'd gone to change. They wouldn't find anything left behind, and Obie was at home in the swamp and had so far been really great at not leaving a trail.

The couple moved on a few minutes later.

For now, they were safe.

They were silent as they continued walking. Obie led the way with Xander occasionally tapping her arm to tell her to change directions. She wanted to be alert for anything in the swamp that she'd recognize as a danger that Xander might miss but she couldn't help her fear of other people.

Something new to add to the list of things that she was going to need to talk to a therapist about. Aunt Karen had taken her and Gator to see one after their parents had died, but Obie hadn't been ready to talk and had started skipping the sessions. She was pretty sure Gator had done the same thing. Eventually Aunt Karen had confronted them about it and told them she wasn't going to keep wasting money if they weren't interested in being helped.

So she'd stopped going. But now she almost wished she hadn't. The last twenty-four hours had shown her how much she had never dealt with. Grief was one helluva thing and it never really went away. It was just softer now. Being in the swamp, thinking of Mama and Daddy didn't hurt the way it used to. But she still missed them.

She didn't need a therapist to tell her that. But she could have used one after Gator left. Obie knew she'd never really be able to forgive herself for letting him go alone. She knew their parents would have wanted them to stick together.

But the unknown had been scarier than staying at

Aunt Karen's with the rules. The woman she was now, who was walking through the swamp with a big man with a gun and a knife at her side, wanted to snort at teenage Obie.

Fear manifested itself in all kinds of ways.

She put her hand up to stop them. The water had been rising and was at her knees now. The area in front of them looked as if it might be getting deeper. The lake was to the southwest of them and she wanted to get to the lake and the marina.

She wanted to be someplace safe and away from everyone who wanted the SD card or her dead.

"Do you think we can start doubling back? It's deeper that way and unless we have an airboat I don't feel safe continuing into that area."

Xander looked at the back trail and then at his compass. He took a few minutes to check the map and the trail again before he put his phone away.

"That should be fine. We are making pretty good progress and we've only gone about forty minutes out of our way if my calculations are correct."

Which she'd lay money on them being right. Xander didn't make many missteps, not when it came to this.

"Okay. With the tide rising I'm not sure what we'll encounter so just watch your feet as we go shallower."

He looked like he was going to say something and then changed his mind. She almost pushed him to say what was on his mind but then stopped. The kiss had been her misstep. Her trying to hold on to someone when life got overwhelming. This morning she'd made up her mind to rely on herself. Just like Destiny's Child had said: *I depend on me.*

She walked south and felt more confident with each step. She started to pick up the pace, the water sluicing around her flip-flops with each step but the sand underfoot was no longer sinking. That was a very a good sign they were getting to firmer land. The swamp was complex and diverse and despite the knowledge she had from her upbringing and the books she'd read there was still so much she didn't know.

She carefully wove them through both mangroves until she saw what looked like a dry path.

It would be nice to stand on firm ground. She took a step toward the path but Xander grabbed the waistband of her shorts and pulled her down into the water using the mangrove roots as cover as a group of four people emerged on the path.

They looked like a mix between the duo from the old camp earlier and the cartel men from the day before. There was no talking or joking between them. They had on khaki shirts and camo utility pants. One guy had his head shaved and had on aviator sunglasses.

They moved in a pattern, searching the area. There was something in the man closest to her that reminded her of her father. Maybe another cop? She looked at Xander but he shook his head. He wasn't trusting anyone other than his team, she guessed.

The water was up to her shoulders so there was no way to get her camera out; she just stared at the foursome trying to remember details. And as they moved past the spot that she and Xander were hiding in, she noticed that the woman closest to them wore a side-arm holstered at her waist.

They had to be police or with law enforcement.

Why wasn't Xander approaching them?

Maybe this group was looking for them and here to help.

Once again she tipped her head toward them and he gave her a hard glare and a short negative shake of his head.

As soon as they were alone she was going to confront him about this. If they were cops they would protect the two of them. Was Xander afraid to admit he needed help keeping her safe?

Xander knew that Obie didn't agree with him that they should stay hidden. She wasn't exactly subtle, and after the third time that she pinched him he knew she was probably going to let him have it when they were finally able to talk. The people looked like law enforcement, which was probably why Obie was keen to talk to them.

But the photos on Aaron's SD card were only a part of the puzzle. And right now Xander was still struggling to figure out if those pictures were important pieces or a distraction. The only person he 100 percent trusted in the swamp was right next to him. She'd come in with him. She'd saved him from being attacked by snakes and crocs, so as far as he was concerned trusting her was a no-brainer.

But these other people? No way.

He wasn't sure if Aaron had been working with the

guy in the suit or if he had been arrested by the guy in the suit, an undercover cop. He should have asked Obie if she remembered what day it was that those photos were taken.

The group moved on after the leader, the bald man in the front, heard from someone via his earpiece.

Damn. These weren't just regular law enforcement and with equipment like that they had the look of some kind of elite team.

He wasn't sure that the team would be working with the cartel but he didn't rule it out either. As soon as they were clear and he felt it was safe, he motioned for her to move.

"Why didn't you let them know we were here? They looked like cops to me," she said, keeping her voice low and still moving cautiously as she led the way out of their cover.

"They look like an elite team. The kind that is hired by someone with a lot of money. I'd say ex–law enforcement. We don't know who sent them. It could be the cartel. They have money," Xander said.

"Or maybe your boss sent them," she said.

Definitely not. As much as they worked with law enforcement a lot in their gigs, Van didn't like working with mercenaries. And other private firms were technically his competitors. "He didn't."

"I'm tired, Xander. If those men can get us back to civilization I wouldn't mind taking a chance. I mean you have your gun… Sorry, I just realized I was thinking if they weren't on our side you could handle them. You're probably tired too."

"I am. If I thought there was a chance they were clean I might have taken the risk. But the truth is I don't know enough to risk it. Do you remember the photos of your shop and Aaron?"

She licked her dry lips and nodded before digging in her bag for her lip balm. "What about them?"

"Do you recall if they were taken on the day he was arrested?"

She considered his question as she found her lip balm and put it on. "I don't think so. Actually it looked like one of the first few days that Aaron started working for us. Why?"

"Just trying to rule out the possibility of him working with an agency or of them trying to turn him," Xander said. "But I don't think that can be done."

"Sorry I'm not more help. And for pinching you. You told me that your job is to keep me safe and you're doing that. I should have trusted you."

He almost smiled. She might have been ticked while they'd been hiding, but now that she was out of the water and on dry ground, she was being fair. He wished for the thousandth time she hadn't been dragged into this mess. But she was making the best of it.

"You should have. But it's okay. Even I wasn't sure if we should make contact," he said. "I'm never going to take any action that puts you in direct danger."

"Thanks for that. Would you have confronted them if you'd been alone?" she asked as they started walking again toward West Lake.

"Yes."

There was no question in his mind that he would

have used whatever means necessary to get information and get out of the swamp. "But I probably would have panicked the first time I saw that croc and gotten bit. So might not have been as tough on my own as you're thinking."

She shook her head as she adjusted the shoulder strap of her cross-body bag. "You would be. I don't think you would have disturbed the croc. You're too calm for that."

He wished he could really lay claim to the calmness she thought she saw in him. Doing a different job in any other part of the world might have allowed him the chance. But he was winging it with Obie, and it was training and skills and her knowledge of the swamp that was keeping them one step ahead of the cartel and this new player who was after them.

It was partially just dumb luck. But then again, Van always said Xander made his own luck.

He would keep Obie safe and deliver her to Van, and then he was going to start talking to the different parties and get the information he needed to solve this puzzle.

Chapter 15

Obie was hot as they continued walking through the swamp. Neither of them talked, but if Xander's mind was anything like hers then the silence wasn't restful. She couldn't help thinking about a third party being involved. What was Aaron into? It had been hard enough to swallow the drug cartel connection, but this seemed to be growing larger.

She couldn't help remembering that her father had been doing a hush-hush investigation when he'd been killed. Officer Wade had told them that he didn't trust the higher-ups.

All of which hadn't really meant much to her at the time. She'd been bereft with grief and not really concerned about her dad's workplace drama. But now she had to wonder if uncovering these memories was helping her make connections between law enforcement and the cartel. What part did Aaron play in it all?

She wanted to ask Xander his opinion, but she hesitated, knowing in her heart that she wanted to find something that would connect the cartel to her parents' deaths. Xander would be honest with her if she was pushing for something that wasn't there.

When they got to the east side of West Lake, she filled his water filtrating bottle while he got out the pack-raft.

"Do you think that the cartel could have ties to law enforcement?" she said, trying for casual and totally failing.

"Uh, maybe. Where's this coming from?"

She shrugged as she put the top back on the water bottle. "Was just thinking about those people we saw… I mean you said they looked like former cops but what if the cartel had guys in law enforcement?"

The more she expressed this theory out loud, the more holes she saw in it. Why would other cops kill her folks when they also saw the cartel as an issue? Unless they were corrupt? Her mind swirled with uncertainty. "Never mind."

The pack-raft self-inflated and Xander turned to face her. "I'm not ruling it out at all. I think you might be on to something. When I called in the first time, Lee mentioned our descriptions had already been given to the cops and they were pretty darned accurate. I'm not sure someone watching from a window would have been that good."

"So the cartel gave our information to the cops," she said out loud. She didn't like the sound of that. "Do you think that's what Aaron found out?"

"Possibly. That would mean that he'd be in real danger. Maybe they aren't sure he has what he mentioned having."

"The actual names?"

"Yeah. And other details. Names from a prisoner aren't enough—he needs evidence."

She wasn't surprised to hear that. "Maybe the encrypted files have it."

"Maybe. I can try another call to Van and see where the team is. I wouldn't mind a pickup out of the swamp," he said.

"Yeah, me too," she agreed. He moved away to make his call and she took her phone out of the dry-bag, putting her SIM in so she could check for missed calls and emails. She had two voice mails, which she listened to. One was a hang-up from an unknown number. The second was from Crispin Tallman's office warning her to be cautious and to go to the nearest police station for her own protection. A shiver went down her spine. Maybe it was just her imagination, but she wasn't as reassured hearing from the DA's office this time. The message's tone was measured but unsettling.

She disconnected the call as Xander walked back to her side.

"What are you doing?"

"Checking voice mails and then emails. I have to let Hilda know I'll be out again today," she said. "Tallman's office warned me to be careful who I trust and go to the cops for my own safety."

"We can discuss it after you take the SIM card out of your phone again. I want to limit the time you are on it."

"Why?" she asked as she texted Hilda she wasn't going to be in the office. Hilda immediately messaged back asking if she was okay.

Yes. Hope to be back to work tomorrow. Watch out for yourself and the staff. Aaron was into some dangerous stuff.

Thanks for the warning. We will. Stay safe. Xoxox

She hearted Hilda's last message and then turned her phone off and removed the SIM. She turned to Xander, who looked relieved as she put both items back into the drybag. "Did your team have any info for you?"

"First tell me what the district attorney's office said. Also, did you call them back?" he asked.

"No, just listened to the voice mail. They just said that I was in danger and to go to the cops so they could keep me safe," she said. "It wasn't Crispin but one of his assistants."

"Okay. Well, that fits a little bit with what Van told me. He hasn't been able to speak to Tallman at all. His office has strongly suggested that I turn myself in and bring you to safety. Van says as of right now they haven't been able to crack the encrypted files. But they are hopeful it will be by the end of day."

"We could just go to the jail and ask Aaron to open it," Obie said.

"Yeah, I'm pretty sure he'd tell them to *f* themselves."

"Maybe. I warned Hilda."

"I also asked Van to send someone over and he's sending Luna and Rick. They'll keep your coworkers safe and be on alert if anyone shows up there," Xander said.

Well, that seemed like a lot of good information. Why didn't that make her feel any better? Probably because they still didn't know what exactly was going on.

"I wish I understood this," she said.

"Me too. There is definitely more to this than Aaron let on when he contacted me and asked for a favor. I'm not sure if he is part of it or just stumbled on to it."

"What *it*?"

"Law enforcement. I think you're right about that. The way the information about us has been disseminated so quickly. The fact that the photos we saw were clearly surveillance photos. I think we've only scratched the surface of the danger that Aaron is in and that we are now involved in too."

Rowing across West Lake wasn't bad. It was hotter than it had been the day before, and Obie was quieter today. She was still trying to figure out things that she might have missed when she'd been younger, before her parents had died.

He wanted to help her, and he really needed the distraction. Their safety was still uncertain, especially while the identity of who was working for the cartel, and how far they were willing to go to silence Obie and him, remained obscured. "Tell me more about what you remember before your parents died. Was there anyone new hanging around?"

She continued to row, but her hands tightened on the oar.

"I was so busy with school that I wasn't really paying attention," she said. "Officer Wade was coming to our house a lot more and he and Daddy would close the door to the study to talk."

He was surprised to hear they had a study. "I guess I shouldn't have, but I assumed you lived in a more bare-bones house in the swamp. This area isn't known for having that kind of luxury."

"Ha. Mama had standards and Daddy built her dream home on the land they bought. It's cheap to live where others only see trouble. It abutted the swamp and spread out for acres behind the house. But it was large, made of wood and glass."

Some of the tension that was almost always present in her dissipated when she spoke that home. He knew she was going through rooms in her mind because that was what he did when he let his thoughts drift back to his own childhood. He could clearly remember the room he'd shared with Aaron, the twin beds on either side of the room, the student desks at the end of their beds and the walls covered in posters.

Both of them had been huge comic book fans and gamers. So whenever an anticipated game was released, they'd go down and buy the posters and put them up. He had stopped gaming for years because it was so closely tied to his brothers. But Kenji played Halo and had challenged Xander to try to best him. So he had started playing again.

He shook off those thoughts and forced his mind back to the puzzle he wanted to solve. "Who was Officer Wade?"

"I'm not sure. He wasn't a deputy at the sheriff's

office because they were all called deputy. Daddy just introduced him and said they were working together."

Interesting. So law enforcement but not local. "You made the connection to the cartel. Was that because you heard your father mention it?"

"Oh yeah, and he and Mama had a fight about them. She said something like 'La Familia Sanchez cartel is going to cost you your own family. Let it be.'"

She'd slipped into a deep Southern accent when she'd spoke her mother's words. "What did your father say?"

"Be easy. He used to do that all the time. Tell us to breathe and that everything would be okay," she said, her tone tightening again. "Guess he was wrong that time."

Maybe. So the mom was worried and there was a new "cop" at her house all the time. He wished she'd been older so she might remember more. It wasn't a lot to go on, but it was enough to prove that he needed to dig deeper. When they stopped for another break he was going to have Lee dig into Officer Wade.

"Did you ever hear Wade's first name?" he asked.

"No. I think Gator knew it. He kept in touch with Wade for a few months after we moved to Aunt Karen's. We both thought that it wasn't an accident. There was no way Daddy would have taken the airboat out without a thorough check and he would have noticed the small hole in the intake pipe."

"That was the cause? What happened exactly?"

"There was a spark from the engine and the fan on the airport flamed it and the boat caught on fire. The report said it was instantaneous and there was not time for Mama and Daddy to jump overboard."

Her tone implied she wasn't buying that either. "What do you think?"

"That they were killed and then someone made it look like an accident. Gator thought Daddy had evidence that involved officers who worked for him and the cartel. But no one was listening to two teenage kids even if they had respected our daddy."

"So then you got sent to live with your aunt, your bother kept in touch with Wade and then what happened to him?"

She pulled her oar out of the water and leaned forward. "He left. It was two weeks before his eighteenth birthday. So the cops and Aunt Karen looked for him for a little while but then he was an adult so they stopped."

"What about you?"

"I knew they wouldn't find him. Gator told me he'd had enough of Aunt Karen and he was going back to the swamp. He wanted me to go with him...but I said no."

"Do you wish you'd gone?" he asked. It had nothing to do with solving the puzzle of her parents' deaths but it would help him in the picture he was creating of Obie in his head.

She shrugged but didn't say anything.

There was something about looking into the past and almost wishing you would have made a different choice. But he was self-aware enough to realize he wouldn't have made different choices. He had the feeling that Obie was in the same place.

She might wish she'd gone with Gator, but she knew that she never would have. She chose to move forward with her life. That didn't mean she'd forgotten her parents, but she'd been strong enough to know that she couldn't go back. That there was nothing for her there.

He respected that. Hell, each new thing he learned about her made him like her more.

Until this moment, she had forgotten Officer Wade wasn't with the sheriff's office. Talking with Xander about the past continued to unlock these pieces of her memory. And the shoulders of the man she'd seen the back of in that photo with Aaron…could they be Officer Wade's?

But without knowing who he worked for, she felt like she was spinning her wheels. "Do you think Wade was talking to Aaron?"

"Perhaps."

She pulled her oar out of the water again and turned to face him, so frustrated. "Can you just give me a yes or no answer?"

"No," he said and for a moment she thought he might be teasing her. "I want to but we don't have enough information."

"I get it. When do you think we will?" she asked.

"We might have to go and talk to Aaron."

She had been wondering if that was the case. He was the one who'd dropped them in his mess and he was probably the only one who could figure it out. "He told me to take the card to the district attorney's office. I'm not going to ask if you think that means they might be working together. I'm pretty sure you'll say maybe."

"Perhaps," he said.

She shook her head, tempted to rock the raft and tip him into the lake. He was being so frustrating. But it was a distraction from the endless rowing and her thoughts bouncing between the present threat and the past. She wished she could remember more of those weeks from the time Officer Wade showed up until her parents had died. But she'd had a crush on a new boy and holed up in her room journaling. It had been the beginning of junior year and she hadn't been interested in her father's work.

"If it is Officer Wade and Aaron is in jail…maybe he's the one we should be looking into," she said.

"I agree. I'm going to ask my team to investigate him. Right now we are coming up with a lot of possibilities and any of them are viable but until we know more, they are just theories. I know you want answers. Heck, I would like them too. But for now getting you to safety is where the focus needs to be."

"Yeah, I get it. I mean I think we are doing everything we can to get safely to the marina."

"We are. And talking about different things that occur to us is a good exercise. It helps to see patterns the other one might not see. Like the one you made with Wade. That's a solid connection. Too bad you lost touch with him."

If she'd gone with Gator would she still have been in touch with Wade? Her life would have been very different, and more than likely she wouldn't be here in the swamp with Xander. Not meeting Xander… She wasn't sure she wanted that path, if that choice would have been better.

It felt pointless to be speculating. She just had to keep trying to figure out what Aaron's connection was to the cartel, and maybe to her parents.

Life didn't work that way. Aunt Karen had told her more than once that fair wasn't something that happened in life. Parents died, brothers ran away and girls had to just figure out how to take care of themselves.

Until this moment she didn't think she'd appreciated what Aunt Karen had given her. The woman had made Obie resilient and independent and as much as she might view her life as just an existence. She was safe and had a roof over her head. And usually no one was trying to kill her.

"Once we get to the marina, what's next?"

"I'm hoping my team will be there with transport. We can get to a safe house, clean up, view the data files and then make a plan."

"If that doesn't happen?"

"Then… I'll get us transport and to a safe house. Same plan except it's just you and me."

She preferred that option. She trusted Xander now but she wasn't sure about his team. She'd always had a very small circle of people around her. And she didn't know about bringing new faces into it.

It didn't matter what Xander wanted. If that SD card held information that his boss could use, who was to say that he wouldn't sacrifice Aaron to get it?

But as Xander said they didn't have to worry about that now. Right now it was just getting across the lake.

"Croc three o'clock," Xander said.

"That's a gator," she said, guessing it was a young adult. Looked to her to be about six feet long.

"Uh, what?"

"Yeah. Once we left the salt water behind we are in gator territory."

"Do they get along?"

"For the most part. They coexist down here. It's the only place in the world where that happens."

"The only place in the world," he repeated.

It made her think this might be the only place where she'd be comfortable with him. This time on the lake and on the run was starting to feel normal to her. Like this was her life from now on.

Her life with Xander? She knew that there wasn't a future in it but at this moment she couldn't imagine him not by her side.

Chapter 16

Storm clouds gathered behind them coming up from the Caribbean, and Xander started to steer them toward the northern shore line. West Lake was bigger than Cuthbert Lake, and though he'd thought they could make it across in a few hours, he had a feeling it was going to take much longer.

Obie was a champ, rowing and digging in stronger as the breeze kicked up and thick, warm raindrops randomly splattered on them.

"That storm isn't moving too fast, but it looks like it's a beast," she said. "This one… We might need to use the tent. Even then…we need to find some place that is sheltered."

"Yeah? I'll let you find that. I'll have to deflate the raft."

The rowed harder. Today he'd stayed more to the shoreline after the storm yesterday, so it only took them about ten minutes to get close enough so that Xander could jump out and pull them out of the water with one yank of his arm. Obie hopped out as soon as they were ashore and started scouting for an area.

This part of the lake was similar to the area near

Lake Cuthbert. There were cypress trees with their knobby knees sticking out of the water near the shoreline giving way to small bushes. The farther she moved from the lake, they encountered larger trees that she recognized as live oak and then one huge orchid tree.

As they got closer to the Everglades new flora and fauna were starting to show up. The area closest to the Atlantic was giving way to the inland swamp. The orchid tree's branches fell to the ground and while being under a tree during a lightning storm wasn't ideal, when she glanced back over her shoulder the wind and rain she could see moving across the lake toward them was fierce.

They might have a better chance under the tree's sheltering branches. She pushed under one in front of her and found that there was room enough for Xander's tent. She heard him following behind her.

"What do you think? It's a risk because of lightning but I don't know if we're going to find something better in the short time we have."

"Let's risk it. I'll pitch away from the trunk and branches," he said.

The area under the branches turned much darker. The storm was getting closer now. Xander pulled a flashlight out of his pack and then the tent. She noticed he'd deflated the pack-raft and just tossed it on the ground while he went to work on the tent. She pushed the pack-raft into his backpack and hefted it on one shoulder ready to get it in the tent once he had it up.

He had the stakes, and she dumped his pack on the

ground taking three from him. "Start pushing that one in. I'll lay the others out."

Last night she'd been too tired to help but today she wanted to pull her own weight. To show him that she was a partner and not a liability. She pulled the ground covering out and pushed the stake in as far as she could, moving on as Xander came up to secure it. Working together, they got the tent secured and up just as the wind swept through the branches bringing rain in on them.

"Get inside," Xander ordered.

She grabbed his pack as he unzipped and held the flap open for her. She pushed his pack in first and turned to take her flip-flops off before scooting backward into the tent. Xander followed a moment behind her. He zipped the opening closed as the wind and rain seemed to build around them.

They were dry for now, but who knew if they were safe or for how long.

Xander opened his pack and took out the blanket she'd used the night before, offering it to her. "Dry off with this."

She wiped her shoulders and legs and then handed it back to him. It might be harder to get back to civilization than she'd thought. The terrain was rough, and with people looking for them they couldn't take the paths and network of trails that would get them out of here with any speed.

"Do you think they mean for us to run out of food and maybe let the elements kill us?" she asked. "Don't say maybe. Just give me your best guess."

"I'm not sure that's the plan but it wouldn't hurt if

we disappeared with the SD card. They won't know we sent the files to Price Security."

No one knew except the two of them. The last day and a half had reminded her of pieces of herself she'd lost. And she knew that she didn't want to die here.

She wanted to get out of the swamp and figure out who Obie Keller really was. She'd thought she'd lost that swamp girl forever but now knew that she never could. It was part of her soul.

"I have some more protein bars," he said.

She opened her purse and dug around in it, hoping to find a candy bar that maybe she'd missed earlier or something. Anything that was tastier than the protein bars. She found a piece of mint gum that had fallen out of a pack. "I have a piece of gum we can split after."

He smiled over at her. "We might need to fish."

"After the rain worms come out and we can get some bait," she said, but she realized that he was pretty much saying they weren't making it to the marina today. She had figured that out too the moment she'd seen the big storm behind them. This was going to be one that lasted for a while.

The two of them were once again in the small tent together with a storm outside and she looked over at him. She tried to tell herself that she was only attracted to him because of the circumstances but that was a lie. She liked the man he was. The way he kept calm and even reluctantly revealed pieces of his past.

Being back in the tent with her was a kind of torture, and he wasn't sure he was going to be able to resist her this time. He knew that if he touched her, if he kissed her again, he wasn't going to be able to stop himself from making love to her. He wanted her and she wouldn't forgive him if he touched her and then pulled back again.

He wouldn't either.

He'd never been a wishy-washy man. That wasn't how he was built. And because he'd always prided himself on his iron control when he was with women, he falsely assumed that he wasn't one to fall. But that had ended today when they'd been hiding in the water watching the foursome clearly searching for them. He could no longer pretend that he didn't want her or that he could resist her. She'd somehow found her way under his skin.

"Should we high-card for the truth again?" she asked. "The only other game I know is Go Fish or Slap Jack."

"Slap Jack?"

"Oh, you don't know the high-skill game?" she asked.

He could tell she was teasing him and wondered what the game was she spoke of. He really didn't care because if he high-carded her for the truth, he was going to ask if she still wanted him or if she'd welcome a kiss from him. He had condoms in his pack because…well, he'd thought he might be out in Miami after he checked in on Aaron. But this wasn't a hookup.

Obie was no longer a stranger and that made everything inside of him tighten with both anticipation and a sort of fear. The last person he'd tried to protect that he cared for had been his brother. The one no one spoke about. The one who was now paralyzed.

But he'd found a kindred spirit in her that he hadn't expected to. One that made the blame he'd inflicted on himself seem less powerful.

"High card," he said, his voice low and gravelly. The lust that he wasn't bothering to temper or hide was there right below the surface.

She arched one eyebrow at him. "What truth are you after?"

"Have you forgiven me for yesterday and will you let me kiss you again?"

She shifted back from him, curling her legs underneath her as she watched him. "Depends."

"Is that your version of *maybe*."

"Perhaps."

This was her way of testing him. To take the temperature of his mood.

He was hotter than he'd ever been in his life and it had nothing do with the Florida heat or the swamp humidity. It came from Obie and he wasn't really in the mood to temper it or hide it from her.

"I want you, Obie. I'm not sure that's the best thing to admit to you but there it is. I know I was an ass last night so if you tell me to eff off I wouldn't blame you."

"And if I told you to eff me?"

Instantly his erection went rock-hard. His mind shifted, and any of the reasons he might have come up with to keep from having sex with Obie were gone.

He reached for her. But she put her hand on his chest. "I'm on the pill and don't have any STIs. What about you?"

"Clean bill of health and I'm not on the pill but I do have a condom in the backpack," he said.

"Would you use it?" she asked.

"Yes."

Of course he would.

He'd been watching her and she'd been slowly working her way under his skin. It wasn't just the way she looked, all feminine and fit. She was capable, and watching her in the swamp had been mesmerizing. She wasn't like any other woman he'd ever met.

He pulled the condom out of his bag and put it in his pocket before crawling over to her. She sat up straighter, then pushed her hair behind her ears like she was nervous. She licked her lips. He had no idea what to do to put her at ease, so he sat down next to her and pulled her against the side of his body. Her head fell to his shoulder, tipping backward to reveal the long line of her neck.

He ran his finger along it and watched as goose flesh spread down her neck and chest. He saw them spread down her arm as well. Her nipples tightened against the cotton fabric of his T-shirt and she shifted her shoulders, turning her head so that he felt the brush of her breath against his neck.

Her hand went to his chest as she turned toward him. He lowered his head, kissing her as he'd been wanting to do since the moment she'd come in his arms last night. He thrust his tongue deep into her mouth. Now that he had her in his arms he wasn't in a rush to get her naked. He took his time with the taste of her and the feel of her against his body.

Her hand was on his abdomen, her fingers kneading him through his own shirt. He put his hand on her breast cupping it and rubbing his palm against her erect nipple.

She gave a slight moan as she tipped her head farther back. Her neck was long and exposed. As he lowered his mouth, the scent of her was intensely arousing while he ran his lips along the column of her throat. She shifted closer to him; he pushed his hand up under the T-shirt at the back feeling the slender line of her spine.

She moved to straddle him but he wanted her underneath him. Wanted to be able to see all of her this time. He rolled her to her side and then to the ground. He shifted up on his knees as he undid the button on her shorts and then the zipper, pulling it down.

She lifted her hips and shimmied out of her shorts and panties, shoving them down her legs and then off. He undid his pants and freed his erection, taking out the condom and putting it on.

"Take your shirt off," she said.

He did, pulling it up and over his head and tossing it aside. She touched him. Her fingers burrowed through the light dusting of hair he had on his chest. She ran her finger around his nipple, which felt odd. He wasn't sure he liked it. But she moved on, her nails scraping down his side as she curled her fingers around his waist and urged him forward between her spread legs.

He took his time, running his hands up her legs. She'd gotten a few cuts and bruises as they'd made their way through the swamp and he lowered his head to kiss each of them. Taking his time to move up her legs from her ankles.

"I'm sorry you were hurt," he said.

She put her hand in his hair. Pulling his head up toward hers.

"I'm sorry you were too," she whispered against his lips. He tasted the passion in her kiss and felt it as her hips rubbed against his.

He'd seen her strength so many times so he was surprised by how small she felt. He kissed and caressed her, moving his hands down the side of her body and then teasingly circling her belly button before moving lower to touch her intimate flesh.

He ran his finger lightly over her clit and she dug her fingers into his shoulders as she pulled his mouth back to hers. Sucked his tongue deep into her mouth. "I want you inside me this time."

His cock jumped at her words and he shifted his touch lower to make sure she was ready for him. She was wet and ready and he pulled his hips back, positioning himself until the tip of his cock was at her entrance.

He sank slowly into her. Her body was tight and resisted him at first, but she dug her feet into the floor of the tent, pushing up toward him until he slid all the way into her. Hilt deep, he rested there. His body was tense and the need to thrust into her until he came rode him hard. But he wanted to make sure she enjoyed this too.

She had her hands in his hair again and arched against him, whispering sensual words in his ear. He stopped thinking about trying to control this and gave in to the power she had over him. He kept one hand on her clit teasing her until he heard her breath catch at the back of her throat and that groan he'd heard last night when she climaxed. He felt her pussy tightening around him and then he put his hand under her hip, lifting her up into his body as he thrust harder and faster into her. Driving himself higher and higher. Sensation spread down his back and his balls tightened before he came. He continued driving into her until he was empty and spent. He heard her groan again and then he collapsed against her, careful to support his weight. He rested his forehead against her and her eyes opened and she looked up at him.

She touched the side of his face with a gentle hand and he knew that he was never going to be able to go back to being just her bodyguard. Not that he'd been since the moment they'd entered the swamp. But he had at least been able to pretend to himself that he still held on to a bit of objectivity.

Now though he saw through that for the lie it was. There was no denying that he cared about her. He wanted to keep her safe and he would kill anyone who put her in harm's way.

The beast that he always kept tightly leashed inside had woken and was on alert now. There was no going back to the Xander that he'd been when Van had sent him to Miami.

He was the Xander Quentin who'd left the SAS and tried to fight the world. Before he hadn't had anything but rage and anger to fuel him.

Now, rather than those dark feelings born from his own guilt and shame, he had Obie and his desire to keep her safe.

"You okay?" he asked her.

"Yeah. That was nice. You?"

He hugged her close as he rolled to her back and she cuddled against his side. He knew he should get up and clean up. Get himself ready to defend her if anything happened, and given where they were and the people after them, that was a very real threat.

But he took these few minutes for the both of them. Just held her at his side and looked down at her. He'd never experienced anything like this before and knew he wouldn't again. He just held her and something like peace went through him.

Which scared him more than anything the cartel or the swamp could threaten him with.

He hoped he hadn't put her in jeopardy by making love to her but he couldn't regret it. Wouldn't let himself.

Chapter 17

"I'd like to know more about your family. I feel like I've told you about mine but there is a lot about you I don't know," she said, her voice soft and husky in the dark.

"What would you like to ask me?"

In the darkness of the tent it was somehow easier to open up. He'd cleaned up and they both were dressed again. He'd wedged his pack under his head and Obie was curled against his side as the rain continued to pound the tent. The wind was scary at moments, gusting and then calming down, but the storm seemed less fierce now.

"How did you and Aaron fall out?" she asked after they'd been lying together talking about her family.

He wasn't sure how to put into words what had happened. The story in his mind was full of emotion and action and, of course, a little blood. "You know I have three brothers. We were just always this rough little group. We fought and tried to best each other. Even when we played a sport, we played hard. The local A&E knew my mom by name because at least one of us was in there every few weeks needing stitching up or with broken bones."

"That sounds interesting. I can't imagine that kind of childhood. If I got hurt it was from brushing against a poisonous plant or stepping on something. Gator and I didn't fight."

"You are a woman," he said.

"Does that make a difference?"

"To me it does. I wouldn't just punch you," he said.

"You would Aaron?"

"Yes. In fact when we get out of this and I go visit him in jail I'm going have to try really hard not to deck him."

She laughed. "Well, don't. He is obviously in over his head, which is why he called you. He must know he can count on you."

"He can," Xander said. Even though they hadn't spoken and he'd been reluctant to come to Miami, he knew he wouldn't have been able to resist for long. That bond formed in blood, sweat and fistfights was too strong.

"See, that's good. So you grew up roughhousing with your brothers," she said gently.

"Yeah, I guess that's a better way to put it. When I was fifteen and Aaron was sixteen we were playing rugby at the local pitch. It was me and Tony versus Aaron and Abe. Do you know rugby?"

He was trying to avoid answering her. Setting up the story so that maybe she wouldn't see that he was the one responsible for everything that happened. That she wouldn't get a glimpse of the monster that he had been. That she'd still see whatever version she'd made him. Because she liked that guy and Xander had never truly been able to like himself after that rugby match.

"Sort of. Isn't it like football without pads?" she asked.

"Yeah, sort of. It's a rough game, sort of a test of strength and power. The game was really just another way for us to fight without really fighting. I hit Aaron hard in a tackle and he hit his head. There was blood."

"And he got mad after that?" she asked. She was running her fingers along the folds in his T-shirt, plucking them into peaks and then pushing them flat. Her touch was soothing and he could almost close his eyes and drift off.

Except that was a lie. Now that he'd let himself start remembering that day there was nothing soothing about it.

It had rained and the field was muddy. Tony high-fived him when he'd taken Aaron down hard. Aaron and Abe were huddled together and looking over at the both of them.

There was no way they'd allow a tackle that hard to go unanswered. But Tony was the biggest and strongest of the four of them, even if he was second oldest. He pulled Xander close and told him he'd take the hit.

Xander disagreed. He could handle Aaron, but Tony didn't argue. When the play started again he just shoved Xander to the side as Aaron tackled Tony hard to the ground.

None of them had paid attention to their position on the old pitch or that they'd drifted toward the side. They were too intent on winning, on beating the other team. When Tony hit the ground it was hard, and at first Xander thought his brother was just dazed. But Tony's neck had hit a large rock and he took damage to his spine and the higher cervical nerves, which left him paralyzed.

"It was all my fault," he said.

"How do you figure? Aaron hit your brother not you and I'm not blaming Aaron either. How could you have known that would happen?" Obie said.

He was surprised to realize he'd been talking out loud, that he was finally admitting the truth. "I knew Aaron would retaliate."

"Your brother did too. He protected you."

"Yeah. Well, that's the last time anyone did. I realized that day that I had to take care of myself."

She pushed herself up with her arm on his chest and looked down into his face. "Why?"

"Because it's easier to handle the pain of broken bones and skin."

The rest of that afternoon was a blur. He knew they'd called an ambulance and their mom. Aaron was in shock and denial. He ran away before the ambulance came. After that they were never the same. He didn't try to talk to anyone; that wasn't what Quentin men did.

He'd helped his brother as much as he could. But eventually seeing big, strong Tony not able to move on his own had broken something in Xander and he had to leave. "I joined the Royal Marines and got a chance to join the SAS. Aaron was chosen as well. We didn't touch each other but we competed in everything. I was determined to beat him and prove I was the better man. Not like that would change what had happened."

"That was the last time I saw him," he said.

"Was that why you were so reluctant to come and help?"

He sighed. "No. Not that."

"Then what?"

Obie's heart ached for Xander and how it had shaped him into the man he was today. It also explained why he hadn't just rushed to Aaron's side. A wedge had come between the two men. She was pretty sure he wasn't going to say any more for now.

She heard a familiar sound and sat up. "Airboat."

"What?"

"That's an airboat."

"Do you think they can find us?" he asked. Scrambling up and getting his weapon, he moved to the opening of the tent.

"The branches are offering some cover and we are on higher ground. The path was dry around us but with all the rain it might be wet enough for them. I don't know. I guess I should have led with that."

"It's good. Let's get out of the tent. We're pretty much sitting ducks here."

She put her cross-body bag on but left her flip-flops in it. She'd need to move quickly and was more sure-footed without them. She moved next to Xander by the tent flap. He started to lift the zipper when the engine of the airboat seemed to get closer and a spotlight moved through the branches of the trees.

Her heart was racing. As Xander had said, this tent wasn't going to offer any protection to them at all. He pushed his body in front of hers, using it to shield her as he opened the flap. She couldn't see anything but his big back and neck. The spotlight moved past them. Xander exited the tent and then offered her his hand. She scooted out and immediately moved back toward the large trunk of the tree. Using it as a shield, she made herself as small as possible. Xander pulled his pack out of the tent and then moved to Obie's position.

He handed her his weapon as he put the pack on. "Let's move away from here, but not too far. I want to get a look at them."

It was dark and hard to see so Obie made her way carefully out from under the orchid tree's sheltering branches. The ground was marshy but too dry for an airboat. She scanned the dark horizon and noticed a clump of some trees a short distance to the left. She had no idea if an animal or snake was already using the area and they wouldn't be able to check before they ducked into cover there.

She nudged Xander with her elbow and he looked at her, eyebrows raised. She pointed to the area and when he urged her to move she leaned closer to whisper in his ear, "There could be something in the bushes. Might be dangerous."

"Understood. I think it's a chance we have to take."

His low tone was confident as always, but she was scared. She was reaching the end of her resilience. There wasn't much more she could take.

Now she was worried about Xander too. Not that

she hadn't been at first, but he'd been a stranger and he definitely wasn't any longer.

She darted quickly across the clearing to the area she'd spotted and it was full of low trees and fallen branches. Not really much of a cover, but they could duck behind the fallen tree limbs and use them as a block from being seen.

Xander was right behind her. "Good job. Duck down so that your head isn't visible."

"How will I see them?" she asked.

"You won't. I will. Take my phone and open the message app and hit SOS and Send."

He shrugged out of the pack and set it between the two of them. She dug out his phone from the drybag, which was near the top. It was password protected.

"Password."

"Checkmate."

Of course it was. She typed it in and then found the message app. There was an SOS button right at the top so she hit it. She watched it send, wondering who he was calling. And why hadn't he done that earlier.

But she was pretty sure she knew why. They'd both been thinking they'd be at the marina hours ago. And whoever was searching for them was out in some really shitty weather trying to find them. They weren't giving up easily.

"Sent."

"Who did you call?"

"My team. I thought we'd be okay but there is something I'm missing if they are searching this hard for us," he said.

"I was wondering that too. I mean you said if we died—"

"Not just that but why not wait for us to come out of the swamp and hit us then?" he asked.

"I don't know."

"I don't either. Those encrypted files are the key. We need to get into them," Xander said.

She agreed, but if his team couldn't crack into them then the only solution was going to get Aaron to talk to him. But Aaron was in jail, so that meant…she'd have to contact Crispin Tallman's office and get him to talk to Aaron for them.

She knew that Xander trusted his team to come and help them. But they might not make it in time to save them from these people who weren't giving up.

Xander took his phone from her and put it back into the pack. She thought maybe the airboat had moved on but it doubled back. She held her breath as two men got off of it and walked to the orchid tree, finding their tent.

Obie was a good partner, staying low at his side. She'd done everything he asked, but he heard her quick intake of breath when the men started to search their tent. There was nothing left inside of it and they could make any guesses as to what they thought happened. He saw them looking for a trail and was tempted to stay put and let the guy find him so he could take care of things once and for all. But giving away their position might be more dangerous right now.

Obie wasn't a fighter and he wouldn't put her in danger. Instead he took her arm and pointed behind them.

She got low and crept forward on her stomach. His pack was big and would raise his profile and he needed to keep his hands on his weapon. He was tempted to leave it but anyone who found it would know who he was and be able to track him to Aaron.

He turned and noticed that Obie was waiting with her arms extended. She'd already figured out his pack was a problem. He pushed it as quietly as he could with one great shove toward her. She grabbed the straps and pulled it toward her body and into some deeper coverage.

They were out of the mangroves. The trees and ground cover here wasn't as bountiful. But Obie read the swamp and found them the best coverage she could.

He kept low, crawling to her spot and ducking into the brush next to her. "I'm not sure if we are going to be able to find more coverage than this."

Her whispered comment only reached his ears and he used his free hand on her shoulder to squeeze, hopefully reassuring her that it was okay. "I'll make this work. Stay hidden as long as you can. I'll take care of them."

He glanced at her to see if she understood. Her face was tight; she just gave him a small nod. The tension was palpable and he felt like he was failing her as a bodyguard. He never should have made love to her. He should have been paying attention to the elements and had them on the move before the airboat came.

But he'd wanted those few moments for himself. Had held Obie in his arms and felt like he was okay. But that had made things worse. Much worse.

The men searched in a pattern, but when they reached the fallen logs where he and Obie had first hid they scanned the landscape. One of them shrugged and then they turned back toward the airboat.

It might be a setup. Pretend that they were going to move on but stay close enough to keep an eye on their target. There was no getting back to the lake since the airboat was between them.

And the brush here wasn't dense enough to provide cover for the both of them. The SOS signal he'd had Obie send would give his location to Van. His boss would be on the way, but he might be leading the team into a firefight, or worse. He needed to get to a spot where he could provide better cover for them.

"We have to move."

"Do you think it could be a trap?" she whispered to him.

"Yes. So when we move assume they are watching us. I need to get to higher ground. My boss will respond to the SOS and I don't want to leave him open to attack."

"What should I do?" she asked.

"Stay with my pack. I think you're shielded for now. I'll watch you as well. But I can move quieter or more easily on my own."

Her lips tightened and her eyes got wide. He put her hand on his shoulder and then on the side of his face. "Stay safe. I don't want you to get hurt," she said.

"Don't worry about me," he said, though he appreciated that she was concerned for him. He was going to make damned sure they were both okay. No matter what it took.

He wished he'd packed a rifle because that would give him an advantage that his handgun didn't have.

"Stay hidden until I come back for you unless they find you. Then run in the direction I'm going and I'll cover you. Leave the pack and everything but the SD card. Okay?"

"Yes." Her voice quavered on the word. "I don't think you'll have to do that but better to be ready for it."

"Thanks," she said.

He leaned in and gave her a quick, hard kiss on the mouth and she hugged him tightly to her. He savored the embrace for a moment and then turned and made his way out of their hiding spot. He stayed low, watching the path in front of him while keeping his senses trained on the direction that the men had gone in the airboat.

Airboats were noisy, which was one thing in Xander's favor. But Xander feared they'd ditch the airboat and come back on foot. He listened until for the sound of the airboat and it seemed to be moving away from their position, but that didn't mean the threat had passed.

He kept moving until he found a copse of trees close enough together to offer him some cover. They weren't large but were big enough he should be able to stand up, which would give him a better view of anyone who came at Obie.

Chapter 18

Obie felt panic rising in her like tidal changes. Xander was no longer visible from her location. She didn't doubt that he was watching over her. But he was one man with a handgun and a knife. There were at least two men who had been looking around their campsite clearly aiming to capture them.

They were officially in over their heads.

The weather hadn't cooperated either. But the weather was the least of her problems. Like her daddy used to say, she wasn't going to melt from the rain. But she could die from a bullet.

She heard the airboat as it pulled away from their area and then moved off toward the east. From growing up in the swamp she knew that the sound could carry for a very long way, so when it disappeared about ten minutes later, she suspected that wasn't good news.

Had the men left to double back? Were they going to wait and see if she and Xander showed up?

An organization as big as the cartel had a lot of resources. They probably had a large number of people they could hire to search for her and Xander.

The storm had moved on but some rain and clouds

lingered, and it was close to sunset even though they couldn't see it.

If they were going to make it through the night they'd need help.

She looked at her hands, which were shaking, and then back across the swamp to where Xander had disappeared. Knowing what she had to do, and even if it was something he wouldn't agree with, she took her phone out of her purse and the drybag. She put the SIM card in.

As soon as it booted up, she realized it was almost dead and she had no signal.

Xander's pack was right there. She knew where his phone was. She'd just used it to send his SOS signal. She pulled his phone out. His signal was weak and the SOS hadn't gone through. Hell.

She hit the button to send it again. While it was slowly trying to connect she made the decision that she'd been debating for the last few minutes.

Getting the number from her phone for Crispin, she texted him from Xander's phone. Said they were being tracked by dangerous-looking men and were heading toward the marina at the west side of West Lake. She hit Send, not sure if either message would get out.

Then she put Xander's phone back in his pack and turned hers off since it was about to die didn't bother with the SIM card. There was no one around and the sounds of the swamp seemed muted. Or maybe that was simply the rising panic in her own ears.

She couldn't sit still much longer and put her cross-body bag on and then moved to put Xander's backpack on, too. When someone lifted it up, she screamed and turned as a hand came over her mouth.

The touch was familiar, and when she gazed up she saw it was Xander. "How? I just looked and didn't see you."

"I crawled. I think it's time to move," he said. "Sorry for the scare. How far do you think the airboat traveled before it stopped?"

She wasn't good with distance. "It's hard to tell in the swamp. It felt like about ten minutes until I could no longer hear them."

"Same. Let's move out. We'll stick to those trees over there," he said.

"Okay." She should tell him she'd sent the text to Crispin.

"Did the SOS send?"

"Not when I first hit it. I just tried sending it again. The storm was probably interfering before."

"Maybe. Either way I'm getting you to the marina tonight," he said.

She agreed. "*We* are getting out of here tonight. I want you safe too."

"I'm used to being in the line of fire."

"That doesn't mean that I like seeing you in it."

He leaned down and kissed her quick and hard like he had earlier. But didn't say another word. He put his backpack on and then held his hand out to her to help her to her feet. He put his hand on the small of her back and pushed her toward the tree line. She moved quickly, watching where she stepped because she was still barefoot.

Running in flip-flops wasn't an option, and until she knew that the men who'd been looking for them weren't behind them, she'd have to leave them off.

They walked along the trees for what seemed like hours until they got to the north side of the lake. Xander was very cautious keeping his eye on the trees, and now that it was twilight there were more shadows.

The sounds of the swamp had always been a lullaby to her but they weren't any longer. Because she didn't want to face another unexpected danger, didn't know what other sounds were hidden beneath.

Suddenly there were lights in the distance.

Xander grabbed her arm and pulled her down behind the large trunk of a live oak. She held her breath as he pulled out his weapon and they both waited.

Van walked into the clearing and Xander let out a sigh of relief. "That's my boss."

He pulled Obie to her feet and led her out into the open toward Van. As soon as they stepped out of the trees, he heard a bullet fly past his head. He pushed Obie behind him and turned to return fire, but men stepped out surrounding them.

Van put his hands in the air and Xander did the same. Obie was between the two of them. "We don't want any trouble."

"We just want the card." The man who stepped forward was one of the two who'd been in the airboat. He had a handgun held loosely by his side and wore a bulletproof vest over his T-shirt and camo pants.

"We don't have it," Xander said.

"We know you do," the man said. "That's why we've been looking for you."

He edged closer, and the other two people they'd seen with the men earlier in the day appeared out of the surrounding swamp as well. The other three were armed and looked dangerous.

Xander liked his odds a lot better with Van by his side.

"Let's keep calm," Van said, his voice low and gravelly but loud enough to be heard. Several people stepped out in to the clearing, all armed with AK-47s and wearing bulletproof vests.

"Give us the SD card," the man closest to them said.

"I already said we don't have anything," Xander said. He shrugged out of his backpack, letting it fall to the ground. There was no way they were getting out of here without a fight.

And that was fine with him. He wanted to know who these men were working for. The only way he was doing that was by getting information from one of these four.

"Then you're useless."

He turned back to the man who'd spoken and saw him lift his handgun and fire, taking aim not at Xander but at Obie. He spun quickly, putting Obie between himself and Van.

He lifted his own weapon and fired back, hitting the assailant in the shoulder, and the other man's gun dropped to the ground. Xander felt the burn of the shooter's bullet in his left side but ignored it, turning to return fire from the woman on his left.

He hit her in the shoulder and was preparing to fire again when he saw Rick Stone come up behind her and put his gun between her shoulder blades. "Drop it. This close, even a vest can't really protect you."

She dropped her weapon. He turned and noticed that Luna and Kenji were there as well. They disarmed the other two men and Van had subdued the guy that Xander had shot.

He turned to Obie, who was white as a ghost.

"I don't know how the hell they found us. I'm glad the team got here when they did," he said.

"I don't know either," she said. Her hands were shaking. "Are you okay?"

Glancing down at his aching side, he saw blood seeping through his T-shirt. The bullet had only grazed him but had burned though his shirt and skin. He pulled the fabric away and knew he'd need some first aid.

But so would two of the people who'd attacked them.

Van took charge. "Rick, you have medic training—see to the wounded. Kenji, get those other two over here. I want to ask some questions. X, you want in on the questioning?"

"You know I do."

"His wound needs to be cleaned first. This is the swamp not some sterile environment," Obie said.

"Of course. I'm Giovanni Price," he said, holding his hand out toward Obie.

"Obie Keller," she said, taking his hand.

"Nice to meet you."

Van turned away and walked toward Kenji to start talking to the men who'd attacked them. Rick stayed with the woman who'd taken a hit in her shoulder and Luna was working on the guy who'd been hit as well.

Obie went to get first aid supplies from Rick and then came back. "That was dangerous what you did. Why did you do that?"

"What was my option, let him shoot you while I stood there?" he asked her.

"No, I guess not. But I don't like seeing you shot."

"Trust me, this is nothing. I'm not bigging myself up and being all butch. It's just that his aim was bad and the bullet barely grazed me."

"You're bleeding," she pointed out.

"It was a slight hit."

He pulled his T-shirt up and off the wound, cursing as the fabric pulled away from it. She gingerly touched it, cleaning the wound before putting a bandage on it. "That will do for now. So are all these people on your team?"

"They are. I'm glad they got here when they did."

"Me too. Do you think those men were following us?" she asked him.

"I know you're not a fan of this answer but maybe. The part that has me not sure is the guy who came from the same direction as Van."

"Do you think they followed your boss?" she asked.

"No. They definitely didn't follow him," he said.

"Then how would they know where we were? Unless...? I turned my phone on."

He looked over at her. "When?"

"After the airboat left. I wanted to call Crispin. You're strong and everything but still just one man."

"Did you call him?" he asked.

"My phone didn't have a signal," she said, chewing her lip between her teeth. "I used yours to text him. I told him we were heading to the marina."

Xander turned and stalked away from her. So angry at the moment he wasn't sure he could control his temper. If she had trusted him she wouldn't have put them in this position. Or was he making a jump to judgment? Maybe it wasn't Crispin who had alerted the men who followed them. Soon they'd find out.

But until then he needed some distance.

Obie moved closer to Giovanni, though she heard the others calling him Van as he was questioning the men. She noticed the gang tattoo that they'd seen on the first day on their attackers.

Xander had disappeared into the trees and she wasn't sure what to do.

Van finished questioning the men who were tight-lipped, then he called a contact in the DEA, who came and arrested the four people. Xander still wasn't talking to her as they all got into the chopper that Van and his team had arrived in. It was some big military-looking one, and they all flew back to Miami, landing at a private gated beachfront house.

It was a shock to her system to step out of the helicopter and feel soft grass under her feet and not the roughness of the swamp.

Xander started to brush past her but she grabbed his arm. "We need to talk."

"I can't. I'm still mad."

She shook her head. "Fine, then just listen."

He took a deep breath as his team moved past them. She led the way to a pool, which was well lit and had chairs positioned around it. She sat down because she was tired and Xander stood there, glowering at her for a minute before she pointed to the chair next to her and he sat down.

"I'm sorry I didn't do what you asked. I was worried for your safety. You are big and capable and you definitely know your stuff and can keep me safe. But there were four of them and only one of you."

He looked like he was going to speak but she put her hand up to stop him. "I'm not sure if they just surrounded us or if they got the information another way but when we were alone in the swamp I felt there was nothing else I could do to actually help other than to call and ask for it."

Xander leaned back in the chair, stretching his legs out in front of him. He had to be as tired as she was. Every part of her ached and she wanted a shower and some food and to never see these shorts or top again. But it was more important to her to set things right with Xander.

It had only been the two of them for what felt like a lifetime, and now that they were back in Miami everything would change. She didn't want to let him leave thinking that she hadn't trusted him to protect her.

She cared deeply for him, and it was only when she'd seen him put himself between her and a bullet that she'd realized *how* deeply.

"I get it. There is nothing that I could have said to make you feel safe—"

"I felt safe, but you proved to me my worst fears. You weren't safe. You would put your life on the line for me, Xander. That's something that I… I just didn't want you to do."

She licked her lips. They were sunburned and chapped and she was tired and wanted something she wasn't sure she'd be able to have. To just crawl into his arms in a real bed and sleep, knowing they were both safe.

"The last person to try to protect me was Tony," he said.

"I know."

She reached out for him and he let her touch him. She put her hand on his arm and squeezed. "Maybe it's time you let someone else do it. I'm fine."

"For now. And it was a near thing. If that bullet had hit you it would have been low in your stomach."

He sat forward and took her face in his hands. "I can't stop thinking about how close he came to killing you. You are under my protection and those men got the jump on us. I wish you hadn't called the district attorney but the truth is I'm not sure he's connected to those guys. No one is. But I do know that I almost let you get injured."

"Almost? You didn't let anything happen to me," she reminded him, shifting forward until she could brush her lips against his. "You kept me safe."

He didn't say anything else, just lifted her out of her chair and onto his lap, holding her tightly, his head buried in her hair. "I would die before I let anything happen to you, Obie."

They held each other for a few more minutes. Then went up to the house to get cleaned up. Van and his team had spare clothes for them. She showered and got dressed and then went out on the patio where Van was at the grill cooking for the team. There was an ice bucket with Coronas in it and music playing from the speakers. It was so normal it was strange.

She looked around for Xander but didn't see him.

"I'm Luna," the woman said. She had long brown hair that she wore pulled back in a ponytail. She had on a pair of khaki shorts and a light green T-shirt.

"Obie. Thanks for coming to get us."

"No problem. How was the big guy in the swamp?" Luna asked. "He hates the heat."

"He was good. He just kept focused on moving us toward the marina. He's really good at adapting."

"Yes, he is. He's done it often enough," Luna said.

Xander came out a minute later and everyone moved to sit at the table. Obie didn't pay too much attention to what was going on around her at first since this was the first meal she'd had in day or more. But then she noticed that Xander seemed to really fit in with this group. The laughed and joked and talked quietly between each other. He made more sense here with these other highly skilled bodyguards than anywhere else she'd seen him. Which didn't bode well for the way she felt about him.

Chapter 19

Lee came onto the patio looking tired and like she hadn't slept in twenty-four hours. "Broke the encryption. Whoever did the coding was really good. And you guys are not going to believe what's on there."

Xander looked over at Obie, who reached for his hand. He squeezed hers and instantly she saw he was worried. But not knowing was worse than whatever was in those files.

"What have you found?"

"Well, that guy from the district attorney's office that you had me contact…seems like he's close with La Familia Sanchez. Like his cousin is the head of the cartel. Your brother stumbled onto some really sensitive information and put it all together," Lee said.

She connected her laptop to the TV on the patio and streamed the information to it. There were the documents, which, as soon as he read the first line, he knew that Aaron had written. The way he strung words together was distinct and it almost sounded like his brother was talking to them.

Lee read the documents aloud:

"The Sanchez crime family has deep connections not just in south Florida but throughout the entire country. Ten years ago Bartolo Sanchez was just a lieutenant in the cartel but made a big move to spread the operation out of south Dade County. The move was profitable, but what really made the move work was Bartolo's idea to have members of the gang take jobs within law enforcement and the criminal justice system.

"Working with DEA officers, I have been able to find some connections throughout Florida. I've passed the positions and the profile types of these men and women on to my counterparts working the operation in other parts of the country.

"In Miami I have gathered circumstantial evidence pointing to Crispin Tallman, who is married to Bartolo's cousin Luisa. However I'm pretty sure my cover was blown when I made contact with my handler two weeks ago. The photos are included on this card. I suspect I'll be arrested. In which case I will reach out to a civilian who I trust to retrieve the card and crack the encryption."

Lee stopped reading then and looked over at him. "I assume he means you."

"Yeah. Does the rest of the file have the evidence?"

"It does. Seems that someone on Aaron's team made sure that his case went to Tallman so that he could mention the evidence," Lee said.

"He was probably hoping that Tallman would go after me knowing I could handle the heat," Xander said. And because he'd hesitated, Aaron had no choice but to send Obie after the SD card. He had to retrieve it so that Tallman would show his hand.

"Why didn't he protect Obie after he sent her in?" Xander asked. He understood that some plans couldn't be stopped once they were in motion, but Obie had no training and if Xander hadn't been at Aaron's house he was pretty sure she would have been killed and the card would have been taken by Tallman's men.

"He did," Van said. "I had a call from the Aaron in jail as well. Your brother told me he needed you for a job. That's why I insisted."

"Did he give you any details?"

"No, just said it was a family thing," Van said. "I didn't push because you are tight-lipped about your family. I knew that you weren't going to want to go but he was insistent you were the only man for the job."

Aaron hadn't been wrong. Obie needed protection and the first moment, he'd do anything to keep her safe. He would have done the same thing for anyone that his brother sent into danger.

"Why didn't you mention this before?"

"I told you to go and I knew you wouldn't disobey an order no matter how much you might resent me for forcing you to leave. Saying your brother had called me wasn't going to help matters," Van said.

"Fair enough. I guess he had Obie call me because he thought I'd say yes to her," Xander said.

"I really don't like that Aaron used me," Obie said.

Lee pulled up another file. "I'm sure he wanted to keep you out of it, but if you read this file you'll see why he thought you were the best person for the job."

Xander's eyes went to the screen as did everyone else's.

Bartolo's big move that had gotten him promoted was infiltrating the sheriff's department in central Florida. The file went on to detail how DEA Agent Wade had been contacted by Sheriff Keller and, once arriving, had found that his suspicion that drugs were being run through the swamps on airboats was accurate. They started their investigation and noticed that two officers—Deputy Lawrence and Deputy Peters— were always on duty when the airboat activity was reported by locals. Both deputies reported nothing to be alarmed about and that the increased airboat activity was down to better fishing in the swamp thanks to extra rains.

Sheriff Keller and his wife started to do extra patrols from their home and Officer Wade's report said that he believed the sheriff and his wife must have witnessed criminal activity and confronted the cartel members when they were killed and it was made to look like an accident.

Officer Wade saw Deputy Peters the next day and the man had claw marks from what appeared to be a human hand on his face and neck and a busted nose.

Obie started crying softly next to him and he pulled her into his arms, hugging her close. She and her brother had long suspected that the cartel was involved in their parents' deaths but this proof had to be hard to take.

She just kept her head in his chest and Lee closed the file and opened the photos, which showed two men that Xander didn't recognize. "Let's take a few minutes before we figure out what to do next."

Obie couldn't help but think of those marks on the deputy's face, imagining her mom in some kind of fight with the man. Her mama was tough and fierce, so Obie wasn't surprised she'd fought the man who had killed her and Daddy. In her heart she'd always known that there was more to it than an accident but she wasn't really sure knowing the truth helped at all with her grief.

It made her mad as hell to think of men who worked for her father betraying him.

Everyone went to take the break that Xander had suggested. Only the two of them remained on the patio.

She lifted her head from his shoulder and wiped her eyes. Later she knew she would go over the details of what had happened, but right now she wanted justice for her parents, and payback.

"How are we going to get Tallman and Bartolo Sanchez?" she asked Xander.

"Straight to that, well okay. The team will come up with a plan and then we will put it into motion."

"I want to be part of it. I'm not letting them get away with killing my parents or with almost killing you and me," she said.

"We won't."

Xander didn't seem to be hearing her, which was very frustrating. She got that he wanted to protect her. He'd done his job well. But they were back in the city and she was the one with the connection, as weak as it was, to Tallman.

"I'm not sitting this one out, Xander. I want to catch him. It's men like him that made sure that Deputy Peters didn't even have a comment on his record after his involvement with my parents' deaths. He was at their funeral."

Her voice cracked and she shook her head, refusing to let her emotions get the better of her. Not now. Later when Tallman was behind bars and Bartolo Sanchez had been arrested.

"I understand. But—"

She shook her head and interrupted him. "No, you don't. That man sent killers to find me knowing I'd be at Aaron's house in Key Largo by myself. He didn't send just one person—there were like what, six? That's overkill. I can't let you do this alone. You look just like those former law enforcement guys who your team captured and like Aaron. You can't go in and talk to him. He'll immediately suspect you and clam up."

Xander pushed to his feet and walked a few feet from her, turning his back toward her and putting his hands on his hips.

"It can't be me," he said at last. "But it doesn't have to be you either. There are other ways to catch him."

Obie got to her feet and walked over to him. Putting her hand on the small of his back, she leaned around to look up at him. "There are other ways, but I have to be involved in this. I want to take him down. To show him he underestimated me."

He sighed and then put his arm around her, pulling her close to him. Lowering his head, she felt the ragged exhalation of his breath against her neck. "I can't let you get hurt."

She hugged him tightly back to her. She didn't want to see him get hurt either. Over the last forty-eight hours she'd fallen hard for this big British bodyguard who was so careful about letting anyone know who he truly was. But she'd seen him from the beginning. Maybe because of her connection to his brother or her own relationship with Gator.

Something about Xander had drawn her to him the first second she'd seen him. And the last two days had put them in a pressure cooker. A place where there was no time for the facade that she usually kept in place. They'd been stripped raw. Her feelings for him were real and would last for a long time.

She had no idea if he'd stay or if they'd end up making a life together. But her love for him was real. She wanted to tell him, but that seemed secondary to getting his agreement that she could be the bait to set up Tallman and get the evidence they needed for his arrest.

"I'm not going to back down on this. Your boss is smart and once I point out that I'm the logical choice he'll agree. And the only way I can do what is needed is if I know you have my back and are watching over me."

He gave another ragged sigh. "You know I will be. I won't let anything harm you."

His words were firm, sincere and she took them as the promise she knew he meant them to be. She put her hands on his dear face. He'd shaved when they got back, making his cheeks smooth after the stubble that had been there for the last few days. She leaned up and kissed him. Taking her time, hoping that he'd understand from this embrace just how much he meant to her, and that as much as he wouldn't let anything happen to her, she was going to do her best to keep him safe as well.

The information Lee had shared with them would have struck Xander just as deeply as it did her. He was protective of his brother, as much as he said he didn't know the man anymore. He would want to take down the man who was putting his brother in danger. Xander had told her he turned into a beast when someone he loved was threatened and she believed him.

She didn't want him to have to do that. It would be violent and there was a chance that Xander could end up getting himself put behind bars. The only way to save the man she loved was to put herself in the company of a man who'd had no qualms about sending her to her death.

Xander wasn't sure he was going to be able to allow Obie to put herself in danger. She wasn't wrong about Van. He'd definitely see the plus in using Obie to get Tallman. Xander was also very sure his boss would keep Obie safe. The part that was troubling him was if he could keep himself under control.

Obviously they were both still tired from the last

two days in the swamp, so his control was hanging on by a thread. But added to that was the fact that he loved her.

She was like the swamp that they'd just traveled through. There were parts of her that were beautiful and breathtaking and parts that were dangerous, which he adored. She'd been so city girl when they first met, and he hadn't been sure she'd be able to cope with being shot at, but she'd handled it all like a champ.

She'd dealt with her fears and emotions honestly, which he couldn't help but respect. But she also made him feel safe in sharing his with her. He hadn't talked about Tony's accident or his brothers since the day it occurred. His mom hadn't been able to talk to any of them, and his father emoted by working more hours and being sullen at home.

Obie was the first one to make him feel okay that he was sad and angry about what happened. She had just listened and hadn't judged, which was something he hadn't realized he'd needed.

He loved her.

He'd known that last night when he'd held her in his arms instead of sitting at the tent flap with his firearm ready to defend her.

They'd forged a bond in the tent while that crazy summer storm roared outside and kept them safely from being found. Those hours together had been what they'd both needed.

A chance to find the human in each other.

He lifted his head and looked down into her big

brown eyes and knew that he wasn't going to be able to keep his feelings to himself. He put his hand on her shoulder, his thumb rubbing against her collarbone, and she tipped her head to the side.

"What?"

"I—"

"Gather up, team. It's time to make a plan," Van called as he came back on the patio.

Xander just nodded. "Later."

His feelings weren't going to change, and once Tallman was captured there would be plenty of time with Obie.

She slipped her hand into his as they walked back to the table. He noticed Van looking at their joined hands and then back to him, raising both eyebrows. Xander just smiled at the other man. She wasn't a paying customer; there was no rule that said he couldn't be with her. And if Van had a problem... Well, Xander wouldn't like it, but he was willing to walk away to have Obie by his side.

Van just smiled and nodded his head a few times.

"All right, so we need to get Tallman to confess to either setting Obie up or to being a part of the cartel. Ideas?"

Obie raised her hand and then sort of realized what she'd done and put it back down. "I think I might be the one to get him to confess. He set me up."

"He definitely did. What are your thoughts?" Van asked.

"She wants to go and confront him with the SD card," Xander said. "I'll keep lookout—"

"I'll help provide cover to," Kenji said. "I think Obie is the right choice. She knows Tallman and he definitely will be expecting her to make contact now that she's out of the swamp."

Xander knew that the DEA agent who'd arrested the people hired by the cartel was going to keep it under wraps for twenty-four hours. They were also interrogating the people to see if they could get a confession that would connect them to the cartel. But the cartel killed snitches so Xander was pretty sure that wasn't going to happen.

"Exactly. I'll go to my apartment and then call him from there. Might be best if Xander drops me off in case anyone is watching it," Obie said.

She had sound reasoning and, as she had in the swamp, was outlining a logical next step.

"I've been working at the coffee shop so I can show up at your place and act as a bodyguard in the apartment. I'm not sure he'll come for you there but that way you're not alone," Luna said.

"You'll have to wear a wire," Van said. "I guess we should get you to your apartment and make the call. Then see what Tallman suggests. Obie, if at any point you want to back out, just say and we will find another way to get him."

Even before she spoke, Xander knew that she wasn't going to back down. That wasn't her way. Obie was in this until Tallman was caught. He suspected it was a little bit about her parents' deaths and bringing some closure to her past as well as making up for not going with her brother. She tied those two incidents together the way he did his estrangement with Aaron to Tony's accident.

Both of them needed to take Tallman down to save their brothers and make some kind of peace with their pasts.

Chapter 20

It had been weird being back in her apartment after the last few days. She'd gotten dressed in her own clothes and that had felt nice. After a call to Crispin Tallman's office, he offered to meet her in a nearby park instead of having her come all the way downtown.

Assuming that the apartment building was being watched, Luna was the only one with her. Obie missed having Xander by her side but Luna was friendly and put her at ease.

"Let's get the wiretap turned on and then we can head out," Luna said. "Xander and Kenji are in position as snipers and honestly those two won't let anyone harm you. I'll go with you and then get out to jog while you go meet Tallman but I'll keep an eye on you as well. Rick's with the DEA agent monitoring the wiretap. As soon as they have enough to evidence to convict they'll come out and arrest Tallman. Lee will be monitoring everything and the smartwatch we gave you will only buzz if you need to duck and run."

They'd gone over the plan earlier and she knew that Luna was just running over it one more time reassure her there was nothing to worry about. "Is the tap on yet?"

Luna shook her head. "I'm about to turn it on. Why?"

"I'm scared. But I don't want Xander to hear that."

Luna gave her a reassuring smile. "That's normal. Fear will keep you alert and on your toes. You've faced tougher in the swamp. After hearing about the crocodiles you encountered I know that Tallman will be a piece of cake for you. But if you want to back out I can take your place. We are about the same height and I can wear large frames to disguise the differences in our faces."

Obie knew that Luna would do that. It was another thing they had discussed. And talking about her fear made her feel better. "I still want to do it but had to say it out loud."

"I get it. My husband was in danger when a madman had taken his father hostage and I was so scared for him because I knew he'd do anything to keep his father safe. It's hard to face that kind of fear but the truth is it made it easier for me to focus. I knew I had to keep Nick safe. That was it. I just focused on him and my fears faded."

"Thanks. It's hard for me to believe that you were ever scared," Obie said. The other woman was clearly well trained and she'd heard the stuff that Luna had done to keep her husband—a former client—safe. She knew that Luna had skills.

"I was. And my husband isn't a cautious man, he's always doing reckless things. Keeps me on my toes," Luna said.

"Sounds interesting."

"That's one way of describing him."

"I'm ready now," Obie said.

Luna turned on the wiretap and then they tested and got the affirmative that Rick was receiving the signal. He and the DEA agent were in a van nearby and would drive toward the public parking lot near the park where she was meeting Tallman.

All that was left to do was go and meet him. She had a blank SD card that she'd give to Tallman—they weren't going to risk giving him the one with the evidence on it. Xander and his team agreed that Tallman probably wouldn't check it at the meeting.

She looked around her apartment, decorated in that boho chic style that had been so popular and was on all the shelves at Target. It no longer suited her. She didn't want to be like everyone else anymore. She was tired of blending in. It was definitely time for her to step out of the shadow of the woman that Aunt Karen had made her.

Once this was over and Tallman was arrested, Obie was going to be make a new plan for her life. One that she hoped would involve Xander.

"Let's go."

Luna just smiled and followed her out of her apartment. The cross-body bag that Obie had used during the two days in the swamp was ruined and she was carrying a bag that Price Security had given her. There was a pouch in it that concealed a small derringer pistol as well as a tracking device and backup recording unit. They weren't taking any chances with her safety.

They walked out of the apartment building and the heat of the day wrapped around her. She'd left her hair curly today instead of straightening it like she used to for work.

She had tennis shoes and socks that made her feet sweat but she wasn't ready to leave her house in flip-flops. Not yet.

Her car was had been brought back to her place by a tow truck that Van had arranged. And waited in her normal spot. She unlocked the doors and realized that she wasn't as nervous now that she was on her way to meet Tallman as she'd been upstairs.

She remembered the way he'd sent her to that house to find the information that Aaron had hidden and to be killed so he could have it. That thought stiffened her spine and her resolve. She'd get him to confess no matter what it took.

She drove to the park and as soon as she turned off the car and got out, she knew there was no going back. She waved goodbye to Luna, who took off for her "run" and then looked around to see if Tallman was there yet.

She noticed a man sitting on a bench reading a paper and drinking coffee. Near the swings sitting on a blanket on the ground sharing a box of doughnuts was a mother and her young son. But that was all.

She didn't see him but started walking toward the picnic tables they'd agreed to meet at. The park was quiet at this time of day when commuters were heading to work and parents taking their kids to school.

* * *

Xander checked the sniper rifle that he'd brought with him, but as soon as they saw the setup of the park it was clear that two snipers weren't needed. Kenji was definitely better prepared than he was. "I'll go and get set up. You going to be okay with me on overwatch?"

"You're the best there is, so of course."

"Yeah, I am. But Obie… This is personal for you, Xan," Kenji said. "Not sure how I'd play this. I'd want to watch over her and still be close by."

"Lucky for me I can do both with you. I trust you more than anyone else, Kenji," Xander said.

Kenji nodded and pulled out a pair of glasses that he wore when shooter and then nodded. "That goes both ways."

They bro hugged and Kenji left. Xander looked for cover. He was too big to just chill on a park bench without drawing attention. He was pretty sure Tallman had his description since it had been sent to the police. Both himself and Obie were scheduled to talk to the local sheriff that afternoon. But for now it would be better for Xander to stay out of Tallman's sight.

The path that led to the tables was well landscaped with large palm trees and hibiscus bushes. After the heavy rains of the last few days, there were branches and leaves on the ground. Van had suggested that they appear to be part of the landscaping crew in the park.

Van had several disguises for the team depending on where Tallman suggested they meet. Xander was zipped into work overalls and had on a baseball cap and sunglasses. He was wearing a blond wig so that the hair visible under the hat wasn't his natural black. There was no way to make himself shorter, but his jumpsuit was a couple of sizes too large and made him seem bulkier than he normally was.

They all had earpieces in except for Obie. So as soon as Luna left her at the car, she let them all know.

Xander moved with his rake to a position closer to the trail. He spotted Obie as she came walking toward him and the tables near the center of the park. She noticed him too but her gaze skimmed over him and she kept on walking.

He turned his back to the trail and made himself busy picking up some fallen branches and moving them to the bin he was using.

"She's almost in position," he said as she moved past his location.

"I've got eyes on Obie," Van said. "X, move around to the trees closer to the tables when you finish clearing those branches. Take your time when you get there. I want you in position as soon as Tallman arrives."

"Will do."

They were all tense until Kenji came on.

"Tallman's here. He appears to be alone. Coming toward your position now, Van."

It took all of his willpower to keep his head down and to keep working on the branches. He knew it was important not to break cover but his instincts screamed for him to tackle the other man to ground and beat the truth out of him.

Which wasn't how this was going to go down, so he kept working on clearing debris.

"Got him. X, move in three, two, one."

Xander followed his boss's orders and moved from the trees he'd cleared, closer to the picnic tables. Obie was sitting on the table, not on the bench. She had the bag that they'd given her next to her.

He'd have to hope she kept it close in case she needed to protect herself. When he walked past he didn't look directly at her, but out of his peripherals he noticed her shrug the bag over her body as Tallman approached.

Xander dropped to his knees close to Obie's location and started to pull debris from the flower bed nearest her.

"Ms. Keller. It's good to see you. I was getting worried about you," Tallman said.

"I was getting worried too. It was so scary when those men were shooting at me. I didn't think anyone knew I'd be at Aaron's house," Obie said.

Xander held his breath hoping she wasn't being too obvious.

"I guess trusting Quentin was a dangerous thing to do. He definitely has enemies," Tallman said. "Was the information where he said it would be?"

Xander turned as if reaching for the bag that he'd brought over with him and shoved the branches slowly into it as he continued watching Obie.

"Yes. But I'm not sure it's going to be useful. It looks like a memory card," she said. "Not sure what kind of reader it works in."

"I'm sure the people who work for me will figure it out," he said. "Let me see it."

"Shouldn't I give it to Aaron? I talked to my attorney friend about it and he said that really the evidence should go through Aaron's lawyer."

Obie was using the scenario they'd talked about. She'd wanted to push him and ask him if he'd set her up. But they'd decided to tail Tallman after the card was in his possession. Chances were that he'd take it to the cartel and not back to his offices.

"I'll make sure the lawyer gets it," Tallman said.

"The last time you reassured me that this was probably nothing, I got shot at and had to spend two days in the swamp. So I think I'll keep it until I've spoken with Aaron."

Obie had gone off script and Xander tensed as Tallman snapped his hand out toward her. "Give it to me now."

"No."

He grabbed Obie, pulling her off the bench. He had his hand around her throat. Obie was clawing at him trying to get it off as his fingers tightened around her.

Xander saw red and left his cover, going straight for Obie and Tallman.

Obie knew the plan they had come up with, but from the moment she'd seen Tallman, she hadn't been sure she could go through with it. Now that she'd seen the pictures of him on the file and read the evidence that Aaron had gathered he seemed smarmy, dirty.

What an ass to think she was just going to hand over the card. That wasn't even the way that evidence was meant to handled. But he probably didn't expect her to think of that.

Pushing back on handing it over had seemed like a sort of good idea. Until he grabbed her off the table and started strangling her. His grip on her throat was hard and he kept tightening it. Her instinct was to try to claw his fingers open but he was stronger than she was.

She kicked backward, trying to knock him off balance, and connected with his leg. He stumbled and then he was pulled off of her. His hand tightened on her neck briefly and then he let go. She moved away from him, struggling to breathe, her eyes watering and as she looked back at Tallman she saw Xander had him pinned to the ground.

He was punching Tallman and Obie quickly realized that he might not stop. She ran forward to try to pull Xander off, but before she could get to him another man emerged from the path rushing toward them with his gun drawn. He fired at Xander, hitting him square in the chest and knocking him backward. Obie rushed to Xander's side as the other man stood over Tallman.

"This isn't handling it," the man said.

"I've got this, Bartolo. We can take care of both of them," Tallman said.

Obie held Xander close to her, trying to see put pressure on his wound but realized there was no blood. He mouthed the word *vest* to her.

He had worn a bulletproof vest, which made relief course through her body. For a moment she almost forgot the danger they were in. Bartolo Sanchez turned the gun toward her.

"The card now. I'm not going to argue with you."

She opened her purse, and as she did so Xander slipped his hand into hers and rolled her underneath him on the ground. She couldn't see what happened next, but she heard bullets being fired and Xander stayed on top of her until Van called an all clear.

Xander got to his feet and offered her his hand. Bartolo was injured on the ground close to them. Tallman had also been shot and was a few feet from his cousin-in-law. More men came streaming into the park from the DEA's office and the local cops.

"Are you okay?" she asked Xander.

"I'm fine. Probably bruised from the shot. You?"

Her throat hurt but she knew she'd be okay. "Yeah. That didn't go as planned."

Xander held her, gently moving his fingers over her throat before calling for a medic to examine her. "That's because someone didn't follow the plan."

"I know. I'm sorry but he was so… I just didn't want him to get away with it. I thought if I put up a bit of resistance it might make him do something stupid."

Xander rubbed his fingers over her brow and shook his head. "Or dangerous. He could have killed you."

"I had you watching over me. You'd never let him kill me."

He hugged her close but in his eyes she saw a fear that hadn't been there before. "I can't lose you."

She hugged him back. There were people bustling all around them but she didn't want to move away from him. "I feel the same."

"Do you?"

She nodded, afraid if she opened her mouth that

she'd blurt out that she loved him. That wasn't something she wanted to tell him in the midst of a shootout. She wanted time to talk to him alone when they both weren't injured and maybe were in a nice place.

"Xander, you two okay? The agents need to take a statement and you might want to go with them when they release your brother from jail," Van said as he came over to the two of them.

"Yeah."

"That was ballsy what you did, Obie. I should have guessed you weren't going to just let him walk away," Van said.

"I should have but I wasn't sure that we'd get any proof he was working with the cartel unless I pushed him."

"That you did. Did you know Bartolo was here?" Xander asked Van.

"Not until the old man on the park bench got up," Van said.

"I didn't really pay any attention to the people already here," Obie said.

"I did, but I'm surprised that it was Sanchez," Xander said.

Van nodded as he helped the two of them to their feet and the medic came and checked Obie out. "The information that Aaron got wasn't just going to reveal a crack in the organization. One of the other files has all the names of the men he'd uncovered. Bartolo's entire operation was at risk. He gave Tallman a chance to get it back but when he failed my guess is that he wasn't going to give him a second shot at losing it again."

Xander had to agree with Van. There was a lot at stake for La Familia Sanchez cartel. Aaron's information, along with the arrests of Tallman and Bartolo, should be enough to give the DEA a good shot at shutting them down.

Chapter 21

Van had them all brought back to the beach house in the gated community where they'd first come after the swamp. Xander had gone with Obie to the hospital, where she was treated and released. He had time while she was being examined to think about his actions. He'd saved her but barely pulled himself back from the rage that had been waiting to consume him.

The only other time he'd witnessed someone he loved being injured that way was Tony. And then Xander had turned into the violent and unpredictable person out of his own shame. He rubbed the back of his neck as he waited for Obie to come back from talking to Luna at the house.

He had changed. His anger was no longer directed at the world, and he knew his limits. Even if he went right to the edge with them.

And whether he wanted to admit it or not, both times the source of the change had been Aaron.

He wasn't sure he could just easily forgive his brother for dropping Obie into such a dangerous situation. But he was glad that he'd had the chance to meet her and that wouldn't have happened without Aaron.

The door opened and the DEA agent who Xander hadn't met yet walked in first. A moment later Aaron was there. His brother was bigger than the last time they'd met, but then he was too. They'd both finished growing into the men they were today. When their eyes met, Xander hesitated for a moment and then went to his brother's side. Aaron pulled him into a hug. They held each other for a minute and then pulled back.

"I'm not sure I know what to say to you," Xander admitted.

"Well, let me start then. Thank you," Aaron said. "When my cover was blown and I was arrested I didn't know who else I could turn to. The other agents who worked with me would be in danger if one of them went to get the intel I'd collected."

"Yeah, so about the danger. You sent Obie in there blind."

"I'm sorry about that. But I had thought you'd be going instead of her," Aaron pointed out. "But you had to be shoved, didn't you?"

"I did. I wasn't ready to talk to you again," Xander said.

"I get it, little bro. I was the same way with everyone until last summer when Tony showed up here. We had a good long talk and I... Well, there's a lot more to discuss but we all need to stop avoiding going home."

"So you got arrested to make that happen?" Obie asked, coming over to them. She hugged Aaron and he hugged her back.

Xander watched them and saw that there was genuine affection between them. As much as she'd said

Aaron was a stranger to her, he clearly wasn't, not in a way that mattered.

"I'm sorry, Obs. I never meant for that to get so out of hand. But I hoped that Xander would keep you safe and he did. Still I shouldn't have sent you in like that," he said.

She nodded as she stepped back by Xander's side and slipped her hand into his. "You could have warned me. But I can't be upset with you. There were answers to questions about my parents on your SD card. I... thank you for that."

Aaron just nodded. "That was nothing. just information I had uncovered as I started working the case. Officer Wade remembered you and when I realized that my cover was being scrutinized I looked you up and got a job at your café."

"Why?" she asked.

"I was going to leave the SD card at work. Figured if something happened I'd have a chance to tell you to take it to Wade but I was arrested sooner than expected and the guards that were put on me worked for Sanchez so I couldn't speak freely when you visited. So I turned to my brother for help."

Seeing Aaron like this, Xander couldn't help sort of being astonished at him. "You've changed a lot since the SAS."

"Had to. It was either get my shit together or just give up and Quentins don't give up."

"Give up."

They both said the last part together.

"I missed you, bro. Heard you have turned into quite the legend as well," Aaron said.

Obie turned and gave him a look with her head tilted to the side. She had a bandage on her arm from a cut and bruises on her neck, but she was smiling at him, and he had never seen anyone more beautiful.

"Who said that?"

"Tony. Apparently Mom has been keeping tabs on you. One of her friends noticed you were at the G7 guarding someone from the US. They didn't know who it was."

"I was just helping out a friend," Xander said. The Secretary of State had requested him for the trip to England because he'd guarded her and her family before she'd taken the role and she trusted him to watch her kids while she was being guarded by the Secret Service.

"Yeah, sure," Aaron said.

Xander was embarrassed at the praise from his brother. Also surprised to hear his mom knew about his work. It was past time for him to take a visit home and renew the relationships that he'd severed out of fear. Aaron moved on to talk to Van and the rest of the team and he drew Obie away from them outside to the patio.

"It's nice to be outside and not running for our lives," she said.

"I agree. I like it here."

"Even though it's hot and things bite you," she teased.

He remembered his cranky breakdown when he'd

said that and started to laugh, then pulled her into his arms. "Even then. All of that means nothing to me when I have you in my arms."

"I like being in your arms, Xander," she said and then took a deep breath. "We haven't known each other for a long time but I feel like you are the person who knows me best."

He felt the same way. He glanced over his shoulder to make sure they were still alone. "I love you, Obie. I'd like to figure out a way for us to be together."

"I love you too, Xander," she said. She'd never thought she could be happy unless she'd changed everything about herself and became a woman who would fit in. But being in the swamp had made her face parts of herself that she'd forgotten she liked.

Xander played a big part in that. He'd just accepted her as she was, swamp girl mixed with suburbanite and all. "I want to figure out how to be together too. I'm also going to try to figure out me."

She'd spent a lot of time thinking about the fact that she didn't want to be a barista for the rest of her life. It was time to stop punishing herself for not going with Gator and to live a life that would be fulfilling to her.

And part of that meant finding a way to be with Xander. He meant the world to her, and she wasn't going to let him walk away again. She'd thought that by helping Aaron she'd find some peace with the decision she'd made the day that Gator had left but in truth it had been going back to the swamp with Xander that had saved her.

She had no idea what she wanted to do, but spending time in the swamp and studying the animals and plants that lived there appealed to her. She'd probably have to take a lot of classes to get a different degree, but she was okay with that. Those days in the swamp had reminded her that she was more important than keeping up appearances.

"I like you. What do you have to figure out?" he asked. "I like you the way you are."

He kissed her deeply and she couldn't help wrapping her arms and legs around him and kissing him back. When she lifted her head, she noticed his eyes were half-lidded and felt his erection between her legs.

"Thanks. But I think I'd like to go back to school and maybe work in the swamp," she said as he set her on her feet and took her hand, leading her away from the main house to the pool house.

"I can see you as a biologist," he said. "You'll be good at that. We might have to do long-distance for a while until I can find a job on the East Coast."

"Or I can go to school on the West Coast," she said.

But he shook his head. "No. You uprooted yourself and changed the course of your life once trying to become what your aunt Karen wanted for you. It's time for you to stay where you are. Let me come to you."

"I just don't want to lose you," she said. "I haven't been in love before, Xander, and I haven't felt this safe and sure of anything since my parents died. I want to be with you."

He hugged her close and he bent his head to hers.

His mouth was next to her cheek, and when he spoke, the words traveled no farther than the two of them.

"I won't let you go, Obie. You sort of make me feel okay not to be perfect and I've never had that in my life. When you are always competing and trying to be the winner... Well, I might have missed out on some things but I won't allow myself to miss out on you."

"Good. So we're agreed. I think as long as we both want to make this work we will," she said.

"We definitely will," he agreed. After all they'd survived two days in the swamp with just her skills, his wits and his backpack. They could manage living on opposite coasts until they got everything figured out.

He made love to her in the pool house and afterward they spent the evening with friends and family. Obie reached out and invited Aunt Karen, who was happy to see her safe and sound.

Aunt Karen showed up no questions asked. She took in Obie with her curly hair hanging around her shoulders. For a minute Obie felt her back go up, ready to defend herself but she didn't have to.

"You look happy. God, I don't think I've seen you this way since your mama died," Aunt Karen said, wiping her eyes with a tissue.

"I don't think I truly have been since then," she said, hugging her aunt. "I realize I never said thank you for that day you drove to Winter Haven and met me at the bus station."

"I should have taken you to look for Gator. I was just scared for you two and afraid that if you went back up there you might be in danger," she said.

"Were you suspicious of their accident too?"

"Of course. Your daddy was never meant to die in the swamp. That man knew it like the back of his hand and your mama and I were raised in it. I figured the best way I could keep you and Gator safe was to keep you with me and help you to blend in."

"Thank you for doing that. Did you ever hear anything from Gator?"

"I didn't. I am sorry I let him go. I just didn't know what else to do."

She hugged her aunt close, accepting that Aunt Karen had been keeping her safe the only way she knew.

"Thank you."

"It was nothing, Obie. You and Gator are my only kin—of course I had to keep you safe," she said.

She introduced her aunt to Xander and the two of them got on well. Obie looked around at the people in the backyard of the big house. The smell of the grill and the music playing made her realize how much of her life she'd spent hiding. She'd cut herself off from everything until now.

"I hear you might be my sister soon," Aaron said, coming up and handing her a beer, while draping one arm around her shoulder.

"I might," she said.

"I knew it. As soon as I met you I realized you and Xander would be good for each other," he said.

Which made her laugh. Xander came over to see what was so funny. "Aaron thinks he set us up."

"Oh, he did."

"Not like that. Like some kind of matchmaker," Obie said on a laugh.

"Hey, it worked. Do you think I could make a business out of it?" Aaron asked in a way that reminded her of Xander when he was teasing her.

"No," Obie and Xander both said at once.

Xander hugged her close. Aaron had put them in the right place, but it was those two days in the swamp, dodging bullets, crocs and alligators and weathering fierce rainstorms that had helped them fall in love. When there had only been the two of them and the elements, they'd had no choice but to lower the barriers they used to keep the world at arm's length.

Surviving the swamp had revealed the truth of who they were. The swamp girl and the beast man who wouldn't have even noticed each other on the streets of everyday Miami. Two soulmates who would have been ships crossing in the night, if not for Aaron and his life-threatening favor.

* * * * *

Romantic Suspense

Danger. Passion. Drama.

Available Next Month

A Colton Kidnapping Justine Davis
Hotshot's Dangerous Liaison Lisa Childs

Stalker In The Storm Carla Cassidy
Undercover Heist Rachel Astor

LOVE INSPIRED

Chasing Justice Valerie Hansen
Searching For Evidence Carol J. Post
Larger Print

LOVE INSPIRED

Shielding The Innocent Target Terri Reed
Kidnapped In Montana Sharon Dunn
Larger Print

LOVE INSPIRED

In Need Of Protection Jill Elizabeth Nelson
Hidden Mountain Secrets Kerry Johnson
Larger Print

Keep reading for an excerpt of a new title
from the Intrigue series,
CONARD COUNTY: MURDEROUS INTENT
by Rachel Lee

Prologue

Krystal Metcalfe loved to sit on the porch of her small cabin in the mornings, especially when the weather was exceptionally pleasant. With a fresh cup of coffee and its delightful aroma mixing with those of the forest around, she found internal peace and calm here.

Across a bubbling creek that ran before her porch, her morning view included the old Healey house. Abandoned about twenty years ago, it had been steadily sinking into decline. The roof sagged, wood planks had been silvered by the years and there was little left that looked safe or even useful. Krystal had always anticipated the day when the forest would reclaim it.

Then came the morning when a motor home pulled up beside the crumbling house and a large man climbed out. He spent some time investigating the old structure, inside and out. Maybe hunting for anything he could reclaim? Would that be theft at this point?

She lingered, watching with mild curiosity but little concern. At some level she had always supposed that someone would express interest in the Healey land itself. It wasn't easy anymore to find private land on the edge of US Forest, and eventually the "grandfathering" that had left the Healey family their ownership would end because of lack of occupancy. Regardless, it wasn't exactly a large piece of land, unlikely to be useful to most, and the Forest Service would let it return to nature.

Less of that house meant more of the forest devouring the eyesore. And at least the bubbling of the creek passing through the canyon swallowed most of the sounds that might be coming from that direction now that the man was there. And it sure looked like he might be helping the destruction of that eyesore.

But then came another morning when she stepped out with her coffee and saw a group of people, maybe a dozen, camped around the ramshackle house. That's when things started to become noisy despite the sound baffling provided by the creek.

A truck full of lumber managed to make its way up the remaining ruined road on that side of the creek and dumped a load that caused Krystal to gasp. Rebuilding? Building bigger?

What kind of eyesore would she have to face? Her view from this porch was her favorite. Her other windows and doors didn't include the creek. And all those people buzzing around provided an annoying level of activity that would distract her.

Then came the ultimate insult: a generator fired up and drowned any peaceful sound that remained, the wind in the trees and the creek both.

That did it. Maybe these people were squatters who could be driven away. She certainly doubted she'd be able to write at all with that roaring generator. Her cabin was far from soundproofed.

After setting her coffee mug on the railing, she headed for the stepping stones that crossed the creek. For generations they'd been a path between two friendly families until the Healeys had departed. As Krystal crossed, she sensed people pulling back into the woods. Creepy. Maybe she ought to reconsider this trip across the creek. But her backbone stiffened. It usually did.

She walked around the house, now smelling of freshly cut wood, sure she'd have to find *someone*.

Then she found the man around the back corner. Since she was determined not to begin this encounter by yelling at the guy, she waited impatiently until he turned and saw her. He leaned over, turning the generator to a lower level, then simply looked at her.

He wore old jeans and a long-sleeved gray work shirt. A pair of safety goggles rode the top of his head. A dust mask hung around his neck. Workmanlike, which only made her uneasier.

Then she noticed more. God, he was gorgeous. Tall, large, broad-shouldered. A rugged, angular face with turquoise eyes that seemed to pierce the green shade of the trees. The forest's shadow hid the creek that still danced and sparkled in revealed sunlight behind her.

This area was a green cavern. One she quite liked.

Finally he spoke, clearly reluctant to do so. "Yes?"

"I'm Krystal Metcalfe. I live in the house across the creek."

One brief nod. His face remained like granite. Then slowly he said, "Josh Healey."

An alarm sounded in her mind. Then recognition made her heart hammer because this might be truly bad news. "This is Healey property, isn't it?" Of course it was. Not a bright question from her.

A short nod.

"Are you going to renovate this place?"

"Yes."

God, this was going to be like pulling teeth, she thought irritably. "I hope you're not planning to cut down many trees."

"No."

Stymied, as it became clear this man had no intention of beginning any conversation, even one as casual as talking about the weather, she glared. "Okay, then. Just take care of the forest."

She turned sharply on her heel without another word and made her way across the stepping stones to her own property. Maybe she should start drinking her morning coffee on the front porch of her house on the other side from the creek.

She was certainly going to have to go down to Conard City to buy a pair of ear protectors or go mad trying to do her own work when that generator once again revved up.

Gah!

JOSH HEALEY HAD watched Krystal Metcalfe coming round the corner of his new building. Trouble? She sure seemed to be looking for it.

She was cute, pretty, her blue eyes as bright as the summer sky overhead. But he didn't care about that.

What he cared about were his troops, men and women who were escaping a world that PTSD and war had ripped from them. People who needed to be left alone to find balance within themselves and with group therapy. Josh, a psychologist, had brought them here for that solitude.

Now he had that neighbor trying to poke her nose into his business. Not good. He knew how people reacted to the mere idea of vets with PTSD, their beliefs that these people were unpredictable and violent.

But he had more than a dozen soldiers to protect and he was determined to do so. If that woman became a problem, he'd find a way to shut her down.

It was *his* land after all.

Chapter One

No.

Nearly a year later, that one word still sometimes resounded in Krystal Metcalfe's head. One of the few words and nearly the last word Josh Healey had spoken to her.

A simple question. Several simple questions, and the only response had been single syllables. Well, except for his name.

The man had annoyed her with his refusal to be neighborly, but nothing had changed in nearly a year. Well, except for the crowd over there. A bunch of invaders.

At least Josh Healey hadn't scalped the forest.

Krystal loved the quiet, the peace, the view from her private cabin at the Wyoming-based Mountain Artists' Retreat in the small community of Cash Creek Canyon. She was no temporary resident, unlike guests in the other cabins, but instead a permanent one as her mother's partner in this venture.

She thought of this cabin and the surrounding woods as her Zen Space, a place where she could always center herself, could always find the internal quiet that unleashed wandering ideas, some of them answers to questions her writing awoke in her.

But lately—well, for nearly a year in fact—this Zen

Space of hers had been invaded. Across the creek, within view from her porch, a fallen-down house had been renovated by about a dozen people, then surrounded by a rustic stockade.

What the hell? A fence would have done if they wanted some privacy, but a stockade, looking like something from a Western movie?

Well, she told herself as she sat on her porch, maybe it wasn't as ugly as chain-link or an ordinary privacy fence might have been. It certainly fit with the age of the community that had always been called Cash Creek Canyon since a brief gold rush in the 1870s.

But still, what the hell? It sat there, blending well enough with the surrounding forest, but weird. Overkill. Unnecessary, as Krystal knew from having spent most of her life right here. Nothing to hide from, nothing to hide. Not around here.

Sighing, she put her booted feet up on her porch railing and sipped her coffee, considering her previous but brief encounters with the landowner, Josh Healey.

Talk about monosyllabic! She was quite sure that she hadn't gotten more than a word from him in all this time. At least not the few times she had crossed the creek on the old stepping stones.

The Healey house had been abandoned like so many along Cash Creek as life on the mountainside had become more difficult. For twenty years, Krystal had hoped the house's steady decay would finally collapse the structure, restoring the surrounding forest to its rightful ownership.

Except that hadn't happened and she couldn't quite help getting irritated from the day a huge motor home had moved in to be followed by trucks of lumber, a noisy generator and a dozen or so men and women who camped in tents as they restored the sagging house. A year since then and she was still troubled by the activity over there.

The biggest question was why it had happened. The next question was what had brought the last owner of the property back here with a bunch of his friends to fill up the steadily shrinking hole in the woods.

No answers. At least none from Josh Healey. None, for that matter, from the Conard County sheriff's deputies who patrolled the community of Cash Creek Canyon. They knew no more than anyone: that it was a group residence.

The privacy of that stockade was absolute. At least the damn noise had quieted at last, leaving the Mountain Artists' Retreat in the kind of peace its residents needed for their creative work.

For a while it had seemed that the retreat might die from the noise, even with the muffling woods around. That had not happened, and spring's guests had arrived pretty much as usual, some new to the community, others returning visitors.

Much as she resented the building that had invaded her Zen Space, Krystal had to acknowledge a curiosity that wouldn't go away. A curiosity about those people. About the owner, who would say nothing about why he had brought them all there.

Some kind of cult?

That question troubled her. But what troubled her more was how much she enjoyed watching Josh Healey laboring around that place. Muscled. Hardworking. And entirely too attractive when he worked with his shirt off.

Dang. On the one hand she wanted to drive the man away. On the other she wanted to have sex with him. Wanted it enough to feel a tingling throughout her body.

How foolish could she get?

ACROSS THE CREEK, Josh Healey often noticed the woman who sat on her porch in the mornings drinking coffee. He knew her name because she had crossed the creek a few times: Krystal Metcalfe, joint owner of the artists' retreat. A pretty package of a woman, but he had no time or interest in such things these days.

Nor did he have any desire to share the purpose of his compound. It had been necessary to speak briefly with a deputy who hadn't been that curious. He imagined word had gotten around some, probably with attendant rumors, but no one out there in the community of Cash Creek Canyon, or beyond it in Conard City or County, had any need to know what he hoped he was accomplishing. And from what he could tell, no one did.

Nor did anyone have a need to know the reentry problems being faced by his ex-military residents.

Least of all Krystal Metcalfe, who watched too often and had ventured over here with her questions. Questions she really had no right to ask.

So when he saw her in the mornings, he shrugged it off. She had a right to sit on her damn porch, a right to watch whatever she could see…although the stockade fencing had pretty much occluded any nosy viewing.

But sometimes he wondered, with private amusement, just how she would respond if he crossed that creek and questioned her. Asked *her* about the hole in the woods created by her lodge and all the little cabins she and her mother had scattered through the forest.

Hah! She apparently felt she took care of her environment but he could see at least a dozen problems with her viewpoint. Enough problems that his own invasion seemed paltry by comparison.

As it was, right now he had more than a dozen vets, a number that often grew for a while, who kept themselves busy with maintaining the sanctuary itself, with cooking, with gardening. And a lot of time with group therapy, helping each other through a very difficult time, one that had shredded their lives. All of them leaving behind the booze and drugs previously used as easy crutches.

Some of his people left when they felt ready. New ones arrived, sometimes more than he had room for but always welcomed.

Most of the folks inside, male and female, knew about Krystal Metcalfe, and after he explained her harmless curiosity to them, they lost their suspicion, lost their fear of accusations.

Because his people *had* been accused. Every last one of them had been accused of something. It seemed society had no room for the detritus, the *problems*, their damn war had brought home.

He sighed and shook his head and continued around the perimeter of the large stockade. Like many of his folks here, he couldn't relax completely.

It always niggled at the back of his mind that someone curious or dangerous might try to get into the stockade. Exactly the thing that he'd prevented by building it this way in the first place.

But still the worry wouldn't quite leave him. His own remnant from a war.

He glanced at Krystal Metcalfe one last time before he rounded the corner. She appeared to be absorbed in a tablet.

Good. Her curiosity had gone far enough.

NEW RELEASES!

**Four sisters. One surprise will.
One year to wed.**

Don't miss these two volumes of
Wed In The Outback!

When Holt Waverly leaves his flourishing outback estate
to his four daughters, it comes to pass that without an
eldest son to inherit, the farm will be entailed to someone
else…unless all his daughters are married within the year!

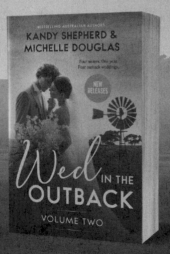

May 2024　　　　　July 2024